THE HILLBILLY MOONSHINE MASSACRE

Also by Jonathan Raab

Project Vampire Killer

The Haunting of Camp Winter Falcon

*The Secret Goatman Spookshow
and Other Psychological Warfare Operations*

The Crypt of Blood: A Halloween TV Special

Camp Ghoul Mountain Part VI: The Official Novelization

More Sheriff Kotto Adventures

The Lesser Swamp Gods of Little Dixie

Freaky Tales From the Force: Season One

Radio Free Conspiracy Theory

THE HILLBILLY MOONSHINE MASSACRE

JONATHAN RAAB

MUZZLELAND PRESS

The Hillbilly Moonshine Massacre
Copyright © 2015, 2023 Jonathan Raab. All rights reserved.
Cover art by Peter Lazarski
Edited by Charles Martin and Jessica Raab
Muzzleland Press logo by Mat Fitzsimmons
Section break icon by Freepik

The original edition of this book was published by Literati Press Comics & Novels in 2015.

All rights reserved. No part of this work, save brief quotations for reviews, may be reproduced without the express written consent of the publisher.

ISBN: 979-8-9879688-1-9

This novel is a work of fiction. Any resemblance to real persons or events is purely coincidental. I am required to put this in the book, Cecil, for liability reasons. Please stop circling the block in your pickup truck while wailing on the horn at all hours of the night. We can talk about this later.

The opening quote from Revelation 12:12 is from the Holy Bible, New International Version®, NIV® Copyright ©1973, 1978, 1984, 2011 by Biblica, Inc.® Used by permission of Zondervan. All rights reserved worldwide.
www.zondervan.com
The "NIV" and "New International Version" are trademarks registered in the United States Patent and Trademark Office by Biblica, Inc.™

Muzzleland Press
Victor, NY

For Tarik and Colin—the original Kotto and Fields.

And for everyone who helped us make backyard monster movies.

Therefore rejoice, you heavens and you who dwell in them. But woe to the earth and the sea, because the devil has gone down to you! He is filled with fury, because he knows that his time is short.

Revelation 12:12

I
You Can't Go Home Again

1. Warrant Served On Quackenbush Road

Larry "Bucky" Green was a two-bit moonshiner with a rap sheet as long as a summer afternoon. Petty larceny, public drunkenness, public urination, illegal discharge of a firearm, and various other typical good-old-country-boy degenerate activities. There was one instance of felony assault (charges later dropped) in that thick folder of his. But, if anyone bothered to ask Sergeant Joe Johnson of the New York State Police, the guy on the bad end of that particular ass beating probably deserved it. But then again, nobody ever bothered to ask Johnson.

This was his turf, supposedly—the deep hills and back roads of central Cattaraugus County, New York. Populated by farmers in old houses, hillbillies and rural folk in single- and double-wide trailers, and effete ski freaks; tourists mostly, slumming it up with the locals in faux-rustic mansions scattered among the foreboding forested hills. Rumor was, even famed four-time-Super Bowl-losing-quarterback Jim Kelly had himself a big cabin out this way. The guy may not have had a ring, but he sure as hell had money.

It was a quiet assignment out here, running the

county and state roads between Salamanca, Great Valley, Ellicottville, West Valley, Little Valley, Machias, Franklinville, and elsewhere—save for the occasional poacher, domestic violence incident, and the constant stream of drunk driving citations. With ski season almost upon them, Sergeant Johnson knew the tourists (and belligerent townies) were sure to keep him busy through the dark and endless gray winter months to come.

The people weren't bad here, for the most part. They just liked to be left alone, to their deer hunting and their cheap beer and their Buffalo Bills football and their pickup trucks and their guns and their John Deere tractors and their four-wheelers. Leave them be, and they were friendly enough to wave as you drove past in your State Trooper SUV, or they might even start a conversation with you while you sucked down jet-black Joe at the Coffee Clatch in Ellicottville. But start mucking around in their business, and, well—it was better not to turn your back on them.

Johnson had been here long enough to know you couldn't solve every problem with a hammer. The SWAT officers who moved into position around the white singlewide trailer at the edge of the clearing did not share Johnson's backcountry diplomacy skills. To those guys with the cool gear and shit-hot attitudes, there wasn't nothing a hammer couldn't fix the hell out of. Most people out here in the deep country were well-armed. They were just as likely to fly NRA flags as they were the Stars and Stripes. Cops had to be careful, sure. But this was overkill. The SWAT team didn't seem primed for a simple arrest; they were arrayed for battle.

State Police Major George Winston's personal dark blue Ford Expedition stood at the entrance of the driveway, flanked by two Trooper patrol cars, one of which was manned by Sergeant Johnson. They were less than 100 yards from the three trailers that sat on each side of the roundabout dirt, mud, and gravel driveway. The target trailer was dead ahead, in the middle, its windows hidden by the swaying fingers of trees just beginning to shed their autumn colors. Gray SUVs, their lights off but their engines running, blocked the adjacent road in both directions—although one direction was a dead end, trailing off into crumbling gravel and weeds. Another pair of State Trooper SUVs stood where Quackenbush Road met Route 242. Early morning traffic buzzed on by, drivers craning their necks to spy on some mysterious manner of local trouble.

The SWAT Troopers, decked out in full kit, wore spit-shined black combat boots that reflected patches of blue morning light. They wore tight-fitting armor and combat gear, webbing loaded with flashlights, pepper spray, handcuffs, ammo magazines, zip strips, flashbangs. They carried M-4 rifles, replete with scopes and lasers Johnson couldn't even begin to identify. They wore jet-black hockey helmets and large wrap-around goggles, their mouths hidden by patches of gray or black fabric. The State Police this far out from Albany may not have had a huge budget for overtime, but they sure had money to buy all the cool guy gear for the SWAT hotdoggers.

Despite their armor and toys, they moved quickly, taking up positions behind large trees and the rusted-out hulks of cars abandoned in the lawns of the other two trailers in the clearing. The assault team moved straight down the driveway, boots crunching on scattered gravel and mud, past sagging mailboxes and an abandoned red tricycle. Behind one of the trailers a dog began to bark, his voice sad and lonely in the cool October morning.

Two men skirted the target trailer, and, ninja-like, dashed into the weeds and trees beyond, hoping to cover any back doors and windows where Bucky might try and skedaddle. A team of four SWAT Troopers stood perched on the rickety wooden staircase that led up to the trailer's lime green plastic door. The lead Trooper turned his mouth toward a microphone clipped to his chest plate carrier.

"Blue team, in position," came his whispered voice over the radio. Major Winston, wearing the same black ninja cammies and kit as the Troopers around the trailer, stood behind the open driver's side door of his command SUV. He pulled the mic from its mount on the dash.

"Roger," he said. "Red team? Yellow team?"

Affirmatives from the other team leaders. Winston turned to the side to spit out a stream of tobacco-brown juice.

"I read all teams in position," Winston said. He turned and looked through Johnson, then his eyes settled on a man at the end of the driveway. That man wore a dark black overcoat and giant aviator sunglasses. His jet-black hair was perfectly parted and slick, shining with oil and specks of dew. The man smoked a stubby Pall Mall, his back to them both, oblivious to the drama that was about to unfold.

Sergeant Johnson had no clue who the G-Man was, or to what department he belonged. He just knew when this guy showed up at the briefing early that morning back in Machias, the SWAT commander's voice had grown a tad shaky. Everybody at the barracks had given him a width berth.

"We're ready to arrest the target, Agent Schrader," Major Winston said, his voice not quite quavering.

Schrader took one last puff on his cigarette. The moon, spectral against the early-morning dim blue sky, reflected in both of his oversized lenses. He let the butt fall to the gravel, and snuffed it out under an immaculately shined black shoe. He turned to face the commander, his shoulders stooped, his head craning forward at an odd angle. The nod was almost imperceptible. Then he ran tar-stained fingers through his hair.

"All teams, this is Six," Major Winston said. "Butterfly. I say again, butterfly."

A hundred yards away, the lead Trooper on the steps nodded and gave his team a thumbs up. One of Troopers moved up the staircase with a cylindrical battering ram. Three sharp strikes against the doorknob and the plastic door crunched and collapsed inward. They were all inside the trailer within three seconds.

Sergeant Johnson watched, his hand on the Beretta on his hip. Water splattered against the brim of his Smokey the Bear campaign hat. He looked up to see the wind shaking the branches above him, dislodging leaves and dew. The colors had come early this year. The leaves would fall off soon, leaving the trees barren and sickly until spring. Early fall through deep winter.

Major Winston, standing next to the driver's seat behind the open door of the SUV, tapped his fingers against the dashboard in an uneven rhythm. Agent Schrader shuffled forward, his fingers wiping at his salt-and-pepper mustache, his mouth twisted into a detached frown.

The SWAT Troopers outside the trailer raised their weapons and scanned windows, looking for targets.

"First room, clear!" someone yelled from inside the trailer.

"Short room! Bathroom, clear!"

"Door!"

"Stacking!"

"Hit it!"

"Breaching!" A crash, splintering wood and plastic.

"Get down, get down!"

There was a loud *pop*, and a flash of light.

"Flashbang," Winston said, a nervous, wrinkled smile on his face. An older guy, sure, but he still had the energy of youth around his features.

Boots stomped on creaking floorboards. Then there was silence.

Sergeant Johnson looked from the trailer to the commander, from the commander to the trailer. The SWAT cops crouched behind cars and trees looked through scopes and down rifle sights. They waited as time slowed to a crawl. The silence was eternal.

The dog stopped barking. There was only the wind, and the sound of Johnson's own heartbeat in his ears. The strap on his pistol holster had come undone, and his hand hovered just above the 9mm, fingertips stealing kisses from cool gun metal.

Five seconds. Ten.

Nothing.

The commander's smile had disappeared. Sweat beaded along the edge of his forehead, trailing down from the rim of his helmet, despite the cool of the day.

Then the shouting. Voices in the trailer, panicked, almost incoherent.

"Put him down! Down!"

"Drop it!"

"Drop him!"

"Oh shit oh shit oh shit!"

And another sound, like the mewling of an injured cat played backwards over grinding metal. Incoherent, unintelligible. Angry.

The hair stood up on the back of Johnson's neck, and he pulled out his pistol by pure reflex.

There was a burst of orange-red light, and the

windows of the trailer shattered and blew out in every direction. The sound of the explosion came next—a muffled boom that followed licks of flame reaching up and out of the windows. Shards of glass rained down on the SWAT Troopers nearby. Handfuls of jagged glass peppered the SUV and men at the end of the driveway. Johnson, not far from Major Winston and Schrader, closed his eyes and ducked, hoping the patrol car would shield him from any debris.

"Hell!" Winston spat.

Schrader carefully picked a few glittering crumbs of window from his hair.

The flames grew. Spectral green and blue fingers of heat, reaching up to massage the roof of the trailer.

"All teams, this is Six! Report! Report! What the hell is going on?"

The SWAT Trooper nearest them turned from his position behind a green Ford pickup with no tires. He held out his hands in comedic confusion.

"Get up there, dumbass!" Winston yelped, his finger still on the transmit key, broadcasting the moment of humiliating terror over the radio. "We've got men in there! Get them out!"

The Troopers left cover and moved toward the trailer. The blue and green flames were now massive claws, consuming the singlewide. Black smoke poured out of the shattered windows.

"Call the fire department," Johnson said to himself, willing his legs to carry him to one of the parked patrol cars nearby. "Call for help, have to call for help …"

There was a low hum, and the air went cold and hard with an electric charge.

Johnson froze in place.

The roof of the trailer exploded, and beams of orange and red light shot straight up into the sky, piercing a low bank of clouds. A wave of shimmering air spread outward from the trailer. The singlewide's walls buckled under some great force, the roof dipping low to the ground and shedding shingles and chunks of flaming jagged wood.

The SWAT Troopers hadn't made it to the door when the second explosion came; they were knocked backwards and landed in the wet grass and muck. The wave of pulsing light and air struck Johnson (*cold, so very cold*), the commander, and Agent Schrader, toppling them. Johnson landed palms-down on sharp stones, his hands and fingers bloodied and raw. The windshields on the SUV and patrol cars burst, as did the windows on the other two trailers. Johnson's breath was suddenly more visible than ever, coming out in near-frozen bursts of white.

The flames churned and Troopers yelled. Winston shouted orders no one could hear or carry out.

Johnson pushed himself up onto his forearms, the sleeves of his uniform torn, his campaign hat missing. Blood leaked out from the center of his forehead and caught along his right eyebrow. Red drip-drip-dripped in his vision, casting the world in ill-focused dark amber.

Plastic siding groaned and snapped; wood splintered. The narrow end of the trailer—from where the explosions had come—curled outward, drawn open by unseen force. Then there was a man—wearing cut-off jean shorts and a faded white undershirt—leaping out of the flames.

The sharp *pop-pop* of 5.56mm rounds from the SWAT team's M-4s echoed in the clearing and off the hills. Men shouted; others aimed at the suspect and fired. After a moment of scrambling to get into a steady firing position along the ground, Johnson's voice and bullets were among theirs. Then his Beretta offered the soft *click* of an empty chamber and magazine.

The suspect was gone, off somewhere in the trees and the hills beyond.

Major Winston's helmet was missing. He pulled himself up to the driver's seat of his SUV, and wiped shards of shattered windshield away from the radio mount.

"All teams, report," he said. Disjointed voices answered him, confused messages on radio waves and in the air around them.

"One suspect running—"

"Shots fired—"

"Officers down, I say again—"

"Paramedics need to—"

"—within the woods—"

The fire moved along the trailer, taking its sweet time with its meal. The smoke hung low like fog. Ashes rained down, orange snow come early to mark the start of autumn.

Agent Schrader pulled off his sunglasses, revealing dark brown eyes that looked black in the dark of morning and shadow. Smoke rose out of one of his pockets. He pulled out his soft pack of Pall Mall cigarettes, which smoldered, set aflame by an errant ember. He waved the fire out, then snapped the top open to see if any of his cigarettes had survived.

Sergeant Johnson pushed himself up to his feet. His ears rang, his eyes burned. Troopers from the checkpoint at the end of Quackenbush double-timed down to the driveway. Sirens began low, long wails from somewhere west—probably Ellicottville. Johnson's hand gripped his empty pistol, the fingers and knuckles turning stark white.

His boots slopped against mud, then came to rest over freshly fallen leaves.

The trailer burned. SWAT Troopers pulled the limp forms of their comrades out of the alien flames and black smoke. Major Winston was shouting again. A neighbor had ventured outside and was spraying his garden hose on Bucky's burning trailer, breaking only to blast away the glowing ash and embers that drifted down onto his own roof. Agent Schrader was on a large rectangular cell phone like something out of an early 90s movie, a half-cigarette dangling from his thin lips. The lonely red tricycle had fallen over, its one wheel in the air spinning round and round.

The wind shook the branches above. It carried the smell of smoke and the sounds of injured men into the deep green hills, into the woods, into the waiting dark.

2. Land of the Free, Home of the Weird

Sergeant Abraham Richards, Alpha Company, 1-107th Infantry, New York Army National Guard, walked down the armory steps into the cool October afternoon, his rucksack weighing heavily on his shoulders, his duffel bag to his side and straining his arm.

"Let me take that, son." His father took the duffel and hefted it over his good shoulder.

"Careful, Dad."

"You can't tell your father to be careful, you know that," Mom said, grimacing and rolling her eyes. She said it as a joke, but she was afraid it sounded like a nag. Everything was tense. Happy, sure, but tense. No one wanted to say the wrong thing, but silence didn't seem right, either. But maybe saying nothing at all was the best thing for it.

Richards shrugged.

"It's your shoulder."

"Darn right," Dad said. A muted grunt escaped his lips.

They walked down the concrete steps to the crumbling asphalt of the armory parking lot. Little scenes of reunion and drama played out around them; soldiers in faded uniforms met parents and siblings, grandparents and cousins, wives and children, friends and dogs. Smiles—nervous smiles—on every face.

Dad opened the back hatch of the blue Honda Fit, and they set the bag inside.

"Do you have everything?" Mom asked.

Richards shrugged.

"If I don't, fuck it," he said, getting into the back seat.

Mom shot Dad a hurt look. Dad held out a flat hand at chest level, calling for calm.

Richards sat in the middle seat. His hands instinctively sought out his rifle, fingers moving over his sides and near his legs.

No, he thought. *That's gone now. That's over with.*

He looked into the rearview mirror, his brown eyes reflecting back at him with dull indifference. Unfamiliar crow's feet had developed at their edges, and the bags underneath had grown dark.

His parents got into the car and they began to drive out of the crowded parking lot. Soldiers and families streamed back and forth. The car crawled along, careful not to hit other vehicles backing out. Wild-eyed children darted back and forth.

As they drove down the long black driveway, the families and soldiers and brick armory behind them, Richards felt the weight of a year and a half of service roll off of his shoulders.

The miles added up. A familiar landscape spread before him. He meant to leave the memories behind him, back at the armory, back with the faceless crowd. He pulled his patrol cap off and set it down in his lap. He pulled the hook and fastener combat patch from his right ACU sleeve and tossed it onto the floor.

They were 10 miles outside of town when Richards noticed he was leaning forward, straining to see out the windshield. His eyes were on the road, on the sides of the road, on trash that fluttered in the wind, on the vehicles that passed by in the other lane. Everything was a threat. Nothing was a threat. He couldn't tell the difference anymore.

Mom asked him questions and he gave short, terse answers. His fingers dug into his thighs, tight, so very tight. Again, he searched for a rifle that wasn't there.

Dad's eyes met his own in the rearview mirror. It was an instant of connection, a moment. Both men looked away.

◬

Kubrick was there to greet him. The old lab mutt had put on a few pounds, and fresh white fur grew out along the edges of his mouth.

"I bet I look a little different, too," Richards said, kneeling down to give the dog a few pats on the head. Kubrick's tail went *thump-thump-thump* on the wooden deck. His pink tongue darted out to steal a few licks on Richards' hands, which had stopped shaking.

Dad opened the door for him and he walked inside, through the front hallway and into the dining room. The house had a childhood smell; an aura of vinegar cleaning solution, fresh bread, and a hint of candle wax. Familiar, but different, like everything else.

Ghosts of childhood played with Ninja Turtle action figures in the living room, or bounded down the basement steps to log some hours with *Donkey Kong Country* on the SNES. And there, another ghost, in front of the bathroom mirror, his father helping him shave his head for the first time before he went off to Basic.

They had laughed then, smiles and eyes proud and hopeful.

The kitchen floor was different; alien white square tiles stood in place of familiar, faded linoleum. The walls were now a dark red. Somewhere under that new skin was the memory of childhood blue, sun-faded and dry.

He slipped his thumbs under the ruck's shoulder straps. Ahead of him was the kitchen table, arrayed with a tray of fresh cookies and a virgin six-pack of Yuengling. The dining room and kitchen sat at the corner of the house, with windows tall and wide facing out to both the south and the west. He faced the western window. Beyond that, the yard stretched down to a wide creek, pregnant with the runoff from an early fall rain. Fallow fields sat beyond, once a source of hay for dairy cows. The beaver dam and marsh encroached on the fields a little more each year.

Then there were the hills—mountains in millennia past, beaten down by time to rounded humps of old earth and rock. Trees, thick as storm clouds, blanketed them, their leaves orange, yellow, and red, with patches of stubborn green sprinkled about. The hills were everywhere, surrounding everything, breaking up the landscape with sharp bursts of color, hiding the edges of the horizon with their ancient heights. Richards had forgotten how much he missed the hills, and the color.

His fingers tapped against the shoulder straps of his heavy ruck. He wanted to take off his patrol cap. He wanted to get out of his uniform. He wanted to take a shower. He wanted to call friends. He wanted to have a beer. He wanted to do everything at once, and, faced with absolute freedom for the first time in a year and a half, found himself frozen at a sudden and limitless crossroads.

"Abe," Mom said, standing just behind him. "Abe."

He turned suddenly, pulled back to this place, to this time, to this moment.

"It's okay," she said, wanting to smile but not able. "Take off your pack. You don't have to stand there, okay? You can relax."

Richards nodded, taking off his patrol cap and rubbing a sleeve along his sweaty forehead.

"Sorry," he said.

"No need to apologize," Mom said. "You're home now, Abe. You're home now."

◭

Michael Bryant sat waiting for him at a corner booth in the Wind Mill Bar and Restaurant in downtown Ellicottville. The oak-paneled walls were decorated with faded black and white photographs of the first years of skiing at Snow Pine Resort, faux-rusted advertisements for gas stations and Pepsi, and a scattered collection of deer and moose heads wearing sunglasses and Mardi Gras beads. Some sort of wild cat stalked above Michael, its eyes glass, its pose frozen forever in time in the moments before a deadly pounce.

Michael smiled and stood up as Richards reached the table. Michael had long, dark, shaggy hair that curled around his shoulders and neck, and wore an XL hoodie emblazoned with "Ellicottville Volunteer Fire Department" above a helmet, axe, and ladder logo. He stretched out his arms and Richards returned the hug, his old friend smelling faintly of cigarettes and beer.

"Hey, Mike."

"Abe. Glad you're back." They broke their hug and took their seats. A waitress in a tight black Wind Mill t-shirt took their beer orders with a smile, her perfume hanging in the air as she swayed her hips all the way back to the bar. Richards tore his eyes from her ass.

"Welcome home," Michael said.

"Yeah," Richards said, another forced smile on his face. He was getting good at that. "It's good to be home."

"How long you been back?"

"Two days at my parents' place. About two and a half weeks since we came back stateside. De-mob was a fucking nightmare."

"De-what?"

"De-mob. Sorry. Demobilization. Fort Dix. They wouldn't let us out of that fucking place."

Michael nodded. The waitress brought them their beers in pint glasses covered in water spots. They were warm to the touch.

"Sorry," Richards said. "I'm working on the swearing."

"Oh, no problem," Michael said, waving his right hand and shaking his head. "I hear worse down at the fire station all the time."

They drank their beers, and they shared silence, and they both made attempts at conversation, idle chatter, Richards asking more questions than Michael, eager to talk about anything but Afghanistan.

More beers. The clinking of glass pints and bottles. As the hour approached dinner, more people, locals and tourists come to see the foliage, streamed in. The air was cool and light with the smell of earth and a hint of fryer grease.

"Things have changed," Mike said suddenly, nodding in the direction of a family wearing matching LL Bean hiking jackets as they walked in. "More tourists last year. More this year, too, probably."

"That's good, right?"

Mike shrugged.

"Good for business. Keeps Ellicottville alive. Unlike West Valley."

"The nuke plant keeps West Valley alive," Richards said. Another gulp of beer.

"The town survives, the locals get brain cancer," Mike quipped. He held the empty beer glass out in front of him, inspecting it like it was the first time he had seen such a thing. "Good thing I'm not on call tonight."

"At least Ellicottville is doing alright."

"Yeah. New development is going up soon, if they get the permits for it. Snow Pine is gonna tear ass up and down those hills on the west side for new condos, new trails. Buying up a lot of property in town, too. Not gonna be a lot of locals left in town, when it's all said and done. They're gonna log about 50 acres of trees, and add in a new lift, a new lodge, the works. It's probably good long term, but it's gonna put some people off their property. Not to mention the environmental costs."

"That'll keep you busy?"

"Maybe. I just run a snow maker part-time. Speaking of which, you got a job? Got any plans?"

"No," Richards said, finishing his beer too, keeping pace.

"I can talk to some people, get you work on one of the lifts. It ain't hero work, but it's money."

"I've got unemployment, and some savings. But yeah, maybe working a little will do me some good. I had the job in high school."

"You mean basket check? Smoking weed on breaks, hassling teenage girls?"

"Yeah, that."

Mike laughed.

"Well, we're hiring early for Octoberfest. And we're due snow soon. They want to be fully staffed by the first week of November."

"Yeah, maybe," Richards said. "What's that?" He pointed to a folded-up newspaper by Mike's elbow. He was searching for something to talk about. The drink made the words come easier, but they also left him feeling empty and desperate for something, something to keep his interest, something new, something to punch through the gray.

"*Ellicottville Events*," Mike said, unfolding the paper. "Check out the front page." He tapped his finger against the headline and the photo underneath.

Degenerate Moonshiner Evades State Troopers, Sets Trailer Ablaze. Cops Killed, Several Wounded.

They ran his mugshot: a gaunt face, pouches under his eyes, uneven mustache perched over thin lips. He might have been handsome if it wasn't a mugshot. Just your average good-old-boy, caught up in some State Boys trouble.

"Looks familiar," Richards said. "'Bucky'?"

"It's a nickname. Making liquor up in the hills somewhere. It was a big fire—ate up the whole trailer in no time flat. They were still pulling Troopers out of the flames when we showed up to put it out."

"Yeah, I think a couple of my uncles used to drink his hooch. Real good local stuff, right? So what's the big deal about 'shining? Why send the State boys after him? That stuff's been around for years."

Mike shrugged.

"Look at the story below the fold."

Richards pulled the paper up. Below Bucky's mugshot ran another headline, smaller, but just as crazy.

Mysterious Lights Continue to Harass Local Yokels.

"What is this? UFOs?" Richards asked. A nervous smirk crept up.

"They've been seeing them around town for a few weeks."

"You're serious," Richards said, shaking his head. "Government planes, maybe?"

"Probably from the Air Force Base in Niagara Falls," Michael said, accepting his fourth beer with a smile. "Or maybe the Calspan contracting facility in Ashford."

"Meteor showers," the waitress said, setting down a saucer plate full of steaming chicken wings. "Google it." She shot them a knowing look, all arched eyebrows and pursed lips. She returned to the bar.

The smell of butter and Frank's hot sauce cleared Richards' sinus cavity and set his stomach to growling. Steam rose up from the wings, fresh from the fryer. He decided to read the article while they cooled.

MYSTERIOUS LIGHTS CONTINUE TO HARASS LOCAL YOKELS
by Hailey Lovering

IRISH HILL ROAD—The continued presence of strange, unidentified lights in the sky in and around the town of Ellicottville has locals baffled.

"They just hovered over my neighbor's garage for about 10 minutes, then we set off some fireworks at 'em, and they just flew straight up into the sky," Martha Walters, a resident of Irish Hill Road, said. "Big, red, glowing balls."

Daniel Yocum, A town worker for the village of West Valley, claimed to have been chased along Route 240 from Ashford Junction to Beaver Meadows Road by a mysterious object.

"Looked like a pair of skeleton hands, floating above the trees," Yocum told reporters. "Floated on out of the treetops, hovered over my vehicle. Made the headlights go crazy. Then I heard the voice of Satan himself come over the radio, telling me to 'actualize my inner self,' whatever that means. Do you know what that means?"

The State Troopers stationed at the barracks in Machias failed to return our phone calls on the issue. It is presumed that their manpower is tied up pursuing known moonshiner and suspected cop killer Larry "Bucky" Green on a manhunt that has dragged on into its second week.

Local conspiracy theorist and Cattaraugus County Sheriff Cecil Kotto was more than willing to provide a rambling statement on the recent phenomena, tying the lights to industrial pollution, climate change, the Nation of Islam, the local chapter of The Order of the Night Moose, and the Green Party headquarters in Olean, just to name a few...

"Wait," Richard said, setting down the paper. "Cecil Kotto? *Sheriff* Cecil Kotto?"

"You remember him, huh?" Michael said, smiling. "I thought you'd think that was crazy."

"He's the *sheriff*," Richards said, not believing the words on the page. "When the hell did that happen? *How* did that happen?"

"Right after you went off for training, what, a year ago? Two years ago?"

"Year and a half."

"Right. So there's this big State District Attorney investigation into the Cattaraugus County Sheriff's Department. Turns out, Sheriff Gifford and most of his deputies were involved in a meth ring. Taking a cut from the local producers, charging them for letting their shipments pass through on up to Buffalo and down to Olean. The scandal wiped out most of the department."

"But Cecil? We went to high school with him. He was a few years ahead of us, right? Guy was a loner. A weirdo."

"Graduated early, too, if you remember," Michael said. "So you got the whole Sheriff's Department going to jail or resigning. The governor steps in, deploys more State Troopers to take over the County, including the jails. We had a special election. Nobody wanted the job—and anybody who did was probably in jail or under indictment anyway.

"Cecil gets it in his head he'll run for sheriff. He got a lot of backing early on, out-of-state money poured into his campaign."

"I'm confused," Richards said. "Why would anyone want to support a local weirdo for sheriff, especially if they are from out of state?"

"*Kotto's Kreepies*," Michael said with a wide smile. "You have been out of the loop, haven't you Abe?"

"I'm lost."

"It's an AM radio show," Michael said, giggling. "Airs every weeknight at midnight on Cattaraugus County Public Access Radio. CCPAR. But the local dumbasses call it 'The Critter,' God knows why. The show got real popular right before the scandal. Fans started uploading the broadcasts to YouTube and iTunes, so it got some national exposure in the underground. It's a call-in program. People share stories about Bigfoot and aliens. That sort of craziness. Then he does a 20 minute rant about secret societies and conspiracy theories. Oh, and he also does movie reviews from time to time."

"Secret societies, in Ellicottville?"

Michael shrugged.

"The Order of the Night Moose, for one," he said.

"That's just a charity thing, right? They wear little funny hats and drive little cars in parades. I think my uncle was a member."

"Ringknockers, sure. But who knows what really goes on behind closed doors, right?"

"Cecil Kotto started a radio show," Richards said. "I can't believe it."

"And it got him elected sheriff. The 'freak vote,' they called it. People here, they were just fed up with the system. Why not hand the reins to the crank who thinks the Loch Ness monster is floating around Lake Erie? He couldn't do any worse than Gifford."

"I don't believe this."

"Listen to the show next chance you get," Michael said. "It's entertaining. Even if he is completely crazy. But it doesn't end there. About a year ago—maybe less—we had a string of murders around the county. Real weird stuff—victims were all slashed up, but their blood was drained out."

"Yeah, that sounds familiar," Richards said. "Did Kotto catch the guy doing it?"

"Not quite," Michael said. "He got in a shootout with some people he said were wearing surgical masks and doctor's scrubs. He said they were driving around in a plain white conversion van, running people off the road and taking their blood. Him and his deputy got on TV and tried to sue the Red Cross, saying they were behind the murders."

"I didn't hear *that*," Richards said.

"No, I don't suppose you would," Michael said. "The story didn't get much traction. But that's the guy who's our local law enforcement now. The guy who accused the Red Cross of serial murders." Michael shook his head and raised his glass. "Ain't that a rip? Welcome home to the land of the free, home of the weird."

3. Octoberfest

The sky was bright and cloudless, and the sun lent a golden hue to the leaves, in full, colorful autumn splendor.

Richards stood at the top of Carnivale, the tallest and longest ski trail at Snow Pine Resort. Chairful after chairful of tourists paid $8 to ride up the shiny-new lift to the top of the hill, to look down over the colorful hills and valley below, and to down overpriced bottom-shelf Canadian beer.

The beer tent was overflowing with Canadians, Ohioans, and yuppies from the Buffalo metro area. A classic rock station had set up a tent next door, with a prize wheel, booth babes in skimpy German attire handing out pamphlets for a deck repair company, and giant speakers that pumped out a steady stream of bland tunes that set Richards' teeth on edge. A pair of Snow Pine Resort flunkies manned the barbecue pit, keeping the coals glowing and the hot dogs and burgers sizzling.

Richards' stomach growled in pain and hunger. Salt and red meat were his preferred hangover remedies. His head pounded, and he considered popping a Sudafed—low-grade over-the-counter speed—to ease the pain.

Despite the sunshine, Richards felt the bitter cold, the wind at that elevation chapping his lips and stinging his face. His red Snow Pine Resort employee jacket kept most of the cold at bay, and his green Nomex gloves—a pair he had worn a handful of times during the deployment—kept his fingers warm.

He stood at the top of the ramp that led down from the lift to the ground below, placing a hand on the metal bars of each chair as it passed over the ramp before slowing down to allow the tourists to disembark and scurry down, pretending they were skiing over snow and ice that was soon to come.

"So you were in the Army, huh?" asked Duncan, the clod-footed ex-jock. Richards knew him vaguely from high school. Duncan had lettered in the holy trinity—basketball, football, and baseball—because Ellicottville High School was so small and he was so damn big. Duncan wore his varsity jacket underneath his Snow Pine Resort coat, which was unzipped so people could see the edges of the school initials on either side of the zipper.

"Yeah," Richards said, grabbing the blue frame of another chair as it came swinging over the ramp. Two young girls, probably just on the early side of high school, giggled as they lifted the restraint bar and jumped out of the chair, squealing as it slowly hovered behind them before swinging around the pulley to head back down the hill. Duncan's eyes followed the girls.

"Look at that pussy," Duncan said.

"How old are you, Duncan?"

"Uh, 29 this year," Duncan said. "That's the great thing about young girls! I keep getting older ..."

"What movie is that from?" Richards asked.

"What?"

"It's from a movie. I've heard it about a thousand fucking times. What movie?"

"Oh, I don't know," Duncan said. "It's just something my dad used to say."

Another chair. An elderly couple, slow to get out of the seat. Richards waved to the attendant in the shack.

"Hey, slow it down!" he shouted. The attendant looked up from his *Guns & Ammo* magazine, a cigarette dangling from his lips, and punched the *slow* button. The lift cable slowed to a crawl, and the old couple shuffled down the ramp, hands firmly locked together.

"What was it like?"

"What?"

"The Army."

"How much time you got?" Richards asked. The lift sped back up.

"We've got another couple hours on shift, right?" Duncan asked. "Did you get scared?"

"It was mostly being bored," Richards said. "And I was angry a lot. But yeah, I was scared."

"Why were you angry?"

"I thought the mission was bullshit," Richards said.

"I almost joined the Army," Duncan said. "But then I got a partial scholarship to SUNY Canaltown. Division III football. Should have put me at wide receiver, but they made me a cornerback instead. I had to tell the recruiter he had to wait."

"That's great," Richards said, not meaning it. "So why didn't you join after college?"

"Oh, I dropped out," Duncan said. "The program was bullshit. Wouldn't start me."

"Right."

"Could've gone pro, if I kept at it."

"Right."

Another chair. Four women in their late forties, reeking of perfume, faces caked with makeup, margaritas and vodka on their breath. They giggled at Richards and Duncan. Richards forced a smile. Another one.

"So what kind of guns did you use? Like the M-60? That shit's the bomb in *Call of Duty*. I think the Marines—"

There was a crash behind them, and shouting. They both looked back at the beer tent; two aging cougars were in the faces of a group of men in black biker cuts, manicured fingernails and bleached teeth flashing. The speakers from the classic rock station blared the virtues of that old time rock n' roll. One of the Snow Pine employees came around the barbecue pit, red hot tongs glowing in his right hand, and shoved one of the bikers.

Most of the crowd started to shout and pull back as the fists began to fly. But some of them pushed forward, turning a fist fight into a full-blown melee. About a dozen people—old, young, men, and women—clawed at one another, smashing glass bottles, tossing beer into faces, throwing elbows, losing teeth. One of the bikers flashed a knife, and then there was screaming.

"Holy shit," Richard said. A moving chair bumped into him, and he caught his balance on its frame. The family on board saw the fighting, and refused to lift their bar.

"We're not getting off!" the father snapped. They sailed on through the roundabout, and began the descent back down the hill.

The attendant in the shack hit the kill switch, and the chairlift drifted to a slow halt.

Another knife. One biker turned on the other, stabbing him in the abdomen.

"Jesus!"

Half the crowd ran away from the chaos; the other half was already fighting, or joined in. An old woman swung her purse at the face of the town priest; the pair of teenage girls bit down on the forearm of the cook; he shook them off and shoved the hot metal tongs into face of the closest girl, who howled in animal pain. Men slugged one another, shattering faces and teeth. The biker group had devolved into a civil war of switch blades and iron knuckles; the women who had been screeching at them turned on each other, ripping the goose down out of tears in each other's designer jackets.

The music played on, inviting the crowd to get those old records from off the shelf.

"We should do something," Duncan said. "Holy hell."

"Like what?" Richards asked. "You want to get in the middle of that?"

The attendant was outside of the shack now, shouting into his radio. A man wearing a Helly Hanson snowboarding jacket, his face covered in blood, his eyes ablaze, stomped up the ramp and made for the attendant. He slapped the radio away, then wrapped his hands across the attendant's throat.

"Hey!" Richards ran over, dropping his shoulder and slamming into the crazed tourist at full speed. The man's hands broke their grip, and all three men went tumbling down the ramp to the moist grass below. The attendant crawled backward while the tourist wheeled on Richards.

Richards shoved himself up just in time to dodge out of his way; then his training kicked in, and he was on the man's back, raining punches down on the back of his head, which spasmed with anger and pain. The man flipped over, but Richards was quick and stood up, maintaining his position above the tourist.

He dropped a knee into the man's stomach, causing a painful gasp to escape blood-soaked lips. Richards dug his knee down into the man's diaphragm, and watched as his eyes went dull with unconsciousness.

Richards let up the pressure, not wanting to kill the crazy bastard.

"You alright?" Duncan asked, running over, fists raised high, ready for someone to rush him.

"Fuck, I think he tried to *bite* me," Richards said. The man's face, neck, and front of his jacket were covered with blood and beer. A liquid leaked out from one of the torn jacket pockets, darkening the orange and white fabric. Richards reached down and pulled out a glass bottle, no larger than a flask. It held an orange liquid that seemed to shine especially bright in the sunlight. On the bottle's face was imprinted a logo of raised glass: a hieroglyph depiction of a man with a long beard, open hands, and massive wings. The image conjured sensations of recognition and lost memory; something about sixth grade history class, and ancient myth. He twisted the cap shut tight.

Beyond the ramp, the melee had devolved further, with a handful of people standing over limp bodies, kicking and tossing wild punches.

"We should get out of here," Duncan said suddenly. "We should call the cops."

"Yeah," Richards said. He stood up, absently shoving the bottle into his work jacket. "Let's pop smoke."

Those not interested in the fight ran down the hill, screaming and crying. People caught on the lift shouted for it to get moving again, seeing the chaos below and wondering why the hell they were stuck mid-ascent. The DJ and the booth babes in the classic rock station tent had fled into the woods, chased by a pair of teenagers flinging sizzling hot dogs and shouting obscenities.

From the massive speakers, the singer declared that new music just doesn't have the same soul.

4. Cattaraugus County Public Access Radio

The voice on the radio was tinged with static and distance, the telling marks of an AM radio station with a limited transmitter pumping out signal over deep valleys and lonely hills. Richards had found the station after some tweaking of the antenna cord, taping it to the wall of his bedroom.

"What witnesses are describing as a flash mob occurred at Snow Pine Resort in Ellicottville today," the dulcet-toned reporter said, her voice tinny and distant. "One Snow Pine employee gave this startling account."

Richards cocked an eyebrow, pausing mid-sip to listen. He was lying on his bed in his underwear and white t-shirt, nursing a good buzz and sore muscles from the day's events. Sure, someone had tried to kill him, but he got a paycheck out of it. Nothing he wasn't used to.

"Man, they just went crazy!" said a new voice on the radio. "Started throwing their beer, scratching each other! It was like something out of a zombie movie, but in 3-D, man!"

"Duncan?" Richards asked the empty room, recognizing the voice. He tossed the bottle up and let the beer cascade down his throat. The reporter resumed.

"State Troopers claim that this was merely another incident of gang-related violence, citing the presence of a local motorcycle club, alcohol, and flaring tempers as the cause of the disturbance. Twelve people were taken to the hospital, and another fifteen were arrested. State Police have released the names of several other suspects ..."

"Bullshit," Richard said, drops of Yuengling spraying from his lips. "There were old ladies going crazy, not just bikers."

But the woman on the radio didn't hear him.

"This is Cattaraugus County Public Access Radio. CCPAR, your local source for culture, education, and news for the Southern Tier." The station cut to light jazz Muzak.

Richards shook his head and finished his beer. He set the empty next to the others—a formation of four green bottles.

Four. Practically a fire team. I wonder if I can get a whole squad of 'em.

He rubbed his hand along his chest, expecting to feel the familiar presence of metal dog tags and chain. No, he had taken them off. They were in a box in his closet somewhere, with this duffel bag, probably. Next to sagging cardboard boxes full of action figures and comic books. Memory and dust.

He reached down the side of the bed and pulled up another beer. Only two left; then he remembered the bottle of Seagram's Seven Crown in the cupboard downstairs in the kitchen. He'd limit himself to one or two drinks from that. He didn't want his parents to notice. It was bad enough with those quick looks of disappointment when he swore too much, and listening to his father ask him questions about his "plans" sent him into a laborious silence in lieu of walking out of the room entirely. Richards knew how to be aggressive, and how to deal with aggression. Passive-aggressive was a style he usually only saw in officers, and thus was normally out of his wheelhouse. His family was working hard to teach him, or so he thought. It was hard to tell the difference between concern and judgment these days; the Army had taught him that nobody gave a fuck about you, except you. You constantly had to prove yourself. No matter what you did, it was never enough.

The beer bottle cap scratched at his palm as he twisted it off, and cool vapors escaped from the green glass neck into the air. The alarm clock read 11:59 in bright green colors. Before he left home for the war, he kept his time by the 24-hour military clock. That had been one of the first things he'd changed when he came back a few days ago, right after he had taken off his boots and sat down on the familiar sagging bed.

The music on the radio stopped abruptly. The woman's voice came over the air again, and Richards wondered what she looked like, how old she was, if she wasn't too much of a goddamn hippie liberal to date a soldier.

No, he reminded himself. *Ex-soldier.*

"Coming up next on CCPAR AM 950, *Kotto's Kreepies*, a call-in hour featuring Cattaraugus County Sheriff Cecil Kotto. Then at one, *Uncle Pat's Car Talk*, followed by 47 minutes of classical polka music. This is CCPAR."

Already halfway through his fourth beer, Richards sat up against the bedpost. He pressed the volume *up* on his stereo remote.

Let's see what all this crap is about.

[Audio transcript of *Kotto's Kreepies*, episode #114. Prepared by Rachel Hawkins, CCPAR intern.]

[Low drums. Crescendo, crashing of symbols. Chorus, singing unintelligibly in Latin.]

ANNOUNCER: "In uncertain times, people cry out for hope."

[Gunfire. Rushing of jets, followed by explosions. Stock sound effect screaming.]

ANNOUNCER: "In the darkest reaches of reality, in the darkest corners of Western New York, one man stands alone. One man dares to speak the truth."

[Music drops out, momentary silence.]

ANNOUNCER: "That man is Cecil Kotto."

[More explosions as the chorus resumes it boisterous singing. Metal guitar riffs screech and grind. Music slowly fades out.]

KOTTO: " ... I know my mic is on. I see the little red light. That doesn't mean I can't ask you for a goddamn cigarette. What, the people don't know I smoke? I appeared in my campaign posters with cigarettes. So what's that ... ? Oh, we're on air? That's going to be an FCC violation, isn't it? I suppose I should ..."

[Audio stream cuts out. Elevator music.]

[Music cuts out.]

[Audio returns.]

KOTTO: "Yes, ladies and gentlemen, welcome back to *Kotto's Kreepies*, the only show on public radio—and I dare say anywhere else this side of the Great Lakes—that dares to tell you the truth. The truth about all sorts of topics of the weird. UFOs, space men, government conspiracies, the Bilderbergers, the Trilateral Commission conspiracy to divide and conquer the world, the Illuminati, the Masons, Scientology, the Boy Scouts of America, the CIA, the Department of Homeland Security, FEMA, EA Games, Reptilians, and other organizations, high strange events, and conspiracies dark and nefarious. I am your host, Cattaraugus County Sheriff Cecil Kotto, broadcasting to you live from the CCPAR studios in lovely Salamanca, New York. If you are hearing this broadcast, *you* are the resistance.

"Now, we've got a lot to get through here, so I'll spare you the clap trap and get right down to the nitty gritty. We've got UFOs over central Cattaraugus County, Bigfoot sightings outside of Humphrey, riots at the ski resort, and men in black buying up all the donuts from Quality Markets down in Ellicottville. There's a lot of topics to discuss. Let's waste no time. We're going to the phones."

[Clicking, murmuring.]

KOTTO: "I understand we have Geoff on the line. Geoff from Peth Road in Great Valley. You're on the air with Sheriff Kotto."

GEOFF: "Uh, yeah, hi, Sheriff?" [screeching, feedback]

KOTTO: "Geoff you old slug, I'm gonna need you to turn down your radio."

GEOFF: "Sorry, Sheriff." [Audio stabilizes.] "Is that better?"

KOTTO: "Yes, much better. What's going on, citizen?"

GEOFF: "Oh, um, I just wanted to call to ..."

KOTTO: "Out with it, young man!"

GEOFF: "I got probed last night, I think."

KOTTO: "Probed."

GEOFF: "Um, yes, yes ..." [Stifled laughter, whispers.] "Sir. Probed. Anally ... In my butt."

KOTTO: "Full anal penetration?"

GEOFF: [laughter in background, multiple voices] "Yes, sir. Very traumatic."

KOTTO: "Who was responsible for this violation? Little green space men? Gray aliens? Mantid overlords? Satanic ritual abuse?"

GEOFF: "Oh, um. It was ... It was your mom."

KOTTO: "Come again?"

GEOFF: "That's what she ..." [uncontrolled laughter] "Yeah, your mom!"

KOTTO: "My mother is not a space creature. That doesn't make sense—wait, you son of a b—"

PRODUCER: "Cut his mike, go to commercial!"

[Unintelligible yelling.]

[Station identification break.]

KOTTO: "Now back to *Kotto's Kreepies*. Once again, I apologize for the technical difficulties. Our call screener will have to do a better job. So while the phone lines are open and we wait for some mature, responsible citizens to call in with their questions about the supernatural, I'd like to present my listening audience an opportunity.

"As you may know, the Sheriff's Department has been reduced in size and budget since the scandal and the subsequent special election that allowed yours truly to take over. I've managed to hire a secretary. Since Deputy Fields moved on to join the FBI, I've been flying solo. We've scraped together enough cash from speeding tickets, civil lawsuits, merchandising,

Kickstarter, and baked good sales to start hiring staff again. It's my vision to hire a few deputies in the coming months. After all, how can I defend you from the coming scientific dictatorship as described by Aldous Huxley, blood moon madness, CIA domestic drug importing operations, skinwalkers, and alien abductions if I don't have loyal officers in the field? So for anyone interested, please email your résumé, cover letter, and martial arts expertise to Kotto at Kottomail dot mail dot Kotto dot com. No drug test required for employment with the County Sheriff's Department. Now, back to the phone lines. Yes, Becky from Machias, you're on the air with the sheriff…"

Becky from Machias prattled on about her missing cat, claiming a pair of men with green, scaly arms and hands, giant fish heads and bulbous eyes, wearing Buffalo Bills sweaters and striped sweatpants, had seized her precious Mr. Mittens. Kotto's response was measured, asking overly-specific questions about the suspects' apparent physiology and whether or not they had New England accents.

Richards laughed, then fished out the last beer from the six pack. He already had designs on the Seagram's downstairs.

"Fuck it," he said to himself. He downed the beer, happy to have some entertainment, happy to listen to people who were way more fucked up than he was talk about the crazy fake bullshit in their lives.

He struggled to remember the password to his email. Then it came to him, and, with a slug of the Seagram's to celebrate, he logged on.

5. Hangover

The pain in his skull called him out of the blissful abyss.

Disorientation came first, followed by swift regret.

"Uhh," Richards croaked. He pushed the covers off of his pounding head, which danced with the vibrations of some subterranean drumming crew deep within his fragile skull. Sunlight streamed in through plastic binds, assaulting his eyes with unwanted light and beauty. His mouth tasted like soap scum and whiskey. At the sight of six empty beer bottles, he closed his eyes and choked back the urge to retch.

Never again, he told himself. *I quit drinking. I friggin' quit.*

It was a prayer he'd prayed before, in high school and in college, one that went unanswered, year in and year out. That was the worst part—knowing that this pain, this fit of rage and roiling in bowels, stomach, heart, and head—he'd do this all over again, sure as hell. He'd do it all over again and again and again.

He pushed himself up, his well-muscled arms shoving into the sagging mattress. He shrugged off the blankets and swung his feet down to the floor. The pounding in his head was almost audible. Tinnitus, which had plagued his ears since that day he stood behind the .50 and ran through two boxes of ammunition in no time flat, pulsed to the rhythm of his heart. It was almost hard to breathe, his body wanted to puke so bad.

That was it, then. His path was clear.

He grabbed his glass of water and walked across the hallway to the bathroom. He set a towel along the immaculate tiles before the throne. He took a few swift sips of holy water from his glass, then bowed his head in worship of the porcelain god.

He puked. Beer and water and bile and pizza clawing its way up his esophagus and splattering onto pristine porcelain, the sound cartoon-absurd. The retches sounded like some Hollywood sound effect, played up for laughs and emphasis for a dull-brained audience come to see a gross-out comedy.

It's all a joke, alright, Richards thought as he paused to catch his breath before the rising tide came again.

Har-fucking-har.

The pulsing in his head was heavier than before, but his stomach had calmed down enough to risk eating something. Sips of water put an end to that course of action: everything that went down came right back up again.

He checked his phone, hoping he hadn't texted or called anyone. Especially any ex-girlfriends.

No. No messages sent or received after 11:45. Thank God for small favors.

Downstairs, his mother had left him a note on the table.

"Leftover burgers in the fridge. Potato chips in the

cupboard. Love you!"

"Love you too, ma," Richards said, grabbing a bowl and the bag of chips. Salt and vinegar. Perfect. His stomach growled in a pain that might have been something approaching hunger. He'd nibble on a few chips and see where that got him. Experience taught him things would get worse as he continued to sober up through the late morning and early afternoon. The key was to get some food and water into his stomach—and keep it down. Then would come the mellow draw out of reduced head and belly-ache, and he'd be ready to drink again—should it come to that—by 7:00 PM. Right as rain, ready to roll.

The thought of a heavy glass of Seagram's in his hands made him gag, and he had to lie down face-first on the living room couch to prevent the vomit from flowing. All was dark and coolness and pain. Seeing things hurt his head. Hearing things hurt his head. Feeling things hurt his heart.

"Ugh," he said into the cool black faux-leather.

The pounding of his head lulled him back to half-sleep. He'd try the chips and water later, if he didn't fucking die first. Not that he'd be that lucky.

───

The knocking was just part of the pulsing and the pain. Then it separated, coming at uneven intervals parallel to the beating of his wicked heart. The knocking became open-palmed slaps against a shaking plastic screen door, and Richards sat up straight, precious saliva leaking from his dry mouth.

"What?" he asked the living room, his eyes meeting the stuffed bear that stood guard over the leather recliner across the room. The pounding on the screen door made his heart jump. He wiped his hands along his face and felt the creases from the couch cushions. What little hair he had on his shaved head stood up or flat down in odd patches. He'd slept fully clothed, so he wasn't completely indecent. Human wreckage and a waste of oxygen, sure. But not indecent.

He walked through the hallway, squinting at the light streaming in through the door's window ahead of him. A shadowy figure leaned against the screen door outside, hands cupped against the screen, head leaning forward, straining to see inside.

Richards pulled open the door and squinted into the shadow.

"What? Can I help you?" Richards said, scratching at his belly. He knew he looked like shit, but didn't care. He just wanted this person to be gone, and he wanted to be face down in the couch for another couple of hours.

"I'm looking for someone," the man said. The light was too bright for Richards to see much more than a tall shadow looming on the porch.

"Who?"

"Richards, Abraham. 8796 Fanciest Track Road, unincorporated Ellicottville, New York."

"Yeah?"

"Sergeant, E-5, Alpha Company, 1-107th Infantry Battalion, 28th Infantry Brigade Combat Team, New York National Guard?"

"Former sergeant. That's me. What do you want?"

"Do you have two forms of ID? I'll accept driver's license, library card, social security card, birth certificate, medical marijuana card, or a letter of recommendation from the local Mutual UFO Network chapter."

"What? What is this?" Richards backed up a step, ready to slam the door on this man's face. "Do I have to call the cops on you?"

The man stepped forward, Richards' eyes fully adjusting to the light streaming in behind him. Just a hair shy of six feet tall, light brown skin, scraggly, unshaven face trying to grow a patchy goatee.

"You can do that, but I'm already here," the man said, pulling off his too-big aviator sunglasses and slipping them into his camouflage military-surplus jacket. "I'm Cattaraugus County Sheriff Cecil Kotto. I'm here for your job interview."

6. Bad Voodoo in the Air

"Whoa, whoa, whoa," Richards said, hammer blows still falling in his brain. "Interview? No, there's some mistake."

"No mistake, got your résumé right here," Kotto said, pulling out a crumpled handful of papers from his BDU-pattern camouflage jacket. "Got this. Not bad, but mine's better. I can tell the difference between real helicopters hovering over my house and fake helicopters which are actually alien spacecraft *pretending* to be helicopters. That's point one on the résumé. Prospective employers are always impressed by that one."

"I'm sure, but …"

"Oh, and I got a poorly-written cover letter in all caps from you. Here, I'll read it to you." Kotto cleared his throat. "'DEAR SHERIFF KOTTO,'" he read, shouting the words, "'VERY MUCH I'D LIKE TO BE A DEPUTY BECAUSE I LIKE YOUR RADIO SHOW … ' blah blah blah hard worker, punctual… 'I HAVE MILITARY EXPERIENCE. FOUGHT IN THE AFGHANISTAN WAR WITH THE ARMY, WHICH IS PRETTY HARDCORE DON'T YOU THINK?' Then a bunch of rambling about working at the ski resort … ah, here: 'WANT TO DO SOMETHING FOR MY COUNTRY AND THE AMERICAN PEOPLE AGAIN.' That's pretty straightforward to me.

Sound like you?"

"Uh, yes, Sheriff, but ..."

"Can I come in?" Kotto asked. "The Constitution is very clear on that. You have to invite a police officer inside. Cops and vampires can't enter your home unless you give them permission. That's in the Constitution, I think."

"Sure," Richards said.

"No, not good enough," Kotto said. "Be specific."

"You may enter my home, Sheriff," Richards said. "That work?"

"Yes," Kotto said, stepping forward as Richards opened the door. "You should really be more concerned about your civil liberties and vampire defenses."

Sheriff Kotto stepped inside. He stood just a couple of inches shy of six feet tall, with light chocolate-brown skin, fleshy cheeks and chin home to a scraggly uneven goatee, and squinting, darting brown eyes. He wore his BDU jacket unbuttoned over a black Misfits t-shirt featuring a grinning skull-like face. His stomach was a classic redneck spare tire, pressing out against the fabric of his t-shirt. His jeans sagged slightly, and he paused to tighten his black leather belt. His tan combat boots were untied, trailing their laces on the floor as he walked. On his head was a "SCHARF BROS. TOWING" red mesh trucker hat, faded and smudged with what looked like motor oil.

"Nice place you got here," he said, looking around. "Who did these paintings on the wall? Monet? Caligula?" He gestured to a framed picture of a fisherman casting his line into an idyllic creek.

"I don't know," Richards said, closing the door behind the sheriff. "My mom won them at some raffle or something. Could be—"

"Can I use your bathroom?" Kotto asked, whirling around suddenly. A cigarette appeared in his mouth.

"You can't smoke in here, Sheriff."

"I didn't ask to smoke in here. I asked to use your bathroom."

"Right." Richards pointed down the hall. "That door on the right."

"Thank you." Kotto tramped down the hall, trailing mud from his boots along the pristine tile floor. He swung the door behind him, not bothering to shut it all the way.

Richards shook his head and walked into the kitchen. He filled a pair of glasses with ice and water, then sat down with a groan at the kitchen table. How long would this weirdo be here? And—wait—

Did he actually apply to be a deputy last night?

He thought hard, fighting through the fog of pain and darkness. He remembered listening to the radio show, and finishing the beer ... Then there was an image of him sneaking down into the kitchen for the Seagram's ...

Shit.

Yeah, he was on the computer. He didn't remember what he wrote or when, but he was definitely on the computer. Did he apply? Did he think it would be funny? Was he serious? Drunk Abe was a very different Abe. Anything was possible in the bottle.

Smoke wafted out from underneath the partially-closed bathroom door. The toilet flushed, and Kotto swung the door open, coughing and waving the smoke from the room.

"I asked you not to smoke," Richards said.

"I was in the bathroom. I flushed the cigarette."

"Come on, man. I mean, Sheriff." Kotto walked forward and took a seat. He spied the glasses of ice water, and reached over and grabbed the one in front of Richards. He held it up to the light, searching for something in the glimmering ice.

"Fluoride in the water was used by Nazi scientists as a means for keeping concentration camp victims docile and stupid."

"It's well water."

"Oh. Bottoms up."

He put the glass to his lips, and proceeded to loudly swallow gulp after gulp, until all of the liquid disappeared down his throat. He slammed the glass down on the table, making Richards jump. Then his teeth ground chunks of ice.

"Oh, dammit," Kotto said, leaning forward, rubbing his head.

"What?" Richards asked.

"Freezy head," Kotto said. "I've got freezy head."

"You shouldn't have drank it so fast."

"I never learn."

They sat there in silence, Richards rubbing his temples, Kotto rubbing his forehead with the palms of his hands.

Suddenly, Kotto sat up straight.

"I know you, don't I?"

"You were a couple years ahead of me in high school, I think," Richards said.

"Yeah, that's it. That's what I meant."

"What else could you mean?"

"Enough with the twenty questions," Kotto said. He squinted, then slapped his cap on the kitchen table, revealing a shaved, balding head. "I'll ask the questions."

"Great. If I answer a few questions, will you go away? I feel like crap."

"You wanted to be a deputy," Kotto said. "Why?"

"Look, I'm sorry to waste your time like this, Sheriff," Richards said, reaching over for his glass and taking a sip. "But I was a little inebriated last night."

"You were under the influence."

"Yeah. That should disqualify me, right? I mean, if I'm applying to be a cop, don't I gotta be morally righteous and all that? Real straight shooter?"

"You were in the Army."

"Yeah."

"That's good enough for me. I don't care if you drink, as long as you don't drink on the job. Except in special circumstances. Of course, there's an awful lot of special circumstances.""Wait, that's it? That's the only qualification?"

"Well, you gotta pass my training course."

"I'm not interested."

"Why not?"

"Because," Richard said, setting the glass down. "Look, Sheriff, don't take this the wrong way. I thought your radio show was great. Real entertaining. But people think you're crazy. The department—it ain't what it used to be. The State Troopers run this county, not you."

"Do you think I'm crazy, Abraham Richards?"

"I didn't say that. Look, I just … Just go, okay?"

Kotto looked away and rubbed at his chin.

"You don't want a new job?" he asked.

"Well, I just started at the ski resort, I—"

"Not what I asked," Kotto said.

"Sure, I'd like a new job."

"Okay. What job can you carry a badge, a gun, and protect people? I mean, *really* protect people? Don't you miss that?"

Richards nodded.

"But I don't miss the Army."

"No, I figured that."

"But yeah, I do miss that feeling. I guess, at the end of the day, I felt like I was a part of something. I dunno. I didn't feel like that toward the end. But, yeah. Sure."

"Look, I'm not gonna lie to you. The odds are

stacked against us. People *do* think I'm crazy. And I'm a one-man operation. And nobody takes my theories seriously. But people need to start to wake up. Because there's all sorts of crazy crawlies out there, Richards." Kotto pointed out the back window, and Richards turned to look at the hills, their trees shaking loose a rain of colored leaves.

"Yeah, space aliens, right? You believe all that crap?"

"Among other things," Kotto said. "But the scariest thing on this earth? It's the heart of man himself. But you already know that."

"Yeah," Richards said. "I guess I do."

"I'm not gonna make you do anything you don't want to. But you sent me an application. You have an impressive résumé, with your military service. I could use a man like you in my operation. I might be wrong here, but I don't see a lot of other applications for an infantryman with an unfinished history degree. So think about it."

Kotto slapped his palm against the surface of the table, shaking the glasses. He stood up, stretching, his stomach pushing out from underneath his Misfits t-shirt. He slapped his cap back on his balding head, then pulled the papers and a pen from his jacket. He scribbled something on the back of Richards' résumé, then set the papers down on the table.

"There's bad things coming, Richards. It's in the wind, man, and everyone knows it, deep down, whether they want to admit it or not. Things are gonna get worse before they get better, and I don't think the State Troopers are prepared for that. I think we need men and women who understand that some things are deeper and darker than drunk drivers and meth labs, although we got plenty of those in this county, lord knows."

"What do you mean?"

"I mean, batten down the hatches, get another dog, lock your windows." Kotto shook his head, looking out at the hills. "There's bad voodoo in the air, man. We need people to stand up to it, to that darkness."

He pulled out his sunglasses and slipped them on, then looked right at Richards—and right through him. Richards saw himself reflected back in those dark lenses, bags under his eyes, weariness painted on his face. When did he get so *old*?

"We need heroes."

"I'm not a hero," Richards said. "I'm just a soldier."

"No," Kotto said, turning to leave. "You *were* a soldier. Now you just work at a ski resort." He disappeared down the hall, trailing an odor of cigarettes and the faint scent of fresh earth, like the sheriff had been doing lawn work all morning...or digging up something all night.

The door slapped shut behind him. Soon after came the revving of a malnourished engine and the squealing of tires. Then the sheriff was gone, and Richards was alone with his pain.

Kotto had left the papers on the table, face down. Richards grabbed them, setting aside his printed-off email, and read the words scrawled on the back of his résumé.

"7:30 am, tomorrow, @ 5701 Beach Shrub Rd. Workout clothes, running shoes, water bottle. Make sure you're not followed."

Richards furrowed his brow, crumpling the paper in his hands. He stared out the window.

The hills shed their colors, one leaf at a time.

7. Training Day

His father dropped him off at the edge of the gravel driveway, which stood at the lip of a curve at the crest of Beach Shrub Hill. Richards waved as his father drove off, concern on his old man's face and a cloud of black smoke trailing from his pickup truck. He hadn't told his parents much—just that this was a job, and it paid more than working at the ski resort. Kotto's reputation notwithstanding, they understood that their son needed some sort of opportunity, and there were slim pickings for opportunity in Cattaraugus County.

Overgrown bushes and skeletal trees hid the property from the road. Richards jogged up the driveway, passing between the bushes to find a squat house and attached garage, patches of uneven and discolored white paint curling off in little ribbons. There was a rusted-out Ford pickup next to the garage. A pair of glowing cat eyes stared out from the darkness beneath the truck, reflecting what little sunlight escaped the gray morning clouds.

A blue tarp covered the corner of the house nearest the tree line. It had come loose in one spot. The wind used it to slap at the roof in an uneven rhythm. Flanked by two square windows was a dark wooden porch, just wide enough to hold a plastic lawn chair on either side of the front door. A coffee can, its blue label faded by sun and rust, overflowed with dirt and cigarette butts. Richards stepped into the yard, past a row of potted plants long since abandoned to the morning frosts, and over a pair of empty Bud Light bottles.

He felt a sudden chill in the morning wind, and he was glad he'd worn his Army sweat pants and his dark green hoodie. He pulled on his Sabres skull cap, then took a sip from his water bottle.

What the hell am I doing here?

As if in response, the door to the small porch swung open. Kotto emerged, pushing open the door with the torn screen, wire mesh flapping loose like a wagging tongue. Kotto wore a white undershirt, black jeans, his untied combat boots, and his aviator sunglasses. He carried a yellow bag of Troyer's Farms salt n' vinegar potato chips. He reached a claw-like hand into the bag and pulled out a greasy fistful of chips, then shoved them into his impassive mouth.

All was silence, save for the whispering of wind among the leaves and the branches, and the crunching of fried potatoes on cigarette-stained teeth.

Kotto swallowed hard, then wiped his hand on his pants.

"You ready to train, cadet?"

"Two miles to go, two miles to go!" Kotto shouted at Richards through a beat-up orange traffic cone, a makeshift megaphone that reeked of road tar. Kotto jogged alongside Richards, the bottom edge of the cone just inches from Richards' ear. "Push it, cadet! Two miles to go!"

Richards hadn't exercised in the weeks he'd been

home, save for walks with the dog. A couple of spare pounds had made their way to his once-pristine abs, a legacy of beer and chicken wings. Still, as his heart pumped hot blood and his lungs pumped cool air, he felt the malaise of inactivity snap its hold on his muscles. He didn't realize how much he'd *missed* PT.

They crested the first short hill, and a quarter-mile stretch of pothole-plagued road loomed before them at a steady upslope. Richards smiled and pumped his legs harder.

"Push it, soldier boy! Two miles to go! Two miles … Two miles to go …!"

Kotto dropped out of his peripheral vision. The sheriff fell back, coughing and hacking. He took a knee, using the cone for support.

Richards turned around and jogged backwards.

"You okay?"

"Keep going, cadet!" Kotto snapped. He held the cone up to his lips. "Two miles to go! Keep running til you hit the burned barn, then double-time it back! I'm timing you!"

"You got it, Sheriff!" Richards said. He turned back to the hill and strode on, shaking his head and laughing.

Kotto caught his breath, and pushed himself back up.

"Damn," he said. "I gotta cut back on the junk food." He fished a cigarette out from a crumpled soft pack in his back pocket, then lit it up. The cadet was already almost out of sight.

They stood on Kotto's back deck, staring at an unkempt yard. The remains of a swimming pool stood to their right, its walls long ago collapsed. An orange tractor stood in a nest of tall grasses at the edge of the lawn. Beyond was a field, home to a pair of deer who moved across the open space before the tree line.

"I've hidden several clues in my backyard," Kotto said. "They're hidden in odd places. Twenty four envelopes containing words, maps, pictures. They're all clues to some mystery, conspiracy, or crime. You'll have to gather the clues and solve the riddle in the time allotted."

"Riddles?" Richards asked. "What's this got to do with police work?"

"It's a mind exercise," Kotto said. "Your mind is your most dangerous weapon. And should we ever encounter MK Ultra brainwashing techniques, your most dangerous liability. Speaking of which, do you watch television?"

"Some sports, sometimes. CNN, Fox News, Comedy Central."

"Jesus," Kotto hissed. He put a palm up to his brow in exasperation. "You may already be too programmed to continue."

"What, that's bad?"

"Television is the primary form of Illuminati meme and thought control," Kotto said. "Do you fall into the false left-right paradigm? Can you name more professional athletes than historical figures? How do you feel about binary post-modernism?"

"I don't know what any of that means," Richards said.

Kotto sighed.

"Never mind. I'll deprogram you later. Have you ever seen *Star Trek II: The Wrath of Khan?* Are you familiar with the Kobayashi Maru?"

"Are you having a stroke, Sheriff? You're speaking gibberish."

"I'll take that as a no. Okay, I'll give you thirty minutes to solve the riddle," Kotto said. "Starting now."

Richards took a moment to take in his surroundings.

"Wait, how many envelopes are there again?"

"Twenty-nine minutes."

"Damn."

Richards pulled off his hoodie and let it drop to the deck. He leapt off into the yard. Unmowed crab grass stood up to his ankles. As he moved, he kept his eyes low, searching through piles of brick and grass, upturned earth and rusting car parts for little white envelopes sealed with duct tape. He found the first couple hidden along the collapsed walls of the empty swimming pool; others hung in withered tree branches at the edge of the yard. In the metal compartment to the side of the tractor's seat was a stack of four, each envelope soaked through with water. Kotto had anticipated this; thus much of the information written inside was done so with crayon.

Kotto stood with his arms crossed, checking his watch occasionally, his eyes hidden behind his wide sunglasses, his mouth a flat line.

Richards jogged back to the deck and dropped his cache of envelopes. He began to sort through them, looking for numbers, letters, or any other clue he could get to organize them. They were shorter than business envelopes; more like something you'd put a small card inside, or a note to your grandmother. As Richards shuffled through the envelopes, he saw no markings of any sort. Just a square of uneven duct tape holding each one shut.

"Time check," he said, shuffling the envelopes into piles. He began to count them.

"Twenty minutes," Kotto said. He gestured behind him. Against the outside wall of the house stood a wide bulletin board made of cork and flimsy wood. Piles of multicolored string were scattered around it, and a small plastic box of colored thumbtacks sat beside it with its flaps open. "You can use this stuff to organize your clues."

"Right," Richards said, not exactly following. He counted 19 envelopes. Not quite all, but it was a start.

He stepped up onto the deck and moved his haul over to the board, which he pulled down and set flat against the ground. Then he began opening the envelopes, tearing away the duct tape, gray residue sticking to his fingers. Richards began to lay the clues out, hoping some pattern would present itself.

"Fifteen minutes," Kotto said.

Richards furrowed his brow and rubbed at his forehead. It all seemed so *random*. There were the familiar faces of celebrities, pictures of historical events, icons from corporations or institutions. Highlighted strips of newspaper marked a series of words or phrases seemingly disconnected from any larger context.

"You have to come up with something," Kotto said. "You're missing a few pieces, but I suggest you work with what you have."

Richards nodded, dribbles of sweat working their way down from his armpits. One last time, he took stock of his clues:

A picture of Bill Clinton shaking hands with one of the Rockefellers.

A highlighted phrase from a *Washington Post* article: "deepest memories abide."

An op-ed from the *Times* about the Iraq War.

A US dollar bill.

A Euro.

A partially-rendered transcript of a Russian TV news broadcast, in Russian.

A faded map of central Africa.

A stock market futures report on natural gas.

An article from *Ellicottville Events* on recent UFO activity. Richards had read that one.

A Polaroid of Ronald Reagan shaking hands with a gray alien, or a man in a gray alien costume.

A stack of post-it notes assessing the Majestic 12 documents, written in crayon.

A VHS case of *Videodrome*, partially flattened.

A press release from the Ellicottville Town Board concerning the introduction of fluoride into the water supply.

A rulebook from the board game *Risk*.

A set of dice, lacking any numbers or markings on their faces.

Pages from a technical manual on a military weather balloon.

The first two pages of Cecil Kotto's 2009 tax return.

Fuzzy photocopies of a Dover Thrift Books edition of *Macbeth*.

A small piece of mirrored glass.

Richards stood up and scratched at the back of his head.

What the hell is *this shit?*

"Twelve minutes," Kotto said, standing beside Richards. "Put it together."

"Put *what* together?" Richards asked, exasperated.

"Something," Kotto said. "Try."

Richards shook his head, then knelt down. He'd worked stupid mind puzzles before, usually in the Army. They'd give you a bunch of boards and rope, and tell you that you had to get a bucket of concrete over some water or something. Dumb stuff, but it made you think, if you took it seriously. Maybe this was like that. Only crazy.

He began to assemble the items into piles;

documents, photos, miscellany. Then he began to post items onto the corkboard. There was no real rhyme or reason at first, but then he organized the political photos and documents in one corner, re-arranged the UFO story and military weather balloon documents near the picture of Ronald Reagan and the gray alien, and connected each group together with string. He stood back, considered his collage with crossed arms and furrowed brow, then moved the dollar bill and Euro to the center of the collection.

"Time," Kotto said, dropping his watch. "Let's see what you got here, cadet." He leaned in as Richards stepped back.

"I know I'm missing some pieces," Richard said. "I'm not sure why I arranged it like I did. Just felt ... Right."

"So what's it about?" Kotto asked. "What's your interpretation of the evidence?"

"Honestly?"

"Yes," Kotto said. "Always be honest with me. It's the only way this is going to work."

"I think it's a bunch of bullshit."

"Hmm, that *is* honest. I guess I walked into that one."

"It's random crap. None of it adds up."

"Are you sure?" Kotto asked, running a finger along the string connecting his tax return to the thumbtack holding up the small mirror. "This doesn't look random to me. And it didn't look random to you, at least subconsciously. You organized it as best you could. Why did you connect these items with the string?"

"Because you gave me string to work with," Richards said.

"Why did you put the money in the middle?"

"It seemed like it belonged there."

"And what do you think now?" Kotto stood up

straight and stared at his trainee. "If you had to put it all together, what would you come up with?"

Richards shook his head, then shrugged.

"I'm sorry, Sheriff. But I don't understand this. I guess maybe I'm not the man for the job."

"Look at it," Kotto said, his voice firm. "You connected the politicians, then ran string to the UFO article, the fluoride piece, the military document… The money's at the center, and the Shakespeare play appears near the news articles and excerpts. You've implied a connection between power, local news events, funding streams, and the fiction of drama."

Richards stared, dumbfounded, at his own creation.

"You've implied that the news is drama, an act. And here," Kotto said, pulling his tax report and the glass mirror from the board. "You've made it personal. Conspiracies start at the top power structures, are reinforced through compliant media platforms which are happy to propagate fiction and news-as-entertainment, motivated by money, with local reach, and funded by my tax dollars. *Your* tax dollars, if you look in the mirror."

Jesus, Richards thought to himself. *Did I put all that together?*

"Well, um," Richards said. "Was I right? Did I solve the mystery, then? Even without the other clues?"

"What?"

"The riddle, the main problem I was supposed to solve," Richards continued. "Did I get it right by doing this?"

Kotto considered this for a moment.

"Sometimes, there's no clear road to the truth. You feel me? Sometimes, we have to come up with the patterns ourselves. Even if everyone else can't see it."

"So I passed?"

"Well, I'm letting you continue to the next phase. So

it's not all bad." Kotto pulled out his .40 pistol from the small of his back. The black gun was shining with oil, glassy to the eye, smooth to the touch. He tossed it at Richards. The gun bobbled in his hands, nearly falling to the deck. "Next up is firearms training."

"You can take off the blindfold now, cadet!" Kotto yelled through the traffic cone, his voice amplified and echoing from somewhere behind Richards.

Richards did what he was told. The blindfold was a Buffalo Bills football handkerchief, faded from years in the sun, stained with salt from sweat (from work) or tears (from watching the Bills). He let it drop to the grass and held his pistol out, pointing down at the ground a few feet ahead of him. Beyond was a field, tall grasses and sunken hay bales peppering the landscape for a hundred yards, a row of trees in the distance with shadows guarding the edge of the forest.

"You ready?" Kotto blared.

"For what?" Richards said. "I don't see anything."

"Engage your targets at they appear!" Kotto shouted. Then there was an audible *click*, and the coughing of a diesel generator signaled its coming to life. Richards checked his ear plugs and waited. He waited for *something*, whatever it was.

"Do you see anything?" Kotto yelled over the thrum of the generator. Richards squinted through the tint of his sunglasses. The only movement was the swaying of grass in the soft wind, and the branches dancing in the forest beyond.

Metal-on-metal groaned and sparks shot up into the air from several points in the field. A tortured whirring followed by the squeal of rusted metal precipitated the rising of a form from the grass 10 yards away. Dracula—rather, Bela Lugosi as Dracula—cape over his face, his eyes alight with hunger, rose from the earth, his black cape spattered with bird droppings, his face sun-faded well beyond his normal pallor.

"Shoot that fucker!" Kotto hollered. "Kill that vampire dead!"

Richards, acting on instinct, brought the .40 up and fired two rounds in a controlled pair, directly at the cardboard cut-out's wavering chest.

"No, no, no!" Kotto yelled. "It's a *vampire!* Shoot it in the heart or the brain!"

"Of course," Richards said to himself. "How could I forget?"

He fired off two more shots, one of which went wide. The second blew out Bela's left eyeball. Grinding metal again, then the target slowly leaned back to rest within the grass.

"Next target!"

To Richards' left this time, only five or so yards away, rose another Hollywood specter. A muscular form, brandishing a mop covered in blood, his face mangled and swollen, rose from the earth.

"Is that the Toxic Avenger?" Richards asked, yelling over his shoulder. "He's a good guy, right?'

"Shoot the damn thing, cadet!"

Richards shrugged and popped off three rounds. Two found purchase in the creature's chest.

I'm a little rusty. Never was much good with a pistol.

"Next target!"

The mutant janitor slowly returned to his resting place. Directly ahead of Richards, no more than 15 yards away, rose a new horror.

"What the hell is this?" he shouted over the whirring target motors and the groans of the generator. "Where'd you get that picture?"

The form that rose from the field was no Hollywood monster; it was a man in a business suit. His face, however, was covered by a black and white print-out of someone else's face. Richards' face. It was his high school graduation photo, blown up to life size.

"I'm not going to shoot myself," Richards said. "Is this some kind of psych test?"

"It's a friggin' pod person!" Kotto shouted through the traffic cone. "He's stolen your identity and works as a bank teller! If you ever meet your doppelganger in the field, you better not hesitate to put him down!"

"Wait, my pod person replacement works at a bank?" Richards said, raising his pistol, but pointing to the side of the target. "That doesn't sound so evil!"

"He's going to steal your brain memories!" Kotto shouted. "Haven't you seen any movies?"

"Weirdest goddamn day of my life," Richards muttered. He fired off the last rounds into the center of the target, watching chunks of cardboard pop up and into the air. His youthful, acne-scarred face stared back at him with a dumb smile. The target went down, and Bela Lugosi came back up for more blood.

8. Run Bucky, Run

An old two-story rail station house guarded the tracks that crossed the intersection of under-repaired rural roads 240 and 242. Most days and nights, it stood lifeless and dark. Although the rail was still in use, it was rare to see many trains or even much road traffic through here, save for the passing of locals to and fro, or the occasional lost tourist.

The trains that did pass through the junction came at night, ferrying cargo under the cover of darkness. Most locals saw in this no sinister intent, the train whistles shrieking out in the late hours and shaking them from uneasy sleep. But if they had been able to see the cargo stored under lock and key, they would have begun to question why so many of their friends and neighbors kept coming down with cancer.

Now, in the bright of day, with no trains in sight, the rail station house was alive with activity. State Trooper Commander George Winston had made it his forward base of operations. With Bucky believed to still be in the area, it was as good as any place to set up shop. The Troopers' mobile command unit RV stood parked on the gravel road below, satellite dishes and antennae fully extended to keep in communication with his superiors back in Albany.

There were a dozen blue Trooper SUVs lined up and down Route 242 just a few hundred feet from the station, along with an MRAP armored vehicle fresh from another railhead in Fort Drum. Around the MRAP were SWAT Troopers decked out in full cool-guy wannabe-Army armor and kit, M-4 rifles with sights and lasers they probably didn't even know how to use held tightly in their over-eager hands. A bunch of their friends were dead or in the hospital, and they weren't in the mood to play friendly neighborhood cop.

They were here to play soldier.

The SWAT team hung back a ways from the road, watching as the other Troopers (most wearing body armor, but uniform caps instead of stormtrooper helmets) waved cars to stop or proceed through a gauntlet of bright orange road cones and aluminum road blocks. Traffic, usually no more than a few cars every few minutes, had become a snarl in both directions along 242 near the intersection. Ellicottville stood to the west and south, the peaks of some of its famed skiing hills visible through a hazy mix of cloud and October fog.

"Here they are," Veronica Cartwright said, leaning forward in the decrepit news van, which sputtered and coughed as the cameraman-cum-driver lightly tapped the brake. "I'm just hoping I can catch Commander Winston out here."

"What makes you think he's not out chasing Bucky?" Dean, the cameraman asked, flicking his cigarette out the window. Their van came to rest behind a rusted-out Chevy Silverado pickup truck, its back window home to a rack full of shotguns. "You gonna drink that coffee I got you?"

"Not until right before I go on camera," Veronica said. "It gives me the farts. Commander Winston will want to meet with *someone*. As far as I know, we're the first media to hear about the protests."

"They don't look like much of a protest movement to me," Dean said, slurping at his gas station mocha latte. "What are they? Occupy Wall Street? Tea Party?"

"Looks more like entrepreneurs," Veronica said. She flipped the sun visor down and checked her makeup and hair in the mirror. Despite all the strides women had made in televised news over the past thirty or forty years, Veronica knew as well as anyone that her beauty certainly didn't hurt. She'd won Miss Cattaraugus County back in 2001 when she was still a senior in high school, her bright green eyes and lustrous blond hair framing high cheek bones and soft, full lips.

Her first big break after graduating with a degree in broadcasting and journalism from the University of Buffalo was as a local interest reporter in Philadelphia. She figured she was paying her dues—three years interviewing hippies at nonprofit fundraisers, huckster community organizers at local festivals, and pet owners who had trained their mutts to do stupid tricks wore on her, but she pressed on, her eye on serious news. She would have taken anything—even the local crime beat—just to get her some exposure on stories that weren't about the newest red panda litter at the Philly zoo.

When the re-assignment didn't come, she took matters into her own hands, taking tips from local residents about police and political corruption, spending her off hours with a handheld camera and asking local aldermen and off-duty cops if they could answer some questions. A few blog posts and YouTube videos later, and she knew her star was on the rise.

Her producer thought otherwise. The discussion was one-sided; her options clear: resign or get laid off. Cutbacks in the news department, and all that.

She packed her bags up and came back to her parents' place, and started looking for work in Buffalo, Erie, or maybe even Hamilton or Toronto. The only place hiring an attractive female reporter with a "resignation" in her history was Cattaraugus County Public Access Television. It was half-time and it wasn't glamorous, but it was work. Since the station was run by a handful of staff and a few incompetent volunteers, she could report on whatever the hell she wanted. If she could find anything to report *on*, that is.

The staff had recommended a few stories—there were seasonal events in the run up to Halloween; people were seeing lights in the sky and getting messages from outer space around Ellicottville. And, of course, the Snow Pine Resort expansion project—hundreds of acres owned by state and local interests were up for grabs by the private corporation. Not everybody was happy about eminent domain being used to provide more condos and ski trails for Canadian tourists, of course. But there was a story there, sure.

But this—this Bucky thing—it was big. It might even be her ticket out of CCPATV, then onto one of the stations in Buffalo, Rochester, Syracuse—or maybe even a prime market again.

Although she saw wrinkles beginning to form around her eyes when she looked in the mirror, and that scrappy, no-sleep-til-the-story's-done energy had begun to fade, she knew she had enough juice left to take one more shot at the big time. Many success stories have humble beginnings, she often reminded herself. Her particular new beginning on the Bucky manhunt story was a crowd standing around a Bud Light half-keg in a pile of ice set inside a kiddie pool.

Someone had tuned their truck radio to an 80s rock anthem station. Tired tunes—overwrought guitar ballads and paeans to loose women anchored the sounds of a party. Hand-painted or drawn signs peppered the yard in front of a house with attached garage, its siding faded and crumbling off like bits of decayed teeth. Twenty or 30 men and women—as well as a roaming pack of dogs—stood about the yard, some carrying signs or shotguns, most carrying beers.

"That's where we start," Veronica said, pointing to the small crowd around the keg.

"They're drinking beer," Dean said. "You sure this is a good idea?"

"This is the story," Veronica said. "We go to where the story is."

"You know, the station isn't going to pay us overtime."

"Then go home to your cats, and tune in later," Veronica said. She picked up her microphone and stepped out of the van. She was careful to avoid mud spattering up onto her ankles and legs, but with the number of tire tracks and footprints in the soft earth ahead of her, she knew that was a losing battle.

As Dean lugged the shoulder camera out of the side of the van and then hurried to catch up with her, Veronica passed two boys—and boys they were, probably no more than 19 at the most—shotgunning cans of Natty Ice. One of them punctured his can with a dull pocket knife, sending a fine foam mist into the air, getting some in her hair and on her face.

This is going to be it, she told herself, not knowing whether it was a lie or not. She wiped the beer fizz from her face and made for the crying woman in the middle of the crowd, sitting near a picture of the suspect blown up to comical size and plastered on a board held aloft by a plastic mop handle.

Dean had already spotted her, and was busy prepping the camera. He may have been an oaf, but he was good at his job.

The woman was old beyond her years, with a lined, yellowed face made sallow by hard drink and cheap cigarettes. Her breath reeked of fried chicken and ash, and her eyes behind her too-thick glasses were large and glassy. Her oversized white t-shirt had a print of Bucky's oversized face, no doubt taken from a cheap digital photograph, his eyes glazed and his mouth hanging open, a Swisher Sweet dangling from the corner of his lips. Beneath the portrait was the phrase, in oversized, all-caps san serif, "RUN BUCKY, RUN."

"He's my boy, and I love him," the woman said. Mrs. Delilah Green, mother of one, 51 years old, unemployed, avid lottery-player and stories watcher.

"Please don't look at the camera, ma'am," Dean said, squinting through the eyepiece and adjusting the focus.

"Sorry."

"It's okay," Veronica said, concern etched on her make-up-caked face. She offered an empathetic smile, and her eyes glanced over at the crowd of protestors and gawkers that stood behind Mrs. Green. They'd taken to gathering directly in the line of sight of the camera, most content to hold onto their beers. Some were holding up the "RUN BUCKY, RUN" t-shirts, stickers advertising them for $10 a piece plastered above Bucky's confused and probably inebriated visage.

"Could you tell us a little bit about why the police are after your son?" Veronica asked. Mrs. Green wiped at her eyes, mascara beginning to smear, with a ratty old wash cloth.

"They say he's a moonshiner," she said, composing herself. "But even so, why would they send the SWAT boys after him? Why not just an APB, one or two Troopers? He didn't bother nobody."

"The State Troopers maintain that your son—Bucky—is armed and dangerous."

"He ain't never hurt nobody. If he's 'shining, that's his business, even if it's criminal, but that don't mean he hurts people."

"The State Troopers have issued a statement, warning people not to drink Bucky's moonshine. They say it may contain poison. Have you ever had any?"

"Lord knows I don't drink," Mrs. Green said, the lie effortless. "I'm a good neighbor, keep to myself. If Bucky made 'shine, which I'm not saying he did, I never drank it."

"Would you tell us a little about why you're protesting the police response?"

"Look for yourself, you got a camera," Mrs. Green said, again, looking directly at Dean. "Does this look like normal police work to you?"

"We see the police out here in force."

"Force is right! They're harassing us! I've had Troopers knock on my hotel room door at all hours of the night, yelling at me, telling me they gotta search the room. They done it six times already, and got snipers in the woods, helicopters overhead. Worse enough they blew up my trailer. I don't know where Bucky run off to. They chased him into the woods, not me."

"If you knew, would you say?"

"I may have, before. But look at this. Is this America? Or communist Russia?" Mrs. Green turned away from Veronica. "I'm sorry. But my boy ain't no killer. A drunk, maybe even a moonshiner. But he would never hurt anyone, not even pig-ass cops."

"Thank you for your time, Mrs. Green," Veronica said. She lowered her microphone and offered the older woman a warm smile. She tossed her head to the side and walked up beside Dean, the two moving away from the center of the crowd.

"We'll cut that last bit out," she said. She pointed to a man in a Dale Earnhardt "NEVER FORGET" short sleeve, selling t-shirts with the "RUN BUCKY, RUN" slogan. "Let's get this idiot on camera."

"My name's not gonna go on camera," the young man said. He had a pile of shirts—all different neon colors—slung over his shoulder. "But boys 'round here call me Cooter." He offered a tobacco-stained smile, his right hand holding a dented PBR can, his left wiping at the side of his unshaven face.

"Oh, okay, Cooter," Veronica said. "Could you tell us why you're selling t-shirts encouraging Bucky to run? Why aren't the people out here willing to cooperate with the State Troopers to arrest an alleged murderer?"

"Bucky is one of us. Alright. I used to buy 'shine off him, back before he changed his recipe. These Troopers, most of them aren't from around here. They don't understand they can't just come into our homes, our property, and act like they own the place. They don't. Just because there's dead cops don't justify how they are behaving." He took a slug of his PBR. "So I'm telling you, one for 10, two for 15." He pulled a t-shirt from the pile near his unlaced boots. "What size are you, honey? Small'll fit you?"

As the morning dragged on, fewer and fewer cars came through the checkpoint.

"We been calling all our friends and family, telling 'em to go around," Cooter told Veronica, after they finished filming. "They ain't done nothing wrong, so there's no need to come through this way."

"What if Bucky's in one of the vehicles? Are you okay with inadvertently tipping him off?"

"I'd call him direct, if I had his number and he'd answer it," Cooter said, his smile becoming a leer as the drink took hold. "But he's too smart to use a phone, let alone his."

Commander George Winston agreed to an interview just after lunch. He was busy taking calls, filing reports to Albany, working the radio, and organizing additional searches for the afternoon. Veronica and Dean killed time by watching the flow of traffic slow to a trickle, and by walking along the edge of the forest, admiring the golden swath of leaves and color.

Winston, escorted by two SWAT Troopers in full combat regalia, made his way to the news van just as the Troopers began to pull their vehicles and road blocks away from along Route 242. They were breaking it down and moving on.

"Look alive," Veronica said. Dean set down the PBR he'd graciously taken from Cooter and worked to get the camera up and running.

Veronica, head up and chest out, her nose just slightly in the air, offered a cool smile and extended hand as Commander Winston approached. The older cop—gruff, with a rugged chin covered in stubble, and ice-blue eyes that spoke confidence and authority—took her hand and gave it a rough pair of tugs, in something approaching a handshake. Veronica refused to wince under the pressure, and smiled her Miss Cattaraugus County smile. He smirked.

"Thank you for agreeing to the interview, sir. I know you're busy running the operation."

"It's no problem. We always have time for the media. It's important that your viewers—your lucky viewers—get to hear our side of the story."

"Your side, sir?"

"That's what I said, isn't it?" He smirk fell and his eyes went cool. "The truth."

"We're ready," Dean said, stepping back to get a close up of Veronica. She closed her eyes, offered a little prayer to whatever god of journalism there may be, and was in the zone.

"In a CCPATV exclusive, State Trooper Major George Winston, the officer in charge of the manhunt here in and around Ashford Junction, has agreed to answer a few questions about the suspect and the operation meant to capture him. Sir, thank you for joining us."

"My pleasure, Veronica," he said, his tone all business.

"Sir, could you describe your operation this morning?"

"In a limited fashion, yes. We're engaged in operations in and around Cattaraugus County, partnering with local municipalities and communities in an effort to bring in known cop killer, moonshiner, and all around degenerate, Larry Green."

"*Alleged* criminal. Your main suspect."

"Of course. *Alleged*. Yes."

"The locals have another name for Larry Green, sir. They call him Bucky, and there's quite a few protestors out near your traffic checkpoint showing their support for him."

Winston frowned.

"Just a few trouble makers, trying to make a buck off of a local tragedy. They're selling t-shirts and violating open container laws." He stopped speaking to offer the camera a wide smile. "If you look to your right, Veronica, you'll see my officers making several arrests. Public intoxication, illegal public assembly, and interfering with a police investigation doesn't sit well with most judges in these parts, does it?"

Veronica pointed, and Dean swiveled on his heels, pointing the camera lens at the melee taking place. Officers wearing full riot gear—including blast helmets, body armor, and wielding clubs—descended into the impromptu protest and camp. As Veronica looked on, the Troopers turned over boxes full of t-shirts, plastic bins full of beer, and dragged Cooter and several of his buddies to the ground. The locals swore and swung and cursed Johnny Law, but in the end, it was Johnny Law who won. And it was on camera for all the world—at least the viewing audience of Cattaraugus County Public Access Television—to see.

Dean captured enough of the ensuing action—a bunch of local yokels getting the snot kicked out of them by riot police—to fill out the piece, and then some. It was great footage, really. The cops were overly aggressive; the protesters were drunk and willing to fight. That is, until their faces were covered in pepper spray and they were tasered or clubbed into submission.

A pang of guilt worked its way up from Veronica's core. These were *people*, after all. And while they had been acting irresponsibly—public drinking, antagonizing the police—they had legitimate grievances. Bucky was probably a murderer, sure. But that didn't justify this.

The Troopers weren't interested in seizing the camera. In fact, while they swept through the yard and dispersed the protest-slash-drinking festival, Commander Winston insisted that they finish the interview. He was confident, calm, and pleased with himself.

"The people of Cattaraugus County are safe, as long as they cooperate with our investigation and operations," he said. "We will not tolerate violence or harassment against our police force. We expect cooperation from everyone in the area. Together, we can get Larry 'Bucky' Green out of your community, and behind bars where he belongs. Everyone will be safer that way."

The only other stories broadcast that evening on CCPATV were an on-the-spot visit to local tourist trap Pumpkinville for a carving contest, and a short report featuring a collection of blurry cell phone camera photos of glowing red orbs appearing in the sky over northeast Ellicottville. The station manager gave her a full eight and a half minutes to run her story. That included all of her interviews and most of the footage of the police moving in on the protestors. The station manager figured that their average viewing audience—maybe about three hundred people per night—just about doubled.

When her report finished, the signal cut to a filmed segment at Cattaraugus County Community College—or C triple C—concerning Bucky's moonshine.

Dr. Christopher Crawbottom, associate professor of general sciences and cryptozoology, was tall and lanky, with a gut that hung just over his belt line, thinning black hair, and thin glasses over a soft face. He wore a brown suit coat (complete with elbow pads, naturally) and black slacks stained with chalk dust. His name and title appeared beneath him in blurry green text.

"This, as you can see, is a bottle of Bucky's moonshine," he said, holding up a small glass bottle. Protruding from its surface was the imprinted-in-glass image of a man with arms and wings spread, a thick beard and a tall hat. Hammurabi meets Dracula. "Ingesting this substance, while initially enjoyable, causes a mild case of food poisoning in the stomach and liver. This isn't your run of the mill 'shine, good viewers. It contains several psychotropic chemical compounds, as well as a few organic molecular substances that we are still attempting to identify. Take it from me—do not drink Bucky's moonshine. It will cause a bout of temporary insanity, followed by several days' worth of delirium tremens. Take it from me, because I am an education authority figure." He paused a moment to set the bottle down on a nearby desk. "But yes, in case you were wondering: it will get you drunk, and it is very cheap. But who would risk their long-term psychological health just for a few hours of fun?"

9. Dog Skulls and Tire Fires

Richards woke up to a painful and unhappy morning in a pile of towels and t-shirts. He'd curled up into a ball against them, arranging the unfolded laundry into a little cocoon around his body. The concrete floor of Kotto's garage was cold, and his neck cracked with a snap of pain as he sat up. The room appeared hazy; light filtered in through old, scuffed up windows riddled with splotches of paint and streaked with spider webs. Somewhere a dog was barking, and a lawnmower was running. They both sounded far too close for Richards' liking. Too close, as in, directly inside the front of his skull.

The pounding in his head came first, and nausea followed swiftly behind. He reeked of sweat and fabric softener; he had slept in his workout clothes from the day before. Keeping his eyes open was a trial.

"What's the last thing you remember?"

"Jesus!" Richards jumped back, falling into a pile of towels. Kotto was there, sitting in a rocking chair, staring out an open garage door. He sipped a Bud Light, then wiped sweat from his brow along the top of his white undershirt.

"Stay alert, stay alive, deputy," Kotto said.

"I remember doing shots. Power hour, right?"

"Yes."

"Why were we doing shots?"

"It was the last part of your training. I had to see how you handled your liquor."

"What's that have to do with police work?"

"There may come a time when you face MK Ultra brainwashing, psychotronic weapons, or even a seduction by demonic or supernatural forces. I had to know what your mental resiliency looked like."

"So you got me drunk? How long did I last? What's my 'mental resiliency'?"

"Slightly above average. Until you threw up."

"I don't remember throwing up."

"It was on the back deck."

"Shit. Now I remember." Richards groaned and rubbed at his temples. "I feel like I'm going to die."

"Drink this," Kotto said. He stood up and walked over, handing Richards a brown glass growler jug of water, and placing a fresh six pack of Bud Light next to him. "Then eat this." He produced a gas station breakfast sandwich, dripping with grease. "Then sleep. You'll be right as rain in no time."

"I'm not sure I can keep any of that down."

"Try," Kotto said, impassive behind his sunglasses. "Try and rest. You deserve it."

"For getting drunk?"

"No," Kotto said. "For passing the training course. Welcome to the force, Sheriff's Deputy Abraham Richards." From the small of his back he brought out a 9mm pistol, three magazines, and a silver star badge. Richards reached up a weary hand and took the markers of his new career. He studied the badge's glistening surface. It read "CATTARAUGUS COUNTY" along the top of the star, with "SHERIFF'S DEPT" along the bottom. They framed an image of rolling hills and a peaceful stream.

"I'm a cop now? One day of training and drinking, and I'm a cop?"

"Budget cuts," Kotto said. "That, and a crippling crystal meth scandal involving half the politicians and police in the county. Til the legislature figures out what to do with the department, we're it."

"No money for training?"

"No money for much of anything. Just a stipend for me, you, a dispatcher, some radios, some ammo, some gas. That's it. We coordinate suspect lock up and court processing with local municipalities and the State."

"This isn't even functional," Richards said, each word ringing in his brain. *Damn*. "This isn't a police department."

"No," Kotto said. "It's the *Sheriff's* Department. And we're what's left of it."

"I feel like I am going to die," Richards said. "Can I throw up in here?"

"I brought you a bucket. Get some rest," Kotto said. "Sleep it off."

"Can you just take me to the vet instead? They can put me down like a sick dog."

"I'll check on you in a couple of hours. Hopefully you'll be ready to work by tonight."

"Jesus. Work? I can barely think."

"There's a manhunt on out there, deputy," Kotto said. "We're needed, hangovers be damned."

Richards dreamed of field and forest. They ran through them, together, Kotto and he, carrying guns, weighed down by body armor and gear. There was an encroaching darkness—an ink stain of pure hate and evil, stretching out from the top of a hill, where a vortex of storm and dark swirled and grew. A nagging, persistent fear ate away at him, making his steps heavy, his breath hot and labored. They ran, and ran, and ran—not from the darkness, but *toward* it. Toward that heaving maw of abyss and dark lines of color that reached up from rotten soil to rip his awareness into purest, coldest black ...

Orange afternoon light stung his eyes. He pushed away a pile of towels, his forehead and legs thick with sweat. The saliva in his mouth had turned into a gooish, bitter paste. The sweat along his forehead and face reeked of alcohol.

The thin plane of glass on the unfinished window set in concrete had magnified the afternoon's light, shining a beam directly onto his forehead. Richards' brain was cooked and there was the weight of a good hangover shit lingering in his bowels. His head didn't pound so bad, and his stomach offered him the first pangs of hunger. Something salty and fatty would do. That, and coffee. Lots of coffee.

After using the bathroom and getting a glass of water to drink (the sulphur smell of unfiltered well water threatening a return to nausea), he made his way back into the garage where he had been sleeping to collect his things. He had a job now, sort of—and plenty of savings from his time overseas—but until he could find a good car, he'd have to rely on his parents. Maybe Kotto could get him a cruiser for his personal use. There was probably a fleet of them locked up somewhere, impounded after the department scandal.

His cell phone read a missed call—his parents, no doubt, wondering how their boy was doing spending his days with the local coot sheriff-slash-part-time-radio-show-host—and he wondered if anyone would be at home to come pick him up. He wanted fast food, coffee, and a shower. Not necessarily in that order.

Footsteps echoed from within the house. Kotto moved along rickety wooden stairs leading from the basement to the kitchen. Garbled voices and static—radio traffic of some sort—followed his footsteps. There was the creaking of cheap hinges in desperate need of WD-40, then the slamming of a door back into place. Kotto opened the side door into the garage and poked his head in, a Motorola portable radio, not unlike those Richards had used overseas, in his hand.

"Hey," Kotto said. "We got a call."

"A call?" Richards asked. "Shouldn't people call the State Troopers?"

"Some do, some don't," Kotto said. "Some people trust local law enforcement more, especially with this Bucky manhunt nonsense. I got Michelle my dispatcher on the line. She's getting calls from around West Valley. We got a riot situation."

"Wait, what?" Richards asked. West Valley was a sleepy little one-light community (a yellow blinking light at that), its only claim to fame the Department of Energy nuclear waste reprocessing facility a couple of miles outside of town. There was the small public school—Kotto and Richards were both alumni—but not much else. If the people rioted, there was nothing to destroy. Hell, there couldn't be enough people to have it even *count* as a riot.

"Sheriff, that can't be right."

"Some concerned citizens say otherwise," Kotto said. "Let's suit up."

Kotto led Richards down into the basement. Occasionally the voice of Michelle—the part-time dispatcher operating out of a radio substation somewhere outside of Ellicottville—piped in over the static to provide small bits of information as calls to the Kottoline came in.

"Fire in the street. Maybe a couple of cars."

"There's an overturned volunteer fire truck just outside of town."

"Cows are on the loose."

"People are clawing at each other in the streets."

Richards wasn't convinced that this wasn't part of his training. Kotto was a weird dude, when you came right down to it. Maybe he was making this riot nonsense up as some kind of test.

Beyond the sagging staircase down into the basement were boxes, bins, old bicycles, car parts, rusted tools. The air in the basement was rank with the smell of sulfur emanating from pools of water littered every few feet.

They made their way back, to a bit of basement sectioned off by chain-link walls on runners. They were all strung together by a Gordian knot of chains and padlocks. Kotto produced a series of old keys that looked like they belonged in a horror movie about an insanity ward. Using each bone-like key in succession, he tinkered and wrenched lock after lock open, chains and locks alike falling onto wet concrete below. Finally the sheriff rolled one of the runners back, revealing stacks of black tough boxes, military duffel bags filled to the brim, and un-opened (but dry) cardboard boxes.

"What's all this?" Richards asked. It wasn't unlike the supply room back in the armory. Except, of course, that this wasn't a National Guard armory. This was the crumbling basement of a local crackpot, albeit a local crackpot with a gun, a badge, and the half-joking backing of the voters of this sad-sack county.

"The County and the State liquidated most of the Department's resources by the time I was elected," Kotto said. "This was all that was left." Kotto stepped inside and kicked back a pile of empty green Genny Cream Ale cans. The screeching of some terrified animal filled their ears. Kotto grabbed a billy club from atop one of the boxes and flailed around behind a pile of duffle bags.

He brought the weapon down, again and again and again, until the screeching stopped.

"Damn basement lizards," Kotto said. He wiped oil-black blood off of the club against his t-shirt. "Now, let's see if we got any riot gear lying around."

Kotto deftly piloted the rickety old VW Van through a winding obstacle course of abandoned cars and unconscious (or dead) bodies strewn about the route into town. They'd met a steady stream of cars, driving frantically, flashing lights and horns blaring, hands waving and mouths shouting to *turn back*.

The van—probably rolled off the line in the late 60s—was a cramped and shaky old number, with torn-up seats and air vents that spit dust. Both men wore body armor—ill-fitting blue and black plate carriers—with mismatched knee and elbow pads. Tactical vests were slung over the armor, holding extra ammo and magazines for their pistols. They kept their side arms strapped to their hips. Around their belts they wore pepper spray, and two billy clubs they'd found under a pile of moldy *Playboy* magazines in the corner of the basement.

It was hard to sit up straight without pain flaring in their lower backs. It wasn't all that different from being on mounted patrol back in Afghanistan, Richards realized.

"There's bad voodoo ahead," Kotto said as they passed the new volunteer fire hall, now ablaze, its bays open and its fire trucks overturned and torched, men wearing hodgepodge firefighter gear pouring gasoline onto the trucks and themselves.

"Jesus Christ," Richards said, leaning back to watch them erupt in flame and screams of maniacal laughter and pain. "They're immolating themselves!"

"The Army teach you those big words?" Kotto said, his voice not betraying a drop of fear or discomfort. His eyes, behind those ever-present aviator sunglasses, were glued to the road ahead.

"Those firemen—they set themselves on fire."

"I know what you meant."

"Why are you giving me a hard time?"

Kotto's fingers tightened on the wheel.

"Just nerves, I guess. Hey, reach in the glove compartment there."

Richards popped the old dash open, expecting to find another gun, or maybe a radio, pepper spray, something.

Just as soon as the glove compartment fell open, an unopened pint of Canadian whiskey rolled into his lap.

"You've got booze in your van?"

"For emergencies only."

"What kind of emergencies?"

Kotto gestured ahead. They were on the outskirts of town now. The damage wasn't so bad away from the downtown core—as if West Valley *had* a downtown—but the smell of smoke and blood was heavy on the air. Ahead they could see the edge of the crowd, stumbling back and forth, some yelling, some screaming, some committing unspeakable acts of violence—or things not quite violence, but close enough.

The crowd grew as the day's light became thin and desperate, drowned out by encroaching black clouds. They were ordinary small-town folk—at least at first glance. This could have been any community gathering along Main Street; a farmer's market, or the Dairy Princess festival, even. But there was no joy, no jubilation. And there was no intelligence in their eyes—just a burning, passionate glow of lust and potential violence. And something else.

"Sheriff. Their eyes."

"I see it."

"What is that?"

"Looks like they're smoking. Green, maybe orange mist."

"What does that mean?"

"Still collating data," Kotto said. "What do you think it means?"

Indeed. Their eyes billowed a steady stream of smoke, a fell light of dancing, dark colors pulsing within. Any semblance of their humanity in those windows to the soul was gone, drifting out and up along that fell fog along with the smoke from the fires that burned all around them. Their words were not the words of friendly neighbors, but a garbled mish-mash of language, something coherent, perhaps, but unknowable to the lawmen.

These were, however, unmistakably the people of West Valley and the surrounding hills. Farmers come into town on tractors whose wheels were slick with fresh blood; a group of parishioners milling around the steps of their burning church; roving bands of young men and women alternatively pulling out their own hair or pulling off each other's clothes in some sick, animalistic frenzy of desire. Old women clutched shards of broken glass and waved them above their heads, spraying out droplets of blood spilled from their own palms; mothers and fathers roasted family dogs over tire fires. Churches and houses burned. The American flags posted on alternating telephone poles waved high and proud over a reverie of carnage and violence and blood.

"I'd say this qualifies as one of those emergencies." Kotto braked and put the van into park. He left it running. He pulled the handset from the radio haphazardly installed above his dashboard. "Michelle, you hear me honey?"

"Loud and clear, Sheriff," came back the only dispatcher on the payroll.

"We've arrived on-scene, time now. We're preparing to deploy. Crowd control operations."

"We're going *out there?*" Richards squeaked. Ahead of them, a little girl bit the head off of a hamster before tossing its jittering body into a pile of burning bodies. Burning *human* bodies.

"How bad is it, Sheriff?"

"Bad enough for me to call in the State boys. We're gonna need some backup."

"Their dispatcher won't put me through to command and control. They keep saying all their Troopers are tied up in field ops, looking for Bucky in the woods."

"Let them know we're in West Valley, and if they decide they want to actually help some folks, head this way with whatever high-speed shit they got from the Department of Defense. They're gonna need it."

"What are you gonna do, Sheriff?" Michelle asked. "Nothing stupid?"

"We're gonna try and make a difference," he said. "Kotto out." He placed the hand set back in the receiver, then grabbed the whiskey out of Richards' lap. The cap popped open with a snap, and Kotto put the bottle to his lips. He drained half of the pint before handing it to Richards. "Whew, doggy, that's some smart stuff," Kotto said.

"You're drinking liquor now? *Now?*"

"Deputy, I couldn't possibly think of a better time." Kotto's voice was soft, proper, polite, and with just a hint of confused defensiveness.

"Fuck it," Richards said. He grabbed the bottle and took a shot. "We're probably not going to live through this anyway." When he was finished, he put the bottle back in the glove compartment.

Kotto reached down for a welder's mask. Richards pulled on his helmet, which was an old-style green K-Pot, without a camo cover. It reminded him of Basic Training. Privates who hadn't qualified with their rifles yet had to wear the naked K-Pot, or Kevlar helmet, until they had proven they could shoot. Unlike the helmet he had worn at Fort Benning, however, this one didn't reek of someone else's sweat and lost hope.

"You ready for some on the job training, Deputy?" Kotto asked, placing the welder's mask, faceplate up, on his head. Turning to face Richards, he looked like some nightmare version of a car mechanic, come to do anything but *fix*.

"Lead the way, Sheriff."

They popped open their doors and jumped down to the road below. As they walked to the back of the van, Richards silently went over the events that had brought him to this moment. There was the training, the email, the riot at Snow Pine Ski Resort, coming home, being in the 'Stan, training, enlisting, leaving college before that. What, exactly, had been the moment of no return? What course had he taken that had led him, inevitably, to this unholy scene of carnage and chaos? Was he really this stupid, that he sought out this dangerous stuff? Did he get off on it? Did he have a death wish?

I could leave right now, he thought to himself. *I could take all this shit off and walk home. I could be back at my parents' place before it got dark. I can just tell him I quit and then it's all over.*

Before they left his house, Kotto had placed portable flashing blue and red emergency lights on the roof above the driver's side door. Now, in the dense smoke and heat, they pulsed bright, ambient light, casting the street in a bizarre dual-toned rhythm of dread. The chaos around them was made absurd by the fun-house strobe effect. Blue and red hues, like 3-D glasses.

Kotto swung open the van's rear doors. Inside was a black weapons rack. He handed Richards a shotgun—complete with nonlethal bean bag rounds—and a grenade launcher.

"This is CS gas," Kotto said, holding up a yellow-tipped grenade round. "Real nasty shit. If this doesn't get them to disperse, nothing will. Except for real bullets."

"I'm familiar with CS," Richards said, thinking back to the gas chamber in Basic. He'd cried and coughed his lungs out while his drill sergeants yelled in his face and called him a pussy. "Wait, we're not wearing gas masks."

"Nope. So try not to fire into the wind."

"Jesus. Jesus Christ."

"I wouldn't credit him for all this," Kotto said. "It's the other guy I have in mind."

Kotto handed Richards a bandolier of grenade rounds, which he slung over his shoulder. The launcher itself was surprisingly lightweight. Richards had fired 203 rounds before, but nothing like this. The gun looked like a giant revolver, but handled like a shotgun.

Kotto slammed the doors shut, and they moved to the front of the van. Some in the crowd had just taken notice of them, pointing bloody fingers in their direction, cackling in some horrible, ancient language of the dark.

"Are you ready, Deputy? You ready?" Kotto flipped the welder's mask down over his face.

"I thought we were going to be doing police work," Richards said, turning to face the mix of horror and the familiar as it began to shamble toward them, one mass of twisted limbs, smoking eyes, and bared teeth.

"This *is* police work!" Kotto said, his voice muffled through the mask. He raised his grenade launcher, and let a round fly with a satisfying *thwump*. It sailed over the edge of the crowd, and landed smack-dab in the middle of the intersection between Main and School streets. Gas billowed up, sending the rioting citizens screeching in all directions. "Let's put it on 'em, Deputy!"

Richards pulled the trigger. The grenade went sailing into the air, and the cylinder cycled a new round into the chamber. He fired again, closer to the edge of the crowd, which advanced on them with a frightening, measured deliberateness.

The smoke seemed to have some effect. Whatever had driven the people to this orgiastic madness, it hadn't turned them into something other than human. Their cries were guttural and animal-like, but their expressions of pain—and even anger—as the gas began to envelop the crowd was unmistakable.

As the two men got the hang of the weapons' arcs, they began to lob rounds between them and the steadily advancing crowd. Soon there was a wall of yellow gas between them. The feral citizens of West Valley coughed and hacked and screamed in pain, but not a word of English could be heard.

"What the fuck are they saying?" Richards called over to Kotto, who was busy sliding fresh grenades into the cylinder. "Sounds like Latin!"

"It's Sumerian, or maybe Babylonian," Kotto said, snapping the gun back up. "I took an online course on ancient Mesopotamian languages." He pointed ahead, to the wall of gas that was beginning to be carried away and off the street by the winds of the approaching storm. "What the hell is that?"

Indeed, beyond the dissipating smoke and the retreating rioters, stood a horrible amalgamation of metal siding, vehicle parts, deer antlers—and bones. Human bones, by the look of things, but Richards couldn't be sure from that far away. The horrific construct was gone just as soon as it had appeared, obscured by a flood of smoke. The crowd rallied and began to push through the wall of gas toward them. Whatever these people were on, the gas was starting to lose its effect.

"Uh, Sheriff," Richards said, firing another grenade straight ahead. Over the din of shouts and groans, there was a sharp crack. A crack like a gas canister smashing someone's ribcage. Or face.

"I see it." Kotto was out of rounds now—Richards estimated they had fired over a dozen gas canisters directly into or around the crowd. That should have been enough CS to pacify a city block, but the wind was carrying the yellow mist northeast and down along the creek bed. Besides, those affected by the gas were starting to get up and shamble toward them, sticks, golf clubs, or metal stakes in their hands and murder in their fiery, smoking eyes. In the looming darkness of the storm, their eyes shimmered hate.

"How tall was that thing they're building? Ten, fifteen feet?" Kotto called over.

"I don't even know what it was!"

Kotto swung the shotgun up, the brown Remington's buttstock pressed against his shoulder where the crook of his arm met the edge of his body armor.

"Halt, citizens! By order of the Sheriff!"

Richards fired his final tear gas canister over the crowd—they had advanced too close, and the wind was too wild to try to put it between them. He set his launcher down on the road. He pulled his own shotgun up—a black, tactical special, unlike Kotto's. Shit, the shotgun Kotto carried looked like an old hunting gun, not something a professional police force would use in a riot situation. Then again, nothing about this operation screamed *professional*.

Richards allowed his mind to wander, for just a short moment, to the paperwork he'd filled out while still intoxicated. Was that W2 even legit? Would he get paid for this, for being torn apart by bloodthirsty rioters in downtown Nowheresville, USA?

The *boom* of Kotto's shotgun brought him back to more pressing matters. The crowd had advanced to within 30 feet of them, and the nonlethal beanbags fired from Kotto's gun caught some in the front row in the face and neck, sending them tumbling. Unlike most rioters that Richards had seen on TV, the mob kept advancing, as if suddenly the pain of the gas and beanbags were nothing to them. They stepped over their fallen comrades, eyes still ablaze.

There was something else, something he hadn't noticed before: glass bottles, everywhere, reflecting the fires from the nearby houses along their curved glass surfaces. There was one near Richards' left boot. The design on the bottle was familiar.

There was an old lady in a blood-soaked flower dress who stepped over one of the fallen rioters—a little girl of no more than 10, it looked like—and reached down to pick up the shovel that the girl had been dragging. She let the blade scrape against the road, sending up little sparks. Never once did she tear her eyes from Richards'.

The air was hot with traces of the CS, and Richards' eyes and throat began to burn. Kotto let loose with another blast from the shotgun, sending shovel grandma and two other murderous citizens tumbling down into the road, clutching at their faces or their chests.

Things hadn't been *good* in Cattaraugus County, not for years. Drugs, a few violent crimes, sure. But this? People tearing each other apart, setting fires in the middle of the street, or going ape shit at Snow Pine during Octoberfest—somehow, in the time that he left for college and then the Army, something had gone wrong. These people, and the gore on their hands and faces, represented some sort of turning point that he had missed.

Kotto was right. There *was* bad voodoo in the air. But it was all around them now, too.

Richards raised his shotgun, and, fighting every decent fiber in his civilized body, fired into the crowd. A retort from Kotto's gun followed, and more bodies tumbled into the road ahead of them. The mob, moving headlong through fire, CS gas, and now the spray from riot guns, closed the distance between them. A firefighter, half of his face burned to a red apple crisp, raised his red axe above his head, just a few short steps from Richards.

"We have to fall back!" Richards shouted, blasting him at near point-blank range. The impact of the blast downed the lumbering volunteer fireman, who crumbled into a mess of uneven breaths and tangled limbs, his axe clattering to the asphalt. Non-lethal rounds or no, Richards knew that a blast at that close range could kill.

No time. He swiveled and fired one, two, three more rounds, watching neighbors—maybe even people he knew—howl in inhuman pain and rage as they fell.

The ranks that followed on finally grew wise. About 20 rioters lay on the road, coughing, bleeding, or worse. The others howled all at once, and broke ranks, retreating for cover or running off to the sides, leaping over ditches and bodies, disappearing behind houses and into backyards.

The CS smoke was gone, but thick gray plumes spread lazily over the street, flowing down from deeper within the town or from the houses nearby. Most of the homes along Main were burning—some little more than piles of torched lumber, melted siding, and ash which the wind and the heat caught and picked up, only to let fall again like dead snowflakes.

The sweat along Richards' forehead leaked down into his eyes. He snapped the K-Pot off and let it tumble to the ground. There was no hangover now, no hunger, no caffeine withdrawal. There was only the beating of his heart, and the rhythmic pulse of blood seeped in adrenaline. He caught his breath, looking around, the violence of the moment passed. This wasn't a battle in some foreign land. This was where he had attended high school, for Christ's sake. How could this happen *here*?

"Whose fire department is closer?" Richards asked, looking off toward the east. "Springville? Ellicottville? Machias?" That dark plume of heavy smoke in the near distance, rising from behind a row of burning houses—shit, that was the *school* over there.

"We're not gonna call the fire departments out here," Kotto said. Richards wheeled on him, only to see the sheriff walking among the quivering bodies of the rioters they had just felled.

"This whole town is on fire!" Richards said. "We went to school here, man! I think—I think I *know* some of these people!"

"Not like this you don't," Kotto said. "This whole show seem familiar to you?"

Glass shattered. There was the screaming of a woman—or maybe of a tortured cat. Then a sudden near-silence; the sounds of crackling flame, and the steady murmur of crowds gathered elsewhere. Shadows dashed between buildings, just out of sight. There were a few individuals, here and there, staring up at the sky or hunched over piles of what could only be viscera. But the danger of being overwhelmed by the horde had passed. For the moment.

"What the hell about this is supposed to be familiar?" Richards snapped. He fed a few more shells into the shotgun.

"You were there when this happened at Snow Pine," Kotto said. He bent down and picked up one of the glass bottles. A high-schooler in a varsity lettered jacket bounded forward and hissed at him through a mouthful of blood. Kotto brought the butt of his Remington down across the kid's twisted face, sending out teeth and a thick mist of red. The teen collapsed, unconscious.

"These are people," Richards stammered. "Shit, these are people I know …" He backed up, staggering, then eased himself down onto the cold of the asphalt. "Jesus." He set his shotgun down and let his head, now heavy, oh so heavy, fall into this hands.

"Look," Kotto said. He held the bottle up. The glass glimmered in the dying light of day and the living fires of home and hearth.

On the bottle's surface was the same faint imprint Richards had seen on the bottle at Snow Pine, the same 'shine those old ladies, yuppies, and bikers alike had been slugging before things went to shit and they started to tear each other's eyes out. It was that old man again—long beard, funny tall hat, massive wings sprouting from his back and stretching wide. Pastiche of ancient Egyptian hieroglyphics, maybe, or something off of the History Channel.

"This is Bucky's work."

"You think the 'shine drove them to *this*?" Richards asked, gesturing around them. "They get drunk and start raping and eating and burning each other alive?"

Kotto unscrewed the cap. There was a small amount of light golden liquid pooled at the bottom of the bottle. He sniffed at the liquor, eyebrows furrowing.

"Huh."

"What?"

"It smells sweet, and soft. Not harsh at all."

"Are you going to take a sip?"

"Nonsense! I don't drink before noon."

"I think it's past that."

"Well, then I don't drink 'shine that has psychosis-inducing hallucinogenic properties." Kotto pocketed the bottle. "Come on. When you're done having a pity party, we've got an investigation to complete."

Richards flashed with anger, ready to lay into the sheriff for being so cavalier about shooting rioters. Hell, they may have *killed* some of these people. But the lawman was already off, stepping over the pile of quivering, unconscious bodies. Richards pushed himself up, then grabbed his helmet and shotgun. He followed.

They passed a burning pickup and an overturned station wagon. Coughing through the smoke, they found themselves face to face with whatever it was the rioters had been gathered around. Seeing it up close and in the full light of its own flames, Richard and Kotto covered their mouths from the smoke and tried not to vomit.

The rioters had built the damned thing out of car parts, scrap metal, backyard grills, and railroad beams and ties. Three such beams stood up together, forming a teepee skeleton over a tangled mess of deer antlers, simmering metal and burning wood; tires, firewood, human bones, family photos, a dog house, a car door—all jammed together to form a base beneath the beams. Some 10 feet up, balanced on the railroad beams and tied down with more wire, was a blue shipping pallet, "WALMART" stenciled along its side. Perched on that was another trio of supports, this time twisted tree branches, at the apex of which was tied string, a leather pouch, and, above that, a dog skull, its bone white and pink and wet from where, just hours before, flesh had hugged its surface.

The pallet and skull totem were away high enough from the flames to remain in place, but still glowed with the orange heat from below. Sparks and ashes passed up through the slits in the pallet, drifting up and around the dog skull with the subtle poetry of fireflies.

"What the hell is this?" Richards asked. He looked away from the totem above, and into the flames. Rows of teeth and black orbs stared back at him, sinister smiles embedded in layers of orange-hot ember.

Skulls. Human skulls.

"Sheriff, inside the fire—"

"I see them, deputy," Kotto said. Standing that close to the fire, he had started to sweat. He wiped at his face, then pulled the welder's mask away from the top of his head. "Now *this* is some shit."

For Richards, operating on adrenaline-time, the sight of the structure had seized his awareness. The longer they stood there, however, the more his other senses began to come to life. Something passed at the edge of his vision, and the scent of burning wood (and flesh) gave way to the sweet whisper of fresh wind, and the crunching of feet on broken glass pulled his attention to the sides of the road.

Both sides of the road.

"Uh, Sheriff, I think—"

Kotto took a step toward the structure, his eyes never leaving the dog's skull on top. A fresh blast of storm air came rushing from the northeast, and carried away the fog of smoke and haze that made seeing much beyond 50 feet difficult. Down the street from the structure, more houses and cars burned—as did more of these twisted fetishes. Kotto estimated he saw four more of those burning obscenities scattered along Main Street alone, stretching the full mile from their side of town to its edge. And gathered around those bone and wood and metal abominations, more of his fellow citizens, each group centered around its own frenzied orgy of violence and degradation. The whole place had gone Spring Break on meth. But instead of pulling apart their toasters, the good citizens of West Valley were pulling apart each other. Or themselves.

"I've seen some freaky shit in my time," Kotto murmured. "But this ..."

"Sheriff!"

Kotto whirled around to see Richards backing up toward him, his shotgun pointing out. On either side of Main Street, more rioters had gathered, men and women and children alike, smeared in blood or filth, missing clothes, some missing teeth, eyes, or limbs, all wielding weapons, whether golf clubs, sticks, or shattered animal bones.

Richards backed up to Kotto, and Kotto put his back to Richards. He raised his Remington to point out, and, doing some quick math (the only practical math he would ever really use, he realized), determined that, between the two of them, they did *not* have enough ammunition to shoot all of these fucking people.

"If you got any orders, boss, I'm open to them," Richards said. "You know. If you've happened to come up with a plan during the last 10 seconds of uncontrollable terror. No pressure."

"The van," Kotto said. "Back to it. Slowly."

Moving together, guns facing out, they began to work their way back to the VW, parked just 50 short feet away. Fifty feet of potholes, unconscious bodies, and tire fires. Fifty feet of blood and dog guts on cold pavement. The van's blue and red lights still rotated, casting that nauseating circus effect on the horror in the street before them.

"They're starting to move to us on my side," Richards squeaked.

"Mine too," Kotto said. "Pick up the pace?"

"I could stand to move faster."

They turned their bodies to move straight on to the van, turning at their hips to keep their shotguns pointed to the sides of the street. The van was only fifteen feet away now, less—and that's when Kotto saw them.

Two men, wearing oversized Buffalo Bills sweaters that read "1990 AFC CHAMPIONS" and camo hunting hats, popped the doors open and stepped out into the street.

"How long were those guys in the van?" Richards asked.

"Long enough to fuck it up," Kotto said. The man in the driver's side had a trail of blood and wires dangling from his lips, and in his red right hand, the van's bony white steering wheel lingered before dropping to the pavement. The other man bent down and shoved a hunting knife deep into the passenger side front tire, which gave up its air pressure with an exhausted fart. Their blank expressions turned at once to toothy grins, each man's weather-beaten and reddened face snapped tight at the same time. Their faces were Jack Nicolson's Joker come to life, wide and sneering, eyes alight with something beyond simple psychosis.

"Hose 'em." Kotto whirled his shotgun around and let loose a pair of blasts, knocking the two men down onto the pavement. They growled with pain; their skulls smacked down against asphalt. "Problem solved."

"The van's fucked," Richards said. He looked past the disabled vehicle. Near the bend in the road, others gathered, but their backs were to the two lawmen. "What are they doing?"

"Tire fires," Kotto said. "Blocking the way out. Not that the van's going anywhere."

They reached the wounded vehicle. Kotto swung his head inside the cab through the broken driver's side window. "Yep." Richards followed him over, pointing the shotgun out at the crowd that had halted just shy of the ditch.

Richards opened fire, one, two, three, four, five shots—he lost count—until he was slamming back the action and nothing came out of the barrel. Six rioters dropped, but others emerged from behind them to join the crowd, melting out of the shadows between houses and from behind fences.

"The whole town is infected."

"Brainwashed, not infected," Kotto said. "We're not dealing with zombies here. That shit only happens in the movies."

"Right." Richards' fingers moved over the pouches on his body armor. "Sheriff, I'm outta nonlethal."

"You got your sidearm, right?"

"I don't want it to come to that."

"Those freakies on either side of the road have other ideas in mind."

Behind the van, the tire fires were alight, and the crowd had turned toward them. A mass of blood-soaked, sneering humanity—men, women, children, the elderly—pressed in on them from all sides. Richards tossed the shotgun and grenade launcher into the van through the smashed window. He reached down to the strap on his hip and drew his pistol.

10. Extraction

"Stop! Police!" Richards yelled to the crowd as they began to advance, ever so slowly—from behind, from the front, from the sides of the road. One mass of grinning, bleeding, blood-soaked, half-naked humanity. Flashes of dim recognition as his wild eyes sped from face to face. The lunch lady from school. The guy who sang too loud in church. A friend's little cousin.

He was about to kill people he *knew*.

"How long before we start shooting?" Richards croaked.

"Use your discretion as a peace officer," Kotto replied. He pulled the welder's mask off, and, opening the van's driver door, reached in for something between the two front seats. He pulled out a green Army combat helmet—some dusty Vietnam-era relic from the now-closed Army/Navy Surplus Supply in Olean, no doubt. He set it on his balding head. He grabbed his aviator sunglasses from the dash and slipped them on, calm as he could be. For a moment Kotto looked as if he was lost in thought, or in prayer, his head tilted down, his lips a straight line. Then he snapped up, drew his pistol, and fired two shots into the air.

The crowd, advancing step by step, didn't flinch.

"Do we shoot them in the leg?" Richards asked.

"Did the Army ever teach you to do that?"

"No," Richards said.

"Good, because it's not a thing. If you're going to shoot, shoot to kill."

"Right." This was it, then. There was no way out.

A small girl of no more than 10 or 11 crawled onto the street, pulling herself up by bloody hands out of the ditch and onto the road. The crowd followed behind, all those same twisted smiles, mockeries of human expression. Richards leveled his pistol and aimed down the slim sights directly at her spattered forehead. Her hair was black, and slick with something darker. Her blue dress was torn and covered in mud or worse.

Jesus. Jesus help me.

At the last moment he swung the pistol over her and took aim at a woman behind the girl. The woman held a gardening spade that seemed to be covered in bits of goo and human hair. Richards fired, once, twice, the recoil of the 9mm light and familiar from his time in the service. The first round impacted just above the woman's right eyebrow, and whatever kind of life animated her limbs drifted out of her. Those menacing, gleeful, green-orange smoking eyes went dark. Her body fell slack onto the asphalt with a dreadful *plop*.

That triggered a cry of anguish—from each individual in the mob on all sides, but as one, their voices roaring together in rage.

Kotto fired too, and Richards swept from face to face, familiar or unfamiliar alike. Golden shell casings ejected from their pistols, flashes of bronze light and the twinkling of soft notes as they struck the hood of the van or tittered down to the road. Still the crowd came forward, with some breaking into sprints; gardening tools, crowbars, or broken hunting rifles raised as clubs. One, two, three, they dropped, whether by Kotto's aim or Richards', limbs flailing, mouths open in animalistic cries of rage and panic.

The little girl's limp form was on the pavement now, too, two red welts of blood bubbling up beneath the fabric of her dress over her stomach.

Richards replaced his empty magazine and charged the 9mm. They'd filled up this side of the street with bodies—but no matter how fast they shot the crowd ahead of them, there were ranks of crazed people descending on them from three more sides.

This is how I die. Fighting zombies—I mean, brainwashed rioters—two streets over from my old high school.

Muscle memory kicked in, and the fear washed away like the morning tide. Kotto pressed up against Richards so that they were back to back. Bodies collapsed in front of them. More kept coming.

The thrumming overhead preceded the explosions. Richards believed it to be his own heart, thumping in panic rhythm. Rows of the attacking, brainwashed maniacs exploded in a flurry of fine mist and chunks of flesh.

Risking a glance up, Richards saw something that didn't make any sense. No more than 30 feet above them, a man leaned out of a Huey helicopter's open side panel door, wearing a gas mask and black business suit. He leaned back within the bird, then re-emerged with a hand grenade. He popped the pin—letting the spoon fall down to the hood of the van below—and gave the green ball of death an underhanded toss to the back of the crowd on the west side of Main Street. From the other open doors emerged a black barrel that spat orange flowers of flame out of its flash suppressor, followed by the familiar tap-dance of 5.56mm shell casings raining down to the van and the street below.

Somebody was firing a SAW—a machine gun whose cadence and firepower Richards knew well.

The grenade detonated, sending a rain of blood and body parts high into the air. The blades caught some of the gore, misting Richards and Kotto in the still-warm ichor. The Huey chopped stormy air, keeping aloft just between the drooping power lines strung on creaking telephone poles.

"Look!" Richards shouted into the din, slapping Kotto on the shoulder to get his attention. The Sheriff glanced up, his face a determined frown, not registering surprise. Above, the man in the gas mask tossed a pair of grenades into the crowd, then kicked at something on the floor. A length of black rope uncoiled and fell toward them, striking the roof of the van and sliding down to linger over the surface of the street. The man waved to Richards, then pulled an M-16 from somewhere and began to pick off more of the rioters below just as the grenades exploded.

The rioters spared the flame and shrapnel turned their feral faces upward, clawing at the air and snarling, some throwing their makeshift weapons into the air in vain attempts to damage the helicopter.

"You first!" Kotto said, pointing at the rope. Richards didn't have to be told twice. The SAW machine gun and the M-16 continued to put down fire in all directions. Richards climbed as fast as he could, convinced that at any moment a bloody hand would latch onto his ankle and snatch him from below, or, worse, that Kotto's screams would follow him as he reached safety.

A soft, hollow, thumping rhythm elicited a glance to his side. Now hanging above the van and halfway to the helicopter, Richards saw a glass Coca-Cola bottle wobble through the air near him, following a lazy arc down to shatter on the street below. From above, it was easy to see the true nature of what they had been facing—it wasn't just a riot on Main Street—the whole town was, indeed, burning to the ground. Little groups of people moved about in the shadows of flame and storm, eyes alight, all facing the center of town, moving slowly, deliberately, toward the commotion on Main Street. This wasn't a simple riot to disperse—this was the *entire population* of West Valley, driven out of their minds by Bucky's moonshine, destroying themselves and their community.

The rope began to swing beneath him. Kotto laid a hand on the rope, pistol arm outstretched. The gun flashed, expelling flame and casings, until the action locked back. The sheriff shoved the pistol into his waistline along his back, then shambled up the rope behind Richards. The deputy looked up to see the man in the business suit and gas mask crouching in the open door of the Huey, arm poised to reach down as soon as Richards was close enough.

"Go!" Richards yelled, waving a free hand. "Take off! We're good!"

There was no way the man heard him over the rotor wash, but, seeing Kotto latch onto the bottom of the rope and the crowd scrambling over the bodies of their dead to within a hair's breadth of the sheriff, the man in the gas mask nodded and moved to get the pilot's attention. Up and up Richards and Kotto scrambled, memories of gym glass in their heads, their arms hot and sore and pumped full of adrenaline. A gasoline-soaked hand reached for Kotto's boot, wrapping fingers around his untied laces.

"Buzz off, you freaky drunken maniacs!" the sheriff yelled, kicking his boot loose. More hands reached up to rake at Kotto's feet. A man in a chef's apron, blood or pizza sauce along his chest, wrapped his arms around the rope and began to shamble up after them.

The helicopter lifted up a dozen or so feet, then dipped its nose forward and its tail up as it made a beeline down Main Street. Richards watched the crowd drift away below, then the bird lifted away from the street and over the power lines, into the stormy sky. He scrambled up through the open panel door, and let the man in the gas mask pull him in.

Below, Kotto struggled to get up the rope, every fistful of progress painful. Images of chicken wings, beer, potato chips, and every other fatty, carb-filled, sugar-laden thing he'd ever stuffed into his mouth flashed through his mind.

"I quit drinking!" he shouted into the wind and the whirring of rotor blades. "I'm going on a diet! I quit smoking!"

But his out-of-shape body cared little for promises.

Kotto crossed his ankles to place the rope under one of his boots to take some of the weight off of his tired arms. Slowly, painfully, he snaked his way up the rope. The helicopter veered east then north, directly into the storm's headwinds. Above him, Richards and the gas mask man held out their arms, shouting deaf encouragements into the swirling chaos. They passed over power lines, trees, bridges, roads—and Kotto recognized they'd be near his home on Beach Shrub Road in moments.

"I'm gonna make it!" he shouted to himself. Foot by miserable foot, he slid up and up. Richards' hand reached down for his. Kotto reached out, but was jerked off his balance by sharp pain from below.

The pizza chef had reached Kotto's feet, and bit squarely into his ankle. Kotto rocked along the rope, grateful for a last-minute burst of strength that allowed him to keep his grip. He kicked the man off of his boot, then reached around to his back for his empty pistol. The man below reached up to claw at Kotto's boot once more, and latched on with a blood-smeared hand. He began to pull the sheriff down.

Kotto groaned, and his left arm, wrapped desperately around the swaying rope, burned. Finally he fished out the pistol, and, taking aim, whipped the gun directly at the man's forehead.

It struck him square between the eyes, just as the helicopter dipped into a gust of storm wind. The pizza chef-turned-blood-freak recoiled in pain and surprise, and his hands snapped open along Kotto's boot and the rope. Separated from his anchor in the sky, the man floated, frozen in time, eyes meeting Kotto's with rage and unthinking hunger.

Then he was gone, tumbling ass over tea kettle, disappearing into the carpet of pine trees below.

Kotto caught his breath, sucking in turbulent air, his right arm swinging up to grasp the next foot of rope.

Richards helped pull him into the helicopter just as it began its descent.

11. G-Man in a Gas Mask

The chopper touched down in the back field where Richards, just a day before, had put rounds into cardboard cut-outs of Dracula and the Toxic Avenger. The whine of the helicopter's engine died down, the blades slowing as the storm above them grew darker and the winds stronger. They'd keep the engine hot, just in case they had to leave in a hurry. Kotto's house was only a couple of miles outside of downtown West Valley. There was no telling whether the brainwashed mob would follow the helicopter, whether they would start marauding beyond the town's limits—or whether they were content to stay where they were, worshiping at altars of human bones and dog skulls.

The G-Man in the gas mask and black suit leapt out first, and Richards and Kotto followed behind, exhausted, covered in sweat, spattered with blood, and coated in a thin layer of gray grime that could only be the ash of those unholy pyres.

"Who are these guys?" Richards asked, once they were away from the rotor wash and he could hear himself think. "Not that I'm ungrateful, but these guys don't look like State Troopers."

"I'm out of answers," Kotto said.

They followed the man in the suit past Kotto's collapsed swimming pool and onto the back deck. Once there, he stopped and pulled off his gas mask and turned to face the approaching officers.

"You still keep beer in the garage?" he asked Kotto. The sheriff stepped up onto the deck, then pulled off his sunglasses and combat helmet. He unsnapped his body armor and pulled it off his shoulders, letting it fall to the gray-stained wood of the deck.

"Couple of tall boys in there," Kotto said, nonchalantly. He fished a bent cigarette out of his BDU jacket, and then cracked a light and took a few puffs.

So much for deathbed promises.

Richards and Kotto had gone into the basement to drop off some of their gear; the G-Man in the suit waited for them at the kitchen table, slow-sipping a Coors Light tall boy. Richards found him poking his gas mask around the table with a pencil stub.

"Thank you," Richards said. "I've got no idea who you are, but thank you."

The man looked up, then ran his fingers through his black hair. He had a thick nose, large round brown eyes, and a pencil-thin mustache straight out of a Whole Foods advertisement for city-dwelling hipsters. In his rain-slicked suit, he could have been any number of things—an investment banker, the owner of a car dealership, or the front man for a kitschy punk rock band.

"It's part of the job," he said, smiling. Kotto emerged from the basement, shirtless, his brown gut hanging over his brown leather belt, another cigarette dangling from his lips.

"And how is the FBI treating you, Fields?" Kotto asked, pulling up a seat at the table and gesturing for Richards to do the same. The man in the suit—Fields—reached down and pulled up two more tall boy Silver Bullets. The cans popped open with a series of satisfying hisses. Richards welcomed the flood of cold liquid.

"It pays well, and the 401k options are fantastic," Fields said. "But I still miss the good old days."

"Amen brother," Kotto said. He raised his can and met Fields', light amber liquid splashing down onto the table. "Fields, this is my new deputy. Richards, Fields. Fields, Richards."

"You guys used to work together?" Richards asked.

"There's some chicken fingers in the freezer. You guys want some chicken fingers? Richards, go make us some chicken fingers."

"What?"

"You're still on the clock, ain't ya?"

"I don't miss chicken finger duty," Fields said. "Does he make you fold his laundry, too?"

"Just during my training," Richards said, standing up and pushing his chair back.

"Oven temperature gauge is a little fuckey," Kotto said. "You gotta pull on it just right, 'til you hear the heat kick on. No, clockwise."

"Like this?"

"Yeah, just a bit more—now back, okay—"

"Got it. It clicked."

"Great. Don't forget the hot sauce."

"Yes, Sheriff."

"Fields!" Kotto snapped, his mind grasping at the conversation at hand. He whirled back to face his former deputy. "What the hell does the FBI have you doing back here?"

"They don't, truth be told," Fields said, tossing his

beer up to drain half of it down his throat. Suds cascaded down the sides of his neck. "Jesus, Sheriff. It was bad out there today. I was hoping it wasn't going to be that bad."

"But you came prepared," Kotto said. "That was some serious hardware you and your boys were packing. FBI know you got a helicopter and some machine guns out this way?"

Fields shrugged.

"You taught me to get the job done, Sheriff. I never forgot that. No matter what it takes."

"That's the Fields I taught you," Kotto said, nodding. "That's the Sheriff Kotto I taught you!"

"Ranch or blue cheese, fellas?" Richards asked.

"*Blue cheese!*" both men at the table screamed, fists slamming against its surface. A salt shaker tumbled over.

"Sorry."

"This is the guy you got to replace me?" Fields asked.

"Nobody could replace you, Fields," Kotto replied. "Someone can take your old position, wear your badge, carry your gun, and I might call them 'Fields' from time to time, but no one can replace you. Unless we get the Clone-R-Ator in my garage back online."

"Shut the whole county power grid down last time, right?"

"Yeah. But what a ride."

With the chicken fingers in the oven, Richards returned to the table and grabbed his beer.

"I know I'm new to this whole law enforcement thing, and I've been away for a while," he said, his neck starting to throb with the same stress-pain he felt when he was overseas, "but I don't remember there being riots and animal sacrifices around here very often."

"You remember when the Senecas shut down the thruway with tire fires?" Kotto asked.

"That was about cigarette taxes, right? This isn't the same thing."

"No, it's not," Kotto said, nodding. "That was about whacky Pataki and his anti-freedom agenda."

"I don't know what that means," Richards said. He looked to Fields. "Is he always like this?"

"He's usually not this lucid," Fields admitted. "Must be all the violence is keeping his head clear."

"Adrenaline and the American Spirit are a potent mix, gentlemen," Kotto said. "Fields, I think it's time you filled us in on what's going on." He pulled the glass moonshine bottle from his jacket and set it on the table. "Bucky's moonshine is driving people mad. But this isn't just a few folks going blind or waking up in the Droopy's parking lot on a Tuesday morning. This is mob violence. It's animal sacrifice. It's pagan altars in downtown West Valley. It's a hell of a puzzle. And while my Sherlock skills are usually sharpest after my morning constitutional, I can't for the life of me put this together. You're a G-Man now. Give me some more pieces to work with."

"Yeah," Richards said. "What in the holy hell is going on around here? I *knew* some of those people back there, I think. And it's not just happening in West Valley, either. It's already happened in Ellicottville, and it'll probably happen again."

"You're right, Deputy," Fields said. "And you're right, Sheriff. This isn't just some bad moonshine. And this isn't just about Bucky." He reached into his black suit coat and pulled out a crinkled manila folder. He dropped it onto the table with a soft *slap*. Fields' dark eyes bore into them. "We're gonna need some more beer."

The files didn't come from an FBI database.

By June 2013, Edward Snowden had released several major national security secrets to the mainstream media, including substantial evidence of government domestic surveillance programs. Fields explained that this information was the tip of the iceberg.

Because of his time at the FBI, Fields already indirectly knew about much of what organizations like the CIA and the NSA were doing stateside. Despite his personal feelings about Snowden's revelatory whistleblowing, he was part of the team assigned to ferret out additional leaks that the former NSA contractor may have been preparing for release.

Their investigation led them to a DARPA-owned backwater server station in Mankato, Minnesota. The station was a cramped concrete room with four server towers, kept behind locked doors underneath the Minnesota State University at Mankato library. While the other two agents ran diagnostics and searched the systems for Snowden's digital fingerprints, Fields discovered a small gray USB stick plugged into a port along the inward-facing side of one of the towers.

Fields didn't have to make the decision. His conscience made it for him. He pocketed the drive and then continued the search, telling the other agents that he'd come up empty. Their team moved on to other servers, other sites, other leads.

A week later, alone at home, Fields pulled the files up on a computer that was disconnected from the internet. The data on the USB wasn't even encrypted; it was open to anyone who knew where or how to access it—or to anyone who pulled it from the server.

There were 20 folders on the drive. Their names were alphanumeric strings. He went through each folder—some contained more files than others—and quickly saw a pattern. The files contained therein were mostly PDFs, scans of copies of copies of copies; digital backups of physical paperwork. A realization dawned on him as he went through each file, sorting through the bureaucratic mumbo-jumbo, the numeric filing codes, the intradepartmental classifications.

They were case files. Specifically, they were portfolios on American citizens. Scans of family photos, military service portraits, transcripts of phone calls, social security cards, reams of emails for the newer cases. Most of it was mundane, but there was a commonality: they were all men and women from Western New York (something that struck him as supremely synchronistic, considering he had grown up there), and, as the hours dragged on, Fields realized something else. While most of the collected data seemed largely inconsequential, there were, buried deeper, implications of something far more interesting and entirely worthy of his attention.

These people were being monitored by one or more government agencies, usually under the guidance of an interdepartmental task force—one of a thousand fire-and-forget teams pulled together in secret, given the authority to use various department resources and personnel to achieve some murky objective before its inevitable dissolution. Fields had worked on such projects before—usually drug interdiction cases, or anti-terrorism task forces—but this one seemed different. This task force—code-named MALTHUS—wasn't conducting a criminal investigation. It wasn't even looking into domestic terrorism.

It was monitoring—and even handling, in the CIA-sense—abductees.

Despite Fields' work with Kotto in years past, when he first started seeing the words "abduction" and "abductee," he assumed it pertained to the criminal offense. But as he read on and poured through file by file, he came across the photographs of strange scars and of small metal implants removed by doctors. He came across the hypnotherapy transcripts. He came across the Air National Guard radar reports.

These people hadn't been kidnapped. They'd been *abducted*. As in, close encounters of the fourth kind.

The next-to-last folder contained reports filed by one Agent Schrader, no first name or agency listed. The subject of his reports was categorized by the alphanumeric sequence LG9844.

Larry Green, and the last four digits of his social security number. Larry "Bucky" Green of unincorporated Cattaraugus County, New York, now wanted for moonshining, assault, and the murder of several State Police.

II
Conspiracy of the Skies

12. Country Boy

Larry "Bucky" Green was born at Springville General Hospital on November 3, 1982, to Delilah Green of Ellicottville, New York. Delilah was a waitress at The Horse Shed Bar and Restaurant in downtown Ellicottville, where she made just enough to keep her and her son in a dilapidated singlewide trailer just off Quackenbush Road. Delilah had never married, and Larry's birth certificate listed no father.

Larry grew up among his cousins and neighbors, running through the woods, hunting, and playing football for Ellicottville Central School. After he started hunting, his friends gave him the nickname Bucky—because of his uncanny ability to land a big-antlered buck every season (and a few out of season).

Like many other young men living dirt-poor lives in the middle of nowhere, he turned to drinking early. His Uncle Bill saw that Larry had a knack for helping make 'shine, as he took the chemistry aspect seriously, and kept finding new and clever ways to flavor his uncle's otherwise bland-if-potent recipes. By the time Bucky graduated high school, they made enough money selling the 'shine to neighbors—and a few cleverly-packaged bottles to local liquor stores for trustworthy customers—that they could live a comfortable, simple life.

    Life was simple. Deer hunting, drinking with the boys, making a little scratch. Things could be worse for a young man out in the sticks, and Bucky was just smart enough to know it.

He first saw the lights just before his 28th birthday. That is, that was the first time he *remembered* seeing the lights.

    He'd been outside by himself, around the burn pit a hundred yards behind the trailer. Bucky and his friends had set it up in an open field, well away from the trees that flowed like shag carpet off the foreboding hills. Route 242 ran along the lip of the field, headlights from passing cars shining through jagged trees and casting larger-than-life shadows on tall grass. The first thing they'd burned, years ago, was an old hay bale wagon, left to ruin by a farmer too old to put it to use. Bucky and his friends, although drunk, were careful to push down the grass around the old wooden wagon, its panels faded and turned to an unpleasant bone-gray after decades in the sun. The flames chewed through it like a starving man's first meal in days. After its hungry work, there was only the rims and the metal support that connected the wheels and the wagon to the tractor. Everything else had gone up in ash and smoke.

    After that first fire, they'd return there—usually once a week when the weather was good, maybe more—to burn paper, bits of scrap wood and materials from drywalling jobs, tires, whatever they could muster up. They'd set it all along the skeleton of that old wagon, douse it in gas, then watch it burn while they slugged down Miller High Life, Milwaukee's Best, or some of Bucky's signature 'shine.

On lonely summer nights when the humidity was up and the peepers sang their swamp songs, Bucky would find himself staring at the sagging ceiling of his room, sweat beading along his forehead. His mother was often at work (or spending her tips at the bar until late in the evening), so when he was alone, he would grab whatever trash they had and junk wood and head out to the spot. He'd crack beers or smoke cheap dope by himself, watching the flames work or the headlights pass by along the edge of the road.

Bucky enjoyed a little time to himself. Time to have a few drinks or smokes and watch the flames dance beneath that great black sky above, starlight competing with the light pollution of Snow Pine Ski Resort to the southwest.

It was on one of those numberless nights, when he was drawn to the promises of ancient fire and open sky and time alone, when he stared up into the abyssal heavens and saw the red lights.

They were larger than stars, and stood, from his position, in a perfect triangle formation, the word *equilateral* echoing back to him from math classes distant. They had been there for a while, he realized. But as time went on they became more distinct, whether growing in brightness or drawing closer, it was impossible to tell. They pulsed a three-burst melody of light, drawing attention away from flame, headlights, and stars alike. Demanding to be seen.

The songs of the nearby cicadas and bullfrogs faded, a gray hand on the volume knob, tuning them out. The wind snapped up and the flames whiplashed. Smoke poured toward Bucky, his nose and throat hot with the acrid taste of ash. Still, he didn't move. It wasn't fear, not exactly, but a cross between fascination and bafflement; a confused sort of *Well would you look at that* across his face. The beer bottle in his hand clinked to the ground, pouring out a bubbling stream into the brown dirt.

The wind stopped. There was no traffic, no sounds from the marsh or meadow. There was nothing, save a low droning, just at the edge of awareness, building and building as the lights grew brighter.

Then they went dim, before flaring up once more. The triangle broke; the lights spun and danced around each other, form and stability washed away in a neon haze. They spun and spun, until all three orbs, satisfied with their dance, shot off in different directions, like embers of a firecracker in the night sky.

The droning stopped, broken by a sharp bullet-crack of the sound barrier breaking.

Something wet and warm moved down the edge of Bucky's hand. He looked down in time to see another drop of blood escape his nose and fall toward his open palm. Blood, gathering along his upper lip, snaking its way into his mouth. He wiped at it, smearing red along his bare forearm.

When he looked up again, the sky was pink with morning, the sun poking its face over the hills behind him, casting the field in a haze of gold. The dew was pregnant with early-morning mist.

The fire was dead. Only a few points of orange light remained within hidden embers, obscured by the blackened bones of firewood left to burn through the night hours.

Bucky's mother was up by the time he reached the trailer. She stood over the stovetop, Spam and eggs sizzling in a twisted skillet that was blackened from a decade of frying food. She shot him a disapproving look as he shambled in, his eyes bloodshot and his skin pale. She opened her mouth to offer him a few words of *you know better you dumb bastard* but when she saw his face, the dried blood and exhaustion hanging off of him like dead skin, she turned back to her breakfast.

Bucky made his way to his room at the end of the trailer. He closed the thin plywood door behind him and fell onto his bed. He didn't wake up until that evening.

It was a week after the lights had made themselves known to him when he had decided to chalk the whole thing up to bad weed. That's when he saw one of the grays for the first time. That is, it was the first time that he could *remember* seeing one.

The sun was beginning its climb down the top of the hills to the west, and the magic-hour timing cast the world in lustrous gold and red hues. Uncle Bill had set up the still up in the woods, just out of sight from casual passersby, but close enough that Bucky could walk up there from his trailer in under 10 minutes. When Bucky reached the still, the sharp chemical smell greeted him, a familiar welcome. The low thrum of the generator competed with the buzz of cars distant on 242, the wind's subtle howls through the twisted branches overhead, and his own footfalls over the dirt and weeds brave enough to encroach on the well-worn footpath. Behind him was the perimeter line of trees, and the muddy footpath that led up from the edge of Quackenbush's dead end.

Bucky had been at the still for a few minutes before

his mind registered the visitor. The shape was in his peripheral vision, just off to his right. It was still at first. Then it moved, slow and gray, thin limbs twisting away from green bushes and brown tree branches, out of harmony with the way the soft wind shook and moved through the weeds and leaves of the forest.

Bucky, seeing something move, walked a few steps forward. Then it registered. He stopped. What had that been?

The golds and reds of the magic hour were fading. In the woods beyond, long shadows crawled out of their hiding places.

It moved again. Unmistakable.

Gray limbs. Impossibly thin. Its body was a wrinkled husk of gray and blue, like someone had wrapped a tarp around a starving African kid's torso, but free of scars or breaks, including where its belly button should have been. Its face was a perfect oval, with a sharp chin that jutted forward, its mouth a flat line across its wide face, puckered in a human expression of distaste, if one could ascribe such things to it. Its eyes were almonds of deep black pools, shimmering with the reflective blue and green scale-glow of insects. It walked away from him, backwards, its eyes—*eyes?*—locked on Bucky. Its legs and arms pumped as if on strings; this was a marionette of some sort, brought to life by a puppeteer hidden in the trees above; a joke, surely, an unfinished dummy from the school theatre department, stolen and spray-painted gray ...

It shuffled backwards, its movements jerky and anything but graceful or fluid, as if it were indeed suspended on invisible strings. It withdrew behind the trees, branches snapping and giving way to its retreat. Then it was gone.

As the adrenaline caught up with him, Bucky

realized why deer would just stop and stare at him sometimes—when they should have been running, scrambling away for dear life. Sometimes, they just held fast, frozen in place, eyes locking with his, recognizing that the form in the tree *wasn't* a part of the tree, but something far, far worse. Something that meant to do it harm. And in that moment of horrible realization, they were powerless to move or react.

Then his legs took him back, his foot fumbling over a root that grew over the path. He struggled to keep his balance, but his eyes would not leave the space between the trees where the thing had been, not until well after he was out of the woods and back to the relative safety and sanity of the paved road.

13. Even Into the Dark

Uncle Bill moved slow; his skin was pale and his eyes were just shy of bloodshot. But as he moved around the still, checking levels and temperatures, he kept stealing glances at Bucky. His nephew was worried about something, agitated. He had called his uncle, telling him about some vague problem with the latest batch. But now that Bill had laid eyes on the still, it was clear that was just an excuse for something else. As far as Bill knew, the new batch would probably be the best they'd produced yet.

As Bucky made his own rounds, he kept his eyes on the trees, and stole glances into the darkness beyond. He didn't keep his back to any one direction. Something was on his mind. Something hounded him.

"You okay, Buck?" Bill asked, hefting a bag of sugar. It was organic, the pricey shit. Bucky had insisted on it. Bill had long ago learned to accept the wisdom of his nephew's decisions when it came to selecting the best ingredients for the 'shine. He hauled it back to one of the small storage sheds they'd set up. That sack hurt like a sumbitch to lift.

Bucky was in another shed, just inside the open doors, adjusting the temperature on their pressure cooker.

"You expecting trouble?" Bill said, dropping the bag inside. Sweat beaded along his forehead. He knew that wasn't good. If he kept pushing it, like the lady doc said, his heart—

"Trouble?"

"Yeah, you got some competition or something? Someone know about the still? You called me up here, and here I am, in my skins and hollers." Bill had been making 'shine since he was in high school, too. There wasn't much of a black market to speak of, but the old fella who had showed him the ropes had warned him to keep the location out of sight, and not to bring strangers around.

"Nothing, no trouble," Bucky said.

"You look like you're on the lookout."

"Nah."

Bill looked off to the west. It was that time of night when the peeper frogs were just getting their chorus warmed up. Cloud tendrils drifted over blue and orange and pink sky. Soon you could see the lights from Snow Pine Resort, running like they did year round (God-knows-why) and maybe the lights to the north, out by the West Valley Demonstration Project. The old nuke plant, where some of Bill's friends had worked most their lives. Most of them folks got cancer, but you didn't hear about that in the news.

If some Seneca got a bug up his butt about cigarette taxes, well, close down the highway and call the governor! But some poor white folks getting that slow-burn death out in the sticks from government nuclear waste? That was just tough nuts, huh Bill?

Bill caught that bitterness rising up in his throat, his eyes going red and wet. He turned away from Bucky and pulled out his flask—the same one his father had carried in Korea, hidden away in his rucksack. He took a swig of 'shine. Newest batch, with blueberry flavor.

When the burning liquid settled into his stomach, Bill tightened the lid and turned back to his nephew.

"We need to move the still? Or we need to bring guns out here?"

Bucky sat down on a fallen tree, his work boots unlaced and the tongues hanging out like tired dogs. He ran dirt-caked fingers through his hair.

"Nah, uncle. Nothing like that."

"Then what's it like?" Bill walked over to him and put a hand on his shoulder.

"It's nothing. I was just hoping you could help me today, is all."

"Buck, I haven't had to help you for a couple of years now," Bill said. "That's being generous to myself. You've always had a knack for 'shining, better than I ever did. You make it best. There's nothing I can help you with."

"Well," Bucky said.

"So what is it?"

"The other day—I seen something, looked like a person, sort of, but ..."

"'Looked like a person'?"

"You ever see lights in the sky, uncle?" Bucky looked up into his uncle's face, eyes wide and hot with something. Boiling over, even. Anxiety. Fear.

No. Bill knew it wasn't fear. It was *dread*.

"You mean the lights from the ski resort? Or the nuke plant?"

"Shit, never mind," Bucky said, standing up. "I'm sorry for calling you out here like this. I know you aren't in any shape to be carrying around all this crap." He stomped off back toward the trail, shoulders sagging forward, head hung low.

"Bucky," Bill said. "Bucky, what's this about?"

He watched his nephew disappear into the trees, the snapping of twigs and the fluttering of birds marking his path. It'd be dark soon, and Bill suddenly didn't take a shine to the idea of being up here all alone after nightfall.

Bucky stayed up late, waiting for his mother to come home. A slow, twisting sensation of something being *off* churned through him, grinding against any semblance of ease. He slugged beers because the thought of drinking anything made at his still was repulsive. The slow buzz started to ease the white-hot animal worry that coursed through his blood.

The night was humid, the air oppressive. The view through the back windows to the field and black sky above left him feeling exposed, like a wounded animal limping through a forest full of coyotes. The occasional sounds from the neighboring two trailers—a dog bark, a screen door screeching closed, the odd clink of dishes—were of small comfort. But as he paced his trailer, stealing glances out into the dark, he was sure that he would see something staring back at him.

Around 10 o'clock he closed all the curtains in the trailer, and locked all the windows and the back door, leaving only the front door to the rickety steps unlocked. This he watched out of the corner of his eye as he sat in the living room watching their small television.

The volume on the TV was up, the highlights from college football games played in loops. He'd heard it all before, again and again, but wanted the facsimile of human company. Calling his friends was out of the question. They'd want to go *out*. Maybe up to the still to sample some of the new batch. Or, worse, out to the open field to start a fire. A fire—somehow that would be a signal, an invitation. It would bring something terrible and dark down upon them all.

Christ, he thought to himself, cracking another beer. *What's got into my head?*

The buzz of alcohol had slipped from keeping him alert and confident down to making him feel bloated and sluggish.

The answer was, of course, to switch to the liquor.

His mother kept a handle of vodka in the cabinets above the fridge. He made himself a screwdriver and dropped ice cubes into the glass, watching them fizz about in the pulpy liquid.

The orange juice-vodka mixture fought the beer. His stomach was an arena of amateur wrestlers, grappling with one another with razor wire and church hall folding chairs over a pile of dirty mattresses. But then the beer was pinned, or flushed down lower, and the stronger, sharper vodka buzz dulled the pain.

He flipped through the channels, even managing to lose himself in a nature documentary, watching bears swipe for fish or majestic elk stalk through remote, green valleys …

The knocks came fast, rapping along the other side of the trailer. *His* side of the trailer. Near his room.

One, two, three …

The third knock dragged out, like a claw scraping against the plastic siding. Just to make sure he knew—he damn well *knew*—that it was for him. Just for him.

His heart leapt into his throat, but the vodka made him brave.

He shot up out of the tattered recliner, then stomped past the kitchen, past the bathroom, past his mother's room, into the thin spread of bedroom at the end of the trailer. Momentum was his weapon against fear and second thoughts; thoughts of stealth or surprise were washed away by the raw energy of the moment. Something was gonna happen tonight, whether that thought made sense or not, and he was resolved to face it head on.

He flipped the light on to his room. Darkness fled to the corners and the secret places. The familiar faces of *Sports Illustrated* swimsuit models stared back at him from the walls, wide come-hither eyes floating over mounds of airbrushed, supple flesh. The bed was still unmade from this morning. His laundry basket overflowed with dirty clothes.

He flung open the sliding closet door, fist raised back. No one inside. He reached back into his closet and drew out a Remington 12 gauge, five slugs already locked and loaded, ready to go. He carried the shotgun carefully, out in front of him, finger on the outside of the trigger well, just like Uncle Bill had taught him. The curtains on his windows were drawn, and those edges of glass that peeked out above or below showed only reflected light from the uneasy bulb suspended in the center of the ceiling.

Outside now. Feet moving too fast down uneven front steps. The motion light clicked on over on his neighbor's nearby shed. Maybe curtains moved and the neighbors looked out; maybe they didn't. Their dog wasn't barking.

Bucky peeked around his truck, thinking he saw eyes staring back at him from inside the cab. No, just his own reflection, disjointed and warped in the slim, competing light from the flood lamp mounted above their front door and the motion detector above the shed.

Bucky cut right and made his way around the trailer, the shotgun's smooth pump perched over his forearm. He was ready to point and shoot at a moment's notice, like he'd drawn down on deer so many times before. But deer didn't come knock-knock-

knocking on your wall in the dead of night, did they? Not even the mutant albino deer over at the nuke plant.

As Bucky stepped out of the perimeter of light splashing along the dirt driveway, he realized he should have brought a flashlight. But damned if he was going to retreat back inside now. If somebody was out here, he was gonna catch them. By God, he was gonna run them down, even into the dark.

He rounded the corner, shotgun raised, hair standing up on the back of his neck, sweat winding its way down his spine like the finger of a teasing lover.

"Come out, motherfucker," he said through gritted teeth, more to steel himself than anything.

In the dark, there was the wind on his face, the smell of the mud of the field. Something else. The scent of … ash. Burnt-black metal, rotten wood.

His night vision opened up, well-honed after a young lifetime spent in and around the woods. *Eat a lot of carrots*, his mom had always told him. *They'll help you see in the dark.*

Nothing. Just the light filtering out through his window, slats of orange spilling onto the unmowed grass.

"Who's back here?"

Bucky expected his words to elicit some sort of response—the scurrying of little raccoon feet over rocks and sticks; maybe a fox darting into the weeds. Hell, he'd settle for a bird.

A bird.

Eyes staring at him from above, catching the moonlight. Wide and intelligent, tracking him, glowing.

The owl sat on a low-hanging branch, one he'd never consciously noticed before. Hell, he didn't even remember a *tree* being there, let alone a branch big enough to hold an owl that size. Its eyes held onto him, then blinked, those moonlight-purple orbs disappearing for one moment before re-emerging and shifting away and around, disappearing in the dark. Bucky squinted and realized that the owl had turned its head all the way around, away from him, and was staring off through the scant trees to the field beyond. Bucky stepped forward, and laid a hand on the tree, which felt different somehow, its bark thin and coming off in rough flakes like ash.

Beyond lay the field, illuminated by a feral moon, and something else—not the lights from the ski resort, but streaming waves of blue and purple light, glimmering hologram ribbons. Were those the Northern Lights, of all things? Here? Now?

The owl shifted above him, raining down flakes of bark. It flapped away, its wings heavy and thick against hot night air.

It never made a sound.

Bucky pulled his eyes from the lights above and made his way back to the side of the trailer. As he passed his window, he tossed a careless glance its way.

Dark, formless; a liquid swirling of black robe, tall and thin, more shadow than solid, moving from the door of his room into the main hallway.

The aggressive panic-heat set in, and he rushed around to the front of his trailer. The neighbor's dog began to bark.

Bucky leapt up the stairs and threw open the screen door, Remington out in front.

There was no one in the hallway.

He whipped around, leveling the gun at the TV, which still chattered meaningless statistics and gobbledygook. No. They must be in the bathroom, or in his mother's room.

"Come out, you son of a bitch!" His voice cracked around the edges. The vodka was no help to him now.

"I've got a big-ass shotgun. I'm gonna blow your fucking head off if you don't come out."

Waiting.

Just the chatter from the TV, and the echoing drip of water falling from the faucet into a pot greased from homemade mac and cheese. The sound bounced around inside his skull, taunting him.

He stepped forward. He'd check his mother's room first, then the bathroom.

The door stood ajar. He kicked it open, mud flinging up from his boot. No one inside. Just the smell of too-sweet perfume and cigarettes.

The bathroom, then. He muscled his way in, determined to knock the bastard down by sheer force of will.

Just the sink, black mold growing along the edges of the drain, and the toilet, flakes of rust drifting across the brown water pool. No one in the shower.

Still in my room.

He moved as if in a dream, his muscles responding a moment-too-slow, snapshots of frustration and fear egging him on.

Inside. The unmade bed, the faint stink of sweat from his clothes. The closet, door open and shadows holding only clothes and boxes of old comic books.

―※―

He slugged vodka and kept the shotgun within reach. He stole glances out into the dark.

When his mother came home, she sniffed his breath and eyed the shotgun.

"Go to bed, Buck," she said. She didn't even lecture him. Maybe she was afraid, too.

"Did you see the lights?" he asked, his voice

slurring a touch.

"What lights?" she asked, going to work on the dishes piled in the sink. She smelled of smoke and fryer grease.

"Northern Lights, out back. I saw an owl tonight, too."

"You've been drinking," she said. Her voice was absent the judgment, the condemnation he was expecting.

Maybe she was just worried about him.

14. Ascension

They came for him when he was asleep. At least, it was the first time he *remembered* that they came for him.

The anxiety of the previous weeks had worn off to a slow drip of general malaise and uncertainty, an iron-tinged undercurrent to his day-to-day. He'd stopped asking Uncle Bill to come by, and, as long as he had the drink, he could fall asleep in a reasonable fashion. He'd even managed to convince himself that he hadn't seen a robed figure in his room that first night. It was just the fear and the drink acting up on him.

But he hadn't been out back to the field. Not since the Northern Lights that nobody else had seemed to notice. Not since the owl.

Gradually, he realized that someone was in the room with him. It was full dark, well after midnight. The haze of Bulleit whiskey hung over him, a slow drum of a burgeoning headache beating within his brain. He'd sprung for medium-shelf tonight; the lower-end stuff was playing hell with his mornings. But soon things began to be clear.

There was a gray face staring at him from the foot of his bed. It caught the blue light (*blue light*?) that streamed in through the window. Its eyes were layered scales, mirrors rippling the illumination into eternity. This creature wasn't as tall as the marionette-thing he'd seen before. It stood about chest-high on spindly legs and arms, leaning forward. It cocked its head to one side, emoting curiosity.

As Bucky's eyes grew wide, the sweat began to drip from his forehead. Movement along the sides of his bed caught his attention. Short, robed figures stood on both sides, gesticulating, chattering at one another.

"Get away from me," he managed, his voice a whine. "Stay away from me. Please. Go away."

The gray thing leaned forward, extending an impossibly-long arm toward him. It held a silver wand that glowed like a tiny firecracker, drifting across inky night toward Bucky's forehead. It touched his skin, and an invigorating shock flowed through his sweat-soaked body.

The robed figures tore away his covers. Fingers that were glass needles poked into his sides, jammed into his rib cage and the soft flesh of his torso and thighs. He made to scream, but his tongue wouldn't move. He could only groan and twist his mouth in horror and rage.

The gray thing looked up to the ceiling, and Bucky allowed his eyes to follow. The white ceiling, the single bulb, the water stains—it all disappeared, revealing a night sky, and a swirling hurricane's eye of clouds, shimmering with silent lightning. Above that, three red lights hovered above the storm, linked together as part of a single metallic superstructure, fading in and out of the visual spectrum. Bucky knew that the storm's center—that impossibly black, localized eye of nothingness—was where they meant to take him.

Please, Bucky thought, eyes bulging, the pain in his sides and legs white hot. *Please, let me go*. The gray thing turned its blank eyes on him, emotionless, utterly

without expression or form.
We have never hurt you, it said.
We will never hurt you.
This is love.

As Bucky shot up toward the swirling void, the lights and the metal and the darkness of the craft rushing toward him, he knew, deep down, that was a lie.

They left him fragments. Bits of broken glass, shattered from a dim mirror, reflecting his own terrified face, a gray hand reaching for him from out of the darkness. When he tried to concentrate on those fragments, things went heavy, gray, black. He had lost a bit of himself. How much more would he lose?

The terror that he had felt during those first few encounters was now dwarfed by the realization that he was no longer simply being haunted; he had entered an entirely new world. Speaking to his mother or Uncle Bill was out of the question. His friends, simple-minded as they were, would take his stories as a joke or as hallucinations, brought on by a problem with his 'shine recipe, maybe, or bad weed. In the years since 9/11, security at the Canadian border became much tighter, and the flow of high-quality marijuana into Western New York slowed to an unsteady drip. Dealers had taken to spraying their supply with pesticides and acid in order to make the highs more vivid. Bucky had just been hitting tainted weed too much, that was all.

But was that all? No. He couldn't lie to himself.

Bucky knew that what was happening to him was *real*, even if it didn't make any goddamn sense. Whatever he was seeing—and whatever was coming for him in the night—was not some hallucination. He was beginning to wish that he was simply going crazy, like maybe his father had, or a distant relative, and this was all just to be expected. Some doctor could give him some pills and he could look at some ink blots and tell the people what he was seeing, and they'd all nod their heads and take notes and they'd fix his brain for him.

He took his pickup to downtown Ellicottville, parking across from the village court and police station. Usually there was a sheriff's cruiser or two parked nearby, supplementing the two village police units. But Sheriff Gifford had gotten himself wrapped up in a meth trafficking thing, letting certain vehicles pass through on the way from the labs down south to markets up to Buffalo, or vice versa. Bucky idly wondered who would be the new top lawman for the county. Probably some tight-necked asshole.

He walked past the post office, then waited for the crosswalk light to give him the go-ahead. He crossed Washington Street to the old brick library beyond. He didn't glance about, afraid that he'd make eye contact with someone he knew, someone who would want to talk to him. Or, worse, they'd take one look at him, his disheveled hair, his bloodshot eyes, his pale skin, those strange bruises along his temples—and wonder and gossip.

Did you see that Green boy? He was wandering downtown like half-dead roadkill. That boy is no good. That family is no good. Never have been, never will be. And I heard he's a moonshiner, breaking the law to make money while the rest of us do the proper thing and keep our heads above water. He probably deals drugs, too.

Bucky shook those small-town phantoms out of his mind.

The library waited for him.

Mrs. Taylor stood behind the polished wood main counter, tapping a keyboard and squinting into a dusty old Dell computer screen. She wore a wrinkled red sweater over a fluffy churchy shirt, cheap fake-gold necklaces hanging around her wrinkled neck. Horn-rimmed glasses (back in style, after all these years) hung over a bird-like nose. Faded blue eyes reflected images of her grandchildren posted on Facebook.

Bucky set his hands on the counter, nervous. He leaned forward, trying to figure out what to say. The old woman looked up at him, eyebrows arched. Dim recognition. She didn't know Bucky, probably, but she knew his family, if only by reputation. Small town librarians had a way of knowing everyone's family, especially by reputation.

"Hello," he managed, an itch in his throat rising up. "Ahem, ah … I'm looking for some books."

"You've come to the right place," Mrs. Taylor said, warmth in her voice and in her sudden smile. Whatever insecurity Bucky was feeling, it vanished. She was surprisingly receptive to his presence. Maybe Bucky had misjudged her judging him. He felt guilty for *feeling* guilty. "Is it … You're a Green, yes?"

"Um, yes. Buck—I mean, Larry."

"Oh, Larry. Yes. Your mother works as a waitress here in town, yes? Delilah, is it?"

"Um, yes ma'am."

"And you played football for a couple of years, didn't you?"

"Yes ma'am."

"You went to school with my granddaughter. Tiffany."

"Oh, yes. She was always a nice girl." Bucky vaguely

recalled a kinda-pretty-blond who was in a few of his science classes. He remembered the periodic table, oddly enough, but didn't remember the girls all that well. Go figure.

"She's married now, you know. Has a baby."

"Oh, jeez, that's great, Mrs. Taylor."

"Yes. Makes me feel so old."

"You don't look it," Bucky said. This old woman was sweet as sunshine. Her warmth and friendliness only made him feel more unworthy, more disheveled. *Normal* people acted like this. Normal people didn't see creatures in the woods or get sucked through the ceiling in the middle of the night.

"Oh, you're too kind. What kind of books are you looking for, dear?"

"Uh, well, you see … I'm not sure you'll have any. And it's not a big deal. I don't read a lot."

"It's always a good time to start. What are you looking for? Books on sports, maybe? Or hunting? We have plenty of those, very popular. We also have magazines."

"UFOs," Bucky said, spitting the word out. "Do you have anything about UFOs? Aliens from outer space? Anything like that?"

Mrs. Taylor smiled and gave him a wink.

"You've been seeing the lights, then?" she asked, her voice a mischievous whisper.

"Lights?" Bucky almost choked on the word.

"Some over Irish Hill, mostly. It's been a few years, but I remember this happening a couple of times. Back in the early 90s was the last time. Folks get all worked up over some things they see in the night. It's fun to think about, but it's probably just the Air Force flying top secret planes. Now they have these drones, which are even smaller. It's amazing what our boys in uniform have cooked up."

Bucky nodded, but felt his face flush red.

"You said ... other people have seen them?"

"Sure! It's nothing new. I've never seen them myself, but my mother talked about them floating over the mill one night. She and her sisters watched them for hours, while they drank lemonade and waited for my grandfather to come home from work." She had turned back to the desktop computer, minimizing her Facebook page and bringing up the card catalog. She made a few deft strokes on the keyboard, and a handful of listings appeared. "Our system says we have several selections. *The Mothman Prophecies* by John A. Keel, *Alien Agenda* by Jim Marrs, *Communion* by Whitley Strieber, and a self-published book by a local writer. *Spooky Lights* by Cecil Kotto. Cecil Kotto. Why, that's that black gentleman who's running for sheriff! What a coincidence." She turned and offered Bucky that warm smile again. "Which one would you like?"

"All of them," Bucky croaked. "Especially that last one."

They moved through the stacks together, pulling each book from forgotten corners of dust and disuse. Mrs. Taylor told him he could read them here or check them out, but he'd need a library card if he wanted to take them home. He signed up for a card—something he never imagined himself doing—and brought the books home in a plastic Quality Markets grocery bag. Mrs. Taylor told him to bring the books back in two weeks, but that he could renew them as long as nobody else wanted to borrow them. She said she didn't think anybody would be checking them out anytime soon, but with the lights in the sky back, that could change. You never really know about these things.

Bucky was a slow reader, so when he got home, he popped a beer and sat down at the desk his uncle had brought home for him from the dump right before he started high school. It was covered in comic books and hunting and fishing magazines, so he swept it all off into the trash and set the books down in a neat little pile. He figured he had about five hours til the sun set behind foreboding hills. He didn't want to be reading those books when it got dark.

15. Special Agent Schrader

Given his recent experiences, Bucky found his mind craving information. With no job other than tending the still and prepping for his deliveries, he managed to finish each book before they were due. He'd blown through *The Mothman Prophecies* in two days, but it was nothing like the movie. Marrs' *Alien Agenda* was a little dry but it was filled with all sorts of weird stuff. Strieber's *Communion* was the easiest to read, as it was more like a thriller than anything. Nothing he read quite fit what he was going through, but some of it rang familiar.

Spooky Lights by Cecil Kotto was the shortest of the books. It was part paranoid rant against the New World Order (which seemed to consist of a guy named Henry Kissinger, a place called Bohemian Grove, and McDonald's) and part collection of UFO encounters. Kotto had collected a few interviews of locals in Cattaraugus County who had seen the mysterious lights, and included a few of his own blurry photographs. Nothing revelatory, really. The author bio at the end of the book said he ran a call-in show on Cattaraugus County Public Access Radio called *Kotto's Kreepies*. Bucky resolved to tune in, especially in light of the news that this crank was running for sheriff.

He didn't understand everything he read, but the consensus seemed to be this: something very *weird* was going on. And now Bucky seemed to be a part of it. Whether these were aliens from outer space, demons from hell, or just something else, he couldn't say. He just prayed to whatever god there was that it wouldn't happen again. Not to him.

The call came just as Bucky had poured himself another drink. The phone gave a shrill ring from its perch on the wall next to the particle board bathroom door. The sound was unhealthy and low-pitched, like it was losing power, or that the call came from some place far, far away. Someplace where phones and trailers and words like "normal" didn't apply.

"It's going to happen again," the voice on the other end told him. It had a soft, Southern accent. "It always does, and it always will. But I can help you."

"Who is this?" Bucky snapped. "Who's calling?"

There was the sound of rustling from the other end, like fingers sifting through papers, or maybe through a smashed soft pack and cellophane, fishing for a cigarette.

"My name is Special Agent Schrader," the voice said. A clicking sound. Definitely a lighter. Then the snapping and popping of that freshly-lit cigarette, bobbing right next to the receiver. "I work for the FBI. I know they've been coming for you. I can help you."

The air went out of Bucky's lungs. He doubled over, clutching the crumbling edge of the plastic countertop.

He didn't feel much like drinking anymore.

◬

FBI Special Agent Schrader told Bucky he'd be making the trip to lonely, lovely Ellicottville in a few days, and that he'd like to have a face-to-face conversation. Schrader told him he knew about the gray creatures and the figures in black robes. He knew about the lights in the sky and the night visits. He knew a lot about Bucky, too.

Schrader arrived early on a Tuesday morning, driving a nondescript black town car, pulling in to the dirt and gravel driveway in front of the trailers at the edge of Quackenbush Road. Bucky was already up (and sober, surprising even himself) and watching out his window. The G-Man stepped out of the car and promptly lit a thin cigarette as he took in his surroundings.

Schrader was neither tall nor short He was devoid of any memorable features, save his jet-black hair combed over the top of his head, and a mustache that had grown too thick for professional appearances. His suit was black, his shirt impossibly white, his tie loose around his neck. He sucked smoke as Bucky walked out of the trailer to meet him.

"Where is the place?" Schrader asked, all business. "Where you first saw them?"

Bucky took him back to the still. It felt weird, giving a man from the FBI a tour of his illegal booze-making operation. Men died over such knowledge back during prohibition. Bucky didn't know this, but the irony wasn't lost on Schrader.

"This is where I first saw it," Bucky said. "It kinda looked like the one in my room that one time, but it moved weird. Like it was a puppet or something. Like it was on strings, all awkward, you know? And it—"

"It doesn't matter what it looked like," Schrader

said suddenly. He'd been quiet, asking a few brief questions, content to let Bucky spill out his answers. "What matters is that they're here."

"Why are they here?" Bucky asked, his eyes pleading with this man, this man from the government, to give him answers. *Any* answer.

"You've been chosen," Schrader told him. He looked at one of the water reservoirs. "Can I try some of your moonshine?"

Schrader explained that Bucky was one of a select few—a couple hundred, maybe as many as a thousand—that the visitors had contacted in recent years. They had been with us for a long time—he didn't say how long, exactly—but they'd always been active in selecting certain people. Individuals with knowledge, skills, or influence. Individuals they could use.

"Use for what?" Bucky asked. He poked at a venison steak on the grill, squinting through the smoke and charcoal fumes. He dipped his Budweiser to splash beer against the sizzling meat.

"Their agenda," Schrader said.

"So Jim Marrs was right. They have an agenda." Bucky nodded.

"A plan," Schrader said. He eyed his Budweiser with a look of something approaching contempt, but took a sip anyway. "They have a plan for mankind. The US government is part of that plan."

"Oh," Bucky said. He stared at the steaks, blood bubbling out of their browning flesh. "These'll be done in a few minutes."

Schrader stared off beyond the trees to the burned wagon and fire pit in the middle of the field.

"Is that where you saw the lights?" he asked, gesturing at the expanse of waving, golden grasses.

"Looked like red orbs, or once the Northern Lights. And there was an owl."

"There's always an owl," Schrader said. "We still haven't figured out why."

"Where are they from? What do they want?"

"They want something from you, Bucky."

"What's in it for me?"

"We get help. Medicine, bits of technology. Quite a bit since 1947."

"Why don't they just give us the answers now? Why make us wait?"

"They want us to figure things out on our own, too," Schrader said, his voice monotonous. Bucky was suddenly struck by the mundanity of it all; Schrader had undoubtedly given this speech many times before. It was all wondrous and a little confusing to Bucky, but it must get tiresome for a trained FBI agent to explain these things over and over again. "So they feed us little bits at a time. Sometimes we'll get a transmission from them—or a small amount of materials—and they won't tell us what it is, or what it means. So we go to work and try to figure it out. Sometimes we get it—like with the microchips—but other times, well … We're really no further ahead than if you gave a monkey an iPhone. Does that make sense?"

"Sort of, sure," Bucky said. Since Schrader had arrived—no, since before then, probably at least since that night with the owl, and for sure since he'd been taken up into the sky—his mind seemed sharper, more alert. The fog and haze of years of alcohol and marijuana use was gone. He'd read four books in a week, for Christ's sake. When had he *ever* done something like that? Not since Chemistry class, when he first saw he could actually *use* something from school.

"We're moving toward disclosure. Soon. A few years, maybe, and we can come out to the public with all of this information. You won't have to be ashamed about what happened. You'll be *proud*. People will be proud to know you, Bucky. You've been *chosen*. Don't you see how special that is?" Schrader delivered this with all the enthusiasm of a DMV employee issuing a registration receipt. He paused, his hands moving about his coat pockets, absently searching out another cigarette. He thought better of it, then clasped his hands together. "There's something else you should know. There are ... forces, factions. Groups of people—and other things—that don't want to see our plans succeed. They will claim to represent your best interests. But they are *not* to be trusted. Their ends do not align with ours. Do you understand that?"

"Yes, it's ... I mean, it's a lot to think about." Bucky flipped the steaks one more time, the scent of seared flesh making his stomach growl. "But ... what do they want me to do? Why me?"

Schrader finished his beer, then tossed the bottle to the edge of the field. It disappeared into the weeds.

"I don't know," he admitted. "But they're going to ask you to do something. It may be strange, it may be hard to understand. It may even be *painful*. But when they ask you to do it, you do it, you understand? It's very important. Whatever work they've prepared for you, you're the only one who can do it."

"Sure, okay," Bucky said, pride and anxiety competing within his mind, within his clouded heart. "But what if I don't do it? I mean, what if I can't? Or I don't want to?"

Schrader slowly turned his head to stare directly at Bucky, all pretense of friendliness gone in a flash of smoke and sudden heat from the grill. His glare was as cold as an Ellicottville winter.

"Are the steaks ready?" he asked, voice flat. "I'm awfully hungry, and it's a long drive back to DC."

16. Secret Ingredients

They wanted him to make 'shine.

They stood around his bed in the dead of night. The little blue-faced gnomes shoved needles dripping with mercury-silver into his arms and legs. But it was the taller grays who spoke to him, their oblong faces obscured by black hoods. Schrader was right—they had something for him to do.

We have a new recipe for you.

The fear was still present. Encountering them wasn't any easier just because he knew that he was *chosen*. They still terrified him. They were frightening to behold, their methods malignant. He had no say as to when and where and why they came; they just *did*, and he was helpless to resist. But now, weeks after Schrader had left him, weeks after he'd mustered up the courage to return to that field late at night, weeks after he'd given up looking for owls or marionette-things that sulked in the darkness—now they came, and they came when he was asleep, helpless, and alone in the dark.

Make your 'shine this way, they commanded. This wasn't a negotiation. A vague uneasiness welled up within him, and what false sense of self-ownership he possessed vanished in the face of their power. What choice did he have? For the first time in his stupid, inconsequential life, he was *somebody.*

He agreed to make the 'shine just as they asked.

A feminine gray nodded her assent, and then gave him what he needed to know. She (*it*) didn't give him some scrap of paper with the recipe on it. No, she leaned forward, stretching over his bed and leaning toward him, her joints and her fragile gray body snapping and bending, until her flat forehead was just inches away from his; her wide, dazzling, scaly, insect-like layers of black infinity boring directly into his own. Staring into those eyes was like drowning in the sky.

This is love, she said in his mind. She was beautiful, in a foreign sort of way, her features indistinct and swirling, pulsing between the rhythms of this reality and the next.

This is love, she said again, in his mind. *Do you accept this?* she asked, becoming something desirable, something alluring, something a far cry from the fear and the nightmare form she had been just moments before. It wasn't sexual excitement, exactly, although his body responded in that way. It was more in his blood; electric, moving, alive. Primed. He did not understand what this all meant. He doubted he ever would.

"Yes," he said. "I accept this."

The creature (*her? it?*) nodded, her forehead touching his, a bright light burning from within the center of her oval eyes, moving forward, firing sparks and strobes of blue and white light across the room. Something passed between them, and Bucky's forehead burned.

He wanted to scream.

They wouldn't let him.

The recipe was in his bones now. Boiling over within his blood. This was something he had to do, whether he liked it or not. He'd said *yes*. Bucky wasn't many things, but he was a man of his word. At least, he was now. They would see to that.

The first step was recruiting his friends. The sudden, terrible sharpness of his mind allowed him to see that most of his friends would be willing comrades. The promise of money, perhaps. An opportunity to join the 'shine business. Once they were involved, they could be marked (what did *that* mean?) and their loyalty would be absolute. It'd be too late to back out.

Bucky needed parts. Fresh. Young.

The visitors had told him where they could find parts. *She* had told him.

Randy's Ford pickup rattled to a halt alongside a crumbling curb. The streetlights along this particular stretch of urban decay in Olean were mostly dead, with a few desperate hangers-on blinking and buzzing against the decay of all things. Houses stood empty or emitting faint lights through barred windows. A dog barked somewhere down the block, and the wind blew through lawns of overgrown grass and scattered garbage.

There were three of them in the truck; Randy driving, Trevor in the middle of the bench seat, chewing his fingernails, Bucky in the passenger seat, staring out at the rot of a once-prosperous small city.

"Why we gotta park here?" Randy asked, throwing

the shifter up and locking it back. "Anybody even live around here?"

"Yeah, where we going, anyway? This ain't close to anything." Trevor spoke without looking at anyone. Whatever drunken resolve had pushed him into agreeing to this scheme had begun to fade.

Bucky stared out his window at the abandoned house beyond the broken sidewalk. It stood on a small piece of property, surrounded by a collapsing wooden fence, dark paint peeling off in little curls. The house's windows were boarded up. Its siding and the boards over the windows were covered in illegible graffiti.

Bucky's mind drifted through the open gate, then up those steps, then through that particle board nailed across the front door. Inside. Dark, damp, the smell of rat piss and bones. Forms flitted about in the shadows. Vermin, maybe, or the memories of the dead. Yes—images, like negatives burned into film, playing backwards across time, showing him things. A family—a little girl, wearing a sundress after church, hair streaming behind her—an old woman, lingering at the top of the stairs, leering down, a crippling black pain in her heart, hard to breathe. Her eyes becoming clearer, sharper, in focus, alight with blue spooklight fire. Peering at Bucky across the haze of ill-remembered past. Hate. Oh yes. *Hate.*

"Buck? *Buck?*"

He came out of it, his mind like a rubber band, snapping out of that house, back to the truck. Back to the task at hand.

What's happening to me?

"It's a few blocks away," he said, wiping a drop of drool from the side of his mouth "You want to park next to the place you're going to rob? Does that sound like a good idea to you?" He turned to set his gaze on Trevor and Randy. If they were going to break already, they were in trouble. He needed them to shut up and do what they were told.

"Sure, but, this is a neighborhood, could be that—" Randy said.

"Does it look like anybody still living in this graveyard is likely to call the cops on a few white guys in a pickup truck?" Bucky snapped. "Really? I count three houses on this whole block with lights on, and those people aren't in the habit of looking for trouble. Probably squatters anyway."

"Ok, Buck. Whatever you say." Randy tapped his gloved fingers on the steering wheel.

"Let's just get it over with," Trevor said. "Let's get moving."

"Good idea," Bucky said. He pushed the door open and set foot down on the ancient curb, then fished out his heavy backpack from the bed of the pickup. The night air was unseasonably cold and sharp; he could almost see his breath.

As Randy locked up the truck, Buck stared off at the house. His mind felt the pull again, but he kept his focus. Whatever was inside that house, he didn't want to see it anymore. He didn't want to give it any more energy.

△

They passed through dark streets, but encountered no one, save a single rusting Oldsmobile that passed by, the sound of deep, rumbling bass and the smell of marijuana drifting over to them. It slowed at the end of the block, then lingered at a stop sign. It pulled away after a moment, as a predator considers the prey not worth the effort. The last thing Bucky needed was a confrontation with bored, wannabe gangbangers.

Bucky spotted the squat, brick building as soon as they turned the final corner. He knew there was an alleyway that ran behind this row of buildings and lead to the fenced-in back lot. He'd never been here before, but somehow, he knew.

"Let's get off the street," he said. Trevor and Randy needed no convincing.

They passed behind the vacant buildings, dumpsters and abandoned cars marking their passage. A cat stared out at them from within a soggy cardboard box, offering a low, threatening growl. Bucky felt the creature's awareness—a set of monochrome senses, sharper than his, but its intelligence dim and easily pliable. He gave that impression a sharp *shove* and the animal clawed its way out of the box and away from them, scampering away between two empty houses.

In contrast to the rest of the row, the back lot of the building was well-lit. Two floodlights—and just below them, two cameras—faced down to the fenced-in area. The wire fence was wrapped in green mesh, with large white signs every 10 feet:

"NO TRESPASSING. PREMISES MONITORED."

"Masks," Bucky said.

They pulled out the rubber Halloween masks. Trevor had a green witch-thing, warts and long nose. Randy wore a floppy Jack-O-Lantern. Bucky donned a leering death's head skull. Inside the fragrant rubber face, his breath was hot and humid.

"I can't see shit," Trevor said.

"Then take off the mask and go to jail," Bucky snapped. He set his backpack down and unzipped it. He pulled out a thick, heavy blanket and proceeded to unfold it. Then he pulled out the bolt cutters. "Trevor, grab those trash cans." His friend did as he was told, his green face floating in the dark. He dragged a pair of big purple garbage bins over to the edge of the fence.

Bucky hopped up on them, careful not to lose his footing, then threw the blanket over the single strand of razor wire that ran along the top of the fence.

Easy as fishing with dynamite.

The clinic's security footage, when it was studied by police, would show three masked figures—the witch, the pumpkinhead, and the skull man—moving from dumpster to dumpster, before they finally settled on the one locked and marked "BIOHAZARD". They cut through multiple locks, and took with them a few unmarked plastic bags. The shift leader filing the report chalked it up to pro-life protesters. No group—fringe or otherwise—ever took credit for the break in.

In a few weeks' time, the case was forgotten.

17. End State

"The rest of the file references a bunch of field reports we don't have," Fields said, laying the folder back down on the table and tapping it with his index finger. "But I think we can fill in the rest."

"This Agent Schrader—he's behind it?" Richards asked. "Not that I really understand what *it* is." Fields shrugged, then glanced out Kotto's French doors to the helicopter, still waiting for him in the field. The storm had moved in proper, and was beginning to send fat droplets of rain down against the glass.

"I'd say he's a part of it. Schrader helped convince Bucky that the visitors—whoever, or whatever they are—were a force for good, not something to be feared. And he talked Bucky into using their recipe for his moonshine. The results of which we've been seeing for a few weeks now, since the State Troopers moved in to arrest him, and failed."

"But wait," Richards said, rubbing at his temples. "Why would the government go after Bucky, if they set him up? They wanted him to make the moonshine. Not that I understand why. But they wanted him to make this poison that's driving everyone insane. If they directed him, why try to bring him in?"

"Maybe they lost control of him," Fields said.

"Or maybe they wanted a problem," Kotto said. "They wanted rioting. Trying to arrest Bucky may have pushed him over the edge. Maybe that activated the—whatever's in the moonshine—that was the trigger." Kotto snapped his fingers. "Jiminy Cricket on a pretzel sandwich! They *wanted* the manhunt. They wanted everyone who'd been drinking the moonshine to go crazy."

"So you drink the moonshine, and somehow Bucky can control you?"

Fields shrugged.

"Maybe Bucky doesn't have that much control. Maybe he can't brainwash people into doing things—but he can certainly stir people up. Make them violent. Or maybe he *can* control them. Who knows?"

"The altars," Kotto said. "Don't forget the altars we encountered today. Those people were crazy, but they were *building* things. We don't know how that fits yet, either. Fields, what do your files say about how he made the moonshine?"

The FBI agent shook his head.

"You now know as much as I do," he said, eyes downcast. "We know a little about his criminal history, such as it is, and we know Bucky stole medical waste from the abortion clinic. Schrader filed these narratives about Bucky's encounters with the ... the visitors. But this doesn't tell us specifically how Bucky processed the moonshine."

"Space aliens," Richards said. "We're dealing with aliens from outer space?"

"That's not what the files say," Fields said. "The files say that Schrader *told* Bucky they were aliens, but there's nothing else in here to indicate that it's the truth. It's possible that the visitors are just some psy-op being run by an intelligence service."

"A psy-what?"

"Psy-op," Kotto said. "Psychological operation."

"So the US government is running ... psy-ops ... against its own people? That's what this whole thing is?"

"Do you really find that so unbelievable?" Kotto asked. "Haven't you been listening to my radio show?"

"Uh ... not that much, Sheriff."

"Think to your time in the Army, Deputy Richards," Fields said. "Don't you think it's *possible* that our government would be capable of this type of deception?"

"Jesus," Richards said. "I'm going to need more beer."

"There's plenty of cases about that sort of thing," Kotto said. "We know the government's done weird stuff to citizens before: sending them phony transmissions from ET to muddy the waters about aircraft testing. Special Forces teams conducting weird tests on cattle. Syphilis experiments. But we don't know that these visitors *are* a psy-op. But we don't know that they're *not*, either."

"All we know is that Bucky and his goons broke into some medical waste dumpsters at the Women's Clinic down in Olean, and somehow that's a part of his moonshine," Fields said.

"What would they steal from there?" Richards said.

"Use your imagination," Fields said. "Police work."

"Police work!" Kotto said, nodding.

"So Bucky stole dead baby parts? And he put them into his moonshine? Oh, Jesus. I'm going to throw up."

"Don't do it on the table," Kotto snapped. "Yeah, it looks like there's human blood in this new moonshine. I wish I could say I'm surprised, but I'm not. The old Middle Eastern gods like Molech and Baal required child sacrifice. People would offer up their children to the dark ones in exchange for blessings and riches. Not much has changed over the last few thousand years. Child sacrifice and blood rituals have always been a part of occult history and power. Hell, they've always been a part of *civilization*. People just don't like to admit it."

"So are we dealing with Molech and Baal, or are we dealing with aliens?" Fields asked.

"I'm not sure," Kotto admitted. "Either or? Both? Or maybe they're one in the same. There's not enough to go on. But the real question here is: what's Project Malthus' end state? We got little spooky space men, abductions, toxic-abortion-mind-control moonshine, and secret government agents. Where's it all going?"

"It's out of their control now," Richards said.

"Maybe they *want* it out of control. Thesis-antithesis. Controlled opposition." Kotto nodded to himself as he spoke. "Yeah, give them an excuse to send in their armored vehicles. Bring out their new soldier toys, fresh from the Department of Defense."

"How long has he been making this kind of 'shine?" Fields asked. "Does it make people crazy the moment they drink it, or is there some sort of catalyst, a triggering event?"

Kotto considered this for a moment, his fingers rubbing the stubble along his chin.

"Well, could be it makes you nuts the moment you take a sip. Or, could be it's a timed thing, like a poison. More likely, it's got something to do with the high strange events around Ellicottville. People are seeing all them lights again—maybe it's the UFOs that are setting people off. People see them lights, or the craft show up and start broadcasting some sort of signal. That activates the 'shine, or whatever the 'shine leaves behind. Either way, it's already started. If there was a signal, it's been sent."

"So we're too late to stop this?" Richards asked.

"That's it, game over, man? End of the world time?"

"It's never too late to turn things back," Kotto said. "No matter how bad or how dark it gets."

Thunder rumbled in the distance. The three men turned to look out the French doors to the storm beyond. Kotto's words hung in the air, small comfort in the face of encroaching darkness.

"Wait," Richards said. "I need to make a call. The storm's messing with my reception. Do you have a landline, Sheriff?"

"Yes, it's the spin-dial mounted next to the toilet."

Richards made his way to the bathroom. Fields and Kotto remained at the table.

"There's just the two of you who know the truth," Fields said. "I have to get back to the field office in Buffalo. I'm gonna be in enough trouble for drawing out a helicopter and a bunch of guns. I can't be here to help you with this one."

"If I can get to Bucky before the State Troopers do, we might be able to stop the rioting, the killing. We might be able to stop this thing before anything worse happens."

"Do you really think you can bring him in? Do you think he'll even talk to you? The Troopers have a hundred men combing the woods for him. There's no way the two of you will be able to track him down before they do."

"I'm not sure they *want* to catch him just yet," Kotto said. "I got a feeling that they want things to get worse before they get better." He tapped the folder on the table. "Project Malthus isn't about just one man."

Richards returned from the bathroom, his face somber.

"I just got off the phone with one of my buddies who's still in the National Guard," he said. "You're not going to like this."

"Out with it, Deputy!" Kotto said, cracking another beer.

"The governor is mobilizing my old unit," he said, "In response to the burning of West Valley, and the violence that's popping up in a few other towns. They're going to occupy the county. That means martial law."

III
Dark of Autumn

18. Shareholders' Meeting

The boardroom at Snow Pine Ski Resort just outside of Ellicottville, New York, boasted a lavish design. A long, perfectly-polished cocoa-stained cherry wood desk dominated the room's center, with wide, tall windows overlooking the main lifts and signature ski trails running down the fall-colored hills of the resort's central hub. The room's wide, expansive walls featured wood panels that hid state-of-the-art surround sound speakers; a black flat screen television stared down from between the mounted, majestic sets of elk antlers that reached out like the grasping legs of massive, bone-like spiders.

Sidney Lovering had shot them both himself, of course. He wasn't much of a sportsman—he found the act of sitting out in the woods all day to be tiresome and uncomfortable—but he knew the value in keeping up appearances, especially to the hicks that populated this town, this town that would be nothing without the business that his resort provided them. Therefore, every few years he spent a few thousand dollars (a few days' compensation, nothing serious) to fly to Canada or the Rockies, have some high-end outfitter park him in a scenic (but comfortable) locale and send giant animals his way to shoot. When he got back to

Ellicottville, he could tell whatever story he wanted.

There was something vaguely alpha male-ish in displaying his trophies in the boardroom. This was a shareholders' meeting, and all two dozen of those attending were equals, certainly, after a fashion. But Sidney, as CEO of Operations and Management of Snow Pine Ski Resort, was first among equals.

"Gentlemen and ladies, thank you so much for your time this afternoon." A sharp crack of light and thunder, just outside the large, curved windows punctuated his remark. "As you can see, we've finished just in time!" Stilted laughter arose from the men and women gathered. "I would encourage you to read the prospectus for the upcoming fiscal year, and to not worry so much about the news. The State Police operation in our good county is going to be temporary. Aside from the minor event that took place during Octoberfest weekend here at Snow Pine, there have been no reports of violence, rioting, or even political demonstrations within our village borders since. The State Troopers have focused their manhunt on locales north and east of Ellicottville. We, as a board, and as corporate leadership, should and do express our complete and continued faith in the efforts of our State Police to apprehend the fugitive Larry Green. As a token of our good faith, the immediate family members of all the fallen officers will receive free night ski passes for the upcoming season, completely free of charge."

Sidney offered a too-pleased-with-himself smile and enjoyed the light applause from the board members. The smile fit smoothly on his tanned face alongside the wrinkle lines of 40-plus years of calculated expression and schmoozing. Of course, what he said was only partially true. There *had* been more violence. Much more. Something big had happened in West Valley the day before—but judging by the polite response from the board, no one had heard about it. Yet. "And in keeping with our scheduled time—and with respect to Ms. Hanson, keeper of this meeting's minutes, our monthly meeting is adjourned."

Forced smiles followed along with handshakes and quickly-recalled facts about children and grandchildren attending school or trying out for high school sports teams. Sidney smiled through a stream of 30-second anecdotes about vacations to warmer climes; then hands clenched and eyes downcast over paltry talk about our fallen heroes in blue; optimistic appraisals of projected profits for the upcoming season.

As the board members filed out, one by one, Sidney let that purposeful smile slowly lose its luster. He was in charge, yes, but even those in charge had to dance the monkey dance from time to time.

Quiet returned to the boardroom as the last couple shuffled out, the smell of lavender old-people lotion tinging the air. Sidney let his face relax, his mouth becoming a flat line. He turned toward the sole remaining board member.

"Warren," he said, walking back toward the wall with the giant-sized flat screen flanked by two of his trophy kills. He drew closer to his reflection in that massive, curved, unblinking black eye. "Can I pour you a drink?"

Inside the stained-wood cabinets below was a mini fridge, which his secretary kept stocked with sodas, bottled water, craft beers, and various mixers. Flanking the whirring black box were built-in shelves, home to a variety of expensive liquors. Sidney didn't see a problem with drinking on the job. And as long as he kept Snow Pine profitable, neither did the board.

"Got any moonshine?" Warren Marks said, offering

a half grin. Warren was just a few months shy of 65. Retirement age for some folks, maybe, but not Warren. He'd been working in and around the county legislature for about as long as he'd been a board member for Snow Pine. He liked to say that he'd never run out of gas while doing the people's work.

The wrinkles marking decades of furrowed brows and campaign smiles in local politics were deeply etched along his face, itself framed by long white and silver hair that he had tied back into a ponytail. His black glasses bobbed slightly as he spoke. His wife said the glasses made him look *distinguished*, just like his graying hair made him look *distinguished*. He didn't particularly want to look distinguished, but considering he'd narrowly survived the meth-trafficking scandal that had gutted county leadership and law enforcement and catapulted a conspiracy crank to the now-ceremonial office of sheriff, he figured he was due for a few personal changes.

"I'd laugh, but it isn't funny," Sidney said. He stood up with a dark glass bottle, a simple white label affixed to its face. "Scotch okay?"

"Yes, of course."

Sidney pulled out a pair of glasses and clinked a single ice cube into each, then set about pouring the drink.

"The meeting went well, all things considered," Warren said.

"I thought so." Sidney carried over their drinks, his visage becoming all at once too-bright when a flash of lightning licked at the top of the main slope in view of their windows. The thunder crack was instantaneous.

Sidney jumped a bit, a drop of scotch dribbling up and out onto his right hand.

"Waste of good liquor," Warren quipped.

"Waste of $340 scotch," Sidney said as he set down

the glasses and took the seat directly across from Warren. He carefully slid a full glass across the table; Warren's eager fingers brought it the rest of the way.

For one quiet moment they considered the storm, the wind whipping up and howling in futile rage against the great glass windows. The rain came in a flat sheet, rolling forward and striking with pebble-sized droplets.

"We have to put this Bucky business to bed," Sidney said. "I can't continue our expansion project if there's a cop-killer in the woods."

"Maybe he left the area," Warren offered hopefully. "There was a possible sighting over in Killbuck."

"Not likely," Sidney said. "You know as well as I. Bucky was—*is*—liked around here. His family, his friends, and every gas station and liquor store owner who ever bought his moonshine. None of them are particularly friendly toward our law enforcement friends. Not after how they've been steamrolling through the countryside."

"The police have a job to do," Warren said.

"Of course. But sometimes that job involves beating up protesters and searching through homes without warrants."

"Tough times, tough measures," Warren said.

"Quite."

The men sipped their scotch, which hung hot in their throats.

"When are they going to bring him in?" Sidney asked. "This has gone on long enough."

"Didn't he tell you?"

"I haven't been to the Lodge since the riot Octoberfest weekend," Sidney said. "I'm feeling a little ... out of the loop. And half of the county has been drinking that psychotic moonshine. Major Winston hasn't checked in lately, but his secretary gave me a call this morning. News out of West Valley. There's at least thirty people dead, and the whole town is up in flames. Fire crews from Machias, Delevan, Ellicottville ... They can't get near the place. Every time they send up a truck, the people—the goddamn crazies—attack them." Sidney took another sip. No, a gulp. "That wasn't part of the deal."

"Three or four days, tops," Warren said. "Our Lodge brother from Washington gave us the impression that once Bucky is out of the picture, things should calm back down."

"And we get what was promised?"

"And the inner council of the Order of the Night Moose will be compensated for the trouble in our beleaguered county, yes," Warren said. "That was the promise." Although, he had to admit, *promises* were far less preferable to material reward, to immediate compensation. But he didn't call the shots, not really, and the others in the council hadn't seemed particularly interested in challenging what their strange, visiting brother from the Washington, DC High Lodge had to say.

We have to do a few things here, he had said in that odd Southern drawl through a mouthful of cigarette smoke. He never did take off that goddamn trench coat. Not even in the inner council chambers. *It will be painful for some of you, for some in your community. But once it's done, you can expect the full cooperation and support from the High Lodge. The DEC, the EPA, the IRS ... No one is going to stop this expansion.*

"If the investors get spooked—or if what happened in West Valley happens here—I think our expansion project will be the least of our headaches," Sidney said.

"At least the media's staying out of the picture," Warren said. "That's one promise he made good on."

Sidney reached over to a black box that sat in the

center of the table. His fingers danced over the soft plastic keys, and the black screen at the end of the room flickered to life.

"Channel 4 or 7 have a weather alert?" Warren asked absently. "This storm won't go away."

"Let me see ..." Sidney flicked through a few stations, the monolith flat screen displaying various images of afternoon soap operas, infomercials, sports coverage, local events—

"Wait," Warren said. "What was that? Go back."

"Where? Which channel?"

"Channel 3, I think it was," Warren said, leaning forward.

"Public access?"

"That's what I'm afraid of."

Sidney typed in the channel number and the screen flickered onto a pair of familiar faces.

"That's the leggy blonde, right? What's her name? Won Miss Cattaraugus County once, I think," Warren said. "I make it a priority to sit on that committee every year."

"I'm sure," Sidney said, smirking. "She's a reporter now? For the public access channel? Kind of a waste of talent. Hmm, the sky's dark there, too. I wonder where she is. Looks like a checkpoint."

"What's she saying?" Warren asked. "And who's that behind her? Is that—oh God. Oh God, no."

The volume bar stretched across the bottom of the screen as Sidney tapped the remote box. Veronica Cartwright, clad in a beige woman's sports coat and skirt, was standing in front of a State Trooper roadblock, which had become a common sight on the roads around Ellicottville and the surrounding areas. Lights flashed, angry motorists exchanged tense words with riot armor-wearing Troopers. Just behind her, waiting with arms crossed, was a man in an old Army helmet, a shotgun perched up over his right shoulder, a military camo jacket hanging loose over his shoulders, a silver sheriff's star clipped crookedly over his left breast pocket. Puffs of blue cigarette smoke rose up over his large black aviator sunglasses.

" … at least that's the story according to the official State Police spokeswoman, who wouldn't field additional questions. However, I have learned that there appears to be a great deal more to the search for fugitive and local hero Larry 'Bucky' Green. In an exclusive interview for Cattaraugus County Public Access Television, we finally have someone from the local government who is willing to give us the inside story."

Veronica turned to the man in the Army helmet and jacket, who flicked his cigarette behind him onto the road before stepping forward to join her. The butt spun up and crashed into the balaclava-covered face of a State Trooper, who swatted away flaming red ash from his nose.

"Hey, watch it, asshole!"

"Cattaraugus County Sheriff Cecil Kotto has agreed to end the media blackout on the manhunt," Veronica said, not missing a beat. "Sheriff, thank you for joining me on air."

"No one is going to see this, right?" Sidney said, his voice low. "Nobody watches public access in the middle of the day, do they?"

"I hope not," Warren said, rubbing at his temples, his eyes closed in pain from a sudden migraine. "Somebody is going to need to shut that crazy bastard up before he makes things worse."

19. Lost Signal

Kotto grabbed the microphone from Veronica and walked straight toward the camera. His face was tinged red from standing out in the cold, and his breath fogged up the lens, leaving only his giant, dark sunglasses and the front of his olive-green Army helmet bobbing in the frame.

"Don't drink the moonshine!" he crowed, his mouth too close to the microphone. Distortion hung on his every word. "It used to be good, I know, I used to drink 'shine, too, until I woke up blind and with a hangover that would kill a Toyota pickup truck. I still drink the liquor, but I know better than to drink that clear devil-juice! And that's just what this stuff is—devil-juice! It makes you fall under alien control. You'll start biting people and building altars out of dog bones and axe-murdering all over the place. We got devil rituals in West Valley happening. That whole town's on fire! The State Police are probably in on it! Stay off the roads! Keep your powder dry! Don't go aboard any alien spacecraft! It's all connected! Remain vigilant people—!"

Veronica moved forward and wrenched the microphone from the sheriff, who stumbled back. Richards caught him from falling. Kotto kept shouting, his voice muffled now because of his distance to the microphone.

"Soylent Green is people!" he shouted. Richards pulled him back toward the road while Veronica got her bearings. She stepped back into center frame, her face a mask of perfect professionalism and composure.

"Um, sorry about that folks. The sheriff seems to have suffered some form of mild seizure. But the fact remains, the disturbances and riots over the past few days and weeks *do* seem to be caused by the moonshine—perhaps some form of psychotropic or methamphetamine compound slipped into the drink. According to the sheriff, West Valley has completely fallen under the control of people affected by the moonshine. And as you can see here, the State Troopers are *not* trustworthy. We've seen them illegally search vehicle after vehicle, and detain people just for passing through. There's been a complete media blackout, with additional reports of—"

From just out of frame came the sound of metal-on-metal equipment tinkling, then the booming voice of a large man with a large gun and a badge.

"Ma'am, we're going to have to confiscate that camera. You need to stop filming immediately, we—" Gloved hands reached from out of frame.

"Hey, let go of me!" Veronica shouted, pulling away. The cameraman stepped back and swung around to capture two State Troopers in full riot gear moving forward, hands on their M-16 rifles, faces covered by balaclava and goggles.

"Sir, hand me that camera," one of them said, hand outstretched toward the lens.

"Uhh, you got a warrant?" the cameraman asked, stepping back.

"Sir, I'm not *asking*."

The gloved hand covered the lens. Flashes of grass,

muddy jeans, black combat boots. Veronica's harried voice over the muffled distortion.

Just before the signal was lost, Kotto's voice could be heard over the scuffle:

"Fight the future, people!"

20. Detainees

"You guys can't do this," Veronica said, her hands zip-tied behind her back. One of the Troopers, clad in full body armor, assault helmet, googles, and black wrapping obscuring his face, shuffled her over to the side of the road with the rest of the detainees. These were the other drivers who had talked back, or asserted their rights to drive unmolested down a public road, and got pulled out of their cars and handcuffed for their troubles. The Troopers didn't call them *suspects*, because that would imply charges were pending. The detainees all sat facing away from the road, their legs dangling over the ditch, grumbling to one another or themselves.

"Sit down, ma'am," the Trooper said, shoving her down into the mud.

"Hey!" she snapped, her ankle bending *just* the wrong way, offering a flash of sharp, twisting pain. She let out a wheezing groan.

"You assholes can't do this, we got rights!" Dean yelled. Her cameraman was already zip-cuffed and sitting on the ground next to her. The Trooper who had shoved down Veronica walked over to him and backhanded him across the face, sending Dean toppling into the mud of the shallow ditch.

Veronica gasped.

"Keep your goddamn mouths shut," the Trooper snapped. "Unless you know where Bucky is, I don't want to hear a fucking peep from now on." He walked away, and another trooper—his face likewise obscured by mask, goggles, and helmet—stepped forward, his rifle pointed slightly above and away from the toes of his black boots, his finger quivering nervously just outside the trigger well of his assault rifle.

"Help him up!" Veronica snapped at the Trooper. She allowed herself to slide down into the ditch, mud spattering up on her stockings and sucking at her running shoes. "You want this man to die on your shift, officer?"

The Trooper hesitated, and then approached the ditch. He pulled Dean—who had been gasping, face down in the mud—back up onto the side of the road with Veronica's help. She got behind him and pushed him up and out with her shoulder, until he was coughing and gasping on his side in the grass.

"You alright?" she asked, pulling her feet out of hungry mud climbing back up onto the shoulder.

"Sit down and be quiet," this Trooper said. A look of hate from Veronica's face was the only reply. He moved down the line, eager to avoid another confrontation.

"Yeah, just got a mouthful of country sludge," Dean said, spitting flakes of grass and chunks of mud onto the grass. "I need a shower."

"You and me both," Veronica said. "Where's the sheriff?"

"If he wasn't yelling his goddamned head off, I think we wouldn't be in this mess," Dean said. "Jesus, what the hell was he talking about? Why did you put him on the air?"

"He's law enforcement, technically," Veronica said. "No one else will talk to me. If even half of what he said was true, we've all got worse things to worry about than being arrested." Veronica scanned the road in both directions. Traffic was still backed up, and the Troopers were pulling more and more people from their vehicles, lining them up in neat little rows along the ditch.

"You think we're gonna get fired for this?" Dean asked.

"You worried you're going to lose your part-time cameraman job?" Veronica said. "Where did you park the van, Dean?"

"Uh, over by that brown house. It was on the left of the driveway, I think, when you're facing the pond and the railroad tracks. I'm not quite sure which direction it is from here." He spit again. "My head's a little fuzzy."

"Think about that next time you consider mouthing off to a Nazi Stormtrooper," Veronica said. She leaned back and looked down the road to her right. There, just beyond the break in the trees, was the house. The driveway was full of Trooper vehicles—including a mobile command unit RV—but beyond that should be their van.

"We need to get out of here," she said.

"And how are we going to do that, boss?" Dean said. "We're wearing plastic handcuffs and surrounded by dudes with guns. Dudes who aren't real happy with us right now."

"If we can get the sheriff, maybe we can talk him into letting us tag along. They might release us into his custody."

"I don't think that's how this is going to work," Dean said. "I just want to go home."

"You're still on the clock," Veronica said. "This story isn't over."

"Yeah, but if I go over fifteen hours a week, the

station manager is gonna kill me."

"I think he'll make an exception for us this time. Is there another camera in the van?"

"Sure, but it's not as good as the one they just smashed. Think I'll have to pay for that?"

But Veronica wasn't listening. She looked up and down the road, straining to see something besides angry motorists, stopped cars, State Troopers in pretend-soldier get ups, and swaying, skeletal trees shedding their colors.

"I outrank you, Sergeant So-and-So," Sheriff Kotto said, poking his finger square into the chest-center of the Trooper's body armor. "Just 'cause you guys got all this fancy gear and this *Call of Duty* shit doesn't mean nothing. This is *my* county, even if this is your manhunt. Where's George? Old George Winston, that old slug? He's in charge of this operation, ain't he? We gotta talk! You boys are going about this all wrong!"

They stood in the manicured front yard, just shy of the driveway that held the State Trooper command RV. Either the Troopers had gotten permission from the homeowners, or the homeowners were nowhere to be found. Away on vacation, maybe, or, more likely, out-of-towners who weren't using their fancy vacation home just yet. Had they shown up and seen the parade of slow traffic, vehicle searches, and an ever-growing crowd of people zip-cuffed and sitting along the ditch, they may very well have turned around and headed back home. Their little country getaway could wait a week or three.

"Sheriff, please," the Trooper said. "You're interfering with our search." He had removed his assault helmet and goggles. Richards stood staring out at the vehicle and personnel searches just behind Sheriff Kotto. The Trooper shot Richards a hopeful look of *help me out here, please*. Richards smirked and shook his head, *you're on your own, buddy*. "The commander has told me to tell you that you're welcome to cooperate with the investigation—all two of you—but you can't be showing up at our roadblocks and yelling at people." His voice dripped with all the practiced reason of a career law enforcement officer, a man with a *future*. And that future didn't involve rocking the boat. It involved doing what he was *told*, and smartly.

"This is horse-cocky," Kotto said, waving a wild finger at the ever-growing line of cars waiting to pass by the roadblocks and Trooper cruisers. "You can't just search every vehicle and arrest everybody. Bucky was last seen on foot, right? What makes you think he'd hop in a car and drive right back into town?"

Richards tuned them out and focused on the traffic stop. He had to admit that the state boys knew what they were doing. The Troopers had about two dozen men on the ground, with more in the command RV vehicle parked in the nearby driveway. There were about half a dozen Trooper SUVs arrayed along the road in both directions along this stretch of Route 242. Richards suspected there were more men in the hills overlooking the road. Possibly snipers, too. That's how he'd play it.

That thought suddenly struck him as odd. He wasn't thinking in terms of being a cop. True, he had a deputy's badge and a county-issued pistol, but his one-day training session hadn't prepared him for much of anything except to get used to Kotto's bizarre leadership style and beliefs. He wasn't thinking like a cop as he analyzed this traffic control point. He was thinking like a *soldier*, like when they used to run these ops in Afghanistan, when they'd search vehicles or pat down passersby, or just hang back and watch while the Afghan National Police guys would shake down old men and women. No, he wasn't thinking like a cop at all, and neither were the State Troopers.

They were thinking like soldiers. Like an occupying force. And they were *acting* like it, too. Shouting orders, grabbing people out of their cars—hell, they were slapping flex-cuffs on people and shoving them down into the ditch. There, just across the road, Richards could see that reporter—the good-looking blond, with the schlubby cameraman next to her all covered in mud. She was looking about as pissed-off scary as an attractive woman could. *Mean*, her face read, and Richards was glad he wouldn't be on the receiving end of that.

"What the hell is happening to us?" he asked himself, a statement more than a question. No, they weren't going to do any good here. If he could just convince the sheriff to pull back, maybe they could regroup, maybe even get the word out as to what was happening. The Troopers hadn't arrested Kotto—yet—but if he kept pushing, they probably wouldn't tolerate his shenanigans forever.

Kotto waved his finger in the air, gesticulating like a fascist dictator giving a speech for an adoring crowd. Traditional lawman Kotto sure wasn't, but Richards could tell that the sheriff took his duties and his responsibility for these people seriously. What the Troopers were doing here was unacceptable, manhunt or no.

Richards walked over to him, trying to find the right words to convince his new boss that this was a losing battle. It wasn't retreat—it was a withdrawal and regrouping. They'd managed to get on TV—even if it was just the public access station. Maybe they could have better luck at the broadcast station itself, or even up in Buffalo with the main three channels. *Someone* had to listen.

Richards reached a hand out for Kotto's shoulder, his mouth starting to open, a look of thankful relief on the State Trooper sergeant's face. But he froze, fingers suspended inches above the lapel of Kotto's faded Army BDU jacket. The deputy's eyes grew large, and his mouth curled back into a feral grimace that reflected primal mammalian fear. The sergeant, seeing the deputy's reaction, ignored Kotto's tirade and turned to follow Richards' gaze.

Route 242 wound away from them to the northeast, following the slope of a hill down to cut over a set of rusted-out railroad tracks flanked by warning lights and CAUTION arms that hadn't worked in years. That is, they *did* function from time to time, but not when trains carrying nuclear waste traveled through at night. No, they came alive at random times during the day and night, flashing their red lights and letting their shaking arms fall to block traffic. Richards, like other locals, had learned to patiently wait for any phantom trains to pass through, or, if it was late enough and there were no cops around, to thread through the arms and keep on moving.

It was these traffic signals that sprung to life now, in the chill of late afternoon, flashing, the tired siren sounds of warning demanding attention. The arms began to descend, and the cars backed up to the tracks gingerly pulled up or back away from the crossing, honking at those in front or behind to let them move away from the descending lengths of metal. The warning sound clang-clanged with malnourished fever, growing in pitch and frequency, the signals' arms and lights dancing with unseen energy, the arms swaying up and down like the blades of impatient guillotines.

The uproar caught the attention of the Troopers conducting the stops and searches further up the road, who turned just in time to see what had caused Richards to suddenly stand in fearful awe.

The craft came from behind the top of a hill brown with the lifeless fingers of dead trees. Its ovoid structure was an offensive contrast in warped metal framed by spires of gleaming bone, eldritch symbols of dread glowing red-hot on each gray metal surface framed by those wide supports of calcium and ruin. Its dimensions were impossible to determine, but the impression it projected in sight (and in the minds of all who looked upon its abominable visage) was that it was *big*. Really big.

As it rotated and floated out over the road, following the snaking of Route 242's disrepaired and crumbling asphalt, it revealed a small dome at the top of the superstructure, an egg-like casing of mirrored glass that pulsed with a faint, blue-orange light.

The damned thing was, quite simply, the stereotypical flying saucer—but dipped in the fires of hell, warped by its arcane energies, and sent back up to our world as an even greater offense to and perversion of logic and reality.

Richards instinctively stepped back, his mouth falling open in utter shock. The Troopers had begun to point at the bio-mechanical monstrosity—some of them going so far as to raise their weapons. The saucer moved over the road silently at first, but then began to emit a low buzzing that seemed to come charging out of the base of one's own skull.

"Well I'll be a milkmaid's college degree," Kotto said, tilting his head to one side and pulling his aviators from his face. "If that isn't the damnest thing."

21. Flying Saucer Terror Attack on Route 242

Veronica spotted the news van just down the road, parked where they had left it, just shy of the driveway. That driveway just so happened to be where the State Troopers had set up their mobile command RV, its antennae and satellite dish pointing skyward.

"There's the van," she said. "Dean, you have the keys still?"

"Yeah, they left them in my pocket." He was squinting up at the bone gray sky, mud and pain etched across chubby face. "I need a drink."

"Maybe the Troopers have some of Bucky's moonshine lying around as evidence."

"I'll pass, thanks."

"Okay, listen, we need to get to our van. We can drive down the shoulder to get past all this traffic."

"How are we gonna do that?" Dean asked. "Maybe if we just sit here and be quiet, they won't go shoving my face into the mud again. Maybe they won't even take us in, right? They've got too much to do. If they arrest us, there will be hell to pay, right? I mean, you're a local celebrity or something." Dean choked out a laugh.

"What's so funny all of a sudden?"

"The idea that a public access reporter is a local celebrity."

"No, I'm not ... But Kotto *is*. You do more than just camera stuff at the station, right?"

"Sure, sometimes."

"How does Kotto broadcast his show? What's it called?"

"*Kotto's Kreepies*. I only listen to it when I'm stoned."

"Does he go into the station to record and broadcast?"

Dean's brow furrowed.

"Uh, no, actually. Maybe a couple of times for interviews. But usually he does it remotely. The station manager had me set up the connection once. He's got a makeshift recording studio at his house, I think. But I don't know where he lives."

"If we can get him on air, can you get ahold of the station? Have them broadcast the signal?"

"I suppose. It's not like the afternoon or evening shows are a ratings bonanza." Dean shrugged. "'Course, I'd need to have my fucking hands untied, first."

"I'm gonna try to flag him down," she said. She scuttled her way back up to the road, like a dog dragging its ass backwards across carpet. The Trooper tasked with guarding them was down the line, arguing with a detainee in a Miller High Life t-shirt and blue, red, and white-striped Zubaz sweatpants. Veronica turned and shouted toward the house and driveway, where she hoped Sheriff Kotto was.

"Sheriff!" she yelled. "Sheriff Kotto!"

A couple of motorists turned to look at her as they slowly crept through the checkpoint, but the Troopers paid her no mind. Aside from the jerkoff who had slapped Dean down earlier, no one seemed eager to bully a pretty woman in professional attire and covered in mud. She yelled for the sheriff a few more times, then stopped.

Something was wrong.

Veronica heard it—or *felt* it, somewhere deep in her heart, and deeper still in that untouched and unconsidered country called her soul—before she saw it. Traffic stopped moving completely. The Troopers conducting the vehicle searches stared off to the northeast, their heads titled up. A few of them even raised their rifles to peer at something through their weapons' optics.

The craft—because it certainly wasn't a bird, or ball lightning, or anything else that mother nature could possibly produce—emerged at the edge of Veronica's vision, spinning slowly and hovering directly over the road. Without reference, it was impossible to tell how far away the bone and metal disc was, but it felt *close*, especially as that fell humming bubbled up out of the back of Veronica's skull, like the rhythm of some great power plant, buzzing with energy deep underground.

The saucer floated into a position above a minivan that sat idling at the base of the slope leading up to the driveway. As the saucer came to rest, so too did its spinning slow and cease, until the craft was completely still, hovering just above the rusting Ford family van. There were runes—what else could they be?—scratched across each metal panel flanked by bone support beams. One rune per panel; each rune at least as tall as a man. They glowed with a soft orange light, but, as the saucer drifted to a full stop and its centrifuge likewise came to a halt, the rune facing Veronica began to smoke and shift, spitting massive sparks until the symbol burned nuclear-hot.

Veronica sat with her mouth open, and her legs,

acting on some fight-or-flight instinct, stood her up in the road, until she was stumbling forward over crumbling pavement. She stood next to a Dodge pickup truck, its driver and the Trooper searching him standing across the hood, likewise staring up at this unholy construct.

Unholy. The word stuck in the center of her mind, branded onto her brain tissue, sizzling hot.

The rune was not a rune at all, Veronica realized. No, it was a symbol that was familiar. It was known to her. Images of hard rock albums and scary movies danced in her mind, released unbidden by some collapse in her mental self-control. Seeing this giant mechanical-organic *thing* in the sky and knowing it impossible, her subconscious released a flood of half-forgotten memories and Jungian fear.

On the frontward face of the saucer was not a rune, but an inverted star, held in the center of a perfect circle, all points alight with terrible power.

A pentagram.

As the symbol grew brighter and brighter, all of the people below imagined—because it couldn't be real—the sensation of heat on their faces, their skin warming to the flames roaring above, their eyes tearing up in defense. The occupants of the Ford Freestar, seeing everyone around them looking up at something above them, stepped out. Twenty-somethings with long hair, Misfits and yellowed-white Young Ones punk t-shirts, faded tight jeans. A band, maybe on their way to a show at the Ellicottville Sportsmen's Club, or headed home from a long tour. Frozen fear was theirs now, too.

The pentagram grew too hot and too bright, until the light flooded the whole valley. Veronica flinched and squinted her eyes, but did not want to look away. No, something pulled her to it. What she was seeing was meant to be seen, as painful as it might be to behold.

Just before the light faded out, a single image, holographic and wide, floated out from its unholy symmetry: that of a Euclidean Baphomet; a goat's face, writ in fire the color of blood, horns curved and tongue dangling out, eyes mere lines but somehow alive and hateful.

The light disappeared, the thrumming sound ceased.

An orange spotlight shot out from the bottom of the craft, a shrill electronic buzzing breaking the silence. The shaft widened into a cone, until the entire van was encased in that terrible, hot light. The band members backed away, yelling in fear or in pain, their hair singed and their skin taking on brown splotches of immediate sunburn. The van's metal chassis groaned, internal pressures building. Then it was lifted into the air, tires just inches off of the pavement. The vehicle turned and twisted slightly, until the side panel door slid back at an angle. A pair of backpacks, stacks of CDs with the band name *The Silver Rockets* stenciled across their covers, and a guitar amp tumbled down onto the road, the amp cracking metal-on-gravel, plastic jewel cases shattering in a rain of indie label rock. Something *whooshed*, and the cone of light lifted and pointed forward, then swung like a baseball bat, carrying the van along its shifting radioactive spectrum. The Freestar floated through the air as if it weighed nothing.

The swinging light carried the van up and to the side. The light disappeared. The momentum of the movement carried the vehicle up and away from the saucer, sending it tumbling through the air over the small pond at the edge of the railroad tracks. The van hit the water headlights-first, the massive splash preceding the screams of the once-silent witnesses, now howling mad with uncomprehending fear.

There was a moment of dread calm. A good four or five seconds of relative stillness, each person seeing what could not be unseen: an impossibility slicing through the veil of our physical world. Those precious few seconds lasted forever to Veronica, her mind racing and heart pumping.

"Dean," Veronica said. "We have to get out of here. *Now*."

"Right behind you, boss." The cameraman scrambled to his feet.

Veronica ran, running shoes hitting pavement and pushing her through the halted traffic and past dumbfounded Troopers. Then the silence was over. Now came the screaming and the howling of mad, delirious fear. Pure, black anarchy.

Veronica and Dean made it to the other side of the road just as the crowd collectively lost its mind. They stumbled over the pavement along the shoulder, which broke off in hand-sized chunks. Sheriff Kotto and Deputy Richards were just ahead of them, staring up at the thing in the sky.

The howls of panic suddenly ceased, and there was only the strained breathing of a reporter and her cameraman.

Then, a voice distant, from where the van had lifted out of logic and sense:

"Hey, my guitar was in there!"

Someone started shooting, and then the screaming began anew.

Veronica couldn't tell if the rounds came from the police weapons or from some overzealous traveler. Someone was shooting *at* the flying saucer, which had come alive again with dread sound and fervent movement, its superstructure spinning, the pentagram on its surface alive again with light and fire.

Another beam of light shot out, droning and zapping, picking up a blue 1994 Chevy Cavalier, its occupants scrambling to get out of the cab, their skin and hair smoking in the searing light as they pushed themselves out of the side doors. They collapsed as they hit the road 10 feet down, then stood up again to dash away into the trees.

People abandoned their cars or drove them into the ditch. The saucer tossed the Cavalier aside, this time toward the wooded hill to the north. Its beam threw the car with such force that it knocked down two pines, grown old and tall and strong over the years, now splintering and shattering as the metal and fiberglass missile impacted and crumpled against their ancient boughs.

"Sheriff!" Veronica yelled. "We have to get out of here!"

Deputy Richards spun around and saw her. He waved them forward, his other hand already clutching his pistol. Some of the Troopers had switched their rifles over to three-round bursts, blasting staccato fire which popped harmlessly against the alien hull. The saucer drifted over to another car, which had been left empty with all four doors open. The beam of hot light enveloped the vehicle, and flung it over the railroad tracks beyond the nearby pond.

As Veronica reached Richards' outstretched hand, more screaming came from behind her. She turned and looked, operating on adrenaline time now, everything happening so slow and so clear.

There were people pouring out of the woods, coming down from the hills. Dozens of them, wielding axes or baseball bats or chainsaws revving up and spewing fumes. They screamed and howled, blood and dirt smeared across their clothes and faces. Their eyes glowed green and orange with smoke that billowed out of their sockets, the flesh on their faces twisted into inhuman gargoyle masks of maniacal hunger.

As the rain began to fall, Bucky's minions descended on the checkpoint.

22. Fight and Flight

Richards saw them pouring off of the hill. A whole mob of crazed people, with those terrible smoking-bright eyes, their skin pale and wretched. Bucky had raised an army of them, neighbors and friends and family, driven mad by his moonshine. These were the folks from West Valley, no doubt, marching south, here, following that flying *thing* that was tossing cars into the trees and pond. None of it made a bit of goddamn sense, but Richards wasn't about to let more innocent people get hurt. He'd seen enough of that today.

He turned from Veronica and aimed his 9mm pistol in front of him. There was a man, tall and fat, his wifebeater turned brown by blood or something else. His eyes pumped that green smoke out, and his mouth was wide open, tongue lolling out like a dog's on a humid afternoon. He jumped out from the nearby trees and lifted a whirring chainsaw into the air. He brought its spinning blade down on the car in front of him—a blue Subaru Outback, a family trapped inside.

"*Thy flesh consumed,*" he snarled, the words deep and echoing with a reverb of multiple voices, like the unified cries of the damned echoing up out of an abandoned well. Sparks shot up into the man's face, burning bits of his exposed flesh, but he didn't let up. There were children in the back seat, screaming. The woman in the passenger seat clawed at the man in the driver's seat. His face was locked in dumb fear.

"Hey, shithead!" Richards said. He walked forward, pistol out before him. He leaned over the top of the Subaru, his sidearm just a couple of feet away from the center of the roof. The chainsaw-wielding maniac pulled the whirring blade away, his face turning from the terrified family to spy the deputy.

"*Godless one,*" he growled. "*We will commit you to the harvest. The threshing floor runs red with the blood of martyrs and sinners alike. Our Father Below grows his kingdom, your lives are ours—*"

Richards fired his 9mm, the bullet splattering the man's face from only a few feet away. The cartridge ejected and clinked along the car's roof before rolling off to the road below.

Green smoke continued to pour out of the man's ruined eyes, and now it billowed from the desiccated black hole where the bridge of his nose should have been. The chainsaw, now idling, clacked down on the car and then into the mud. His lifeless body fell straight back.

"He blew his nose right off!" one of the kids said from inside the car. "Did you see that, Daddy?"

Richards reached down and tried to pull open the driver's side door. It was locked. The man inside had a face warped with fear, his wife sobbing next to him.

"Get the fuck out of here!" Richards snapped. "Get your family out of here!"

Already vehicles were pushing against one another, driving madly down both lanes and the shoulders in both directions, edging forward and colliding bumper to bumper. But no one got out to exchange insurance information. It was a snarl, but it was moving.

"Deputy!" a voice said. "Cut us loose!"

Richards turned to see the reporter and her chubby cameraman standing behind him. He pulled his K-Bar knife from his vest, then cut the plastic restraints from their wrists. Dean rubbed at his hands. Veronica grabbed Richards by the shoulder straps on his black tactical vest.

"We have to get Kotto on the radio!" she said. "We have to warn people!"

"Right with you, darling," Sheriff Kotto said, stepping past them and firing his pistol at a woman with a pitchfork who emerged from the trees. Two sharp cracks. The woman, her sun dress torn to expose her flabby flesh, collapsed into the ditch with an inhuman moan of terror. "But we gotta survive this first."

Staccato rifle and pistol fire echoed up and down the road. Some motorists had taken to fleeing into the woods; others honked their horns and tried to push through the traffic. Deep thrumming came from the flying saucer above, which seemed content to hover and spin and observe the chaos below, its cone of light no longer wreaking radioactive havoc.

"My whip's in that mess down the road," Kotto said, pointing to a pickup boxed in by abandoned cars. "We're gonna need another vehicle to get out of here."

"Here," Dean said, pulling the van keys from his pocket. "I'll drive."

"Shouldn't we assist the Troopers?" Richards asked, holding his pistol with both hands low in front of him, his head on a swivel.

"We don't have the firepower," Kotto said. "They've got rifles and armor. As much as I don't like seeing people getting cut up or eaten alive, they should have seen this coming."

"Tactical withdrawal," Richards said. "Again."

"Hasn't been our week so far, Deputy," Kotto said. "We can't stop this by shooting our way out. Hell, I wish that were the solution. But I don't want to kill all these people. And that flying saucer up there—I don't think bullets are any good against it. Let's get in that van, and—"

"Sheriff, look out!" Richards shoved Kotto down, who hit the pavement helmet-first. A man came shambling out from behind an abandoned car, a garden hoe raised over his head, his eyes locked on the unsuspecting sheriff. Richards made to raise his pistol, but he realized he was too slow. He wouldn't get the round off in time—

A sudden blast of heat and air knocked Richards aside. From the shoulders up, the maniac disintegrated, blood splattering out in a rain of diseased ichor and iron-tinged heat. The gardening hoe clattered to the road, and his headless corpse stood in place for a moment, swaying back and forth, pumping out black and red blood in shallow little arcs from the top of his severed neck. Then it collapsed, green smoke rising from its ruined flesh.

Veronica stepped forward, then pumped the riot shotgun taken from some fallen Trooper, ejecting a red casing onto the road.

"Where'd you learn to shoot, honey?" Kotto asked as Richards helped him back up.

"I was Miss Cattaraugus County," she said, resting the barrel against her shoulder and flicking away a loose strand of blond hair from her face. "You don't get the crown without knowing how to handle a gun or skin a deer. Besides, Grandpa was a Korea vet. He didn't talk about the war, but he did talk to me about guns."

"I like her," Richards said. "Can we take her with us?"

"In the van, assholes!" Dean yelled from the vehicle's open driver's side window. "There's more crazies coming out of the woods! Let's go!"

The engine was already running. Veronica followed Richards and Kotto to the sliding panel door, then turned to see the flying saucer above. The metal and bone saucer flickered and faded into the dark sky, no more than a phantom image on an old VHS tape …

Dean pulled the van into the driveway, then completed an elegant 10-point turn to face back out onto the road. The State Trooper commander himself, George Winston, had left the command RV to lead the counterattack, gathering scattered police officers and forming small fire teams to push back the brainwashed psychos.

Bucky's minions poured off the hill by the dozens, wielding gardening tools and chainsaws, or clawing at Troopers and citizens alike with their bare, bloody hands. But what the Troopers lacked in numbers, they made up for in firepower. But if there were more moonshine-crazed folks in the hills, the battle would eventually turn against them.

Richards stared out the back window of the news van as they pulled away from the driveway and the central checkpoint, Dean keeping the van in first gear as they drove along the mud-ridden shoulder.

"Sheriff, we have to get you on the radio," Veronica said from the front passenger seat. Richards and Kotto sat on the bench seat just behind her. "They cut off our signal mid-broadcast, so I'm not sure how many people got the message."

"What's the message again?" Richards asked,

counting how many magazines he had left on his vest. "Even I'm losing track."

"People need to arm themselves, and stay indoors," Kotto said. "Who knows how many of them creepy-crawlies are running around out there, killing people or making folks drink moonshine so they become one of them."

"They've already got the whole population of West Valley," Richards said. "That's what? A few hundred people? Minus the ones we cancelled just now and yesterday?"

"And they've been on the move. No telling how many people they've killed—or added to their ranks—since. Jesus on a jetpack! We don't have enough ammunition to kill them all."

"There's another way, right? Is there any chance of … you know … de-crazifying them? Bringing them back? Making them human again?"

Kotto tilted his head down and let his helmet slide off into his hands. Despite the cool of the autumn evening, there was a shine of sweat, not just rain water, along his wide forward, making his short, black hair glisten. He leaned forward and groaned, letting his helmet fall to the floor of the van.

"You gonna make it, boss?"

"Yes, I'm fine. I just need a cigarette. And maybe a milk bath enema."

Veronica curled up an eyebrow at Richards, who shrugged his shoulders.

"Bucky's the key to all of this," Kotto said, sitting back up. "The visitors—whatever they are—they picked him to make the moonshine. And we know that Bucky's got some weird powers, right? The people we saw back there were working together, speaking English, even. At the riot yesterday, it was more chaotic. Someone's controlling them. That someone is probably Bucky."

"Hold on back there," Dean said. They had reached the railroad crossing. Most of the drivers there had turned around and driven away at the first sign of trouble. Only a couple of cars were left abandoned in the road, doors open and blood streaked across their hoods or windshields.

Dean maneuvered the van through the lowered arms of the railroad crossing guard arms, then snaked through a pair of abandoned pickup trucks on the other side.

"Stop here," Kotto said

"Are you crazy?" Veronica asked. "More of those … those crazed hillbillies might be out there."

"I see some of them right now," Kotto said. "Hand me that shotgun."

Veronica didn't hesitate. The riot gun she'd taken off the body of some fallen State Trooper had been an object of sanity and protection during their escape from the battle. When Kotto asked for it, she suddenly felt sick by what she had done with it. Necessity and bravery in the moment was one thing. Post-adrenaline reflection was another. They were all learning that lesson.

Kotto slid back the pump action with deliberate speed to make sure there was a shell in the chamber. As Dean slowed the van to a halt, its brakes protesting with squealing fear, Kotto slid the panel door open and stepped out onto the road. He rubbed one hand over his face and hair, letting the cool, light rain patter down on his skin. Richards pushed himself off of the bench seat and stepped out of the van. Above them the clouds were gray, with streaks of deep black. The wind was a frozen blade, cutting to their cores.

"It's getting worse," Richards said. Kotto said nothing. He pointed to a spot somewhere behind a short field of weeds, where the tall grasses fell away.

Brown forms bobbed up and down, but Richards couldn't make them out.

"Come on." Kotto led him down the shoulder, his shotgun at the low-ready, his finger hovering just over the trigger guard. Richards likewise drew his pistol. He checked the chamber for the fourth or fifth time since hopping in the van. Yes, he had a round ready to go. Yes, there was a magazine in the grip. But memory and adrenaline sometimes played funny tricks on you.

Behind them and up the hill, the gunfire became less sporadic. The command RV was still parked in the driveway, an ominous black monolith jutting up over a few short pines that flanked the yard of the house. The occasional vehicle—including State Trooper SUVs and patrol cars—darted past them, drivers eager to be away from the chaos at any speed. Either the Troopers had rallied and repulsed the attack, or …

There was a small creek that ran parallel to the edge of a mowed lawn, bubbling with volume and the patter of rain. Kotto pointed to the forms bobbing at the edge of the lawn, just beyond the limit of the weeds and grasses. The two lawmen raised their weapons. Richards sidestepped to get a better angle as they came around the edge of the weeds. The rain striking pavement and the rushing water of the nearby creek covered the sounds of their approach.

Ahead of them were three people—their clothes likewise shredded, their hands and faces covered in slippery gore—bent over the convulsing form of a State Trooper, his black and blue uniform torn away, his body armor and helmet lying forgotten and bloodstained a few yards away. One of his outstretched hands—still tittering with errant signals shot from a dead brain—was still wrapped around the handguards of his M-16 rifle. The weapon's fire selector switch had been set to three-round burst, for all the good that did him.

Richards turned his head, slightly, removing the image of carnal degradation from his vision. He had seen dead bodies before, sure. But that didn't mean he ever got used to it.

"Jesus."

"I'll take the two on the right," Kotto said. "You ready, Deputy?"

One of those feeding—a teenaged boy, with ruined black teeth now dripping red—perked his head up and emitted a low growl. The other two turned from their meal, rain washing away caked-on blood from their twisted mouths.

"We can be wolves or snakes. We can be pigs or swarms of flies."

"Deputy."

"Our harvest is nigh."

"Deputy!"

"Drink the 'shine, join the crowd. Become one with us."

"Hey!"

"Yeah. Yeah. Let's get it over with."

They fired until their guns ran dry and the smell of cordite hung heavy in the air.

23. You Are the Resistance

The red "ON AIR" letters kicked on, illuminating the dark guest bedroom-turned-podcast studio in a dread glow. The curtains hung open, but with night coming on and the storm clouds obscuring the sky, it was pitch black beyond the limits of the motion sensor lights on the back deck and front porch. Richards and Dean drank beers and glasses of water tinged with iron in the kitchen. Veronica sat on the edge of the guest bed, watching Kotto's hands dance over the dials on his mixer and tap commands on his keyboard. The station manager had been furious to learn that she'd been arrested—or detained—and that the police had smashed her camera. But when she told him what was happening—or what their star conspiracy show host *thought* was happening—he agreed to clear the station's schedule (a rebroadcast of the Buffalo Philharmonic's summer patriotic performance series) to allow him to broadcast a special edition of *Kotto's Kreepies*.

"You want real news, right?" she'd asked him over the landline. "Not just crap about community events and local politics? This *is* real news. Even if it's straight out of a bad horror novel. And we're the only ones covering it."

That had won him over. That, and, since their aborted live broadcast from the State Police checkpoint on Route 242, the station had been inundated with calls from worried viewers about what their half-mad county sheriff was ranting about. Other calls came trickling in about increasingly dangerous weather conditions. A few had come in to report seeing flying saucers in and around Ellicottville. The station manager couldn't make heads or tails of it. He figured that if anyone could, it was Sheriff Cecil Kotto.

"Good evening, good citizens of Cattaraugus County," Kotto said into the microphone, his right hand on the mouse to control the on-screen levels, his left clutching an ice-cold Coors. "This is Sheriff Cecil Kotto, coming to you live from my secret command bunker, with a special emergency edition of *Kotto's Kreepies*. If you happened to be tuned in to Veronica Cartwright's broadcast earlier today, you saw the Gestapo come down hard on us. But they can't stop the signal. If you are hearing this broadcast—yes, each and every one of you—you are the resistance."

He does have a flare for the dramatic, Veronica thought. She found herself wanting one of those beers. Richards walked into the room, his shirt soaked through with sweat from where his tactical vest had sat on his chest and shoulders. Veronica reached over and plucked the beer from between his fingers and took a long sip. She gave him a bright, innocent smile. He shrugged and walked back to the fridge to get another.

"I don't have a lot of time, and if this storm is what I think it is—and what I think it is is the result of occult forces summoned from somewhere deep in the hills of our good county—we're going to lose power, we're going to lose telephones, we're going to lose it all. Night is falling, and morning may be a long ways away.

We've covered a lot of serious topics in my years as your host. But tonight, gentle listeners, tonight might be different.

"What we have here is a full-on apocalypse scenario. At least, that's what my gut tells me. I can't see all the pieces. There's too much interference in the ether. Too much smoke, too many mirages gumming up the old brain-bucket circuits. Where this thing is going, I can't say. But I can say that it feels bad. Real bad.

"We know that the government is involved. Somehow. And those weird lights that've been floating through here—going back at least to the time of the Senecas, and probably before them—they have something to do with it. The authorities are telling you that it's just bad moonshine, like some sort of PCP or crystal meth thing. Let me tell you, that's half true. Drinking the moonshine *will* make you go crazy. It'll turn you into something else. Something not-quite-human. But there's more to it than that.

"Yesterday evening, we saw the entire town population of West Valley turned into these rampaging maniacs. Now they're on the march. We were just present at a State Trooper checkpoint. And dozens—maybe hundreds—of the bloodthirsty bastards came running out of the woods, waving chainsaws and gardening tools. And they *talk*. First it was some ancient language. Ancient Sumerian, maybe Babylonian. Now it's weird King James Bible stuff, about a 'harvest' and souls and all that.

"And they weren't alone. One of them UFOs you've seen—or one maybe your parents, or your uncle, or a friend has seen—one of them flying saucers showed up. It was a friggin' bio-mechanical aircraft, part bone, part metal. And it tossed around cars with some ray gun radiation beam like they were nothing. Then it disappeared into thin air, right after the crazies showed up and started sawing through station wagons and eating State Trooper guts.

"It's bad out there, folks, and to be frank, your old pal Cecil might not be able to handle this one on his own. If you got guns, keep 'em handy. Stay indoors. Don't follow the lights. Close the curtains. Act like nobody's home. I *think* that army of crazies is moving on to Ellicottville, but there's no telling who's been drinking that devil 'shine, and if they're coming your way.

"Is Bucky guilty of all this? Is he in control? We have information that indicates that he was an alien abductee. This could be prelude to an extraterrestrial—or even extradimensional—invasion scenario. Or it could just be good old-fashioned Illuminati scheming.

"I don't know what the next play is. I don't know if I'll be able to broadcast again anytime soon. What I *do* know is that we are better than this—better than illegal checkpoints, better than dead cops, better than tearing each other's guts out and building sacrificial altars to demon gods. We're better than all of that. We don't have to live in fear of the dark. We don't have to live in fear of each other."

Kotto paused, letting the dead air hang with the memory of his words.

"This is Cecil Kotto, your sheriff, signing off. If you're hearing this transmission, you are the resistance."

Kotto's fingers danced over the keys, then brought the levels on his on-screen mixer down. The "ON AIR" sign dimmed out, leaving the room in darkness once again.

"What?" Veronica said, her voice breaking the long silence that followed. "That's all you got? Half of that didn't even make sense."

"Half of what happened today didn't make sense,"

Kotto said. "You saw that thing in the sky. You saw them insane-o's eating people. What did you want me to say?"

"That you've got a plan," Veronica said. "Something besides 'grab your guns.'"

"I do have a plan," Kotto said, standing up. "We're going to find Bucky. We're going to bring him in. And we're going to put an end to this hillbilly moonshine massacre, once and for all." Kotto pointed at Richards, who had returned with a fresh beer. "Deputy! Head down to the basement and grab a few more boxes of ammo. I've got some parachute flares down there under a stack of old *Penthouse* magazines. Grab a few of the magazines, and then maybe a few flares. You, reporter lady! You need to record our mission for posterity. You have to tell our story."

"This story is insane," Veronica said, leaning forward to rest her head on her hands. "What was I thinking?"

"Thinking isn't gonna get us out of this mess," Kotto said. "Stopping Bucky will."

"How are we gonna find him, Sheriff?" Richards asked.

"He's probably somewhere nearby. I think *they* need him. Did you notice anything about how those crazies smelled? Besides the reek of blood and guts and generational poverty?"

Richards considered this for a moment.

"They smelled like booze," he said. "Yeah, that's right. Whenever you got close to one, it came off their breath, real hot."

"Right," Kotto said. "The psychosis is induced by the moonshine. What happens if they run out of the liquor?"

"Then they might return to normal," Richards said. "Assuming they don't remember what the hell they've been doing."

Kotto snapped his fingers.

"And who's the only one who knows how to make the moonshine?"

"I'm guessing it's Bucky," Veronica said. "Unless he's got his minions cooking it for him now."

"The State Troopers are all over his old still," Kotto said. "So that's out. If he's gonna keep feeding his army his specialty hard liquor, he's gonna need another still. Someplace nearby, but off the grid a bit."

"And someplace with a lot of water," Richards said. "And a power supply. Or a road to bring in fuel and ingredients, at the very least."

"That's enough to go on," Kotto said, walking toward the door that led out to the kitchen. "Come on."

"Where are we going?" Richards asked. "That's not enough to narrow it down."

"No, but it'll get us started," Kotto said. "Go grab that ammo. And some porno, for the ride over."

"The ride over where, Sheriff?"

"We're going to the only man who can help us," Kotto said. "The only man in Cattaraugus County who grows reasonably priced, high-quality, hallucinogenic magic mushrooms."

24. Magic Mushrooms and Mescaline Tea

The house was a blue doublewide trailer laid over a cheap and crumbling concrete foundation. Rusted-out cars sat in the front lawn, suffering a beating from golf ball-sized hail. Lightning reflected off cracked windshields and tinted windows.

Dean pulled the van into the dirt driveway, careful to avoid a circle of shattered glass along the ground that reflected his headlights, which were woefully suited to pierce through the dark of the storm. A shaved head emerged from behind thin curtains draped along the front windows of the doublewide. Eyes reflected headlights. He disappeared, and the light in the living room went out.

"Let me do the talking," Kotto said, tossing the *Penthouse* into the back seat and reaching for the panel door's handle. "Willy can be a little skittish." He slid the door open and stepped out into the hail.

"Who is this guy?" Veronica asked as Dean shifted the van into park and killed the engine. Balls of half-frozen water pattered against the metal roof of the van, the sound like sizzling bacon. "Are we coming here to buy *drugs*? I thought you were police officers."

"Ma'am, this is my third day on the job," Richards

said. "I'm exhausted, scared, and a little drunk." Richards watched through the windshield as Kotto scurried up to the front door, his BDU jacket pulled up over his head to shield himself from the white ice that fell from the sky. "I have no idea what we're doing, or what is going to happen next." Veronica scowled at him, her brow furrowed and her mouth hanging open. But she considered his reply and remained silent.

Richards caught his reflection in the rearview mirror. Dark eyes, perched over hollow, pale cheeks stared back at him. He hadn't been this tired since his time overseas, when they ran operations for five days straight with no sleep, driving from one end of the valley to another, burning fuel and daylight because the commander said so. Now he had a new CO, and once again, what they were doing didn't make much sense. But they'd made it through so far, out of a couple of situations that they probably shouldn't've survived. The only thing keeping him going now was forward momentum. Maybe inertia would catch up with him eventually—with them all, with this whole county—but until then, he'd keep driving on. He didn't have much choice.

Richards stepped out into the barrage of hail and ran up to the front door, which opened just as he reached Kotto. The sheriff, not waiting for an invitation, shoved forward, pushing the door open and the house's owner into the darkness of the living room. Richards followed.

"Hey, easy!" the man said, his form cast in darkness and shadow. Van doors slammed shut, and Veronica and Dean jetted up the gravel path and into the open door. Dean came in last, closing the front door behind him with a shudder.

"How many people you bring here, Sheriff? You know I don't like people I don't know." The man's voice dropped to a growl. "People I don't *trust*."

"Spare me the Walter White stuff," Sheriff Kotto said, peeling off his BDU jacket, balls of ice rolling off of him. "You'd already be in jail if I wanted you there."

"You got any lights in here?" Richards asked, aching to be out of the dark. Instinct and recent memories sent his hand to the pistol perched on his hip.

"Power's out," the man said. Something snapped, and the glowing orb of a lit match appeared across the room. He lowered the flame to a set of votive candles arrayed in stained glass holders along the surface of a coffee table. The room emerged from the darkness in waves of soft gold and filtered multi-colored light, greens and blues and reds dancing along them and the walls like the first rays of sun through church windows.

They stood in the open living room of the doublewide. Near the coffee table and along the interior wall was a sagging couch, musty with the smell of cigarette smoke and wet cat. A recliner sat with its foot rest out and up. A big screen TV was perched atop an entertainment center overflowing with green Xbox 360 and black DVD plastic cases. A few TV dinner tray tables stood scattered around the room. Ashtrays and empty (or half-empty) beer cans and bottles everywhere. The smell of piss hung over everything. Richards, his nose tingling, guessed—*hoped*—it was the cats.

"This is Willy," Kotto said, gesturing to the pale, feral-looking creature before them. "Willy, this is my new deputy, a sexy-lady news reporter, and her oafish cameraman."

Willy stood over the coffee table, his arms crossed over his chest. He wore a ragged black Dead Kennedys t-shirt, the trademark black-white-red "DK" logo punched full of small, moth-eaten holes. He was white—even in the dark, he looked pale, like he hadn't seen the sun since before a sudden lifestyle choice of vampirism. His head was unevenly shaved, his big eyes nervously flitted from person to person, his big lips bulged with either chancre sores or last night's bar fight. Richards recognized him as someone who had been about six or seven years ahead of him at West Valley Central. He had been built solid, once—almost six feet tall, with linebacker's shoulders. But most of that had melted away over the years, muscle and vigor replaced with a soft layer of bulge from too many Budweiser and Miller and Ice House 30 racks, too much greasy pizza ordered from the gas station outside of town along the 219, too much post-high school partying and not enough direction or purpose. Just another casualty of low-horizon aspirations.

Richards didn't remember Willy all that well—just that he had gotten into trouble quite a bit, and he always reeked of cigarettes. He was someone the underage kids could get to buy them a bottle of cheap vodka, if they let him have half of it.

The five of them stood in silence, letting the shifting light and shadows dance over them, the patter of hail from the roof above a soothing, sleepy wash of white noise.

"What's this about, Sheriff? I ain't involved with moonshine. I don't even know Bucky. I told them State boys everything, told em that—"

"It doesn't matter if you know Bucky or not," Kotto said. He pulled off his sunglasses, then tossed his BDU jacket over an unused lamp fixture, which fell to the floor under the coat's dripping weight. "But you're the only one who can help us find him."

Willy pulled in chairs from the adjacent dining room. Veronica and Dean sat on the creaking wooden seats at opposite ends of the coffee table, now cleared of all debris. Kotto and Richards sat on the couch. Willy sat cross-legged on the floor opposite them. Candlelight, filtered through stained glass, glowed from locations all around the room, casting everything in a soothing haze. That many candles in that many places could be a fire hazard, sure, but it was better than the near-total darkness.

The storm itself had relented, content to carry its payload of hail elsewhere. Now just the wind and the chill remained, pressing against the house, wood creaking and groaning and popping. Veronica shivered, pulling her blazer-blouse tight around her. Dean had fished out an XL Buffalo Bills hoodie from the van, and had eagerly taken the cup of equal parts Sunny Delight and vodka Willy had offered shortly after Kotto laid out his plan. Willy offered Veronica wine. She soon discovered that he meant MD 20/20 poured into a plastic cup. But the cheap alcoholic juice warmed her up and calmed her nerves all the same.

Kotto asked for water for himself and the deputy, which surprised the reporter. Neither of these yahoos had been particularly concerned with maintaining sobriety during this series of violent and bizarre escapades. Hell, they had smelled like booze since they had linked up at that doomed State Police checkpoint on 242, and, as far as she could tell, they hadn't stopped drinking. Then again, she didn't really blame them. They had all journeyed far into a territory far removed from any semblance of logic or professional decorum. There were men with chainsaws attacking families in station wagons. The State Troopers had become a roving army. Flying saucers buzzed traffic and used tractor beams to throw vehicles into the air. None of the rules—for professionalism, for logic, for reality—applied anymore. And now, sitting in this double-wide trailer somewhere outside of West Valley, with an eldritch storm overhead, the power out, candles lit, and bottles of booze and bags of what Veronica could only assume were drugs on the table before them, they were all about to go *further* into the madness.

When, exactly, did she set off on the course that would lead her to this moment? Was it when she lost her job because she took her responsibilities as a reporter too seriously? Was it when she decided to move back here, despite the fact that there were few jobs, and fewer opportunities? Was it when she decided to repeat those mistakes by covering a story—a manhunt, weird lights in the sky, a deranged local lawman spouting nonsense about conspiracies—that no one else would touch?

She should have listened to her mother and just become a nurse. Nurses worked long hours, sure, but they made money. And they had good job security. They helped people, too. In ways more tangible than writing on the crime beat, or covering local events for public access television. Sure. A nurse. She could do that.

"This is all I have," Willy said. "You're cleaning me out." He gestured to the gallon-sized plastic bag, stuffed half full with shadows.

"Looks like a good harvest to me," Kotto said. He picked up the bag and snapped open the seals that ran along the top lips like tiny plastic railroad tracks. He leaned in to let his nose get a brief whiff of the contents, then turned away. "Pew. Smell's ripe."

"Picked them last week," Willy said. Kotto offered the bag to Richards.

"Want to smell?"

"What am I smelling?" Richards asked, leaning forward. He scrunched his face and turned away. "Ugh. Smells like cow shit."

"That's because they grow in cow shit," Willy said. "The richer, the better, man."

Even Veronica could smell the nitrate-laden odor from across the coffee table.

"What is this? What are we doing here, Sheriff?" she asked. "I thought we were going to find Bucky."

"*Psilocybin semilanceata*," Kotto said. "Right, Willy?"

"Shit, I don't know all that. I just grow the fucking things."

"Wait, is this ... ?" Richards said.

"Magic mushrooms," Kotto confirmed. "One variety of them, anyway."

"And the water should be ready for the tea," Willy said. "I'll go check the kettle."

"Tea?" Veronica asked.

"Mescaline," Kotto said. "The mescaline will push us into the mushroom trip faster, and open a few more gates along our journey."

"We're taking mushrooms and mescaline tea," Richards said. "Tell me that isn't what we're doing."

"Of course not!" Kotto said. "That would be ridiculous. We're taking mushrooms, mescaline tea, *and* drinking some Genny Cream Ale. This combination, when used in conjunction with local Seneca nation chanting and meditation techniques, will enable us to enter the psychosphere."

Dean laughed, then slapped Veronica on the shoulder.

"These guys are awesome."

Veronica stared dumbfounded at Kotto.

"You're going to take a bunch of drugs," she said. "This will help you find Bucky how, exactly?"

"'Hey Abe, how was your first few days as a sheriff's deputy?'" Richards asked himself. "Well, thanks for asking, Mom. I almost got eaten alive by brainwashed maniacs, then I was attacked by a guy with a chainsaw, and there was a goddamn flying saucer, and then I took a bunch of hallucinogens with my boss right before the apocalypse. All in all, I'd say it's been pretty average so far." He leaned forward to let his head rest against his outstretched hands.

"I've assumed that that UFO we saw scaring folks is probably not a purely physical object, at least most of the time," Kotto said. "I have reason to believe the source of Bucky's power is spiritual, drawing energy from ley lines and the psychoactive superstructure of our local consciousness fields."

"What?" Veronica said.

"*Psychosphere* is a term coined by pulp science fiction-horror writer Richard Lumley," Kotto said, matter-of-fact. "It's a plane *above* our typical consciousness level, which can be accessed by people with varying ESP abilities. Or if you take the right mix of hallucinogenic drugs and regional, award-winning beer."

"You guys are hearing this too, right?" Richards asked. "I'm not going crazy, am I? He's really talking like this?"

"I've only recently discovered it myself," Willy said, returning from the kitchen with two steaming mugs of mescaline tea. He set them down on the coffee table. "Has to be the right mix of all this shit. If you get it wrong, you can't reach it."

"Wait, when you say reach the psycho ... psychosphere," Veronica said, "you mean trip your balls off, right? That's what's going to happen?"

"Yes," Kotto said, sipping his water. "And no. The event will begin as a relatively normal hallucinogenic experience, but will quickly transition into the metaphysical. Of course, I've never done all these drugs at once before, so this might just be a six-to-eight hour waste of everyone's time."

Dean laughed.

"This is crazy," Veronica said.

"What's crazy is a flying saucer with a pentagram on it, and people tearing each other apart because they drank bad moonshine," Kotto said. "This? This is just business as usual."

"You're going to pay me for this stuff, right?" Willy asked, his voice betraying what he knew to be the answer.

"Now citizen, the fate of the entire county—maybe even the whole country—depends on me using this motley collection of questionably-legal substances to project myself into the astral plane. Don't niggle over compensation!"

"Illegal," Richards corrected. "This isn't 'questionably legal.' It's definitely *illegal*."

"'Astral plane?'" Veronica asked. "Excuse me, but I'm just trying to keep up. I thought you said 'psychosphere.'"

"Yes, that, and 'consciousness superstructure,' a term coined by John Keel when he was researching the Mothman of West Virginia. Whatever you prefer."

"And whenever you get there, you'll be able to find Bucky."

"Possibly, yes. It will allow us to achieve a state of remote viewing—at least it should—not unlike the CIA program of the mid-twentieth century that enabled psychic explorers to identify the locations of Russian military and nuclear assets. But we'll be using more potent drugs. Call it a shortcut." Kotto backhanded Richards' chest. "You got any experience with hallucinogenic drugs, Deputy? Or am I gonna have to be your guide the whole time? Do you have a spirit animal?"

"I've never done anything like *this*," Richards said. "It's not too late to back out, is it? I mean, I can just go home, and get a job at the ski resort again when it's all over, right?"

"Never tripped face before, huh?" Kotto said. "Oh, this could get ugly. Alright, one piece of advice: stay out of the dark place. You'll know what I mean. And yes, it is too late to back out." Kotto handed Richards one of the mugs of steaming, stinking tea. "If we don't do this, there won't be any ski resort to return to."

Richards took the cup in his hands. The heat of the steam felt good on his face.

"Bottoms up, pinkies out," Kotto said, grabbing his own mug. "Willy, we're gonna need more candles."

Willy had overloaded the mescaline tea with sugar in an attempt to mask its taste. It was too-sweet, the sugar a sludge at the bottom of the mug, a saccharine head rush following on the heels of the burnt-vegetable syrup. The tea wasn't too unlike the chai Richards often drank in Afghanistan, sitting with the Afghan National Police or Army soldiers, staring off at the mountains beyond the sand wastes and contemplating the utter hopelessness of war and the human condition and all that pretentious bullshit he used to like to kick around his tired little head.

Kotto gulped down his tea with one effort. While Richards let his stomach settle, the sheriff began to spread chunky peanut butter across slabs of stale white bread. Then, laying each brown-slapped slice face up on the table before him, he reached into the plastic bag of psychedelic mushrooms. He ran the dry stalks and caps between his palms and fingers, sending down a rain of crumbs into the chunky landscape of each slice.

Kotto offered Richards one of the sandwiches.

"Chew really fast," he advised.

The mushroom dust and chunks were masked by the peanut butter, but Richards often caught the taste of something acrid and unpleasant, vaguely like a mown lawn of wet grass on a weekend morning. His stomach had begun to dance a little unpleasant number by the time Kotto shoved a six pack of Genny Cream Ale across the coffee table at him.

"Drink up."

Veronica thought she would be relieved when Willy left them to it. Instead, she began to wonder how she was going to care for two drug-addled police officers for six hours. Willy was a burnout, sure, and possibly dangerous—but at least he knew what to expect, and maybe he knew how to help someone get better if they got sick or had a full-on freak out. Veronica's experience with drugs started and ended with that one time she smoked pot in college and ended up crying in the rain for an hour, lost and confused in the middle of campus.

"I don't want to be here when it starts," Willy said, not looking anyone in the eye as he left the living room. "There's some joints on the table for the come down, if they want 'em. There's enough for you guys, too." Dean reached for one of the rolled joints and grabbed a blaze orange lighter from the carpet under the glass coffee table.

"Where are you going? What are we supposed to do

if they need help?" Veronica asked.

"I'll be in my room behind a locked door, smoking weed and watching *The Transporter 2* on repeat," Willy said. "You can come with, pretty lady."

"I'll pass."

"You might change your mind once they enter the psychosphere," Willy said, a mischievous smile creeping across his dumb face. "Things can get a little … weird."

Smoke wafted into Veronica's face from Dean's lit joint, and Willy disappeared into the darkness of the hallway.

"Just make sure you keep the candles lit," he said from somewhere in the dark. "Otherwise they might not be able to find their way back."

Dean sputtered out a painful cough.

"You want some, Veronica?" he asked, offering her the joint.

Her face was a scowl. But the smell of the smoke and the amusing, bewildered look on Richards' wide-eyed face softened her attitude and expression.

"Sure," she said, taking the paper joint in hand. "Why the hell not?"

25. Through a Glasse, Darkly

Kotto finished his third Genny Cream Ale right around the time the mushroom cramps kicked in. His guts were churning; that old, familiar kick in the core, nausea moving up and down his torso in unfriendly waves.

"We're experiencing some tremors in the deep earth here," he muttered. He looked at Richards. His deputy. Richards. What was his first name? Dick? Deputy? No. Abe. That's what he put on the W-2. Abraham. Like the vampire hunter. Jesus. What an appropriate first name. Couldn't have picked a better one if he made it up. Must be a sign. A symbol. A synchronicity. But they hadn't fought vampires together. Yet. Oh yes, that would come, and many more battles to follow. How long could they keep this up, fighting against the forces of darkness? How long before something gave, before he made a mistake that could cost them both their lives? Responsibility. Leadership. There were more battles to fight if they survived this current conflagration. This messy soup of noxious spiritualism and over-violence.

A lot riding on this, eh, Cecil? Don't screw it up. Everybody's counting on you.

Abraham Richards. Good, solid, *Dracula*-inspired,

Biblical name. A man of the desert, sure. Warrior-type. Fought in the goddamn *war*. Overseas. Iraq, was it? Afghanistan? Pakistan? Kuwait? Eastern Canada? The War of Northern Aggression? The greater middle-eastern religious conflict. Lines of blood and dishonor stretching back a thousand goddamn years. Back to Bible times and before. Crusades. Shades of Christian-western guilt. Internecine conflict between Muslim-Arabs. Arabs killing Arabs. Muslims killing Christians, and vice versa, all coming from the same lines, same root families. Battle over resources. Battle over religion. Same old story. *Old Testament*.

His deputy was oblivious to all of this. His deputy was a part of—or had been, at one point in space-time—all of that. Others took his place, sure. New battles to fight. Old battles to fight.

"Richards!" Kotto said, the name coming out of his mouth too loud. Veronica and Dean, sharing a joint, jumped.

"Yes, yes sir?" Richards said, his slack face becoming red. He leaned forward and hid his eyes between his fingertips.

"This is hitting me pretty hard," Kotto said, trying not to stammer. "This—this—we're going to be entering new phases of consciousness soon. Yes sir, very soon. Have you started to experience time compression?"

"Time compression," Richards said.

"Yes! Out with it, Deputy! Are you experiencing a sense that time *is not as it should be or as it seems?*"

"My stomach hurts."

"That'll pass. Drink more beer." Richards groaned and reached for his can. He took a small sip, his face transforming into a bitter scowl.

"Can I have some water?"

"Sure, you sure can," Kotto said. "Yes, good idea! And you two!" He waved a wild finger at Veronica and

Dean. Their eyes grew large and frightened. "Are you smoking that reefer?! That's not going to do you any good, it's not ..."

Veronica and Dean, stoned-horror on their faces, began to wither and pixelate, like photographs texture-mapped to a dancing digital flame. The room's dimensions bent and twisted. A low hum like the song of a whale echoed out from all corners of his vision.

"Elastic," Kotto managed. "Everyone's going elastic. Deputy, pay attention. This is the apex of the psilocybin come-on. It's here the mescaline will push us up to the next level, through the door of perception that is otherwise locked." Kotto burped as Veronica and Dean wiggled like spaghetti noodles, then shot away into the darkness, speeding out and away from the couch with the walls and the ceiling and everything else that we might call reality.

Everything stretched, then it snapped. Good and lost now. Out in the ether. There was the couch, sagging cushions, piss smell, and all. There was the glass coffee table with the contraband and the bag of cheap bread, a half-eaten jar of peanut butter, a few empty beer cans, white and green and silver.

Was he alone?

"Richards?" Kotto said. "Richards, are you there man? We're in the soup!"

"What?" From far away.

"Come back to the couch. Follow the candlelight."

"Where, Sheriff?" Closer now.

"Up, Deputy. Go *up*."

Abraham Richards floated up through the cushions, his blue spirit form coalescing around a glowing core, fortifying itself and becoming form and flesh again. Or it looked to Kotto that way. Hard to tell what was real in this time-space. Or lack thereof. Whatever. He was *rolling*. Hard.

"We're in the psychosphere, I think," Kotto said.

"You think?"

"I've never actually done this before."

"I can feel my blood. I'm afraid I'm going to forget how to breathe."

"Focus on the moment. On the now."

"The now?" Richards asked, reaching for his beer. He lifted the can and emptied its contents into his throat. The beer glowed a dead green, working its way down his esophagus, which had become a series of twisting green pipes like in *Super Mario Bros*. "The *now* is meaningless, Sheriff."

"Now you're getting it."

"Did I *think* that, or did I say that?"

"Doesn't matter. Look around. Where are we?"

"On a couch. Willy's couch. Remember that guy? I think he used to sell my cousins cheap liquor and dirt weed."

"It was a different time for all of us, Deputy." Kotto stretched his arms out, his muscles popping. Fatigue was setting in, hard. He needed to sleep. They both did. The toll the last couple of days were taking on his body was suddenly a definable, numerical thing, expressed in colorful digits that danced along each joint and bone and stretch of skin. Something out of *Final Fantasy* or whatever. They needed some tonics. Some elixirs, even. Hopefully not a phoenix down anytime soon.

But there was no time to be tired. If he was where he thought they should be, they had to act fast. Six hours' real time was nothing here. It could be over in seconds. It could be over in days. They had to act while they could. Sure, being *here* meant that he recognized that acting was often just the result of environmental factors and philosophical meta-physical constructs making themselves manifest through particle physics in his brain ... But dammit, he had never been a math realist, and wasn't about to start thinking in those terms now. He had to *do something*.

"Do something," Kotto found his lips saying, the words coming out in a colorful, crazy font like something out of Windows 3.1, running for all it was worth on his parents' old 486. First time he'd ever played *Doom*, it blew his fucking mind.

"You're thinking in terms of your digital consciousness history, too," Richards said, nodding. "Yeah, I'm seeing reality through the lens of ... It keeps shifting, drifting away."

"Where are we?" Kotto said. "Pay attention! Look around! We're on Willy's couch, but we're not *at* Willy's anymore. If that mescaline did its job, we should be Elsewhere."

Richards considered the couch, then the coffee table. Beyond that ... Kotto followed his gaze. Carpet, yes, dancing in and out of the black as the candlelight flickered. But where were the other candles? Surely the ones on the table were not enough to cast that glow.

"It's full of stars," Richards said, then giggled.

Not quite. Beyond the reach of that arcane dance of shadow and light, swirled vortexes of barely-discernible purples and blues, white-hot lights like stars being born (or dying) traveling to them from across an array of cosmos. If up close they saw digital information, in the great Beyond they saw things as a proto-history of the cosmos text.

"It's whatever we think it should look like," Kotto said. "Come on. Let's go find Bucky." He stood up on the couch, then jumped. Richards stared up, wide-eyed, as Kotto drifted further and further out, leaving the comfort of warm candlelight and cheap beer for the deep unknown. "Come on, Deputy! We don't have much time!"

"Time's meaningless!" Richards said. He jumped. Kotto was far away—miles—and then he wasn't. Richards *willed* himself forward, because it seemed like The Thing To Do. And you know what? It worked. He was very pleased with himself. Kotto could read that on his deputy's face.

"Picture this," Kotto said, waving his hands in the air. A map of Cattaraugus County, drawn out in crayon on cheap poster board like a kid's science project, shimmered before them. "Think of the landscapes. The hills. The people. The violence."

Richards did. Indeed, the swirling cosmos and void gave way to waves of brown and green and golden-autumn reality.

"No, this isn't quite right. There's a storm overhead, right? Or at least clouds." Neither of them was sure which of them had said the words. It didn't matter. It was True All the Same. But as they recognized this, the ether formed clouds from whispers of light. Dark, heavy, rumbling with fury.

"Now someplace specific," Kotto said. "This is the general scope… the essence. But it's not a *place*. Not yet."

"Where?" Richards asked. "Where should it be?" He paused. "I'm really, really aware of my tongue right now."

"Language is the intersection between biomechanics and abstractionism," Kotto remarked. "What's a place you can picture? Really well?"

"My parents' house," Richards said. He rubbed his stomach. The nausea had passed as they entered the superstructure. He had expected a loss of physicality as they entered this primordial, plastic arena. Like the trip would make him a being of pure spirit or essence or mental projection or whatever. But it was nothing like that at all. He was sure—more so with the side effects of the psilocybin—that he maintained his physicality, even in this weird place. Sure, maybe his limp and unconscious, drooling body was still sitting on Willy's couch somewhere outside of West Valley, but it sure didn't feel like it. He felt *here*, in this place, in his body. "I think I peed my pants. Do you feel like you peed your pants?"

"That's just the mushrooms making you aware of the moisture on your skin," Kotto said. "Don't worry about it." But he shoved his hands down his pants to check all the same. "Nope, all clear. Your parents' house? No, I don't know it that well. Let's try something else."

"West Valley," Richards said. "We both went to school there."

"More specific," Kotto said. He snapped his fingers. "You a good kid in school?"

"Uh, I graduated."

"Did you ever go behind the barn?"

"Smoked cigarettes a few times. Or hung out with the kids who did."

"There. Behind the barn. Focus on that."

The hills moved away from them as if projected on a treadmill. Air and ether rushed and flowed, but they felt no chill. The flickering of candlelight underpinned each image as it sped by: roads, houses, barns, fields, State Trooper vehicles with lights flashing. Then West Valley, most of it a smoking ruin, small bands of roving moonshine maniacs scurrying from pyre to dog-skull altar to shadow and back again. Kotto and Richards saw the gray, spray-painted, rotting walls of the barn reach up to them, and they were floating behind the abandoned structure.

"The graffiti's still here," Kotto said. "No one ever bothered to paint over it. The kids just keep adding more."

"There," Richards said. "The pentagram. I remember that. I know the kid who put it up there."

At the center of the barn's outer wall was the blood-red pentagram, spray-painted with an uneven hand.

"Evil always manifests. It always shows you what's coming," Kotto said, shaking his head.

"This is just some kid copying a heavy metal album, trying to piss off the adults," Richards said. "It doesn't mean anything."

"Everything always means something," Kotto said. "It doesn't matter what your intention is—especially when it comes to symbols and words of spiritual evil. People mock God, joke about worshiping the devil. That gives evil power all the same." He turned away from the graffiti-marked wall and looked around them. Cigarette butts on the ground, Coca-Cola bottles and Keystone Light cans littered the area. "This is solid. This is definite. Good." Kotto looked to the sky. "We have the physical presence represented. Now we need to find ley lines."

"Lay-what?"

"Ley lines. Channels of invisible energy, usually centered on places of historic or religious importance. If we can find those, we can follow the draws to sources of occult power."

"The drugs are making what you're telling me make perfect sense."

"Where's the nearest church?"

"Catholic church is over there," Richards said, pointing through a row of bushes and houses to their left. "I went to Sunday school in a building not far from here."

"Take me there."

"What?"

"I don't have a good picture of it in my mind. It'll get murky. If you know it, we can get there easier."

Richards closed his eyes. Fractals and faces greeted him.

"I'm experiencing mild hallucinations when I close my eyes."

"We're in one giant shared hallucination," Kotto said. "Situation normal. Act like a professional."

"Right," Richards said. "Of course."

The world moved, color and form flowing away along rivers of temporal distortion. They were outside the church, freshly-painted white, tall and sharp spires, smoke curling up out of smashed stained glass windows.

"Good job, Deputy. You're getting the hang of this."

"Does this mean I get a raise?"

"Let's try to survive this end-of-the-world nonsense and we'll talk about compensation."

"Hmm."

"Ah, there. Do you see it? Beneath the stairs, leading up to those big-ass wooden doors."

"I only see the sidewalk, the church…"

"Open your third eye. Let the mescaline and the Genny Cream Ale expand your mind. Beneath the materialist substrate."

Richards frowned, then crossed his eyes, like he was looking at a *Magic Eye* book.

"That's one method," Kotto said, nodding. "Use the force, Deputy. Try to *feel* the thing. You've got a connection to it, too."

"I'm a Jedi Knight," Richards whispered.

"Yeah. Sure. Whatever works for you."

The sidewalk, grass, stairs, door, church—it all began to peel away in perfect-square layers, tiles floating up and spinning away into the clouds or out of their vision. Beneath was a blue field of impossible beauty and energy, pulsing and moving from point to point, arcing and colliding with itself and moving on again. Richards was dumbstruck; how could he have never seen this? How could he have walked these stairs, and never noticed the impossible beauty beneath his very feet?

"Is it … Is it God?" he asked.

"Jesus, man, no! Although the pagans seemed to think so. Think of it more as a representation. It's a signifier your brain cooked up. Power, sure, energy, sure. There's science in there, I'm sure of it. Moon phases and electromagnetic fields and psychic energy. If we had some DMT we could … Well, that's a different story. Now, we just have to follow it."

"It goes in a hundred directions," Richards said. He walked forward and bent down, reaching his hand into the blue light. Veins and arteries glowed blue through his skin, but he felt nothing.

"But it's flowing south. And those fingers of green and red—you see them? Siphoning away bits and pieces of it."

"Yes."

"Those are synthetic draws. It ain't flowing into trees and shit from there. I'm guessing if we follow those streams, we'll find Bucky. Just gotta follow the negative psychic energy. Are you still with me?"

"We're all connected, man," Richards said. "And it's all connected to us."

"Jesus. First-time psychedelic trips. Keep it together, man. We gotta follow those fingers. Let's *fly*."

26. Feeding the Beast

They soared over rows of trees, hills, and roads, the storm clouds to their backs. The façade didn't always keep; they were moving along a landscape, sure, but all was dim and shifting. Candlelight flickers from behind the walls of reality reminded them that they were also somewhere *else*, despite what their bodies and minds and the drugs told them. The effect was that of light moving behind a movie screen. The images still held, but you could tell that there was something beyond. Something *beneath*.

Kotto flew ahead of Richards like some post-apocalyptic Superman, his BDU jacket (when had he put that back on?) fluttering over his form like a cape, combat boots unlaced, aviator sunglasses catching raindrops and sending them arcing around his face. Richards could *feel* Kotto near him (and next to him on the couch), and he held onto that knowledge of nearness and essence.

Kotto kept his mind on the energy draw from the ley line they had discovered back in the smoking ruin that was West Valley. Richards felt the desire—the deep urge to *know*—to stretch his mind out in all directions at once, to go exploring beyond this simple shared hallucination-projection that was before them. He'd smoked weed a few times before, sure. But it was nothing like this. Something pulsed and vibed in rhythm with his own essence, something deeper in his own mind *and* out in that world that he now knew to be much larger and deeper than he could have ever possibly imagined.

"There, ahead!" Kotto shouted. They flew over a massive hill that dwarfed all the others for miles. As they drifted to a stop, a pond, some railroad tracks, and a line of abandoned cars came into view below.

"This is where we were earlier," Richards said. "What was that—a week ago? Two?"

"A couple of hours," Kotto said, eyes on the clouds above them. Flashes of blue-green light charged across a field of black and gray. "You're experiencing time compression."

"Hours..." Richards said. "We haven't slept in a while. What time is it?"

"It doesn't matter," Kotto said. "Look. Over the ridge."

"Ellicottville. Looks like they still have power."

"No, they don't," Kotto said. "Those aren't the lights from the resort."

Richards squinted through the storm. Fractals and spinning orbs and cubes formed out of the cloudscape. He shook his head and looked again. Sure enough, the light that colored the dark blanket of sky was not yellow or orange, but a deep, foreboding red, with cerulean sparks that fired up and across the clouds in little jets of beautiful fury.

Richards reached for a strand of blue-red energy—the one Kotto had been following to bring them here—and plucked it like a guitar string. A low, droning note hummed within his mind. The vibration carried on, heading straight toward those nightmare-lights, not so many miles distant.

"That's it alright," Kotto said. "Whatever Bucky is cooking up, it's happening there. He's drawing power from the ley lines... And something else. We're missing something."

Kotto frowned, and put his hand to his chin.

"Damn! We've been too focused on the visual substrate. We're going to have to change our perception again. We need to find another layer. Shift focus."

"To what?"

"We'll know it when we see it."

"See what, Sheriff?"

"Close your eyes."

"There's the fractals again."

"Clear your mind. Let the mushrooms bubble up whatever they want."

"I'm starting to see the creatures from *Aliens*. They're crawling around my parents' closet."

"No, don't go there! That's the dark place. No. Think positive. Think *expansive*."

"I have no idea what you're asking me to do!"

"Excellent. Now, open your eyes."

Richards did as he was ordered. The landscape was still there, complete with the road below, the cars, the bodies, the trees shedding leaves. But it had become less distinct, retreating back into the formless ether from which it was conjured.

"No, this isn't quite it."

Kotto clapped his hands and whistled, then shook his head back and forth. He let his aviator sunglasses fall to the earth below.

"My eyes are open!" he bellowed, his words echoing off invisible walls of stone. "Richards, open your third eye! Look with what you can feel, what you *know*, not what your eyes tell you."

"Sheriff, I ..."

"There. You're seeing it, aren't you?"

"It's ... It's horrible."

Richards saw the world awash in black and white, a photonegative of the chaos of the road below and the storm above. The lights emanating from somewhere over Ellicottville were still there, and so were the strings flowing from nearby ley lines—but now it was something else, too. Something else feeding the fires of wrath and fury that Bucky and his minions were gathering. Strands of shimmering non-light were suddenly visible, running like silken spokes around an onyx spider's web. Those fell strands grew and expanded, and the conflux ahead sucked up energy from ley lines and this newly-visible source alike.

"What are we seeing, Sheriff?" Richards asked. He caught sight of the black, glimmering strands near him, pulling taught and sharp. He floated up and away from them, but found that they were everywhere, flowing toward that horrible pyre from every imaginable direction.

There was one flowing from *him*. From right out of his guts.

"Sheriff, one of them's got me," he moaned. "Oh God. Am I gonna die? Is that what this means?"

"Deputy," Kotto said, tears bubbling up from the corners of his eyes, "we're all going to die. You know that better than most, right?"

"Oh God. What *is* this? You've got one too."

Kotto looked down. As he floated toward Richards, he realized the band of darklight moved with him, not affecting his movement in any way... It flowed *from* him.

Kotto reached down and tried to pull the thing from him, but his hands went right through it.

"It's no use," Richards said. "I can't get mine off, either!" His hands were out of his control now, clawing and scratching at his rain-soaked shirt.

Kotto floated closer to him, then let himself drop to consider Richards' strand. The more furious the deputy's movements, the louder his cries, the more he lost control—the more the strand *grew*, and pulsed, and carried out points of non-light away from him.

"Richards, calm down!" Kotto snapped. When Richards didn't respond, Kotto grabbed the deputy's hands and held them fast. Richards looked down with an animalistic sneer, his face twisted and his teeth bared.

"Deputy!" Kotto yelled, his voice almost carried off by a sudden wind. "Abraham Richards! Look at me! *Look at me!*"

Richards, feeling the press of the psychedelics turning sour, his heart racing, the absurd surrealism of his present circumstances, was granted one last moment of sanity before the darkness overtook him and the trip went totally south.

His eyes met Kotto's, which were streaked with tears.

"It's our fear," the sheriff whispered. "Look." He pointed off to the distance behind them. Kotto carried them through the psychosphere-space, following a fiber of the glistening black until they were face to face with a woman staring at an emergency radio in the kitchen. Richards heard Kotto's voice coming over the speakers, followed by an official-sounding monotone as Someone Important told everyone that the governor was sending in the National Guard, and that martial law was being declared.

The woman wasn't alone. Her family was frozen around her, eyes weary and concern stretched across canvas-like flesh. Strands of the black—of their *fear*—stretched out of them, invisible on the material plane, leading to someplace in Ellicottville, someplace where a man who made moonshine commanded a legion who built altars of human bones.

"We're feeding his power," Richards said wearily. Kotto nodded.

"We have to find out exactly where he is," the sheriff said. "We can follow these lines to—"

But a shadow had fallen over Kotto and Richards. They looked up just in time to see the ceiling and roof phase out of the visual spectrum. Above them floated a disc of metal and bone, flaming orange runes, a low drone rumbling in their quivering skulls.

Kotto screamed something. A pull. Force on Richards, drawing him up like he was falling down stairs. Richards tried to hold on to Kotto's hands, tried to reach out for the kitchen table, yelling in terror for someone to *help me please God someone help me*. But Richards' hands were spirit as much as they were flesh, and, as his id registered this, he went tumbling up, up, up, into that vast shadowlight that waited for him within the open maw of the flying saucer.

27. Temptation in the Wilderness

The ley lines were gone; the tendrils of fear-energy were gone. Kotto was gone.

Richards was aware of himself, lying on his back on a cool metal table. A corpse on a mortuary slab.

But there was no smell of death here; in fact, there was no smell of anything. Not even the musk of his own sweat, caked into his shirt from days of fighting and running around and chasing monsters. No, he felt clean, and rested, as if someone had done his laundry for him while he slept a deep sleep, then clothed him again in warm fabric fresh from the dryer. No burn in his muscles, no fatigue in his mind. Just clear, empty neutrality.

Black borders of null stood beyond the cone of light shining from above. Richards squinted into the light. No fixture, no bulbs. Just that dull glare, a dim impression of cheap hospital light filtered through weathered glass.

From beyond, a grinding metal sound. Mechanical grinding; maybe a door opening somewhere. Maybe hideous machinery springing to life—he couldn't be sure. Nothing serious enough to trigger The Fear. No real sign of danger. Yet, Richards recognized that he *should* be afraid. He had been doing something important, and it had been interrupted. Something about a radio and terror from the sky ...

Footfalls on tile. Richards let his own feet—clad in perfectly-clean Army tan boots (*they should be caked in mud*)—dangle over the floor. He stood up, resisting the urge to stretch and yawn. He looked off into the darkness, assuring himself that he had indeed heard the sound from in front of him. But the truth was, that grinding sound—and the echo of footsteps that followed—could have come from anywhere.

His field of vision warped and twisted like a balloon's surface pressed by invisible fingers. With sure but even force, he felt himself turned to his left, his eyes finding the figure that strode out of the darkness, clicks and echoes and echoes of clicks following its every step.

Within the darkness, the form was vapor. Gray. Long limbs swinging in a deep fog of shadow.

Closer now. At the edge of the light. Familiar features. A figure in a blazer, dressed like—

"Veronica?"

She stopped at the edge of the light to consider him. She looked around.

"You're here, too?" she asked. Her voice came to him all funny; all metallic and lined with rusty notes. Something about the acoustics of this place, surely.

"Yeah," Richards said. His hand went to his side, expecting to find purchase on his pistol grip. His holster was there, but no 9mm. "I'm not sure how I ended up here. What's happened? What do you remember?"

"Remember," she said, her eyes pulling back from their lazy rolls from side to side, settling on him. Richards felt his blood respond to some humming in the floor, as if his whole circulatory system was harmonizing with the working of great machinery below. Electric, aware, *amped*. Jesus. He was getting aroused. Not so much because of Veronica, (although, now that he thought about it, had she been wearing a low-cut top and skin-toned stockings under a miniskirt last time he saw her?) but because of that energy. It was like an amphetamine charge laced with a Red Bull-and-Viagra cocktail. Good God, what was happening?

"Look at me," Veronica said. She reached out a finger and turned his chin toward her face. Her eyes bore into his; shifting, swirling, growing. Eyes yellow and wide, wolf's eyes, set in a human face. A human face that bled color and light, rearranging itself in shifting tiles, spreading from her chin to her forehead and back down again. Until her face was supple instead of thin and refined. Until it was younger. Until it was a shade older. Until her hair was in flowing red locks. Until her hair was in a neat blond bob. And back again and back again, ad infinitum.

She wasn't Veronica. She was every woman Richards had ever loved or lusted after (he was unable to tell the difference for most of his life); she was whatever ...

"...you need me to be," she whispered, her voice less human and more mechanical, more *cold*, than it had been just moments before.

The pulsing from beneath his feet was more insistent now, louder, *louder*, the hammering of war drums of some dread army, come to wage cosmic war.

Her face settled on a form, each piece of her flesh agreeing to be one thing, the amalgam fading. She wore the face of the first naked woman Richards had ever seen: flowing brown hair over bare white shoulders, her smile impossibly bright, her flesh airbrushed and shimmering with flowing color. An image in a dirty magazine, come to life.

She leaned in. Their lips met. Richards lost himself

in the moment, the pulsing and thrumming and dread rhythm from below a crescendo of fury; the percussions suddenly joined in by wild yelling and howls of orgiastic delight; of victory, of blood, of a thousand nameless desert nights under misaligned black stars, of men and women offering themselves to one another and to their terrible spirit-gods of the wilderness, of the screams of infants sacrificed to cosmic malignancies over altars of bone and dripping human fat. *Rebellion* and *excess*.

And the phrase, whispered into his mind by a voice at least as old and twisted as death itself:

AND YE SHALL BE AS GODS.

On the table now. How had they ended up here? Memory was listless; shifting, smoky, like the edges of the darkness around them. There was only the howling and the pounding of drums, and the *pulse* of his own blood to the rhythm, his own body betraying him to the moment, the promise of pleasure and communion with something great and terrible pushing all other ideas out of his throbbing skull.

"*Richards!*" came the cry, from somewhere at the edge of the cacophony. Distant, full of reverb and terror.

The voice pulled his awareness out of the rush of physical heat and pleasure. The deputy turned away from the sweet kisses of the woman above him.

"Who?" he asked, but the woman—her face changing again—silenced him with her lips.

"*Abraham Richards!*" Again, closer now, more insistent. Richards pushed the woman away.

"Someone is calling for me," he said.

"No one is here but us," she said, her face flipping and morphing again, becoming indistinct. Except for the eyes. The eyes didn't change this time. Yellow and wide. Terrible.

"Someone—someone called ..."

"*Deputy Abraham Richards!*"

"Kotto?" Richards said. "Sheriff? Where are you?"

"*Don't do it!*" came the voice, closer than ever. "*It's a goddamn succubus! It ain't worth it! I'm speaking from experiiiiiiiieeeeence!*"

"A succu-what?" Richards looked to the woman, whose yellow eyes met his own. She hissed, her face twisting into that of a half-human, snarling beast, her hair becoming twisted and black as swamp rot hanging over her shoulders. The illusion of her beauty floated off like the night's fog. As Richards scrambled out from under her, he rolled off the table and stood up, only to see a withered, gray thing before him, its face wrinkled and horrible, any sense of longing or sexual desire in him suddenly suffocated by the sight of her water-logged, mottled flesh. The pounding and the howling around them had turned to dismal shrieking; howls not of pleasure but of frustration. She hissed at him again, a foot-long serpentine tongue dancing out at him from between the lips of a corpse. She clambered off the table to the floor with a wet plop, then galloped off into the darkness beyond. The music and the screaming disappeared with her into the dark, and Richards was left in utter silence.

"Holy shit," Richards said. "I almost had sex with that fucking thing."

"*Riiiichards!*"

"Kotto! Where are you?"

Footfalls on tile again. But from behind him now. Richards turned and braced himself for that she-devil to come back for him, this time not with kisses and caresses, but with tooth and claw.

Instead, Sheriff Kotto emerged, his BDU jacket open to reveal his gut protruding from under his white undershirt, his aviator sunglasses and army helmet on him once more.

"Deputy!" Kotto said, speeding toward the island of light. When he reached the light, he stopped. "Wait. How do I know it's really Deputy Richards?"

"Uh," Richards said. "Sheriff, I almost had sex with a shape-shifting woman alien thing. And then it turned into a hag and I wanted to throw up."

"Good enough for me," Kotto said, stepping into the light. "Where did she go?"

"Into the dark," Richards said, gesturing behind him. "Back there. Or maybe over there. Uh, I can't really tell. It's hard to remember."

"You've noticed that too, huh? Good. It's the first sign your mind is fighting back."

"Fighting against what? What's going on?"

"We escaped a cannibal holocaust-slash-UFO terror attack to the residence of a known drug dealer. We ingested mescaline tea, psychedelic mushrooms, and Genny Cream Ale to achieve a sort of ESP-transcendence. That propelled us into the psychosphere, or consciousness superstructure, allowing us to use CIA remote viewing techniques to find the source of Bucky's psycho-spiritual power. Then, a flying saucer came along and sucked us up, hammering our brains with illusions and mischief, including that she-beast that almost got you to copulate with it in some bizarre cosmic horror ritual. Is any of this coming back to you?"

"Yes," Richards said flatly.

"Great! Now we have to escape from here," Kotto said.

"How do we do that?"

"We blast our way out," the sheriff said, looking around him. "Nothing around here, huh? Just this sex-slab?"

"I didn't have sex on it," Richards said.

"No?"

"Scout's honor."

"This is the only time you'll ever thank me for cock-blocking you," Kotto said. "Although I will probably do it again at some point. Hopefully that won't involve succubus soul-suckers."

"How did you know what she was?"

"It's all fun and games at first, but then comes the larva, and the hatching period, and then there's talk about getting a cat together—"

"Do you hear that?" Richards asked. The drums and the howling had disappeared with the woman, but now there was something else. Whispering. Words hissed in shadow. Getting closer. Louder. Angrier.

"I'd say they know we know the jig is up," Kotto said. "Come on out of the shadows, you big pussies! We're not buying it! Time to send us back home!"

"Why would they do that?" Richards asked. "Am I missing something? I mean, if they can't seduce us, or trick us or whatever, they're probably just gonna kill us. Right?"

"A reasonable risk assessment on your part," Kotto said. "Here they come."

Out of the dark, they crept.

28. Crossing the Streams

Grinding metal. A taste of ozone on the air. The light above them pulsed and shimmered, cascading from one spectrum to the next. It settled on red. Deep red; a light no longer like that of a hospital room. Now, a light fit for an Italian horror film—the color of movie blood, vibrant and obscene. The light fluttered and flickered, bathing Kotto and Richards in its fell waves.

Ahead of them, the shadows shifted. Richards turned from side to side, leaning back against the metal slab upon which he had found himself moments (*minutes? hours? days?*) before. From all angles, they crept forward. Hunched, arms ahead of them, spindle-like fingers twittering furtively in anticipation of the hunt.

"They're gonna grab us," Kotto said. "Don't get grabbed! It's bad news, man!"

Richards processed nothing his boss said. He understood nothing. They'd entered the crazy zone. Nothing made sense. Maybe it was the drugs that had propelled him to this place. Maybe it was the darkness, maybe it was the fear. But as the gray, skinny, inhuman figures with wide faces and wide, limitless scaly almond eyes moved out of the dark toward that island of light in the middle of that infinite black gulf, Richards felt a physical *scrape* within his own mind. Something was slipping. In his brain. He was losing it.

This is what it's like to go mad, a voice that sounded like his mother told him. *You always knew it had to happen, sooner or later.*

His mind, in some misguided act of mercy, pulled his consciousness into the deep recesses of memory.

Abe was a child—seven, probably—small enough to be ignored most of the time, but just becoming bright enough to realize that the world his parents and his teachers had sold him didn't quite exist. Because if the good guys always won, if everyone got their happy ending, if justice and peace prevailed—then there would be no need for a room like this.

Clean. The institutional blue paint on the walls faded from years of open curtains letting in indifferent sunlight. The air tasting of solvent tinged with poop. His mother held his hand, walking him forward to the end of the room. That bright, golden light of early sunset over a snow-caked landscape filtering to him over the rows of hills and buildings beyond. It would be dark soon.

The light above him crackled. A pair of flies dueled around the narrow fluorescent tube. For a moment the light seemed wider, seemed red, his favorite color (this week) … but then it was just a hospital light again, cold and blue-white.

"Abe, say hi to your grandmother."

This moment had been coming. He hoped he could avoid it. That maybe if he stared at the buzzing flies long enough, that maybe if he ignored that poop smell long enough, they could go without passing through this moment. They could walk out of the hospital and never return, and never talk about it ever again.

"Abe," his mother said, more insistent, the strain of her job at the Springville ER, raising a son who didn't fit in at school, and the impending death of her mother drilling fractures in her voice.

He looked.

Grandma sat up in her bed, the mechanical reclining portion propped up to let her watch TV. What remained of her wispy, white hair hung off of her head and face like Halloween party cobwebs tossed up for decoration by an impatient child. Her face was marked with lines of blue and red, as if the network of arteries and veins beneath sensed the impending doom of the larger body, and wanted *out*. Her eyes still held some spark of intelligence, but they also seemed foggy, distant, not unlike those eyes of glass set into the frozen faces of his father's taxidermied trophies: deer and elk and moose alike, forever witnessing, never allowed to sleep or shut their eyes, even for a moment.

"Hi Gramma," Abe managed. He forced himself to look into those eyes. He wanted to show her that he wasn't afraid. That he wasn't bothered by how she looked. That he could love someone in his family, even if they had become as twisted and horrible as the thing before him.

These ideas, he knew, while honorable, were lies he told himself. If he admitted what he thought of her—what he *really* thought about this woman who had once been so full of life and love for him and his cousins and now spent her days locked in this room gibbering to herself—he would never forgive himself. So he wouldn't acknowledge the lie. He would bury it and not think about it. Not until decades later, when he was lost, floating among the astral plane on a mental projection of a flying saucer, with little feral gray creatures closing in all around him.

"Joshua," his grandmother said, eyes on him. Spittle dripped down her chin. Abe didn't know who Joshua was, but her eyes were on him. They didn't let him go. They would never let him go. "Joshua, come inside for dinner."

His mother was crying. He looked up at her, ashamed and not knowing why.

"Who's Joshua, mommy?" Abe asked. His mother put a hand to her mouth. Her blue nurse's uniform smelled like vinegar.

"Nobody else is home," his grandmother said.

His mother put a hand on the woman's leg—mercifully covered by a thin blanket—before pulling Abe away. They walked out of the room, into the busy hallway, a doctor with his face buried in a clipboard stepping to the side to avoid them. His mother leaned against the wall as his grandmother called for Joshua, whoever he was.

They cried together.

◢◣

"Richards! *Richards!*" Kotto again, shaking Richards' shoulder. "Come back to me, deputy!"

"Oh, sorry," Richards said, remembering that he wasn't seven, that he wasn't full of hate and fear of the living corpse in that hospital bed. She was gone now, dead, no longer a burden on his mother, no longer crying out for Joshua or for anyone else, ever again. The madness that had crept into her brain had spread to the rest of her body, shutting down its systems one by one.

"Don't go to the dark place, Deputy!" Kotto said.

"Stay with me, here, or we've got no chance!"

The grays were closer now. Moving in unison, a wall of paper-thin flesh, eyes catching the red light from above and swallowing it whole. They were only a few feet away.

"How do we get out of this one, Sheriff?" Richards said.

"We're still in the psychosphere," Kotto said, calmly. "We can use that. We have to find something that will push them back. Push the negative juju back."

"Like what?"

"Think of something that gave you hope. Something that made you unafraid. Something *deep*, Deputy. What made you brave? When the monsters closed in, what kept you safe?"

One of the grays took a step into the edge of the red light. Its mouth was flat, its eyes unblinking and without pupils or color. And yet, within that impassive visage, hate and menace lurked. This moment would be nightmare fuel for Deputy Richards for years to come.

"Umm …"

"Think of something," Kotto said. "Visualize it. Let the mushrooms do the work for you."

"Wait, why don't you think of something?"

"If we focus on the same thing, it'll grow stronger," Kotto said. "Besides, that mescaline is hitting me pretty hard right about now. I can barely string together a coherent sentence, let alone manifest some sort of spirit weapon to fight off aliens or whatever the hell these things are."

Richards closed his eyes. He shut out the thought of those things creeping toward them. He shut out the sound of their leathery feet shuffling along on the hard, cold floor. He looked past the memory of his warped grandmother. Deeper.

What made me feel safe in the face of fear?

His parents, sure, but they couldn't help him now. There was Teddy, the grocery store bear that had been his nightly companion until he was nine years old. There had also been a saintly glow about the old family Bible. But no, he needed something more direct. Something born for battle. Something that could keep him safe from the terrors of the deep dark.

Got it.

"Sheriff," Richards said. "Look."

Kotto turned to see what Richards was holding. It had materialized out of nowhere, becoming form and mass the moment Richards' mind seized on the idea. Of course. There could be nothing else. Kotto saw it and smiled, another appearing in his own hands, shimmering into existence from the dark.

They were wands—rubber handles on the far and near ends for their hands to wrap around, with a boxy metal middle lined with wires. The rear grip attached to a black tube containing wires that ran to the power source on their backs, held to them via shoulder straps. The black metal power source was lined with colorful wires, screws, buttons, and rectangular compartments for who-knows-what, with a circular base that held four alternately-flashing red lights. Kotto and Richards leaned slightly forward against the weight of the proton packs as they came into being.

"They're heavier than they look," Kotto said. "This switch here, right?" he asked, pointing to a metal toggle on the wand in his hands.

"That's what they did in the movies," Richards said.

"Then what are we waiting for? Heat 'em up," Kotto said, flipping the switch. A high-pitched whine filled their ears. A sense of power and heat flowed through the wires, the wand suddenly becoming heavier in his hands.

"Smokin'," Richards said, activating his own.

"Make 'em haaaard," Kotto said, twisting the wand with a mechanical snap, a small silver muzzle extending out from the tip. Richards followed suit.

"Ready!"

The grays had stopped moving forward. Now they lingered just within the perimeter of the light. Their smell—ash, burning metal—drifted over to them.

"Let's show these space critter bastards how we do things upstate!" Kotto shouted. The creatures tilted their oblong heads, their almond eyes betraying nothing. "Hose 'em!"

Richards fired first, the wand unleashing a thick stream of yellow-orange-red light, around which danced blue-purple claws of static. The force of the blast pushed him back a bit, so he leaned forward against the pressure.

Kotto fired next, ready for the pushback. He laughed, sweeping the beam from side to side. Richards turned away from him, sending waves of energy into the gray forms, who exploded and gibbed into a thousand messy, dripping pieces as the proton streams tore apart their molecular structures. The grays, not comprehending what was happening, stood in place like frozen automatons with a sudden glitch in their programming. Richards swung the proton stream into the head of the nearest one, popping it like a birthday balloon full of black oil.

"Yeah!" Kotto shouted. "Sending you creepy-crawly fuckers on a one-way trip back to *Hell!*"

Suffering the fury of the cascading orange-blue light from the proton streams, the grays broke ranks. They retreated into the darkness, unleashing whines of pain and terror. Richards and Kotto stepped out after them, tagging as many of the little bastards as they could, slicing off mottled limbs and sawing in half gray alien faces, black blood like tar popping and sloshing everywhere.

Soon the grays were gone (or incinerated, or dismembered by laser fire), leaving Kotto and Richards panting, their packs hot against their backs, the barrels of their neutrino wands smoking with the smell of ozone. They stomped around a perimeter of black ooze and gray gore, kicking aside body parts and black sludge.

"We did it!" Richards said. "We fucking did it! Did you see them run? Dude, I cut like six of them straight in half! That was fucking gross!"

"Hold your horses, Deputy," Kotto said. He flicked the power on his wand to OFF, then set the blaster in its carrying latch behind his right shoulder. "We turned back the tide, but we're not out of the woods yet. We gotta find a way off this ship."

Richards nodded, the adrenaline coursing through his system, making it hard to think.

"But we're not on a physical ship, right? This is all in our heads?"

"Sort of," Kotto said.

"So if we can—I don't know, maybe blow a hole in the wall or something? We could get out of here."

"Right," Kotto said, snapping his fingers. "You see a wall this whole time?"

"Uh, no," Richards said. "Just this light, this slab. No walls."

Kotto considered this, staring up into the red light that emanated from somewhere within the darkness above.

"I've got it," Kotto said.

"What? You want to venture out into the creepy-ass blackness?" Richards said, gesturing to his side. "It's dark as shit out there. I don't think I want to know what's out there."

"No, not quite," Kotto said. "If we can't find a wall

…"

Kotto climbed up onto the slab. Its surface was suddenly slick with condensation and cool to the touch. The entire room was growing warmer, more humid.

"They're changing something," Kotto said. "Let's hurry." He offered Richard a hand, and, despite the extra weight of the proton pack, managed to pull his deputy up. The light above them flickered, growing dim. The darkness around them moved in waves. Whispers of hatred; the insect chittering of claws and gray limbs in the black. Something was coming for them. Something from the dark.

"Heat 'em back up," Kotto said. The familiar whirring and whining of unlicensed nuclear accelerators filled their ears. "Let's blow this popsicle stand!" Kotto yelled, letting loose a stream of light and energy from the neutrino wand. The beam arced down, and Kotto aimed the barrel out a few feet beyond the slab on which they stood. Richards followed suit, bracing against the pushback of the weapon. Sparks flew up as their lasers chewed through the first few layers of whatever-the-hell-it-was that made up the flying saucer's floor.

Their beams worked like welder's torches. Waves of molten metal—or what appeared to be metal—rolled away from their blasts. Richards took a moment to glance over his shoulder, away from the light. His eyes didn't adjust to the darkness right away, but they didn't have to. Something was moving back there. The darkness had begun to drift like fog moving in from the old swamp behind his parents' house. The red light above had almost gone out, leaving them in darkness save for the light from their streams.

"We're gonna have to hurry this up!" Richards yelled over the blasts. Kotto nodded, then let his beam go out. Richards likewise pulled his finger off the firing button. Smoke drifted up from their barrels and from where the laser arcs had cut into the floor. A smell of burnt plastic and ozone. The men looked around them, the chittering and whispering no longer a soft backdrop; there was a sense of movement, of *mass*.

They were coming back, and they were *pissed*.

"Sheriff, I don't think we're alone."

"Start shooting."

"What, into the dark?"

"No. At the floor. Fire. Do it, Deputy!"

Richards did as he was told, the beam blazing bright in darkness. Kotto moved next to him, then placed his barrel inches away from Richards'. When he fired, his beam caught and wrapped around its twin, sending sparks and fingers of blue-purple light out in angry waves.

"Cross the streams!" Kotto yelled. "Don't let up!"

Their joint beam grew and snaked, pulling them from side to side, threatening to knock them both off the slab. But its force and heat chewed through layer after layer of now-molten metal, cutting down a melting hole into the depths of the ship. The voices of anger and hate and hunger came to them, even over the din of the destruction they were laying down in wide arcs of laser and light. The wands grew hot in their hands, and the joint beam began to grow and expand. Soon the beam was impossible to look upon. The packs whined and hummed, louder and sharper, threatening to deafen them.

The hair on the back of their necks stood up. Their eyes watered. Their teeth and bones vibrated and chattered, calcium and enamel growing hot—

Inhuman hands reached for them from the darkness.

29. Detective Work

There was light, and then there was the force and heat of an explosion, skin pressed hard against bone, limbs limp and flailing in the air.

They fell. First through clammy cold and impossible silence. Then through fields of cloud that pulsed with the rhythms of blue lightning. Tree limbs like arms, branches like gnarled fingers, scratching against flesh. The ground below, hard and unyielding, soaked with rain and waiting for their bodies to impact, the promise of quick death.

Kotto sat bolt upright on Willy's couch, gasping for air, shaking his head and holding his arms out in front of him in a vain attempt to break his fall. The crack of thunder as he came out of his fugue echoed the explosion of the UFO that they had so narrowly escaped.

Richards came to more easily, sitting up and rubbing at a string of drool that had descended from his lips.

"They're awake," Veronica said, smacking Dean, who rested in a moldy recliner.

Veronica walked over to Kotto and put a hand on his shoulder as the sheriff struggled to regain his sense of place and self.

"Drink this," she said. She handed him a glass full of a cool, thick red liquid.

"What's this?" Kotto rasped, breathing heavy. His body shook with the aftershocks of death-fear. He had been about to splatter against the ground, and now he was safe in a living room. His body and mind struggled to keep up with such drastically changing circumstances.

"Bloody Mary," Veronica said.

Richards groaned.

"I feel like the floor of a taxi cab …"

"You might have a bit of a hangover from the … whatever the hell it was you just did," Veronica said.

Kotto accepted the glass and took a sip. Richards found one waiting for him on the table, and gulped half of it down without a break.

"Water, too," the deputy said. "Please."

Dean got up and went into the kitchen.

"What happened?" Veronica said. "You guys were out for a while. Lot of twitching and mumbling."

"How long were we gone?" Kotto asked.

"Gone?" Veronica offered a raised eyebrow. "You were here the whole time."

"We floated through the air," Richards said. "It was pretty wild."

"You were passed out for about five hours," Veronica said. "By the way—your friend Willy? He's a creep. Hospitable, but a creep."

"We don't have much time," Kotto said. "The forces of evil are growing in power every moment we dilly-dally."

"Did you find out where Bucky is, or not?"

"Somewhere nearby," Richards said. "We tried to follow—what were they? Ley lines. They're being drained somewhere south of here."

"Somewhere just outside of Ellicottville," Kotto

said. "I can't be sure. We were attacked. Goddamn creepy-ass grays showed up. Richards had sex with one."

"She was hot before you showed up and scared her off," Richards said. "And I *almost* had sex with her."

"What am I doing with these people?" Veronica asked herself, shaking her head. "So you *don't* know where Bucky is? Then what was the point of you guys ingesting illegal drugs in the first place? Just wanted to kill an afternoon?"

"Where would Bucky be?" Kotto asked. "He'll need power and water to run his still ..."

"Wait," Veronica said. "Dean! Is that paper still in the van?"

"Yeah, probably. Why?"

"Go and get it for me, will you?"

"I'm getting water for the deputy."

"Go get the goddamn paper!"

Dean, mumbling, made his way back through the living room and back out into the night. The rain had slowed to a trickle in the hours since Kotto and Richards had gone on their psychedelic journey, but the sky remained black with clouds.

Kotto and Richards sipped what remained of the Bloody Marys. Richards, being reunited with his body, felt a sudden weight about his limbs and mind, as if inhabiting a flesh construct took *effort*. There was so much pain and friction. Their experiences in the psychosphere had been terrifying—but also liberating. He wondered if he would ever feel that free again.

Dean returned with the paper—a folded up copy of *Ellicottville Events*.

"I've read that one already," Richards said. "My buddy showed it to me."

Veronica snatched the paper out of Dean's hands, and started flipping through the pages.

"So you said Bucky's probably set up somewhere to the south of us, right? Near Ellicottville?"

"That's where the energy lines took us," Kotto said. "And that's where the psychic flying saucer showed up."

"I don't know what any of this means," Dean said, holding up his hands. "For the record."

"And you said he'd probably need a power supply and water to operate his stills," Veronica said. "Which means he needs to have generators someplace. But he'll still need a road to bring in supplies, so he can't be too far off the beaten path. But he'd also need to be someplace that the State Troopers wouldn't think to look, right?"

"You've got the makings of a fine deputy there, missy," Kotto said. "Jesus, my head hurts. Why did I let you talk me into this, Deputy?"

"So you guys went off on your little mushroom adventure and almost got killed by 'creepy-ass grays,' and accomplished not a whole lot," Veronica said, holding up the paper for them to see a particular headline. "Meanwhile, the answer was right in front of us the whole time."

Richards squinted in the dim candlelight. Kotto stood up straight, then took the paper from Veronica's hands.

"'Snow Pine expansion project put on hold,'" Kotto read. "'Construction equipment, generators sit idle while EPA and DEC conduct environmental impact study.'" Kotto snapped his fingers. "I've got it! Bucky's somewhere near the Snow Pine construction project! They haven't cleared out that many trees yet, and there's all this equipment, power … And probably fresh water, too."

"Guys, I just gave you the answer, you didn't figure it out."

"Richards, you still got contact with your National Guard buddies, right?"

"Yes, sir."

"Is your cell phone working?"

"The storm's let up a bit. I've got a few bars."

"Start making some calls," Kotto said. "Where's my gun? You guys seen my gun? We're gonna need to get it together. No time to waste!"

"What's the plan, Sheriff?" Richards asked, standing up and trying to maintain his balance. "I think I'm still a little high."

"That's just the mescaline wearing off," Kotto said. "Just try to keep it together for another couple of hours. You'll be fine. But see if that drug-addled brain of yours can operate your cell phone. Find out what route your old unit is taking into the county. I'm willing to bet the governor knows more about this than we do. He's probably sending those soldiers right where the action is. We have to meet up with those boys and get them to help us stop Bucky!"

"How is stopping Bucky going to stop ... whatever the hell is going on?" Veronica asked.

"This isn't about Bucky, not really," Kotto said. "They're using him to raise an army, an armed insurrection. Then they move in with the National Guard. They want to start a war here. I can feel it. And you can bet those goddamn FEMA trucks will be right behind! This is a New World Order plot, man! We gotta stop this thing!"

"Why here?" Veronica asked. "I mean, what's so important about Cattaraugus County? There's nothing here, nothing important, anyway. Why not try a city? Buffalo, Rochester?"

Kotto scratched at the scraggle of a beard along his chin.

"For starters, Catt County is heavily armed,

independent-minded. You got poor trailer trash, wealthy ski yuppies, whites, black folk, Seneca Nation reservations. Lots of people who don't like to be pushed around. If they can pull it off here, they can do it anywhere. This is a test-run for the whole state. Maybe the country."

"Pull *what* off, Sheriff?"

"Full-on takeover. Martial law. Suspend the Constitution, bring in the FEMA trucks, round us all up!"

"That's crazy," Veronica said. "The government wouldn't do that."

"Hurricane Katrina ring a bell?" Kotto said. "What about Japanese internment camps during World War II? Or the entire history of contact with the Native Americans? 'It can't happen here?' *It already has.*"

"Wait," Richards said, setting down his cell phone for a moment. "What about the UFOs? The altars we saw in West Valley? How does that crap fit into all of this?"

"I think it goes back to this Agent Schrader character—whoever he really is, he's into some bad voodoo. He got Bucky to contact those aliens, or demons, or visitors, whatever they are. I think he's harnessed the powers of Hell to implement his agenda of control."

"You're incredibly lucid for someone coming out of a mushroom trip," Dean remarked.

"This is unreal," Veronica said.

"Oh, this is very real!" Kotto said. "Schrader's got connections. Probably to the Order of the Night Moose, which was infiltrated by the European Illuminati right after the time of the American Revolution. They're Satanists at heart, man. Dark rituals! Child sacrifice! Blood orgies! It's where they get their power. And the fear—Richards and I saw it in the psychosphere.

Flowing in from all directions. The more they spook us with those damn UFOs and the moonshine-crazed murder-horde, the more power they gain!"

"So, let's lay it all out," Veronica said. "We're dealing with an Illuminati government agent who is using the dark power of Hell to manifest UFOs, alien abductions, and create mind-control moonshine in order to cause fear in the population, which in turn contributes to their supernatural power, which leads to civil unrest, which will justify a government implementation of martial law and suspend American freedoms and the democratic process. Am I missing anything?"

"I'd say that about sums it up."

"Shit," Veronica said. "I don't think I'm on board with this."

"What choice do we have?" Kotto asked. "You're on board whether you want to be or not, missy! And this ship is sailing straight into one hell of an iceberg!"

"So what does all that mean?" Richards asked. "What's our next move? Does it involve more drugs? Please don't say that it involves more drugs."

"It means, Deputy Richards, that we have to stop Bucky," Kotto said. "Tonight. Before there's any more killing. He's gathering power at Snow Pine, right? That means he's going to use it, or Schrader is. We have to stop him before he pulls off whatever ritual it is that Schrader needs him for. There's no telling how much chaos that whacky fear-magic is gonna cause! He might be opening a portal to Hell, or some higher dimension full of those spindly-armed creepy-crawly gray bastards. We don't need any more of those little shitheads running around my county, grabbing folks and probing them! No sir!"

"But if Bucky and Schrader are secretly working for the government," Veronica said, "then why would the governor send in the National Guard? Wouldn't he *want* things to get more out of control?"

Kotto considered this.

"Yes. Unless they need something else. Something more. Maybe it's not just the fear they need for their ritual. Typically, there needs to be some sort of sacrifice for these kinds of things."

"Typically," Veronica said, rolling her eyes.

"Right. Just like Bucky's moonshine doesn't work without baby blood. So they've been killing folks for a couple of days now. But maybe they need something more. Something big. Where a lot of people would get killed, all at once. Lots of blood, lots of guts."

"Like a battle," Richards said. "Like hundreds of brainwashed crazies with pitchforks and chainsaws going up against armed National Guard soldiers? You mean like that?"

Kotto's face fell.

"Get on the horn, Richards. We have to reach those soldiers before they get into Ellicottville. They may be walking into a goddamn goat rodeo of Biblical proportions!"

"So, wait," Veronica said, her face a sudden scowl. "We could have just *called* these people, and that would tell you where Bucky is? And I figured out where Bucky is by reading the newspaper. And yet you decided that taking illegal drugs and fighting psychic aliens was the best course of action?"

"A good lawman knows when to take risks," Kotto said. "Besides, if we hadn't tripped balls in the astral plane for the last several hours, we may never have figured this whole thing out!"

"That's really not likely," Veronica said.

"Richards, get on the horn! We've gotta get to those soldiers sooner rather than later!"

"What do you want me to tell them, Sheriff?"

"That the mission's changed," he said. "I have a feeling they're going to be walking into a meat grinder. We have to stop that from happening. For their sake, and for the people that Bucky's moonshine has corrupted."

Kotto stomped over to grab his BDU jacket and helmet.

"Willy! Thanks for the 'shrooms. Put it on my tab! Also, I may or may not find my gun in the next 45 seconds. Keep an eye out for it!"

"What have we gotten ourselves into?" Dean asked Veronica.

"We're either going to win a Pulitzer, or we're going to prison," she replied.

Kotto already had the front door open.

"Are you people coming or not? We've got a county to save!"

30. Convoy

Captain Jimmy Hagerson of the New York National Guard *hated* rain. That might have come as a surprise to people who thought all soldiers were tough as nails, masochistic gluttons. But the truth was, bad weather, the cold, the wet—one could never quite get used to them, no matter how much experience you had.

And did Jimmy ever have experience. As a company commander, he'd been through a lot just to get to this lowly station. He'd gone through the Infantry Officer Basic Course, Army Ranger School, and an overseas deployment to Afghanistan, all before reaching the rank of captain. That was pretty typical for a lot of officers in his class. Joining the military during a time of war tends to accelerate experience, maturity—and burnout.

He'd settled in as Alpha Company commander not two months ago. The old captain moved on, and Jimmy got a promotion. He'd left Second Platoon to become the executive officer, and then he found himself with the command a year later. One hundred and thirty men looked to him for leadership and guidance. Many of them were combat veterans, having put years or even decades into military service. It was an honor to lead them, Jimmy knew. But he also knew a lot of the men were tired. Truth be told, he spent more of his time at drill filing paperwork, administering discipline, and supervising re-integration and counseling classes than he did preparing his men for combat.

They'd been home from Afghanistan less than a year, and it was clear that the unit was tired, chewed up. They needed a break. Truth was, so did Jimmy. At 28 years old, his back hurt, he didn't sleep most nights without a few drinks in him, and that ringing in his ears always seemed to pick up when the stress piled on.

That ringing came on strong when he got the call. His battalion commander sounded worried, his voice hushed, his words coming out monotone.

"The operations order is in your AKO inbox," he said. "The governor's activating your boys."

There wasn't much more than that; the OPORDER didn't have many details, either. He was to move Alpha Company to a little ski town called Ellicottville, and support local law enforcement efforts in restoring social order, whatever the fuck that meant. He figured supply would have to break out the armor, helmets, shields, and batons. Instead, he discovered that the governor wanted them to carry rounds. Lethal rounds. And not just one magazine each, like they did in New York City for special security missions. Each soldier—even the SAW gunners—were getting a full issue. Two hundred and ten rounds for the riflemen; 400 rounds for the gunners.

The ammo supply truck was at the armory before he was. The driver was dressed in a black sweater with a black flat-brimmed cap that read "MALTHUS" which was probably the name of some defense contracting agency formed by ex-Green Berets. The driver claimed he'd been put on notice about the operation the day *before*. That meant that somebody at the 42nd Division knew the governor would be mobilizing Alpha Company at least 24 hours before the operation had been officially ordered.

That didn't smell right to Jimmy. But he was used to things being fucked up. That was the National Guard for you. Hell, that was the Army for you.

The news wasn't saying much about any riots in Cattaraugus County; coverage was instead mostly about a freak storm that had parked itself there. By the time all of his soldiers made it to the armory and they held first formation, the State Troopers had issued a full travel ban on any and all roads leading to and from Ellicottville. Calls from Battalion informed him that they'd have a State Trooper escort into town, leading them from the edge of Springville in Erie County south on Route 219 and into Cattaraugus County. Details were scant, but Ellicottville was near the heart of the chaos.

There were rumors flying around about a large-scale riot in the hamlet of West Valley the day before. Other stories were coming in about people rampaging through the back roads, attacking motorists with chainsaws and axes. Real crazy shit.

Nobody would give him a straight answer as to what they were walking into—but it sure as hell didn't sound like a standard riot situation. If things were really that bad—so bad that the governor was sending them down there fully stocked with enough ammo to take on the Taliban—why wasn't it on the news anywhere?

Their convoy consisted of four deuce-and-a-half supply trucks, a government agency conversion van, and a soft-skinned Humvee at the front and rear of the formation. When they hit the county line, Captain Hagerson ordered the gunners in the Humvees to stand up and lock and load. Lucky for them, the rain had oddly tapered off by then.

At the other end of a long bridge that connected Erie and Cattaraugus counties, they linked up with a single State Trooper patrol car, its red and blue lights flashing in the dark. Jimmy rode in the lead Humvee—more out of curiosity than protocol—and ordered the convoy to a halt as they pulled up to the police.

Two officers waited for him, standing to the front of their vehicle. As Jimmy stepped out into the rain, the two men stepped forward to meet him halfway. The officers, not unlike the captain, wore body armor and M-4 rifles slung over their chests. They didn't wear combat helmets—those were in the car—but aside from that, they wouldn't look out of place on a battlefield. Jimmy didn't like that one bit. He knew, then, that his company was deploying for one reason, and one reason only: escalation.

"Good evening sir!" one of the cops barked through a thin layer of fabric covering the lower half of his face, not unlike that which the Afghan interpreters would use to hide their identities. "We're glad you boys are here!"

"Good evening, officer," Jimmy said, shaking the man's hand. The other officer kept glancing behind them, his eyes scanning the darkness of the tree line. Scant drizzle dripped down from the impossibly black clouds above. "What's the situation here?"

"We're to escort you down to Ellicottville," the first officer said. "Major George Winston is on-site. He'll fill you in on the situation, then you boys can dig in."

"Dig in for what?" Jimmy asked. "I'm a little confused as to what is going on down here. I'm told a riot, but we get issued ammo, not riot gear. This whole things feels more like we're going to war than we are going to restore order."

"You're not too far off, sir," the officer said. "We'll lead you the rest of the way south. Once we're in town, the commander can fill you in."

"Why isn't this on this news?" Jimmy said suddenly. "This is pretty serious stuff. I had to collect my soldiers' cell phones and lock them up back at the armory. What don't you guys want getting out?"

"We should move, sir," the other officer said, eyes still on the tree line. "It might not be safe here for long."

"I agree, captain," the first officer said. "I'd prefer to let the commander fill you in."

"Right, of course," Jimmy said, shaking his head. "Lead the way."

They drove on. Route 219 wound south, a lazy gray snake curled over foreboding hills, once pristine in full autumn glory, now dark as death with no light from the moon or stars to shine upon them. The highway lights were all out, too, and any house they passed stood in solitary darkness.

As the convoy made the turn off the freeway portion of 219 and onto the old road, the oppressiveness of the night storm hit home. There were more homes here—and a few businesses—but they were all dark. Some had cars parked out front, some didn't. Once, Jimmy caught what he thought was the flicker of candlelight pulsing against the curtains inside a home—but the convoy sped on, and he couldn't be sure. Occasionally their headlights would splash against the porch of a home, illuminating Halloween decorations that should have been lit with orange and green lights; instead, they were dark with undefined menace.

The State Troopers had handed him a Motorola, not unlike the ones they'd given the 'terps to carry in Afghanistan. A static-tinged voice came over the air:

"We're about 10 minutes out from Ellicottville," the Trooper said. "We're taking it kind of slow for those big trucks of yours. Roads are still pretty slick, and it's hard to see in this muck."

"Roger."

Indeed, "muck" was as good a word as any. Although it had stopped raining, their headlights had to fight for every inch of space ahead of them. The darkness threatened to swallow them whole.

But then, just ahead, a pair of dim headlights blazed out from the dark. There was another vehicle coming toward them. Jimmy grabbed the Motorola.

"Trooper One, Alpha Six. I thought there was a travel ban here. Is that one of yours? Over."

"Negative, Alpha Six. We'll push them off the road. Give us a moment, over."

The convoy slowed to a crawl. The gunner standing in the hatch behind Jimmy shifted, pointing his SAW toward a line of sickly trees that stretched out along the road to their right. The Trooper vehicle ahead of them stopped, then blared its horn at the oncoming vehicle.

The vehicle appeared to be a conversion van. It stopped just a few yards from the front of the Trooper car. Both officers stepped out into the dark, M-4s up and ready.

"Get out of the goddamn road!" one of them hollered. "This is official police business!"

The panel door on the van's side slid open, and a single figure jumped out onto the road. He walked forward, hand extended out, holding something that glinted in the dark, reflecting silver in the headlights.

He approached the two officers, who lowered their rifles. An argument ensued. Jimmy watched the exchange—the two State Troopers yelling and shaking their heads, the other man waving his silver object in the air and pointing at the convoy. Finally, he gave the Troopers the finger and stomped toward Jimmy's Humvee. The Troopers made no move to stop him.

"He's got a gun, sir," the gunner said.

"That doesn't look like he's holding a gun," Jimmy said.

"It's a sidearm, on his hip," the Humvee driver said. "He's not holding it."

The man walked forward, then stood directly in the beams washing out from the Humvee's headlights. He wore a Buffalo Bills fitted cap, black plate carrier stuffed full with pistol magazines and red shotgun shells, and Army tan combat boots under ACU pants.

"Friendly coming through!" he shouted, his words just audible over the idling engine. He held up the object in his hand.

A star. A silver sheriff's deputy star.

"Hey, isn't that—hey Specialist Swell, isn't that your old team leader?" the driver asked the gunner.

"Holy shit. It's Sergeant Richards!" the gunner exclaimed. "Sir, that's Sergeant Richards."

The former team leader walked to the side of the Humvee, then tapped on the glass. Jimmy rolled down the window.

"Captain Hagerson!" Richards shouted over the drone of the diesel engine, leaning into the Humvee.

"Richards?" the officer choked out. "What the hell are you doing? Is that a badge? You with the Troopers now?"

"County Sheriff's Deputy," Richards said. "Sir, I'd love to catch up, but there's no time. The situation has changed. If you do what those assholes up there are telling you, a lot of people are going to die."

"Sergeant—I mean, Deputy—I don't even know what the situation is," Jimmy admitted. "I got a vague goddamn OPORDER and a bunch of ammo, and nobody's telling me shit. You want to fill me in?"

"We don't have a lot of time, sir," Richards said. "But you've got bad intel. It's not the riots you have to worry about. Something worse is about to pop off, and you boys are a big part of it."

"I can't *not* follow orders," the captain said.

"No sir, I'm not asking you to do that. I'm telling you some creative interpretation might be in order."

Jimmy smiled.

"You mean like that time in Pul-E-Salam?"

"Just like Pul-E-Salam, sir. You can still follow orders, Captain. But unless you listen to me and the sheriff, there's gonna be a whole lot of folks who are gonna end up dead who don't deserve to be."

Jimmy considered this. He glanced at his driver, who just shrugged.

"You're gonna tell me just what the hell is going on in this county?"

"Yes, sir. Hell *is* going on. That's why we need to move fast. Ditch these State Police assholes and follow our van."

"The sheriff drives around in a conversion van?"

"It's actually from the local public access TV and radio station," Richards said. "Long story."

Jimmy raised an eyebrow, then shook his head. Radio traffic was starting to come in from his platoon leaders, each one asking for a SITREP. What would he tell them? What *was* the situation, anyway?

"Alright," Jimmy said at last. "So we got work to do. What do you need from me?"

IV
The Beginning of the End of All Things

31. Saving the Day

"Signal's piercing the storm," Dean said. "I'm not sure how, but they're ready to relay the broadcast to the radio waves—and anybody who's got a TV should be able to see it, too."

"So we're audio only?" Veronica asked.

"Probably. But some people might have a generator. If they tune in, they'll see your smiling face."

"How do I look?" Veronica stood in front of the side of the van, the CCPATV logo emblazoned behind her in broad strokes of red and yellow. The light from Dean's camera was nearly blinding in the pitch black of the night.

"Like you've been through hell," Dean said. "But that's good. Makes for a more authentic, war correspondent look."

"You think I should wear a helmet or a flak vest or something?"

"Nah. This is fine. Don't want to push it."

"Got it. Let me know when we're live."

Dean nodded, then put a finger to his headset. The voice of the station manager buzzed in his ear.

"Okay. We're live in five, four ..." He held up his fingers, going from three, to two, to one.

"This is Veronica Cartwright, reporting live en route to Snow Pine Ski Resort," she said, leaning her head forward ever-so-slightly, her eyebrows arched. Her go-to *I'm-serious-this-is-serious* look. "Sheriff Cecil Kotto is asking that the people of Ellicottville and the surrounding communities join him to put an end to the chaos that has gripped our county for the last several days. He's asking that all citizens who are capable, to go out into the night, armed with flashlights or even candles. He's asked that you get with your neighbors ..."

"Get out there and show them you're not afraid!" Kotto yelled from off-camera. He bounded into the frame, wrapping his hands around Veronica's microphone and pulling it too close to his mouth. Veronica grimaced, but didn't let go. "Show them that you don't need the State Troopers or the feds or anyone else to tell us what to do! This is our town, and we're gonna take it back! I need you out there, people! We're rolling into town and I want to see you out there and unafraid. We're not gonna let a few chainsaw murders and demon-UFOs scare us into submission! Show your support! Get out there, and show them what us country folk are made of!"

Veronica shouldered Kotto away, and pulled the mic back.

"You've heard it here first, citizens. Grab whatever source of light you can, and take to the streets. We'll be reporting live as Sheriff Kotto leads the National Guard into downtown Ellicottville, presumably to put a stop to the riots, the murders, and maybe even the UFO sightings. Who knows what will happen next? Certainly not this exhausted and underpaid reporter. Stay tuned for more as the situation develops, on the only news station willing to cover the true events behind the Larry 'Bucky' Green manhunt and riots. For Cattaraugus County Public Access TV and radio, I'm Veronica Cartwright."

"Aaannd ... we're clear," Dean said. The red flashing light on his camera rig went dark.

"Do you think they'll go for it?" Richards asked. He stood just behind Dean.

"From the looks of the psychosphere when we were tripping balls, I'd say if they don't, we're fucked," Kotto said. "How'd I look on camera? Did I keep it professional?"

"You guys are the weirdest goddamn cops I've ever met," Dean said, lowering his camera.

"Come on, let's run some red lights!" Kotto shouted from the front passenger seat of the news van. The State Troopers in the patrol car had sworn up and down that *they* were in charge, and that the sheriff had no authorization to lead the convoy. Kotto, in a rare moment of self-aware humility, offered to let them lead the way further south. But he had Richards tell his National Guard buddies that they'd be heading straight to Snow Pine Resort. If the State Troopers wanted to join them in saving the world, they were welcome to come along.

But as it stood, the Troopers insisted on stopping at the traffic light where old 219 met 242. They came to a full and complete stop and looked for nonexistent traffic. Ahead of them, the old Catholic graveyard loomed in fog and dark, stones and eyeless statues keeping vigil in the night.

Something had changed. Cell phones were working, radio waves were broadcasting. And, deeper into town, lights danced in the darkness.

Finally, the patrol car crept forward. Kotto leaned out the front window and waved to the Humvee and the rest of the National Guard convoy that followed.

"Fuck this light!" he hollered.

Richards, now in the driver's seat, hit the gas and the news van rounded the turn with a squeal of tires.

"That's more like it, Deputy!" Kotto said. Ahead of them, the State Trooper car's emergency lights spilled over onto the town. The convoy passed a row of vacant rental properties, then an auto mechanic's hop. The Lutheran church was on their right. Soon they were passing the turn to Delity soccer field, and downtown Ellicottville waited for them.

"What's that ahead?" Veronica asked from the bench seat. She leaned forward to peer out the front windshield. "Dean, get the camera going."

"You think it's the crazies?" Richards asked. Instinctively, his right hand left the steering wheel and grasped the pistol at his hip.

"It's not the moonshined monsters," Kotto said, a broad smile breaking across his face. He reached up to the army helmet chin strap that dangled along his neck, and secured it under his chin. "Those are my constituents!"

The State Troopers slowed their speed as people moved in from all sides. They had gathered in the parking lots of the corner gas station on the left and the small grocery store to the right. Bonfires blazed up and down the main street, but stood well away from the buildings lining the downtown corridor. The people themselves stood around the fires or held flashlights, candles, glowsticks—and a few, adults and children alike, carried Jack O'Lanterns, smiling with the light of candles within. They threw up arms and cheers when the State Trooper car made the curve to the straight shot downtown, and the news van and National Guard vehicles followed behind.

"Slow down," Kotto said. "Let's enjoy this." As their

van moved past the grocery store parking lot, Kotto leaned out the window, sitting on the edge and waving to the crowd. Dean had the camera rolling the moment they hit town.

"Hello Catt County!" he shouted over the thrum of diesel engines and the cheering of the crowd. The people—young, old, kids, adults—saw their sheriff and let out another ecstatic roar. Dozens—hundreds—pressed into the street to greet the convoy as it roled in. Kotto waved and shook hands as the convoy slowed to a crawl. Even Richards shook hands and smiled as the people of Ellicottville pressed their hands in through the driver's side window.

"Thank you!" they shouted, smiles on their faces, flashlights and cheap beer cans in their hands. In the middle of what was about to become a war zone, with the threat of Bucky's minions in the dark hills around them, they'd responded to Sheriff Kotto's plea to take back the night—and they threw a party.

"You're getting this, right?" Veronica asked Dean. He slid the side panel of the van open to get a better shot of the crowd, then, realizing they were going less than five miles an hour, hopped out to get the scene on foot. His camera caught it all—the bonfires, the kids decked out in their winter Buffalo Bills or Sabres gear, the coolers overflowing with cheap beer, the old men in blaze orange hunting jackets with rifles and shotguns slung over their shoulders, the grills firing up venison and hamburgers. Some of them even broke out their Halloween costumes, wearing demon and skeleton masks; children dressed up like Harry Potter or Clone Troopers from *Star Wars*, moms lighting candles inside hollowed-out pumpkins.

And at the center of it all, at the center of the mass of citizens who pressed in to greet their heroes and shake the hands of the soldiers pulling into town,

Sheriff Kotto. Kotto leaning out the van window, army helmet just slightly askew, his open BDU jacket flapping in the breeze to reveal a pistol tucked into the waistline of his pants, his hands in the air and a smile on his face that would put any aspiring politician to shame.

The crowd had even taken up a chant as the convoy passed through downtown:

Ko-tto! Ko-tto! Ko-tto!

"This is kinda amazing, Sheriff!" Richards shouted from the driver's seat. The crowd was so loud, it was hard to hear inside the van.

"We're gonna change the psychological landscape with this one!" Kotto said. "If Bucky's power is fear-based, he's gonna be hurtin' after this!"

They passed the last of the shops and hotels, leaving much of the crowd behind them to cheer on the National Guard convoy as it snaked its way through the celebrating citizens of Ellicottville. Ahead, the State Troopers pulled off to the right, headed to the command center set up on the lawn of the town offices.

They had set up pickets and rolls of razor wire around the town center, transforming it from a bureaucratic brick building to a forward command post. The Troopers must have salvaged their mobile command RV from the last moonshine maniac attack, as it stood idling on the front lawn of the building, somehow no worse for wear. Groups of Troopers in full combat gear and rifles stood all along the property. Floodlights from mobile generator units illuminated the grounds and the streets adjacent.

When it became clear that Richards was turning the van—blinker flashing, and the rest of the convoy to follow—left, in the direction of Snow Pine Resort, the Troopers ahead of them got out of their car and waved them right, toward their command center.

"No chance, fellas!" Kotto shouted. "We've got a war to win!"

With that, the Humvee carrying Captain Jimmy Hagerson followed their lead—as did the rest of the convoy.

A group of Troopers rushed toward the road, waving for the National Guard drivers to go *right*, not left. But the young specialists and privates at the wheels of the big deuce-and-a-halfs smiled and waved, pointing to the Humvee ahead of them: where their commander went, they went.

"We're growing a tail," Richards said, looking out at his side view mirror to make sure every Guard truck made the turn. "Looks like a few pickup trucks falling into the convoy, too."

"Patriots," Kotto said. "We'll put 'em to work."

"Hey," Veronica said suddenly. "Have you guys seen Dean?"

"Must be he got caught up in the moment," Richards said. "Want to go back for him?"

"No," Kotto said. "This thing is rolling now. We couldn't stop if we wanted to." Kotto pointed ahead of them, to the darkness of the hills beyond. "And by now, it's a good bet they know we're coming. No time to waste."

32. Digging In

Underground generators pumped juice for the emergency lights at Snow Pine Ski Resort. The hotel stood dark, save for the lights from the lobby. Condos that lined the northern side of Snow Pine Road were dark as the rest of Ellicottville, with only a few showing signs of life and candlelight within. With Octoberfest over, the fall seasonal staff was nowhere to be seen. The pickup trucks and minivans of the mountain maintenance crew and full-time management stood scattered about the resort's various parking lots, testament to the life still pulsing in the hibernating husk of Western New York's most popular skiing attraction.

Beyond the lodges, condos, hotel, and administrative buildings laid out along the valley's floor, the hills stood dark. The chair lift motors stood still and silent; the chairs themselves suspended on steel cables, overhanging streaks of grass cut wide through thick forest; these crooked fingers of slope would be covered with white and full of skiers and snowboarders in two months' time, maybe less. But for now, they looked like burn scars among the trees, as if some great fire had ravaged the hillsides, leaving empty space where once mighty trees had grown.

"The main lodge parking lot," Kotto said. "There." He pointed ahead and to the left, just beyond the limit of the hotel parking lot. The main lodge itself was one of the resort's older buildings. In recent years the company had given it a facelift—replacing its old wood panel siding with expensive layers of pine panel that glistened in the light of winter moons, the withered "SNOW PINE RESORT" sign replaced with an updated logo designed by a team of corporate graphic artists.

"The design firm that made that new logo also designed materials and art for Lockheed Martin, Harris Radio, and the Church of Scientology," Kotto remarked, pointing to the sign as the van pulled in and its headlights passed over the logo. "Makes you wonder."

The National Guard convoy pulled in as well, making the sharp turn left and down a small decline into the main lodge's parking lot. Soon the trucks slowed and soldiers in full body armor, helmets, and carrying rifles hopped out, guiding the Humvees or deuce-and-a-halfs into parking spots spread out along the freshly-paved lot. Richards pulled the news van up to a space between the main lodge and the new admin building where families lined up to get their smiling faces photographed for ski passes. The van's headlights washed out into the darkness beyond a large patio, and, below, an open courtyard home to a solitary stone clock tower. In each direction beyond stood the silent and brooding chair lifts, the wind sliding along surfaces of blue-painted metal, plastic, and glass housing the mighty machines that pushed and pulled steel cords up and down the slopes.

"That clock tower has a State Trooper stingray unit mounted inside of it," Kotto said.

"What does that mean?" Richards said, sending the shifter into park. The van wiggled to a halt.

"Spoofing," Kotto said.

"You mean like when you smoke weed and blow the smoke into a Gatorade bottle full of fabric softener sheets? Spoofing."

Kotto stared at his deputy for a moment.

"No."

"Oh."

"The police can collect phone call information—metadata—with those towers. Then they can construct warrants around this illegally-obtained information."

"Do you have that capability, Sheriff?"

"What? I can't even remember my Reddit password. You think I'm capable of illegal surveillance? That's for the 'professional' police."

Veronica slid the side panel door open and stepped out.

"Anyone seen Dean?"

A pickup truck full of men with guns pulled down into the main lodge parking lot. It puttered to a halt behind the van, and Dean jumped down from the side, panting.

"Hey, guys!" he called over. "What did I miss?"

Within the hour, Captain Jimmy Hagerson and his staff had occupied the main lodge. His men moved crates of ammunition, computers, flares, food, water—and even a copy machine—into the restaurant portion of the lodge, a wide and open space with huge glass windows that offered a commanding view of the valley before them and the hills beyond.

Outside, machine gun teams and scouts moved into positions all across the compound. A SAW gunner perched with his ammo bearer on the patio above the swimming pools. Sharpshooters with night vision goggles and M-16s occupied the roof of the hotel. Two-man teams with radios and binoculars slipped down into the valley, taking up positions in and around the abandoned ski lifts and warming huts. A squad patrolled up and down Snow Pine Road, while another set up a cordon at the intersection where the road met 219. The Joes joked about occupying the Burger King across the street, but the first sergeant had briefed them on the risk of psychotropic contamination in the water and food in the area, so that put a stop to that.

Several pickup trucks full of men and women with hunting rifles and shotguns had parked near the National Guard trucks. Sheriff Kotto lined up the volunteers—about 20 in all—in the parking lot behind the news van.

"Repeat after me," Kotto began. "Raise your right hands."

"*Raise your right hands.*"

"No, sorry, I meant—"

"*No, sorry, I meant ...*"

"Dammit!"

"*Dammit!*"

"Ahem. I do solemnly swear to obey my lawful orders, to serve the people of Cattaraugus County ..."

"*I do solemnly swear to obey my lawful orders, to serve the people of Cattaraugus County ...*"

"... to defend the Constitution of New York and of the United States ..."

"*... to defend the Constitution of New York and of the United States ...*"

"... and to oppose any and all forms of malicious supernatural, occult, or alien activity. So help me God."

"*... and to oppose any and all forms of malicious supernatural, occult, or alien activity. So help me God.*"

"You okay with that last bit, Chip? I know you're an

avowed atheist." An old man holding a jet-black AR-15 rifle, with a long gray beard, black leather Road Boys biker jacket, and a bandanna around his head, smiled and nodded.

"Agnostic, Sheriff, but I appreciate the gesture all the same," he grumbled.

"Okay, that's it! You're all official reserve deputies. I want four of you headed down to the roadblock at the end of Snow Pine Road. You are to observe the soldiers and make sure they don't conduct any illegal searches, seizures, or try to violate the Third Amendment. The rest of you, you'll be here, assisting in the defense of the main lodge. This is our red line. We don't give up this post. Not even if the forces of Hell herself come screaming out of those woods. You get me?"

"*Yes, Sheriff!*"

Veronica and Dean were busy getting the shot ready for another live report, this time in front of the Snow Pine Resort sign posted on the front of the main lodge. Behind them, an Ellicottville Volunteer Fire Department truck and ambulance had pulled in and parked just a few spaces down from the National Guard trucks. Volunteers in fire helmets and bulky jackets as well as the EMTs from the ambulance crew milled about and smoked cigarettes, shooting the shit with each other and with nearby soldiers assigned to guard the trucks. The now-deputized volunteer militia mingled about, telling jokes or staring off into the darkness beyond their little perimeter.

One of the volunteer firefighters laid eyes on Richards and Kotto, who stood just outside the main doors to the lodge. He made his way over to them.

"Abe!" the volunteer said, holding out a gloved hand. His fire jacket hung over his bulky frame.

"Mike?" Richards said, smiling. He stepped forward to embrace his friend with a handshake and a hug. "Jeez, I had forgotten you were a volunteer."

"Assistant fire chief, actually," Michael Bryant said. "Glad to see you're okay. I was just thinking we should get beer and wings again, and then all this craziness kicked off. And here you are, joining the Sheriff's department." Michael nodded to Kotto. "Sheriff."

"Fire-person," Kotto responded.

Richards nodded, his smile falling.

"The work's not done yet," Richards said. "We have to stop Bucky."

"What's the plan? Sending in the cavalry?"

"Not quite," Richards said. "Kotto and I are going up. Alone."

"That sounds crazy," Michael said, shaking his head. "There's gotta be a better way, right? Why not just flatten the whole hill if you think he's up there? I'm pretty sure these guys have enough firepower to do that."

"Maybe," Richards said. "That's Plan B. Plan A is we take out Bucky, and this whole thing goes away. No one else has to die."

Michael nodded.

"You don't have to play the hero, you know," he said.

"Says the guy wearing a uniform, who practices running into burning buildings." Michael smiled at that. "And you're right. This whole thing *is* crazy. When you told me Kotto was the sheriff now, and all that crap he believes … But with all the things I've seen in the last few days, I know it isn't as clear-cut as the State Police want us to think. It's not just drugs in the moonshine. It's deeper than that."

"People are seeing UFOs again," Michael said. "You know, I laughed about it when I showed you that newspaper article last time we hung out. But after all this ..." His voice trailed off. "My dad saw a UFO, once. Saw the lights hover right over the house when I was a baby. He never told me that story. Not until tonight, when the call came in to report for duty, not long after Veronica Cartwright and Kotto got on the radio. No shit, he sat me down, and told me about how those lights were over the house, a few weeks after they brought me home from the hospital. He said it scared the hell out of him. It made him feel vulnerable. Like, no matter what he did, he couldn't protect his son. Not really."

Michael turned away from Richards. He watched as Dean changed out the battery pack on his camera.

"He looked scared when he told me that," Michael said. He shook his head.

The two men stood in silence, content to be distracted by the activity and the drama around them.

One of the main glass doors to the lodge opened, and a soldier leaned out.

"Excuse me, Sheriff? Deputy? They're waiting for you."

Richards nodded.

"Time to go," he said.

"Yeah," Michael said, voice low and solemn. "I suppose we've all got our parts to play."

"Listen," Richards said. "We might be taking casualties. There's a lot of firepower here, and if Bucky's up there, he's got a whole army of crazy people. If there's a battle here, it's going to be bad. Just promise me something."

"What?"

"Promise me that you'll treat everybody who comes in, whether it's a soldier or one of *them*. You can do that, right?"

"I'm trained to do two things," Michael said. "Put out fires, and keep people alive until they get to the hospital. And I'm pretty good at both."

"Then you're probably going to do more good for this community than I can," Richards said. He extended his hand. "Good luck, Mike."

"You too." They shook hands, and Michael returned to the fire truck. One of the newly-sworn in reserve deputies handed him a bottle of water, which he took with a smile.

Kotto approached Richards, the scent of dead cigarettes wafting over with him.

"You ready to go brief these guys?" Kotto asked. He put a hand on his deputy's shoulder.

"Aren't you laying out the plan?"

"You know it as well as I do. Besides, these soldiers are your people, not mine. They'll follow, if you're ready to lead."

Richards looked over to Michael, who was giving orders to the volunteer firefighters and EMTs around him. Michael directed them to lay out stretchers, to prep supplies, to lay down tarps.

As long as the rain held off, they'd triage right there in the parking lot.

33. We Need Heroes

The emergency lights cast the dining area in a pale orange glow, lending their faces a spectral, Jack O'Lantern quality. Halloween had come early to Snow Pine Resort.

Captain Jimmy Hagerson, his first sergeant, his platoon leaders and platoon sergeants, old man Chip of the reserve deputies, and the volunteer fire chief gathered in a semi-circle around Kotto and Richards. The sheriff and deputy stood with their backs to the tall glass windows that stretched wide to reveal the valley and hills upon which the fate of the county would be decided. Veronica and Dean stood to the side; the light from Dean's camera spotlighted Richards and Kotto, washing away the orange light from the emergency lights above.

Captain Hagerson nodded to Richards, who cleared his throat and stepped forward.

"Good evening gentlemen. My name is Deputy Abraham Richards, and this is Sheriff Cecil Kotto. Thank you for your support of this operation." Richards took a moment to let this words sink in, to give the delay of introduction before the actual brief. He made eye contact with everyone in the group as he spoke, telling himself to keep his words slow and his voice clear. It was funny how easy it was to slip back into soldier-leader mode. It felt like coming home.

"We've got one main road in and out of here," he said. "We need to keep it secure. We've got a cordon of Alpha Company soldiers and some volunteer deputies at the intersection of 219 and Snow Pine Road. Their orders are to let only law enforcement, military, and emergency personnel through. All others will be waved off. If more volunteers show up, send them to defend the Burger King." He smiled, and a few soldiers offered muted laughs. Richards pointed to the windows behind him. "We've set up our defense here, in and around the main lodge complex. Captain Hagerson's men have established zones of defensive fire up the ski slopes, with the weapons-free red line just beyond the creek at the edge of the courtyard. That means if anybody sets foot that far down, abandon your sectors of fire and focus on keeping them out of the complex.

"National Guard medics and local fire and EMT service personnel have set up the casualty collection point in the parking lot in front of the main lodge, directly behind you. Keep them safe! Volunteer deputies will be defending that area. Most of them can probably shoot better than you weekend warriors, so don't worry about that."

More laughter. Good. They were keeping it light.

"At about 2200 hours, Captain Hagerson is going to give the order to fire off flares, and do a probe-by-fire into the hillside. We're not looking to start a battle, but if Bucky's army is in those hills, we need to draw their attention here. My guess is that they already know we're here. So all we gotta do is poke the bear.

"By that time, Sheriff Kotto and I will already be about half a mile up Snow Pine Road, headed toward the Christmas Tree Lodge. We plan to follow the service road there up to the abandoned construction site. We believe that's where we'll find Bucky."

"And what are you going to do once you get there?" Captain Hagerson asked. "Arrest him?"

"If we can, yes," Kotto said, stepping forward. "I have reason to believe that the suspect is not acting of his own free will. There are larger forces at work here. Now you soldier boys just showed up, so you got no idea what we've been dealing with. But for those of you who've been here for the last couple of weeks, you know that the story the State Troopers are putting out and the news media is ignoring ain't adding up. It's horse puckey, if you'll pardon my Latin." Kotto gestured to Veronica and Dean. "You see that sexy lady reporter over there? Well, she's the only one who's interested in getting the truth out. I'd appreciate it if you all gave her some of your time when you got a chance."

"I can give you two til dawn," Captain Hagerson said, his arms crossed in front of his chest, all business. "After that, if we know Bucky's forces are up in those hills, I'm going to take the fight to him. I've already been in touch with the State Troopers, and they're going to be deploying their men here in a couple of hours to join us in the big push. I can't delay an attack any longer than that."

"Roger that," Richards said. "And one more thing—stay positive. If people start getting scared, if things go bad and people begin to panic—we could lose this thing."

"So you want us to think happy thoughts, Richards?" Hagerson asked, smirking.

"That's exactly what I'm saying, Captain. You have a problem with that?"

Hagerson nodded, the smile not leaving his face. "Ha. No, I guess I don't. But I don't get it."

"There's a lot about this situation we don't

understand," Kotto said. "But I can tell you that we need to hold the line here. If Richards and I don't make it, your best hope is to take that hill. And whatever you find up there, you destroy it. Don't let anyone take any of that moonshine or anything else you find up there. Burn it. Burn it all with fire."

"What else would we find?" Hagerson asked.

"I don't know, rightly," Kotto said. "But whatever it is he's doing up there, it ain't good. We've got to stop him, tonight, one way or another. Otherwise all the firepower in the world ain't going to be able to stop what's coming. Any other questions, people? No? Alright. Then let's get moving." Kotto clapped his hands together, and the group broke. The soldiers huddled around Captain Hagerson; the fire chief and others made their way back outside.

Kotto clapped Richards on the back.

"Here goes nothing, Deputy."

Dean flicked off the camera light, and the room fell back into that quiet orange glow.

"You two are going up alone?" Veronica asked, stepping forward. "That's your big plan? Go it alone? Why not take some soldiers with you at least? Or some of these crazy militia people?"

"Bucky's one of ours," Kotto said. "He's from here. He's one of us, even if what he's done is terrible. Besides, I work better alone. Or, almost alone. We take half a dozen guys up there, it's likely that one of them starts shooting. We can move faster alone, quieter. I don't want to start a battle here. I think that's what *they* want."

"But why do this? They're cheering for you, following you now, but ..." Veronica let her voice trail off. "Just a few days ago, they all thought you were crazy. I mean, I *still* think you're crazy, and I've seen as much of all this as anybody else. When this is all over, they'll go back to laughing at you. You know that, right?"

Kotto turned away from Veronica. He stared out into the darkness.

"Why do this for them?" she asked, placing a hand on his shoulder, briefly, before pulling it back. "Do you think they deserve it?"

"Maybe we deserve a lot worse than what Bucky's done to us," Kotto said. "I'm thinking we may have had this coming for a while. You can't build a castle on sand. And you can't build a country on blood. Sooner or later, that bill comes due. Looks like maybe now, we're the ones to pay it."

"So why do this?"

"If there's a chance we can save Bucky and those people under his control, I've got to take it. We need people willing to stand up for the little guy, even if the odds are against him. Even if it costs us everything." Kotto pulled a cigarette out from his BDU jacket and stuck it between his lips. He pulled up a metal Zippo lighter and leaned the cigarette into the flame. His face was framed by light and shadow. He clicked the lighter shut again, and let the smoke escape out his wide nostrils.

"We need heroes," he said.

"And you're it, huh? You're gonna save the world with a shotgun and a burnout for a sidekick?" Veronica cast a glance at Richards. "No offense."

"None taken."

Kotto shrugged.

"Depends on how you tell the story, I guess." Kotto pulled his shotgun from his shoulder, and pumped once, chambering a round. "But that's your job. Now we gotta go do ours."

34. Probe-by-Fire

The lights of the main lodge complex faded behind them. Ahead, the night waited.

They followed the fresh pavement of Snow Pine Road deeper into the valley. The road was a straight shot west, past empty parking lots cut into the hills, waiting for the inevitable yearly rush of cars and skiers and snowboarders piled into family SUVs, buses, cars.

Soon, they were in near-complete darkness.

"Let's pop the IR sticks," Richards whispered. They paused, standing in the middle of the road. It reminded Richards of being a teenager again, walking along the country roads into deep midnights, no traffic or people out for miles. It felt like youth. It felt like breaking the rules.

He snapped the glowstick, then shook it. He stared at the plastic cylinder, expecting some sort of illumination, despite his knowledge that the only light it emitted was outside the visual spectrum. The soldiers wearing their night vision goggles would be able to see the stick as a glowing streak. The idea was, if they had to rush back to the main lodge, the scouts and gunners would see the glowsticks and hold their fire. Richards tucked the stick snugly into the vest he wore, placing the glowstick in an empty magazine pouch and buttoning it shut to secure the source of infrared light. Kotto slipped his through an empty slot on his shotgun shell bandoleer.

"I hope Bucky's minions can't see infrared light," Kotto said.

"Is that possible?"

"Anything's possible."

They walked on.

They stuck to the center of the road, as their footfalls on wet pavement were quieter than trying to push through brush and bush. The parking lots gave way to stretches of trees hiding private condo drives leading up to lavish weekend cabins built in the Alpine style. Richards realized that, despite working here, despite his friends and family working at or around Snow Pine—few of them would ever be able to afford such luxuries. What were seasonal, weekend getaway cabins for the out-of-town folks cost just as much, or more, as the houses that many people in and around Ellicottville owned and struggled to maintain. The resort brought opportunity, sure. But it also highlighted disparity. Richards didn't have an answer for that.

The lights behind them were lost to curves in the road and the weight of the trees pressing in from all sides. Kotto and Richards both moved with their shotguns bared, barrels pointing forward or at a slight angle toward the ground. Every snapping twig, every falling branch, every erratic drumbeat of dripping water on fallen leaves implied menace and threat.

Richards knew that this plan was no plan at all. They were flying blind—almost literally, as they could barely see a few feet in front of them at a time—and for all they knew, they could be walking right into an ambush. The events of the past few days played out again in his mind; memory conjured the images of men with chainsaws, women shoving gore into their mouths, families tearing apart their victims, eyes alight with smoke and fire.

Snow Pine Road stretched on further west, leading up to more private drives, cabins, and condos. It wound up like a crooked finger into the tall hills. As Kotto and Richards set foot onto the access road that led down to the Christmas Tree Lodge parking lot—which provided access to the ski lifts that stood deepest within the woods—machine gun fire echoed throughout the valley. At first, Kotto mistook the distant, dull booming to be a part of the cacophony of water dripping down from the tree branches all around them, but the intensity and volume soon overshadowed his first impression.

"That's the probe-by-fire," Richards said. "If there's anything hiding in the trees on the hillside, it's gonna get real dead."

The chattering of the SAWs continued. From the sounds of things, Richards figured, they were firing from three different positions. But it was hard to tell at this distance.

"Look, a light," Kotto said, pointing behind them. A red-orange glow grew from behind the trees, faint and distant. "Jesus, I hope it's not another flying saucer."

"Just flares," Richards said. "The soldiers are letting Bucky know exactly where they are. I hope he's stupid enough to go for it."

"I think he's been expecting it," Kotto said. "I think a battle is all part of the plan."

Richards thought back to the time, only a few days ago, when Kotto gave him newspaper clippings, money, string, photographs, articles. Kotto had told him to figure it out, figure out the conspiracy. The big picture. He'd done his best—he'd done *something*. Kotto had seen something in what Richards strung together. Richards wasn't sure there was anything *to* see.

"Do you still think I'm crazy?" Kotto asked. Richards shook his head, but his gesture was lost in the dark between them.

"Let's keep moving," Richards said.

The ski lift was a holdover from the 1980s—blocky construction housing wheels, gears, and a metal engine that roared too loud when the doors to the machine's guts were left open. The thin metal chairs clinging to steel wire could hold only three skiers at a time as they carried their payload up the long trip to the top of the Christmas Tree trail. A dim memory haunted Richards, emerging from the dark and tugging at emotions and images that stirred to half-life. His mother and his father, sitting on either side of him, his face cold, his little legs dangling over the edge of the chair as it lifted higher and higher, the lift pulling them up and along the slow incline of the hill. The ground seemed so very far away to his child eyes.

Kotto led Richards along a side trail that weaved away and back onto the main run of Christmas Tree along its western side. The grass was overgrown and wet, soaking their camo pants as they made their way up. They stuck to the edge of the trees, the dark of night sufficient for stealth, with additional concealment from the low-hanging boughs of pine trees that twisted and swayed over the swath of open trail. Richards would have preferred to move through the woods, but Kotto had nixed that idea. They'd make more noise traveling through thick brush, and they would never reach the summit in time. But even in the full dark with clouds overhead, Richards felt exposed. Eyes were upon them from every direction. Or so his instincts screamed.

Kotto walked ahead of him. In the darkness, Richards could only make out Kotto's dark form ahead. Mostly he followed the soft *swish-swish* of Kotto's BDU jacket, and the soft footfalls his boots made on grass overrun with rainwater.

The path they followed curved away from the main trail, then arced back in a lazy loop to reconnect at a point higher up. Both men huffed with effort; although Christmas Tree was a Green Circle—low skill—it was much, much steeper than it seemed. Sweat was gathering along their foreheads; Kotto stopped at several points to remove his helmet and to silently curse his smoking habit. Richards appreciated the short breaks, but the tension of time hung over their efforts. Every moment spent resting was another moment Bucky could use to complete whatever it was that he was doing up on that hill, assuming he was even up there. Every moment moved them closer to some bloody confrontation. They hoped the soldiers positioned at the main ski lodge would distract Bucky's psychotic moonshine army, but they didn't want there to be a full-on battle.

What if we get lost? Richards found himself thinking. *What if we can't find Bucky's still?* And then: *What if Bucky isn't up here at all?*

Those thoughts entered Richards' mind as Kotto halted again. He walked back to Richards, who took the opportunity to catch his breath.

"We'll cut across the hill here," Kotto whispered. "I'm pretty sure the access road is just a hundred yards that way."

"Are we halfway up the hill?" Richards asked. "I could have sworn we passed that point already."

"Slow going in the dark," Kotto said. "No, the access road to the construction site should curve this way. We just gotta cut through that scrub to get there."

Richards looked around, for all the good that did him.

"And if Bucky's got eyes on that road?"

"Then we're all gonna die," Kotto said, matter-of-fact. "We'll burn that bridge club when we get there."

"What?"

"I said, 'we'll burn that bridge club when we get there.' It means we'll deal with it then."

"No, that's not what that means."

"What's it mean, then?"

"A 'bridge club' is a bunch of old ladies playing cards."

"Right."

"So you want to burn a bunch of old ladies? Why would you say that?"

"It's an expression. Blame the culture for giving me such sick words to use," Kotto said.

"That's not the expression."

"We'll debate the finer points of ancient Greek when this is all over," Kotto said. He stepped into the tree line. "In the meantime, let's fiddle this dally-do."

35. Blood Moon

The trees themselves conspired against Sheriff Cecil Kotto and Deputy Abraham Richards. Branches scratched at their faces. Trunks barred their paths. Fallen leaves concealed deadfalls in the dark. Their progress was slow, painful. Kotto had estimated the access road was only a hundred yards away; it took them an hour to find it.

When they emerged onto the narrow open space, Richards breathed a sigh of relief. Each step through that treacherous grove between ski trail and access road was bought with the price of sweat, of burning muscles, of twisted ankles, of scratches in flesh of face and bruises beneath rain-soaked pants. The jacket Richards wore under his assault vest was soaked through as well, and hung limp and heavy over his shoulders. His skin was beginning to itch, his feet were burning with growing blisters. He'd been through Hell these last few days, and it was finally catching up with him. He just wanted to tumble down into the weeds and sleep—or die, whatever came first. But Richards was a soldier—or had been, not too long ago—and he had learned early on in his time in the military that exhaustion was just something to be ignored.

To Kotto's credit, the sheriff showed few signs of

slowing down, and hadn't complained or second-guessed the plan, at least not out loud. They'd moved along the main road then cut up the ski slope, then cut over to the access road. That offered them an easier path to the summit, but also gave them erratic movement and kept them close to concealment. If anyone was following them, they hadn't let on, or had been lost behind them. It was a dangerous mix of speed and stealth, definitely tilted in the former's favor. But they didn't have much choice. Sooner rather than later, the National Guard unit would break their defensive positions and go hunting for Bucky and anyone else who was still under his control. That, or the fight would come to them.

As they made their way up the access road, which transitioned into a switchback that wound and curved and twisted at seemingly impossible angles, they heard the gunfire. It came from well behind them, to the east. The gunfire, such as it was, was sporadic. When it popped off the first time, Richards stood still and listened.

"Rifles," Richards said. "Firing M-4s, maybe M-16s from the sharpshooters. They're saving the SAWs."

"Might be just a few bad guys, then," Kotto said, hope in his voice. He turned and looked up the road, which curved back around and led back above them. "There's not much time. We have to keep moving."

The orange light ahead was no flare. Fire, unmistakable in scent and sight.

Kotto had spotted it first, the fingers of light scratching at the boughs and sky above. He led Richards off the unpaved road, just on the inside of the forest's edge. The trees pressed together here, despite the elevation.

"How much you wanna bet that's our boy?" Kotto asked, kneeling down in the dark. He slipped off his helmet. Steam drifted up from his scalp. "We better be ready to shoot." He swung the shotgun from his shoulder down, and ran his fingers along its familiar stock.

"What's the plan, then?" Richards asked.

"We gotta scout it out first," Kotto said. "We'll move up this side of the hill, away from the trail. Real slow. We gotta see how many of them are up here."

"And if they're all just standing around up here?" Richards asked. "What if Bucky's still got a security detail hanging around? Or if he didn't send any of them to go fight the soldiers?"

"We'll burn that bridge club when we come to it," Kotto said. "Alright. Let's go."

The earth flattened out. The trees became thin.

A massive fire illuminated the quarter acre-wide clearing. It cast sinister light and fell shadow on a pair of bulldozers parked side-by-side. Stacks of concrete bricks, bundled metal cables, piles of lumber covered in plastic tarps, mobile light generators, felled trees, and piles of bulldozed dirt stood in concentric circles around the center of the clearing, at which the sinister heart of flame burned and pulsed.

At the edge of the clearing, Kotto and Richards leaned out from behind withered trees, their leaves long since shed.

"Do you see anyone?" Richards whispered. Kotto shook his head *no*.

The flames burned bright, stuffed full of fresh wood from the construction caches and felled trees. A few of the generators hummed diesel power. Barrels of what Kotto presumed to be shine—or the ingredients thereof—stood in little groups of six, scattered about the area. People *had* been here. Had they all simply left the moment they heard the machine gun fire? Was their ruse too effective?

The fire cast the whole area in that wicked Halloween-pumpkin orange. The only movement the two men could discern was that of the trees rustling in the wind, and that of shadow.

Kotto waved Richards to follow, then he darted over to the first pile of wood wrapped in plastic. The men cut across the open, hunched low, shotguns at the ready, hearts pumping oil. Richards hadn't been this tired since the war, and Kotto hadn't been this burned out since his last all-weekend bender, staying up late listening to old episodes of *Infowars* and *Coast to Coast AM* on YouTube. But at the sight of the fire, at the sound of the generators, at the feeling of being *here*, where Bucky had been, they were energized with a perverse mix of fear and anticipation. Reality took on that iron-tinged spark, the taste of blood almost in their mouths, the sharpness of the cold air cutting through their lungs.

They reached the long band of wood; two-by-fours cut into planks over a dozen feet in length. Lumber used for framing buildings. Maybe the bones of a new mountaintop coffee spot, or even a new stretch of condos, high among the snow-capped hills of Snow Pine's luxurious winter nights. But for now, it was merely cover on a battlefield.

Kotto peeked up over the edge. Richards made to inch up as well, but just as fast as Kotto went up, he dropped back down behind the planks.

"One, in front of the fire," Kotto said. "Did you see him?"

"I didn't see anything," Richards admitted. "Are there any more of them?"

"Just the one I saw," Kotto said. "Stay down. I'll check again."

Kotto creeped up again, staying low. Richards estimated they were about fifty yards from the edge of the fire. If someone was standing there, it was unlikely he'd seen them as they left the concealment of the trees and made their way closer.

Kotto bent back down.

"Yeah. Just one. Can't see much of him—or her. No one else's home."

"What are the chances it's Bucky?"

Kotto shrugged.

"Let's take this bastard down and sort out the rest later. If it's him, great, we get to go home. If it's not, well …"

"We'll burn that bridge club when we come to it," Richards said. "Okay. I'm ready."

"I'm gonna cut right, you go left," Kotto said. "But keep me in the corner of your eye. Don't drift too far off target and get grabbed by some shadow person lurking in the dark."

"What's a shadow person?"

"Hopefully you won't have to find out," Kotto said. "On three. One. Two …"

The sheriff popped up, shotgun raised. Richards stood up and went left, staring down the barrel of his shotgun at the dark form ahead of them.

They moved slow, deliberate, their footsteps in the wet leaves and grass drown out by the crackling and roaring of the pyre ahead of them, that great ball of flame that burned orange and evil.

Kotto's eyes darted from side to side, keeping

Richards in his peripheral vision, his shotgun pointed at the man standing ahead of them, and casting an all-too-frequent glance into the dark at his flank. They hadn't come all this way just to get chainsawed at the last moment by some moonshined crazy who caught them unawares as they closed in on their suspect.

Each step forward took an eternity. Each breath in and out was louder than ever before. His finger caught rainwater or sweat along the rim of the trigger well, aching to press up against that little lever and let the man ahead of them eat a deer slug to the chest.

The figure's features and form were pure night-black against the heavy light of hungry fire. The adrenaline-fear-excitement in Richards' mind shifted *just enough* to let a single, coherent thought through:

Something's not right.

Fifty feet away from the person ahead of them.

Forty.

Thirty.

Ten feet, the fire hot on their faces now. Kotto's eyes fought the light from the fire, then stretched open again when he looked away. It was hard to see, but the form was right in front of them, Richards moving in from the left, Kotto on the right. He could reach out and almost touch the suspect—

"I sent them away to fight your army," the man said—clearly a man, his voice low and throaty, his words tinged with a bit of that anachronistic Western New York country folk twang. "We're all alone now, just you and me, just us three …"

"Hands up and turn around!" Kotto shouted. But truth be told, he couldn't see if the man was turned away from them or not.

"Hands up!" Richards echoed, giving his best command voice.

Kotto's eyes adjusted to the dark. The figure before

them let his head droop forward, but then he turned around. His hands slowly drifted up in mock surrender.

"I knew you were here the moment you stepped foot in these woods," the man said, his voice soft and confident, carrying to them over the din of the fire behind him and the generators running somewhere in the darkness beyond.

Kotto focused on the man, squinting against the fire. His eyes adjusted, revealing the features of the figure before him.

"Bucky. Jesus, it's him."

"In the flesh," the fugitive replied. "Or, as my uncle Bill used to say: 'in my skins and hollers.' I never understood what he meant by that."

"Keep your hands above your head, and get down on your knees," Kotto said, the calm in his voice hovering over a pool of chaos and uncertainty beneath. "No sudden moves, Buck."

"Sheriff Cecil Kotto," Bucky said, more to himself. "We played football against each other once, did you know that? You were a senior, and I was a freshman. No, wait, they're telling me you graduated early. You couldn't have been a senior. Maybe a junior, then? What position did you play? Wait, wait, don't tell me. They will. You were a running back, and you played outside linebacker. A starter, too, that last season. And no wonder you guys did so well that year—and you beat us—you wrote the playbook, didn't you? How'd you ever get the coach to go along with *that*?"

"I never told anyone that," Kotto said. "Are you in my head, Bucky? Those alien bastards give you telepathy, too?"

"Alien bastards?" Bucky said. He lifted his head up to look Kotto square in the eye. Kotto saw now what a sorry shape the fugitive was in—he was rail thin, his skin was pale, his hair wild and unkempt. He'd been on the run too long. And something else was wrong. Something else was drawing out the health from his bones. Something within, causing him to wither.

"I used to think they were aliens, too. Did you know that's what that government agent told me? They were aliens, and they were here to help. They've been here since the beginning—our beginnings, man and woman and all them babies they had back in Bible times and even before. That government man told me half the truth. Lies go down sweeter that way, don't they? When they're mixed with the truth? That's your specialty, isn't it Sheriff Cecil Kotto? You go on your little radio show and people laugh at your crazy theories and your stories, and some people even take them seriously. And you *know* half of what you put out is BS. Half of what you put out is *lies*. But you say them anyway, because those lies give you a sort of *power*, right? A sort of magic. And people will listen."

"Buck, I need you to keep those hands up," Kotto said, his voice beginning to shake with anger. "Richards, get the cuffs ready."

"They won't let you take me alive," Bucky said.

"I don't care what the State Troopers want. If you're my arrest, they can't touch you."

"I'm not talking about the State Troopers," Bucky said, shaking his head. "Sheriff, they tell me so many things about you. How *smart* you are. How much you've managed to piece together, just outta bits of lie and crumbs of truth. But I'm wonderin' if maybe they give you too much credit."

"Shut up."

"Sure, it's the Troopers who want me dead," Bucky said. "But the visitors need me to keep going. They need me to complete *my work*."

"Shut up, Bucky. I'm not gonna tell you again."

"They won't let me *stop*, Sheriff. They'll never let

me stop. They want me to keep working til the flesh falls off these fingers. Til the whole damn county drinks my shine, and keeps drinking, and keeps killing, and their fear keeps spreading, til every last one of you is theirs—"

Richards brought his balled fist across Bucky's face. He fell down into the leaves and mud. Richards slung his shotgun over his shoulder, then sat down on top of Bucky's back, forcing his knee into the moonshiner's spine.

"That hurts," Bucky said.

"You've killed a lot of people," Richards said. "Why'd you do it, man? Why'd you do it?" Richards pulled Bucky's hands down and to the base of his back, then snapped the metal cuffs over his wrists. The deputy realized this was the first time he had actually done this to someone. Not bad field experience.

"They have many names," Bucky said, his voice flat. "They gave me so much. They took more, sure, but who's countin'?"

"All of these people dead," Richards said, rage bubbling to the surface. "They tried to kill *me*, the Sheriff. I don't even know if my parents are okay."

"They know the names of your parents, Abraham Richards," Bucky said. "They tell me to tell you that they know their names, and they've visited them many times. Did you know that your mother saw them, once? Ask her about those three lights in the sky, Christmas Eve, 1973, over your grandmother's house."

"Shut your mouth," Richards said.

"Your grandmother," Bucky said. "You know. The one who went *crazy*. What name did she call you, Abraham Richards? What name did she call you when you saw her that last time, before the rot in her brain and bones took her to the worms of the earth?"

"*Shut the fuck up*," Richards snapped. He shuffled

back and pulled Bucky up by his cuffed wrists. The suspect grunted in pain, but stood up as well.

"Where's your cadre of crazies?" Kotto asked, lowering his shotgun.

"I told you," Bucky said, spitting out a mouthful of leaves and wet dirt. "I sent them down the mountain. They should be walking into the fire soon."

"Why would you do that? If you knew we were coming, why'd you send them to get slaughtered?"

"It wasn't me, not really," Bucky said, his voice sounding hollow and distant. "Do you think it'll be enough of a sacrifice to complete the spell? I don't understand the ritual here, no more than you do." The handsome, smart-aleck smirk on his face disappeared, replaced with a flat, terrified expression, his eyes bulging wide. "I don't want those people to die," he said. "I didn't want any of this—" Bucky twisted his head to the side, his eyes slamming shut. "Oh, *fuck*," he said. A tremor shook through his limbs. Richards put a hand on Bucky's arm to steady him. "Help me, get them *out* of *me* or please God just *kill me—*"

The convulsion ceased just as suddenly as it had started. Kotto walked forward and lifted Bucky's head up by his wide chin. The suspect's eyes slapped open, wide pools of glass reflecting Kotto's face in the light of the fire.

"I'm feeling much better now," he said, his voice a monotone. He turned to stare at Deputy Richards, Bucky's sudden nonchalance and dead voice sending a shiver into the deputy, cold sweat washing down his spine. For just a moment, his hands rebelled, threatening to release their grip on Bucky.

"I don't like this, Sheriff," Richards said, not sure why, but meaning it.

Bucky's head snapped up, fast, *too fast*, so that he stared at the sky above. Richards and Kotto followed his gaze.

Trails of smoke from the wide fire clawed their way skyward. In the glow of the flames, Kotto and Richards did not notice that the clouds above the clearing had parted. But the mystical light that soaked the clearing didn't just come from the fire Bucky had built. It also came from above.

"My God," Kotto said.

The leering red face of earth's moon grinned down at them, large, far too large, its surface dripping with a red-orange radiance. It was closer and bigger than Kotto had ever seen, making the typical harvest moon appear slight in comparison. This moon threatened to engulf the sky; it threatened to *fall out* of the sky, its every detail on its pockmarked, familiar surface suddenly grown to impossible size and clarity.

"The sky is theirs and the moon is hollow," Bucky said, his words like a recited prayer. "Everything we've been taught is a lie."

Heat and smoke bubbled out of Richards' left hand. The metal handcuffs had grown red-hot, searing his palm and fingertips, even through his gloves. Instinct pulled his hand away; Bucky simply wiggled his wrists and the handcuffs melted off, leaving searing trails of blackened flesh to trail smoke where the cuffs had met his skin.

"Sheriff …" Richards said, backing away.

"That's the biggest goddamn blood moon I've ever seen," Kotto said.

"Sheriff!"

Kotto looked down in time to see Bucky outstretch his left hand. The man's face was completely blank: no triumphant, sinister smile; no pained expression of sorrow. Neutral. Smoke began to rise from his eyes. Something deep within glowed, and glowed hot.

Beams of blue-green light sprouted from Bucky's

fingertips, joining together in a five-pointed star in the center of his palm. Then the *rush* of air crackling with force and fury, and the bolt of gathered light hit Kotto square in the chest, sending him flying back endlessly into the dark.

36. Congregation of the Night

Richards didn't hesitate.

He brought the butt of his shotgun down on Bucky's head, once—sending him staggering—twice—dropping him to the earth. He flipped the gun around and leveled the barrel at Bucky's back. The safety was off; his finger did a nervous little shake as it caressed the trigger.

"Don't make me blow your head off, man," Richards said. "We didn't come here to kill you."

"No, I suppose you didn't," Bucky said, that voice still flat, emotionless. "And you didn't come here at all, at least not in the way you think." With a crack of bone, Bucky turned his head to peer over his right shoulder. Blood dripped down from the back of his skull, leaking down to the collar of his shirt and arcing over his right ear. "*They* sent you here. Did you know that? They wanted you here. Wanted you to see more of the board. More of the pieces moving."

"*They* nothing," Richards said. He looked off in the direction in which Kotto had gone flying—really *flying*. Whatever that juice was Bucky had hit the sheriff with, it packed a punch.

"Sheriff Kotto!" he yelled. "You alright?" Richards glanced around. The fire was still roaring, and the moon leered bigger and brighter than ever. The deputy realized he could see all the way to the edge of the trees now. Everything in the clearing was so ... sharp. Brighter, even, in that orange-red incandescence.

"That hurt!" Kotto yelled back, from somewhere distant. Maybe from within the trees. "Jesus!"

"You okay?"

"He fucked up my jacket and my glasses," Kotto shouted from the dark. "I think they melted off. Is my gun back there?"

"They know so many things," Bucky said, his voice quivering. The impassivity melted away from his face, and his words turned to groans of pain and anguish. Tears trickled out of his fiery eyes. "Kill me, Abraham Richards. Please, kill me."

"What?" Richards asked. "What the fuck is wrong with you? You just tried to kill the Sheriff!"

"I held it back as best as I could ..." Bucky let out a gurgling scream that grew into a roar, his throat shaking with inhuman force. Richards stumbled back, the air around Bucky suddenly charged with blistering static and blue sparks. The roar echoed out over the clearing; the trees along its perimeter shook with the force of the cry, shedding whatever leaves remained, branches snapping off and tumbling to the wet earth below.

Bucky's slumped body jerked up, as if pulled by invisible strings. His arms shot out and braced him against the mud, and he pushed himself to stand back up. Richards aimed the shotgun directly at him.

Fuck this, he thought, his finger finding the trigger once more. *No more chances.*

The orange glow came to him as he aimed down the shotgun's sights. The front sight post wormed its way from side to side, then dipped low to the ground. Richards scowled and looked up from behind the rear sight post just in time to see the shotgun's barrel drip, blazing orange and hot, down like lava to pool on the ground below.

The orange light along the barrel slid back toward him, infusing the metal chamber with that inward glow. Smoke rose from the gun and Richards tossed it aside. Heat from dripping metal.

When Bucky spoke again, his voice was different. Truth be told, it wasn't Bucky speaking, and it wasn't his voice at all. It was the voice of a thousand insects, swarming over desert carrion. It was the voice of the unrepentant murderer on Death Row, cracking jokes before his time in the chair. It was the voice of wild dogs tearing into their own flesh. It was the voice of War and Ruin, and of all the harm and evil that had piled itself onto the blood-soaked countryside.

"We know your name, Abraham Richards. We know so much about you. We love you, Abraham Richards. We will embrace you. You and the Sheriff and your parents and this whole county and everyone within and beyond its borders. We are here for you."

Richards wheeled back. Bucky—or whatever was controlling him now—turned his body to face Richards. Flames licked out from his eyes, his nostrils, his leering smile. His hair burned off in plumes of thin black smoke. The skin along his skull boiled and dripped down onto his shoulders. His right ear glided down a river of melted fat and flesh.

"We have so many names," he said. *"Every name of every murderer, of every rapist, of every tyrant, of every little rebel-god that you make yourselves to be, and every one you will ever spawn. We have your name, Abraham Richards. And we see so many things ..."*

Richards, terrified beyond the capacity for rational thought, backed up. The humming from above jerked his attention away from the hideous specter before him.

Overhead, the flying saucer. Bone-white framing superstructure; panels of gray metal that glowed with unholy fire. One panel rotated into view, revealing a perfect pyramid cut into its side. The fire within started at the bottom and worked its way up, sparking a flaming torch at its apex: a pair of concentric ovals. An all-seeing eye.

The saucer revolved into view, clearing the trees and moving to settle over the clearing, framing itself over most of the blood moon, turning that hideous face into a bright and terrible blood-red sickle.

"Harvest time is here."

The light from that all-seeing eye grew too bright to look at; Richards shut his eyes hard and turned away, the light after-burn lingering in his vision, even as he closed his eyes. He stumbled back, disoriented, desperate to keep any distance between himself and whatever Bucky had become. When he managed to open his eyes again, he was facing the edge of the clearing.

Red eyes, reflecting the fire below and the moon and unholy light from above. Long faces, bodies hunched low. Teeth, flashing sharp and bright.

Wolves, Richards' mind sputtered. It spit out any phrase that came to mind, desperate to assign meaning to what he was seeing: *The Boy Who Cried Wolf. Little Red Riding Hood.*

Waves of heat radiated around them. From the fire, or from something else—perhaps reality itself shifting and writhing in tortured holographic expression. They became indistinct, forms within and of the darkness. Wolf, yes, and then man—bipedal, at least, but with those same yellow fire-mirror eyes. Then snakes, large and perched back, ready to strike, hoods wide and glowing with blood. Then worms, piles of writhing and mottled mass, a thousand hungry maggots or worse, stretching out and reforming into new and hideous shapes and forms.

Richards turned from that rank of unspeakable phantasms. Bucky had done nothing to follow him, but that grinning skull's head remained trained on him.

The blood, next, it said, not with words, but with image, with impression. *We'll start with yours, son of man.*

Bucky reached out a shaking arm, palm open, fingers extended. The spectral blue-green light glow from each fingertip cascaded down to form that perfect pentagram in his palm. What flesh and muscle remained on Bucky's face formed an imperfect grin; blackened, fire-soaked teeth cracking in a horrible pastiche of human delight.

Richards, horrified, his vision wavering between shifting realities of heat and primal fear, stood helpless as the light in Bucky's palm grew.

"Kotto-Fu, motherfucker!"

Out of the shimmering dark, Sheriff Kotto, his jacket gone, his body armor vest burnt and black, flew through the air to deliver a downward thrust from his own mangled and melted shotgun. The crack of spectral energy shook the air as Bucky misfired the bolt of malignant light, sending the eerie stream harmlessly into the forest beyond. Bucky's form staggered under the blow, and, before he could recover, Richards ran forward, full speed, his K-Bar knife held out before him.

The blade pierced Bucky's rib cage, releasing a torrent of specters and spooks—long-limbed spirit-things that howled and cried and opened mouths of feral, gnashing teeth, eyes yellow and large and bodies dripping with ectoplasmic sinew. These spirits drifted out and up toward the flying saucer above, screaming bloody hell and murder, shaking the forest with their groans of rage.

Fire shot out from all sides of the UFO—each panel's symbol alight with fury; orange sparks and streaming liquid flame to the earth below. Fire and death rained down around them. Smoke and ash filled the air, heralding doom.

The wolves—or the snakes, or the men, or the worms of the night—moved in from all sides of the clearing. Jaws snapped and morphed, twisting into long, large things full of hideous orange teeth. Howling, hungry, preparing to cross the threshold between worlds, impatient for the blood and the ritual, satisfied instead to dine on the two interlopers attacking their avatar.

Kotto dropped the shotgun and pulled out his pistol. Bucky's skull-face turned toward him in that final moment, rage etched along bits of fat and flesh still clinging to his brow and cheeks; those fire-eyes brighter and more furious than ever.

Kotto fired. The powder ignited; the bullet propelled forward. The pistol's slide flew back, ejecting the empty casing from the chamber, then slid back forward once more. Kotto fired again, and again, until the skull-head disintegrated, and collapsed, blood and bits of brain and bone spattering out in all directions. Bucky's body—still in flames—fell in slow motion to the waiting earth.

A voice on the radio:

"Jackrabbit Six, this is Sharpshooter One, reporting in from the east tower, over."

Captain Hagerson turned from the windows. He—

and everyone else in the room—stared out at the moon which had appeared in a sudden break in the clouds. The sight of that big red orb emerging out of the total darkness had drawn all of their attention, sending fear into the hearts of his already-jittery men. Combat veterans or no, something that goddamn weird had an effect on anyone.

It had even managed to shut up Major George Winston of the State Troopers, who had come by to personally berate the company commander for not following *his* owners. The State Trooper commander followed Hagerson over to the radio station.

The Jackrabbit platoon leader was at the radio console, mic in hand.

"Go ahead Sharpshooter One," the young LT said. He nodded as Captain Hagerson and Major Winston approached to listen.

"We've got dismounts moving toward our position from the south," came the reply. "Looks like—two, maybe three. Check that. Five dismounts, moving out from the tree line, walking toward our position, over."

"Roger Sharpshooter One. Are they armed, over?"

"Looks like one of them is carrying a weapon. Could be a rifle."

"Tell them to light those fuckers up," Winston grunted. "If you don't send your boys to take out those psychotic zombie bastards, I'm gonna send my men out there to do it *for* you."

"Tell them to get confirmation on the weapons," Hagerson said, calmly.

"Sharpshooter One, this is Jackrabbit Six. Alpha Six wants you to get confirmation on the weapons, over."

"Roger, wait one."

The restaurant-turned-tactical command center had fallen almost completely silent. Static hissed softly from the radio consoles. The moon was larger than ever.

Kotto stared down the sights of his pistol, watching the smoke trail up and out of the barrel. Bucky's lifeless form sat twisted and broken in the dirt. The flames along his skull and limbs began to whisper out in black tendrils of dead smoke.

Richards pulled back, his K-Bar knife still dripping blood and gore. Beyond them, the shape-shifting shadows rushed forward, crying out in fury and hate. But with each step those hideous forms took forward, they became less and less tangible, until, like the spiritual flames that flickered out on Bucky's corpse, they were nothing more than smoke and ash, blown along indifferent wind.

Above them, the humming and droning of the rotating alien construct likewise shimmered in and out of the visible spectrum. The flames on each of its side panels subsided, leaving bare faces of steel to face over the ruined landscape below. Then it, too, was gone, blinking out with little fanfare, revealing the moon—smaller now, its face white and familiar instead of red and malignant, holding celestial court among bright, bright stars.

Richards, breathing heavily, threw his knife to the side, where it embedded in the dirt, just to the side of Bucky's smoldering body. An impromptu cross for the dead.

Richards sat down in the mud, his head leaning forward, gasping for air. Kotto moved to him, knelt down, and put a hand on his deputy's shoulder. Richards looked up and met Kotto's slim smile, an exhausted beacon of hope along a face smeared with black ash and blood.

"Nice shooting," Richards managed.

"It was point-blank," Kotto said. "If I'd missed, I'd have to quit this sheriff business. Probably would have to become State police."

"Yeah, but State Troopers can't drink on the job."

"Jeez, you're right. Well, fuck that idea."

Richards allowed himself a laugh. Kotto, too.

"It hurts to laugh," Kotto said, sitting down in the mud next to Richards and leaning back.

"I bet it does," Richards said. "He hit you with that spookbeam right in the chest. I thought you were a goner."

"I think I broke a few ribs," Kotto said. "It hurts to breathe."

"Yeah," Richards said. "And to think."

"Yeah," Kotto said. He cocked his head back and looked at the sky.

The black clouds broke ranks and drifted away, melting like candle wax in a Halloween pumpkin.

"You should tell your boys to start shootin', I'm telling you," Major Winston said, shaking a finger in Hagerson's face. "You boys don't know what you're up against! Why do you think you've got all this goddamned ammo? The governor wants you to clean house!"

"Officer, you are not to interfere with the operation of my TOC," Captain Hagerson said. "Now keep quiet for a few minutes."

Right on cue, the radio crackled back to life.

"Jackrabbit Six, this is Sharpshooter One. There's more of them coming out of the trees. And that's a negative on the weapons. They're men, women, kids. Dozens of them. None of them are armed. They're waving and yelling, too. I think they're trying to get our attention."

More reports began to flood in from the other positions. Men with binos, NODs, and high vantage points called in men and women on foot, moving down the valley toward their positions at the main lodge. None of them were armed.

Hagerson leaned forward and grabbed the mic tied to the company radio frequency.

"All Alpha Company units, this is Alpha Six," he said. "Hold fire. Do not fire unless attacked. I say again—do not engage unless attacked."

"Jackrabbit Six, Alpha Six, this is Sharpshooter One," came the soldier's voice over the platoon net. "We've got people down just below us, moving toward your position. Some of them are limping. They look wounded. I think they're calling for help."

"Then let's give it to them," Hagerson said. He cradled the radio mic and turned toward Major Winston. "You and your Troopers are welcome to join us in rendering aid to these civilians," he said. "Unless you're still set on fighting a goddamn war." He turned to address his platoon leaders. "Get me a fire team from each platoon, and grab a couple of those militia and volunteer emergency workers." He patted the M-9 pistol slung at his hip, then strode toward the main doors of the lodge's restaurant. "Let's go see if this is for real."

37. Memories in Smoke and Fire

In the years that followed, Kotto would dream that, as he stared into that terrible death's head, as all Hell rushed toward him, he saw not a demon, or a monster, or an alien intelligence staring back at him.

What he saw, instead, were the eyes of a very scared, a very tired young man.

And as Kotto pulled that trigger, those eyes spoke gratitude.

They spoke peace.

38. Local Jurisdiction

They dumped the barrels out, one by one, until the whole clearing reeked of alcohol. They tossed bags of sugar and grain into the roaring fire. They smashed the glass bottles and jugs that held the image of the old god, that strange man with beard and wings. Inside plastic hard boxes were the bags of blood and dismembered body parts from the abortion clinic. These went to the flames next.

When they were sure they had dumped out every stash of 'shine, and burned every bag of foul ingredients, they walked to the edge of the clearing. Kotto had taken a flaming tree branch from the fire, and, wielding it like a torch, set fire to a trail of generator fuel. The fire snaked back toward the center of the clearing, crawling over every barrel, barrier, pile of wood, tree stump, and every inch of blood-soaked earth. The whole clearing went up in bright, purifying fire.

Kotto had insisted that they not burn Bucky's body. They had dragged his near-headless corpse to the edge of the clearing, setting it against a withered tree.

They watched the place burn. Neither man said a word.

The way down was easier, with no need to keep out of sight. The light of the moon and stars showed them the way.

Kotto was hurt; the closer they got back to the main lodge complex, the more he leaned on Richards for support. His breathing had become raspy and laborious, but he did his best to keep himself up on two feet. Bothering with subtlety or stealth was a lost cause; if they encountered any of Bucky's moonshine crazies who still wanted to eat their flesh and grind their bones, there wasn't a whole lot either of them would be able to do about it.

The two lawmen saw the lights from the main lodge. The emergency lights were overpowered by floodlights stretching from the parking lots down through the entire complex; the whole valley was aglow as if this were a regular night of skiing. Red and blue lights from State Trooper vehicles flashed up and down the road; cops, soldiers, and emergency workers alike moved about.

"You hear any shooting, Deputy?" Kotto asked as they shuffled forward.

"No, sir."

"Then maybe we got a shot."

"Hey, Mike, I know you're busy, but we could use some help here." Richards guided Kotto forward, and let him set down on an open stretcher. Michael Bryant turned from a group of militia volunteers, and stared with wide eyes at his friend.

"Abe! Jesus, I thought you were dead, man. All these people, they said they'd been doing terrible things."

Richards looked around. There were dozens of people here, covered in emergency blankets, sipping little cups of soup and coffee served by a couple of National Guard guys out of plastic green field rations containers. Richards had eaten that kind of food once too often, but he knew the power of a hot meal and warm drink. These people—familiar, yet haunted and distant—looked like they needed it. Most of them were covered in blood and dirt, or were injured themselves. Their eyes were distant, and they huddled together, most of them crying in small groups. The EMTs and fire crews kept their distance.

"This is fucked up," Michael said. "Bucky fucked these people up pretty bad."

"What do they remember?" Kotto asked, wincing.

"Everything," Michael said, shaking his head. He stared down at his mud-stained boots. "They remember everything."

Major Winston got wind of Kotto and Richards' return. With his SWAT entourage in tow, he made his way out to the triage area, where he found Richards sharing a beer with some of the local militia, and Kotto sucking down a cigarette while an Army medic wrapped his ribs.

"George, you old slug!" Kotto shouted. "I was wondering when you were gonna show up!"

"Cecil," Winston hissed, stopping just a foot away

from the sheriff. "You want to tell me what in the seven goddamned hells happened up there?"

"Sure," Kotto said, taking another puff and blowing it into the State Trooper's face. "We got our man."

"You got your man? What does that mean? I got all of these people coming off the hill, talking crazy stories about flying saucers and demons from Hell. I think they might still be dangerous, and you're giving them food and medical care!"

"I'm not doing much of anything except getting shouted at, at the moment," Kotto said. "But the stories aren't so crazy. Why don't you ask some of your men what they've been seeing these last few weeks? You can put that in your report to the governor."

"And say what, exactly?"

"The truth, or not," Kotto said. "That ain't my business what you tell your boss. What *is* my business, is this is my county, and I finished this manhunt for you. There's a body up top there. Got a couple bullets lodged in the brain, just like you wanted. You can send your boys up there to clean up the goddamn mess. But you're going to leave these people here alone."

"The hell I will," Winston fumed. "I've a mind to arrest *you*."

"See, I'm not so sure my deputy and his militia friends are gonna like that move too much. Are you boys?"

"No, Sheriff," the men with guns and beer said at once. Winston shot them a sidelong glance and shook his head.

"You killed Bucky, is that what you're telling me?"

"Had no other choice," Kotto said. "I'll put that in my report. I'll send you a copy, if you like."

"Who the hell do you report to? You're just a crank radio show host! I don't care if you got elected or not!"

"To the taxpayers," Kotto said. "If they don't like my

story—the truth—that's on them. But I don't report to you or to any other goddamn agency. I report to the people. But you can take Bucky's body, if you like. Leave everybody else outta this."

Winston stepped forward, bringing up a balled fist.

"We could use the body," a new voice said. Soft, with a Southern twang.

Winston froze in his tracks, and turned to consider the man behind him. He emerged from the entourage of SWAT commandos. The man wore a thick, bushy mustache, wide glasses, and jet-black, parted hair sprinkled with gray. His black suit hung loose on his shoulders. Gleaming black shoes reflected the depths of space itself.

"We could study the brain tissue," the man said to Winston, but considering Kotto. "It would be ... useful."

Winston swallowed his anger, but glared at Kotto.

"If you say so, sir," he said.

"Send your men up to the hill. I'll be up shortly," the G-Man said. Winston shot Kotto one last *this isn't over* look, and off he went, stormtroopers following close behind.

"Well, Bucky's head got a big fucking hole in it, so good luck with that," Kotto said.

The man in black offered a sly smile.

"You killed him, Sheriff Kotto? It's an honor to finally meet you."

"In my skins and hollers," Kotto said. "Give me one guess." Kotto held his right index finger up, and turned away, feigning deep contemplation. "Agent Schrader, right? Department of Homeland Security? National Security Agency? Something like that?"

Schrader offered him a wide, down-home smile.

"Why, yes sir, something like that."

"Which one?" Kotto asked. "Who do you work for?"

"Do you have a cigarette, Sheriff Kotto? I'm afraid

I've gone through all of mine while waiting here for you heroes to save the day. And the gas station in town is shuttered. Due to the violence."

Kotto smirked, then offered him a smoke.

"Thank you kindly," Schrader said. He produced a square metal lighter, which glimmered silver in the parking lot lights.

"What's that design on the lighter?" Richards asked. "On the side there."

Schrader offered him that same friendly smile, the cigarette bobbing between his lips. He offered the lighter to Richards, who held it in his palm, moving it to help the etched design catch the light.

"I've seen this before," Richards said, holding up the lighter. "The guy with wings. Big hat. Hieroglyphics or something. It's the design on the moonshine bottles."

"Excellent detective work, Deputy Richards," Schrader said. "I see your talents were wasted by serving in the infantry."

"Who do you work for, Schrader? Which alphabet soup Nazi fascists sent you to do this to us?"

"You know my name, Sheriff Kotto. But you don't know much else, do you?"

"I know enough to know that this whole county is my jurisdiction. And we still got a few cells downtown I could throw your ass inside for a few days, if I had a mind to."

Schrader offered a laugh, his eyes alight with good humor.

"Sheriff, I'm disappointed in you! I don't scare so easily. But since you've been such a good sport about all of this, I'll give you a clue." He took another drag of his cigarette, then blew the smoke straight up into the air. "I don't work for any of them." His eyes grew wide behind his owl-rim glasses, then he leaned forward to rest face-to-face with the sheriff. "They work for *us*."

"What's left for you here, Schrader?" Kotto said. "It's over. We killed Bucky, though Lord knows we didn't want to. All these people are returned to normal. We burned the still up there. I'm gonna make sure that any moonshine left in this town is put to the flame. It's over."

"Over?" Schrader asked. He stood up straight, letting his eyes fall straight on Sheriff Kotto. "This? All this? Because you stopped one man?"

"His ritual," Richards said. "He never completed the ritual. We stopped the fear, and we stopped the blood sacrifice. Bucky's dead, and the moonshine recipe dies with him."

"Do you really think you've stopped *them*?" Schrader asked. "Two local lawmen, drunks, known drug users to boot—you take a few pawns, maybe a rook off the board—and you think it's all over? The things you two have *seen*, what you've felt, what you know to be true—and you think it's *over*?"

Schrader dropped the cigarette and extinguished it under his impossibly-black shoe. "They—the visitors—they don't think like you and I do," he said. "Days, months, years—meaningless. Theirs is a perspective of millennia, of eons. You look around tonight, and you see a victory. They see a bump in the road, the buzzing of a fly in the dark, soon forgotten." Schrader dropped the pretense of Southern-boy charm, and leaned forward, waving a furious finger at Kotto and Richards. "You honestly think this was their big plan? Here? In this place, where no one cares whether a few hundred hillbillies and rednecks and yuppies and trailer park assholes tear each other apart? Their reach extends into every institution, every government, every major religion. Outside of today, sirs, you've accomplished *nothing*."

Schrader leaned back, running his hands along his sport coat, regaining his composure.

"Then we'll take today," Kotto said, standing up, ignoring the pain in his side. "We'll take today, and tonight, and tomorrow, and every day that comes after. I'll be here—*we'll* be here," he said, putting a hand on Richards' shoulder. "And until those alien-demon-visitor bastards put me in a grave, I'll fight. This is *our* county." Richards stood next to him, his head held high, his arms crossed over his chest. "Go take your body, and get the hell out of here," Kotto said. "And don't let me catch you in Cattaraugus County ever again."

Schrader nodded, then offered Kotto a warm smile, dripping with venom.

"Sheriff, the world is a more interesting place with you in it. I admire your ... vigor." He nodded to both men, then turned to leave. "I'll be out of your jurisdiction by dawn, Sheriff. But we'll see each other again. I'm sure of it." He began to walk off, his gait slow, his shoulders hunched forward ever-so-slightly; poor posture belying his simmering confidence.

"Why would you tell us all of this?" Richards asked. "If you're some man in black with all of these secrets, why come here? Why tell us anything?"

Schrader stopped, then turned his head to speak over his shoulder.

"Because you've earned a little of the truth," Schrader said. "Because, maybe winning all of the time gets a little boring. And because there's nothing you can do to stop what's coming. Not in the end." He began to walk off again.

"Here," Richards said, holding the lighter out. "You forgot this."

"Keep it," Schrader said, not breaking stride. "If you ever want to come to a meeting—here, anywhere there's a lodge—show that to them and mention my name. They'll let you in."

"Lodge?" Richards asked. "What are you talking about?"

"The Order of the Night Moose," Kotto said, voice low. "Dammit."

"Why the hell would I want to come to one of their meetings?" Richards asked.

"Because maybe you'd like to join, Abraham Richards," Schrader said, his voice diminishing with distance. "Because maybe you'd like to learn a little more about this great and terrible world."

Schrader walked off, his heels clicking against wet pavement. As he disappeared into the crowd of victims, soldiers, and firefighters gathered around the entrance to the main lodge, Veronica emerged from the main doors. Dean followed, and the reporter directed him to get coverage of the crowd. She turned and spotted Richards and Kotto, then grabbed Dean and jogged over to them.

"Hey!" she said. "I thought you guys were dead."

"We're getting a lot of that lately," Kotto said. "People usually think I'm dead at least once every six months or so."

"What happened up there?" Veronica asked, catching her breath. Dean stumbled up behind her, his face flushed. "You stopped Bucky?"

"We stopped something," Richards said, staring off at the crowd where Schrader had disappeared. "But I'm not sure what."

"How'd you do it?"

"I think Bucky wanted us to stop him," Kotto said. "I think—I think he was fighting *with* us, not against us."

"I don't think I follow."

"I'm not sure I do, either," Kotto said, shaking his head.

"What happens here?" Veronica asked. "To the resort? To Ellicottville?"

"What do you think happens next?" Kotto asked. "They're going to sweep it all under the rug. Their precious development project can go forward."

"But this is too big of a story," Veronica said.

"Not if nobody tells it. You're the only reporter that's been here—everything from the manhunt, to the police abuses, to this. You're the only one here."

"Then I'll tell the story," Veronica said.

"Even if no one listens?"

"They'll listen to you," Veronica said. "Look, Sheriff—even after all I've seen these past few days, I still think you're crazy. I mean, maybe not as crazy as I first thought. But you were right about a lot of things. You found Bucky, and it looks like you've freed these people from whatever psychosis was controlling them. I'm willing to put you on camera. Full interviews. I want you to help me piece this story together, from your perspective. You can be the face of this thing."

"Is that a good idea?" Richards asked. "Won't people just dismiss it, then? Kotto's got a reputation."

"But you've been right about so much," Veronica said.

"Abe's right," Kotto said. "I get on camera, and start talking about State Troopers and alien abductions and demon altars and UFOs and possessed people, and you cut it down to a 10 second sound bite. You run the story, you make me look like a crazy person. Everyone forgets about it in a week." Kotto turned to look out into the darkness of the hills. "We deserve better than that. The people of this county deserve better than that."

"Bucky deserves better," Richards said. "If he really was fighting their control—then he's as much a victim as everyone else. Or maybe as much a hero as anyone here."

"It won't be like that," Veronica said. "I promise." She looked back at Dean, who nodded. "Look, we've been talking. You've already got a relationship with the station, right? Just on the radio side of things. But I'm pretty sure that your broadcasts—and my reports—we can do something else. If I talk to the station manager, I think we can get a new arrangement. Something that will benefit the both of us."

"I've already got my radio show," Kotto said. "And all those stoned teenagers keep uploading them to the YouTubes, so lots of people hear my theories."

"That's not enough, Sheriff. We can do more."

"You'd help me do that?"

"Sheriff, working with you idiots is way more entertaining than doing stories on Pumpkinville and waterskiing squirrels," she said. "Right, Dean?"

"Yeah," he said. "I mean, I got to smoke a joint and drink beer while you guys were on acid or whatever, and I was getting paid the whole time."

"Magic Mushrooms, not acid. Big difference," Kotto said.

"Right."

"You'd really put me on TV?" Kotto asked. "And not make me look like an idiot?"

"You do a good enough job of that all on your own," Veronica said, smiling. "I'll even let you have final cut, if you'd like."

"What do you get out of this?" Kotto asked. "Better ratings? Maybe a promotion up to a news station in Buffalo?"

"Maybe," Veronica said. "Yes, that, maybe. But I've been thinking a lot about what you said. 'We need heroes.' I think you're right. I think the people here need something they can believe in."

"And you'll help us give them that, huh?"

"I'll do my best," Veronica said. "But I can't really do it without you."

Kotto looked at Richards, who shrugged.

"Don't look at me, Sheriff," Richards said. "I'm just a burnout alcoholic veteran with a gun. This is an executive decision."

Kotto smiled.

"Alright Veronica," Kotto said, hands on his hips. "What exactly do you have in mind?"

39. Freaky Tales From the Force

Partial Transcript of FREAKY TALES FROM THE FORCE S1E1 "PILOT". Originally aired at midnight on November 25th, 201X. Broadcast on Cattaraugus County Public Access Television (CCPATV), with audio simulcast on Cattaraugus County Public Access Radio (CCPAR). Additional sources include unauthorized distribution on YouTube, Vimeo, and various other video hosting services. As of this transcription, copyright complaints have not been lodged against any unauthorized distributors.]

[The scene begins after a brief break for station identification and local sponsorship promo graphics. This episode's sponsor was a small grocery and sandwich shop in Machias, New York, known as "Lil's Deli." They advertised their location, phone number, and the "$14.95 Dozen Wings and a Six Pack of Yuengling Mid-Week Sheriff's Special."]

BEGIN TRANSCRIPTION.

BLACK.

OPEN ON African-American male, dressed in old-style

army fatigue jacket, wearing large black sunglasses, Vietnam-era military helmet, smoking a cigarette, holding a large gun, presumably a shotgun or deer hunting rifle. Crouched low, he is hiding behind a large tree.

Text appears beneath the figure: "CATTARAUGUS COUNTY SHERIFF CECIL KOTTO"

KOTTO:
"Utilizing secret techniques we found on the internet, my deputy and I have managed to track this creature to a part of Allegheny State Park just outside of Salamanca, New York."

VOICE, FROM OFF SCREEN:
[Whispering] "Sheriff, I think I see the [unintelligible]. Looks like he's sitting down to take a [BLEEP]."

KOTTO:
"That's good work, Deputy. Great work." [Turns back to camera.] "Okay, look, we're gonna move in real quiet like. Dean, keep that [BLEEP] camera on me and make sure you get that hairy [BLEEP]. This is gonna be bigger than the Zapruder film and the Patterson footage put together!"

VOICE:
"I think he saw me."

KOTTO:
"Get down! Get down!"

CAMERA drops low, KOTTO goes prone.

KOTTO:

"Shh!"

Several moments of relative silence. KOTTO's face dominates the frame. Twigs snap from somewhere out of view.

VOICE:
"He's moving."

KOTTO:
"Go! Let's go! Dean, get your fat [BLEEP] up and get that [BLEEP] camera rolling on that [MULTIPLE BLEEPS]!"

The camera scrambles up alongside KOTTO and the other officer. They leap over a fallen log and into a small clearing. Ahead, we see a gray-brown figure, but the camera movement is too erratic and out of focus to see much detail.

KOTTO:
"Oh [BLEEP]! He's coming back!"

UNIDENTIFIED OFFICER:
"What do we do?

The camera focuses on a two-shot of Kotto in the foreground, his deputy in the background. The deputy has his pistol drawn. Kotto unnecessarily pumps his shotgun, ejecting a round.

More growling. The camera swings over to the right. The gray-brown figure—still fuzzy and out of focus—charges them.

Gunshots. Unintelligible screaming, growling. Several

uses of the FCC censorship "BLEEP."

The camera tilts down. We hear the cameraman breathing heavily as we see his boots. He is running away.

KOTTO:
[Off-camera] "He's got my gun!"

Heavy breathing, running. KOTTO reappears, pulling the camera to his face.

KOTTO
"Shoot that son of a [BLEEP] or we're all gonna get anal probed!"

BLACK.

Funky rock, upbeat blues number. The show's iconic theme song.

Blurry neon, multi-colored text DISSOLVE FADE IN:

"CATTARAUGUS COUNTY PUBLIC ACCESS TELEVISION PRESENTS"

"A VERONICA CARTWRIGHT PRODUCTION"

[Title Card] Slime-green letters in cartoonish font DISSOLVE IN:

"FREAKY TALES FROM THE FORCE"

Roll Opening Credits over stock footage of clearly-staged action scenes (a la popular television programs such as *Cops* or *America's Most Wanted*) involving

Sheriff Kotto, Deputy Abraham Richards, and local citizens. Jumping over car hoods, firing guns, moving through dark graveyards, a traffic stop for a man riding in a pickup while wearing a rubber "gray alien" mask, etc ...

Epilogue

Sidney Lovering, CEO of Operations and Management of Snow Pine Ski Resort, pressed the "POWER" button on the jet-black remote. The big screen, high definition television mounted on the far wall of the Order of the Night Moose Ellicottville Lodge's boardroom flickered to black. Small motors whirred and gears spun, and the giant television receded into the wall, wood panels sliding back down and out to cover the space it had occupied.

"They're planning on airing a new episode once a week and playing it every goddamn night," Sidney said, tapping the wide triangular table at which they sat. His position was just off to the left of the vacant Grand Moose's chair. A place of honor, bought over the years with loyalty, access, and money. An achievement, to sit at the table. An honor, to sit just to the left of the ceremonially-empty seat of the Grand Moose.

Unlike his boardroom at Snow Pine Resort, this one carried none of the accoutrements of his station or position. Here, the brother-elders met, and they met as one, and in truth. *Weaving Spiders Come Not Here*, and all that. No pretense or intrigues tolerated.

Also unlike that boardroom, this one housed a much smaller table. Shareholders were a dime a dozen.

Brother-elders were few. Very few. Six, to be exact. Six men gathered around the triangular table, with an empty seat at its apex. An empty space for ceremony, mostly. But should the Grand Moose or one of his emissaries ever decide to grace one of their meetings again, that place was reserved for them.

"We were promised this would be over quickly," Warren Marks said, taking his cue from Sidney and standing up. Rehearsed, confident. Warren had managed to modify the County Legislature's normal schedule for a week while the area recovered from the crimes and freak weather that had plagued their beloved home throughout the month of October. Closed-door, emergency sessions only.

Of course, the *real* power in Cattaraugus County rested here, in this room. With these six.

"Instead, it dragged on, and a lot of people got killed. Now, we knew that was a possibility going into this deal, but we've got state and national news outlets picking up the story. *This* version of the story." He pointed to the blank space on the wall from which the television had receded. "That's the face of our community now. That drunken game show host for a sheriff."

The other men nodded or looked into their drinks. The fog of cigar smoke hung desperately in the air.

"Well, if I may," one of the men spoke up. "It's on public access television. Who watches that?"

"Apparently, a couple of million people," Sidney said. "And counting. On YouTube alone."

"This is a problem," Warren said. "Sure, the expansion project at Snow Pine is going forward, and we will all benefit from that. But it's an issue of branding. Right, Sid?"

"You're correct, Warren," Sidney said, leaning forward on the table. His hand tapped over ancient runes carved into its glossy Redwood surface. Lines of meaning, icons of sin. Of *power*. "We estimate it'll cost us a few hundred thousand dollars in PR to mitigate the stink this Bucky incident has stuck Snow Pine with. No one is going to want to go skiing where the rumors are spreading about Satanic rituals and massacres."

"We have to do something about the sheriff," Warren said. "And we have to put a stop to that stupid show of his before it gets out of hand. I know you don't like to move openly, but I don't see how we have any other choice—"

"Gentlemen, if I may," said another voice. Soft, amused. A bit of a down-home drawl, a charming affectation.

All six of the board members turned to see the man in black standing at the entrance to the room. None of them had heard the doors open. The sergeant-at-arms posted outside had clearly not wanted to stop this interloper.

And for good reason.

"Brother Schrader," Warren said, his voice betraying his sudden unease. "We welcome you to our council." He swallowed hard, then extended a hand toward the empty seat next to Sidney. The next words came from ritual and memory: "Would you join our council, as is your right, in the seat of the Grand Moose, peace and enlightenment be upon him, as his duly-appointed emissary?"

The other men rose immediately, leather farting and wheels squeaking over waxed-wood floor.

Schrader offered the room a bright smile.

"How kind of you, Warren." He strode around the table, careful to make eye contact with each man—two sitting at each side of the triangle. When he reached the empty seat at the triangle-table's apex, he put both hands on the chair's back.

"What are we talking about here, boys?" Mock-concern flashed across his face. "Please, gentlemen, take your seats."

"After you, sir," Sidney said.

"Of course." Schrader beamed wide at the room, then pulled the chair out and sat down, silent as a mouse. The others followed suit.

The air had changed; the smell of slaughterhouse fear was suddenly upon them.

"Now, about this meeting's business," Schrader said.

The others looked down, or pretended to check messages on their phones. Warren shot Sidney an arched eyebrow. Sidney grimaced, then cleared his throat, and turned to face Schrader.

"We think Kotto's a problem," he said. "And the stigma about what happened at Snow Pine—that *ritual*, or whatever it was that Bucky was trying to accomplish. We think it's bad for business. Bad optics. We were discussing possible solutions."

"You gentlemen don't like the results of our little deal, is that it? You're getting the construction go-ahead. No more Department of Environmental Conservation or Environmental Protection Agency interference."

"Yes, sir," Sidney said. "But please consider what might happen if more people listen to Kotto. His stories—"

"They aren't stories," Schrader said. "You folks here know that better than most."

"Yes, sir, but—"

"Your profits, yes? You're concerned that folks won't flock to your expanded resort? That your town won't recover its family-friendly image and reputation, simply because of a few dozen violent homicides, a couple UFOs, and one aborted Satanic ritual. Do I have the long and short of this here particular Tomcat, Sidney?"

Silence. It dragged on for a moment too long.

"Yes, Brother Schrader. You have ... the Tomcat."

"Brother, your fears are misplaced." He extended his arms outward. "These are not *problems*. These are *opportunities*. Do not be so shortsighted. You now have free publicity. The rumors will swirl. The good sheriff killed a man on your mountain, and stopped an evil end-times ritual. Sirs, you have verified *o-ccult act-vity* in your town, and you think people won't flock to that? Boys, you disappoint me. You're misreading the times."

"Sir?"

"Oh, you can drop the 'sirs' and the formalities if you like, Sidney. Gentlemen, I am here to express the Grand Moose's personal gratitude for your cooperation in facilitating this operation. Why, we in Washington consider this a great success. A great test-run of a much wider, and much more overt program."

Warren's eyes went wide.

"This was a success?"

"In a way, it was." Schrader turned that warm smile on Warren. "You see, brother, we aren't concerned with covering our tracks any more. Now, I know some of you old-timers may find that hard to swallow. I certainly did. In my hundred and fifty-some-odd years as a member of our worshipful Order, I've seen a lot of changes, a lot of new directions. And this, my friends, is the most radical of all."

Schrader considered the room. All eyes were on him. Curiosity had replaced—or at least temporarily outweighed—their fear.

"Brothers, men—what I mean to say is, we aren't going to be hiding this sort of thing much longer. It's a *good* thing your local drunk crackpot is shooting his mouth off on TV and the internet. The more people who hear what he has to say—and the more we *deny* it—the more people *believe it*."

"But sir," Sidney said. "The Grand Moose has said—the texts say—we have to keep the sacred things hidden—"

"Oh, don't misunderstand me. There are certain things that we must withhold from the people. Why, without our guidance and heavy hand, they would be lost. Civilization would descend into bloodshed, anarchy. Chaos. We all know that. But we want to reveal some of it—a little at a time. We've been programming them through film, music, television, books—to accept the things that we are to reveal. We just need a little more time before we reveal some of our most sacred rituals, our most sacred knowledge, of how things really work and humanity's true place in this world. The time when we reveal ourselves to the rest of the world is rapidly approaching.

"Sheriff Kotto's show—and others like it—will help generate the predicative programming that is required for the mass' psyche to absorb the revelations to come. For now, we keep the source of our power—and our alliances with those that give it to us—shrouded in shadow and rumor. But soon, gentlemen—and a few of you will live long enough to see it—we will bring these things out into the open. Illumination of the masses, in a sense, is coming. But we have to get the timing right. When we present our priesthood and our gods to them, they must be prepared to accept them. Everything hinges on that. Show them too much, too early, and they will rise up against us. Show them too little, and our memetic viruses will fail to take hold.

"Rumors of magic and murder will *draw* people here, brothers. The development land has been touched by blood, by magic, by fire. The ritual was never completed, true. But that doesn't mean there's no power there. Build your condos, your lodges, clear your new ski trails. But build something else. Can you imagine it? Bohemian Grove East, but open to the public several times a year. When the moon and the stars are right, of course. Imagine the *power* something like that could generate.

"You'll make all the money you want. Ellicottville will develop a bit of a reputation, sure. But in the years to come, I can guarantee you, it'll be the *right* reputation. You boys are so concerned with commercial interests—and I don't blame you for that. But the real money isn't in ski resorts and condo construction projects. The *real* money, the real *power*—why, that's in spirituality. Religion. That's in the promise of transcendence. And Ellicottville—soon, real soon—may just be one of few sources of that. That's what Bucky's ritual was all about. Then we will harvest the real rewards of our efforts. Rewards everlasting. Rewards spoken of in our secret texts. Rewards that, because of the generosity of our dark masters, I have already tasted. And brothers, let me tell you—that taste is *sweet*."

The men began to nod. Some prematurely finished their drinks.

"Forgive us for being shortsighted, brother," Warren said. He looked around the room. "But I speak for all of us when I say that we remain loyal to the Grand Moose, and to the Order. And we remain loyal to you."

"Why, Warren, that's just the kindest thing anyone has said to me all day," Schrader said. "So, with the knowledge that the Grand Moose and the High Council holds your cooperation and loyalty in high regard, will you do me this little favor, and drop any plans to interfere with the good sheriff?"

The men nodded.

"Good! It's settled." Schrader rapped his knuckles against the table. *"Freaky Tales From the Force* stays on air, and Kotto remains the sheriff. At least, that is, until the next election. Right, boys?"

Nods and polite, forced laughter.

"I'll leave the local politics to you, Warren. But for now—leave Kotto alone. We've got more important work to do. Like finding me a stiff drink. Who's taking me downtown? Who's buying? I need a *steak*. All this business is making me hungry."

"A steak, sir?" Sidney asked, his voice practiced, avoiding that nervous fear that was clawing at the back of his throat. "Are you sure you wouldn't prefer something a bit more ... rare? It would be my honor to find something that might suit your particular tastes. Sir."

Schrader turned to the man on his left.

"Ah, Brother Sidney. You know me so well." He parted his lips, his smile never wavering.

The canines on both sides of his mouth stretched and snapped and grew, wide and sharp, reaching down below to the upper edge of his chin. His next words came through with a touch of slur, his tongue struggling to form the words over the sudden and drastic changes in palate, teeth, and jaw:

"I could always be persuaded to have something a little more appealing. A little more *fresh*."

The finely-polished surface of the Redwood table reflected only an empty suit, animated with invisible force. The half-reflection moved over deep, eldritch etchings. Etchings that told a story of ancient rebellion, power, illumination—and the fury of Hell against the world itself. Fire and light to come, mankind ascendant in the cosmos, led by the great Light Bringer, their final victory over the Lying Tyrant God of the Desert at hand.

catastrophic social breakdown and environmental degradation as merely differences of partisan opinion.

The national and international events of the years since this book's release demonstrated how conspiracy critiques of legitimate problems can be used to funnel support for reactionary and anti-human political movements and policies. That is, acknowledging the problem, for some, can lead to doubling down on the problem. That belief in UFOs is somehow being used to justify ballooning military budgets, for example, might make even Sheriff Kotto think twice before speaking on the subject.

For a time I was content to let the novel fall out of print, mostly due to my unease about reader interpretations and my own embarrassment about some of its content. Surprisingly, a good number of readers reached out about finding copies of the book. Eventually, I decided that all good literature should be at least a little problematic and uncomfortable—especially horror literature—and so this new edition is widely available, and will continue to be, despite my reservations.

I'll trust Sheriff Kotto to speak for himself, even if I've changed since 2015, and so has the rest of the world. Who knows—maybe we'll hear from Cecil again, someday, and he can let us know how he's changed, too, in the years since the world as we know it ended.

Keep watching the skies—

Jonathan Raab

Gothic Upstate New York, 2023

Acknowledgments

My wife Jess is my best editor and critic. Her wisdom, kind words, and support throughout the writing and editing of this novel helped make it possible.

Colin Scharf helped me develop what would become the weird world of this fictional Cattaraugus County back when we made backyard monster movies. He also created Special Agent Steven Fields, and co-created Freaky Tales From the Force, when it was just a fun little vignette in one such DIY film.

Tarik Ramadhan was the first actor to play Sheriff Cecil Kotto, and helped infuse the character with life, humor, and manic charisma.

Thanks to Mer Whinery and Matthew M. Bartlett for throwing their good names behind the book.

Charles Martin deserves credit for taking a chance on such a bizarre and personal novel. His faith in my writing and my vision for the story and themes presented here is greatly appreciated.

Thank you also to everyone who asked about getting the book back into print.

About the Author

Jonathan Raab is the author of *Project Vampire Killer*, *The Haunting of Camp Winter Falcon*, and more. He is the editor of *Behold the Undead of Dracula: Lurid Tales of Cinematic Gothic Horror, Terror in 16-bits,* and others. His short fiction has appeared in numerous magazines and anthologies, including *The Best Horror of the Year, Volume Fourteen*. He lives in Gothic upstate New York with his wife, son, and a dog named Egon. You can keep up with his new projects at www.muzzlelandpress.com.